OUR LIMINAL SPACES

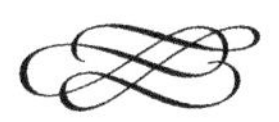

POORNIMA MANCO

Book cover by MiblArt

For my Family

The truth is, indeed, that love is the threshold of another universe.

—

Pierre Teilhard de Chardin

RADHA

1996

CHAPTER 1

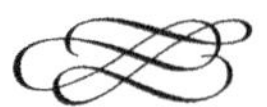

"*Ae gaandu! Kidhar ko jaata hai tu?!* Bloody idiot! What do you think those rear view mirrors are for, you jackass?"

Radha had just finished her first round of yoga sun salutations when she heard the expletive-filled shriek followed shortly after by a loud bang. It was only 9am. Shyam had warned her before leaving for work that the new neighbours would be moving in today. That seemed to be going well!

She sighed and positioned herself once more in the downward dog *asana,* wondering what sort of woman was brazen enough to use such foul language so loudly. From the dialect, it appeared she was from Bombay. No one said *gaandu* in Delhi, or even Haryana for that matter. Radha had to keep reminding herself she lived in Gurgaon now, which was in Haryana. It was so easy to forget this simple fact, as nearly every weekend they drove into Delhi, which was only forty-five minutes away by car.

Another crash, more expletives. What on earth was going on next door? Radha rolled up her yoga mat and stepped out onto her balcony. The truck trying to back into the neighbour's drive had crashed into the wall, not once, but twice. She had to agree with the unknown woman's assessment. The driver was clearly a jackass!

A chunk of the wall had been taken out. Even though the truck looked no worse for the wear, the wall had seen better days. She was glad that Shyam's buddy from school had offered them the services of his removal company when they had moved here six months ago. She could not imagine having to deal with crazy truck drivers on her own.

Where was this woman's husband, anyway? Shyam had said it was a couple in their thirties, but she had only spotted a woman briefly. Now the woman emerged from the shadows again, gesticulating and pointing to the wall. Thick curly hair piled on top of her head, sunglasses perched on her nose. She was wearing a lime green *khaadi kurta* with jeans and *Kolhapuri chappals.* Even though Radha couldn't make out her features, she liked the mishmash of the Indo-Western outfit the woman was sporting. She wished she still had the guts to wear stuff like that. Shyam had once said he preferred her to dress in *salwar-kameez* and *sarees.* So she did. Maa had drummed it into her from a very young age that it was important to keep your husband happy. Radha had given up her jeans and skirts, and much else, to keep Shyam happy. But she still envied this woman's insouciance and flair. In another life, she would have worn an outfit like that with loads of silver bangles and a big chunky silver necklace. In another life. Radha sighed again.

Almost as though she felt her eyes upon her, the woman shielded her eyes and looked up. Radha took a step back, but not before being spotted. The woman raised her hand and waved. Self-consciously, Radha returned the wave and retreated indoors. Had she come across as a nosy neighbour? She hoped not. First impressions were important, and if they had to live next door to this mouthy woman, she hoped she could maintain a cordial relationship without it spilling into over-familiarity.

Radha put her yoga mat away in the spare room which was still cluttered with the detritus of their move. So much needed doing but somehow this one task seemed insurmountable and she knew she would have to handle it alone. Shutting the door to the room, she felt instantly relieved. Today was not the day to begin the work.

She was not an untidy person by nature. Living in a small house with her parents and two brothers had made her acutely sensitive to utilising space efficiently. Perhaps that was the very reason she could not tackle the task of this spare room. She had never had a spare room before. The intention was to convert it into another bedroom, but where was she to store the writing desk or the ironing board, the large trunk from her in-laws' house or Shyam's cricket bat?

Later, as Radha chopped the vegetables for the curry she was making for dinner, she wondered how the woman was getting on next door. What was the protocol in a situation like this? Would it be better to go over with some food to welcome her or leave her be to settle in first?

She set the knife down, wiped her hands on the kitchen towel, and went over to the phone on the side console. With every 9, the rotary dial took forever to move back into place. She wished Sangita's phone number had fewer 9s in it.

"Hello?"

"Sangita?"

"Yes, dear?" There was a laugh in her voice, almost as if she was saying "what now?", except she wasn't.

"The new neighbours have moved in..."

"Mm-hm."

"Actually, only the lady has moved in. I don't know where the husband is."

"Okkkay..."

"Are you free to talk?"

"*Arrey baba,* I wouldn't have answered if I wasn't. So, what's the problem?"

Radha recounted the morning episode to her, then paused for a breath before asking, "Should I go over today and greet her? Is it rude to leave it for later in the week? Should I take Shyam with me?"

"So many questions, T. I don't remember you being so indecisive before."

"I just don't know what to do in situations like these."

"And you think I do?"

"Well, you're working and dealing with people all the time. Whom do I deal with except the maid and the *presswallah*?"

"Out of choice, may I remind you? Okay. Here's my two *paisa* worth. I'd leave the couple to settle in, and maybe go over on the weekend and welcome them to Gurgaon, or your community, or whatever."

"With flowers?"

"Yeah, with flowers, if you like. That would be a nice touch."

"Not too much, *na*?"

"I think it's nice. Who doesn't like flowers?"

"And should I go with Shyam?"

"Is he into all the neighbourly stuff?"

"Not really. All he wants to do is watch cricket on the weekends."

"That sounds like my brother! Nah, leave him out of it. Just do your thing and quit worrying about it. Also, she does sound a bit of a handful, this neighbour of yours. If you get strange vibes, just back away, okay?"

"Sangita, not without just cause. The idiot driver ruined their wall." Radha wondered why she was defending the woman, when she had been judging her only a few hours ago.

"Right. I'm just going by what you told me. Anyway, if she's a Bombay *waali,* she's going to find Gurgaon really backward and boring."

"Oh, but it is!"

"Oh, but you chose to move there!"

Radha didn't have the heart to tell Sangita that it had never been her choice. Shyam had chosen, and she hadn't objected. Sangita may have been her dearest friend, but Shyam was Sangita's brother, and blood was always thicker than water.

❖

"Are gladioli better or roses?"

"What?"

Shyam had his legs up on the settee, a bowl of peanuts and a chilled beer on the side table, and she could tell he was only half-listening as he watched Tendulkar score another six.

"Yes!" He jumped up, nearly knocking the side table over.

Radha made a lunge for it, catching it in the nick of time, rescuing the peanuts and the beer alongside.

"*Wah* Radha," Shyam grinned at her, "Such impeccable timing. You should be in the women's team."

"Shyam!" She groaned. "Please, I just want an opinion."

"Are you still worrying about the flowers? Just buy anything. What does it matter? Not like we're going to be best friends with these people."

"But we are living next door to them for the foreseeable future, and they are our immediate neighbours, not like the Mehtas or the Advanis."

"Just get them the gladioli. That'll do."

Shyam ran his fingers through his wavy brown hair, his attention back on the screen.

"Have you seen the husband yet?"

"Hmmm?"

"The woman's husband?"

"Yeah, saw him briefly the other day."

"What's he like?"

"Who?"

"The *husband*, Shyam, who else?"

"Okay, I guess. A bit fat, a bit balding."

Radha sighed and went into the kitchen. It was impossible to have a conversation with him when he was glued to the television. She would just have to find out for herself.

She did not know why she'd been thinking so much about the couple next door. It wasn't like she'd seen much of them in the last five days. On one occasion, she had seen the woman get into her car and drive away, but things had been very quiet all week, unlike the explosive start to their move. She had spotted no children either, but there was a small yappy dog that ran to the gate every morning and grabbed the rolled newspaper from the ground, and ran around with it till the maid caught hold of him. The dog's name was Batman. Strange name for a dog.

She let herself out quietly and walked to the market nearby. It was 5pm and the flower seller was just setting up on the roadside. The oppressive heat of the day had retreated and a gentle warmth had replaced it, turning the evening quite pleasant. In June, she rarely left the house during the day. On the unlikely chance that she had to venture out, the heat outside felt like stepping into a furnace, and she kept herself protected with a *dupatta* over her head and an umbrella alongside. Her brothers had always loved poking fun at her, but Maa had supported her by saying that a girl needed to protect her complexion.

Radha stood and watched the flower seller set up his roadside stall, sprinkling his flowers with water, placing the others in buckets dotted along the pavement. She had always loved watching the sellers put the bouquets together, and today was no exception.

"I'll take the white gladioli, and some of the red carnations, and yes, add some pink roses, too."

Radha watched as he laid out a cloth on the ground, then put the first layer of clear cellophane down, followed by the printed cellophane, before starting with positioning the gladioli at the bottom and then building the bouquet as per her instructions. The air was redolent with the fragrance of the fresh flowers and she breathed in deeply, watching the bouquet come alive under the man's ministrations.

Lugging it back, she wondered if she had gone a bit overboard. She loved flowers, and Shyam rarely bought her any, so the only pleasure she could take in them was when she got one made for a wedding or an occasion like this.

She let herself into the house to find that he had fallen asleep in front of the television. The match was long over and the men were droning on about how each of the players had played and what their chances were in the upcoming India-Pakistan match. She took the remote out of his hand and lowered the volume. She wouldn't switch off the television or he would get annoyed. Heaven knew why. He nearly always slept through the commentary.

Then she went into the bedroom and brushed her hair before twisting it into a bun. She put some kohl in her eyes, applied a small yellow *bindi* to her forehead, which matched her *salwar-kameez,* spritzed a bit of perfume, before picking up the bouquet from the bed and making her way over to next door.

Shyam was snoring as she shut the door. She giggled to herself. Fast asleep, he looked so much older than his twenty-eight years. Sometimes, she felt they had turned middle-aged in their twenties.

"Rubbish!" Sangita scoffed in her mind. "We're only twenty-two. Don't you forget it!"

She nodded in response and smiled to herself. It was funny how sometimes one could foresee the future in a single moment.

The wall had been temporarily plastered over, and as Radha walked past it, she grimaced. It was really quite bad. No wonder the woman had lost her temper. Then she clicked her tongue. She really needed to find out what their names were. She couldn't keep referring to them as the woman and the man. There was a nameplate on the letter box and she leaned forward to peer at it. 'Das', it said in a pretty red cursive. Oh! So they were Bengalis.

Suddenly, the little black dog was at the gate, barking and jumping up. Startled, Radha took a step back. The maid came outside brandishing the leash and calling out, "Batman? Batman!" She stopped short, looking directly at Radha.

"*Namaste,* are your *sahib* and *memsahib* in?"

The maid nodded, grabbed the dog, and scurried back inside. How odd!

A minute later she was back, apologising profusely and opening the gate. A torrent of words issued from her mouth, but her thick accent made it difficult to decipher what she was saying. Radha followed her towards the main door, which was to the side of the house.

All houses on the street were facsimiles of each other. The gate led to the drive, which then led to the main door. The front of the houses had large French windows that fed into a patio area and a small garden. Downstairs, there was a kitchen and dining room, a drawing room for entertaining and a storeroom for all the kitchen and dry goods. Upstairs, there were three bedrooms, one with a small attached ensuite, and a larger bathroom with doors that opened into the other two rooms.

Shyam had said they were lucky to find such a spacious home in Gurgaon. It was thanks to his job as a systems analyst in the burgeoning IT space. Nearly all the IT sector had relocated to Gurgaon, and the once sleepy little village on the outskirts of Delhi had transformed into a hub for all things information technology. This was the 90s and India seemed to have suddenly leapt into the 21st century with countries like the USA, UK and Germany turning their gaze towards the sub-continent.

Radha wondered whether Mr Das was in IT, too.

The dog's leash was tied to the leg of a chair and it growled at her as she walked behind the maid, clearly displeased at being sectioned off in this manner. She skirted him, scared he'd nip her ankles. Radha had never had any pets. Her family thought all animals were dirty, and they did not belong in a house. Her own feelings were ambivalent. There were times she had wished she could have kept a cat for company, but all that was in the past, anyway.

The maid took her into the drawing room where Mr Das was smoking a cigarette and reading his newspaper, while Mrs Das was lying on a *divan,* eyes closed, listening to western classical music. As soon as the maid walked in, her eyes snapped open. Upon spotting Radha, she sat up, pulling her shorts down and running her fingers through her hair.

"Well, hello, what have we here?"

Mr Das looked up from his newspaper, a puzzled expression on his face.

"Hi!" Radha stammered, "I'm your next-door neighbour, Radha Misra. I just came by to welcome you here."

The woman smiled as she appraised her.

"I saw you the other day, didn't I? On the balcony?"

"Y...yes, that was me."

"Are those gorgeous flowers for us?" She jumped up and took them out of her hands, burying her nose in the bouquet.

"Yes, I just..." Radha ran out of words.

Mr Das stood up and walked towards her. He ushered her into the room and directed the maid to bring some water.

"Oh no, I'm fine," Radha protested.

"Nonsense, darling," the woman twirled with the bouquet, "no one is fine without a drink in their hands. Monish, water? Really? Don't you want to offer our guest something stronger? What would you like? Some wine? Whisky? Rum?"

"No, I don't drink alcohol. Water is fine." Radha fidgeted in the chair. This wasn't what she had expected at all. She'd hoped for a quick introduction, a bit of polite conversation and a fast getaway. Instead, here she was sitting with these people who she surmised she had nothing in common with. The woman was decidedly strange—hyperactive and watchful, all at the same time.

"Oh, look at us. We haven't even introduced ourselves to you yet. I'm Mira, and this is Monish. M&M." Her eyes twinkled as she said this. "Sorry, the house is still quite a mess, but we haven't really had the time to set it up yet."

Radha looked around. Aside from the *divan*, a few armchairs and a lamp, the room had no other furnishings. Around twenty boxes were piled up in a corner.

"We were like that for the first few months, too. It takes time," Radha said.

"How long have you lived here?" Monish asked, stubbing his cigarette out in a mug.

"Only six months. My husband, Shyam, just got a new job in RevZone and the commute from Delhi was proving too difficult, what with the long hours..." Radha trailed off.

"*Chai*!" Mira yelled, and Radha nearly dropped her glass of water. "Sorry, that came out louder than I'd planned. Monish, I swear, this maid pretends she's deaf half the time. Tilo! Tilllooooo!!"

"Calm, my pet. She's probably taken Batman for a walk. I'll get the *chai* started." Monish stood up and made his way to the kitchen. Radha watched him, open-mouthed.

"What? Never seen a man make tea before?" Mira laughed at her.

"I...I...No." Radha blushed, discomfited.

"Don't worry, I've trained him well. The *chai* will be very good, you'll see. Now, tell me all about yourself."

Radha observed the woman sitting across from her, trying to decide which bits of her life she wanted to divulge. Dressed in an oversized striped shirt and short shorts, hair in a messy ponytail, and her large amber eyes that were gazing intently at Radha, she decided this was the sort of woman she needed to steer clear of. There was something wild and unpredictable about her, as if societal rules did not apply, and she could and would do anything she liked. She unsettled Radha, and that was a feeling she was not at home with.

❖

"Not our kind of people? What does that mean, Radha?" Shyam spooned some more of the *daal* into his plate.

"I just mean they are very... liberated. He is making the *chai* while she is drinking whisky. She says she doesn't cook because she doesn't like to. They are both professors, but she's taking a hiatus to write a book."

"Hmm, well, nothing wrong with any of that."

"Wrong?" Radha spluttered. "You've never even set foot in the kitchen here!"

"I don't need to. You take care of me like the good little wife that you are." He grinned at her, the dimple in his left cheek deepening. Radha couldn't help smiling back. He was so devilishly handsome that she could never resist his charms.

It was funny that she hadn't encountered Shyam until her third year in college. Not funny in a comical manner, but ironically funny as Sangita was her best friend and it would have been natural to run into him much earlier. Sangita and she had spent almost every waking hour together, discussing Freud and Jung, and whether eating another one of the greasy patties in the canteen would affect their figures adversely. In their very first month in college, as Psychology Honours students, they had bonded over their love of old Hindi movies and obscure Phantom comics. Sangita often spoke of her brother, who was studying in IIT Kanpur, but as Radha had two older brothers of her own, she paid little attention. Brothers were just irritating, noisy, condescending characters who made her life a misery every time they were around. Of course, it didn't help that her brothers were a decade older than her. With five years between Sangita and Shyam, she had assumed that they weren't that close either. How wrong she was.

That night, as she cleared up, leaving the dishes in the sink for the maid to wash the next morning, she wondered what had brought such disparate characters as Monish and Mira together. One was so grounded and placid, the other so fiery and volatile. Perhaps it was those differences? Opposites did attract, didn't they?

Was she just as different from Shyam? She couldn't tell. It felt as though she had just drifted from one home into another, never quite knowing her own mind. How did Mira see her? As a good little wife, a boring, typical young Indian woman slave to the men in her life, or just an acquaintance to wave and smile at occasionally?

With a huff, she switched off the light. Why was she fixating on this woman? She wanted nothing more than a cordial, neighbourly relationship anyway. So what did it matter what she thought of her?

She climbed into bed with Shyam, who set his book down without a word and turned towards her. He loosened her bun and let her hair tumble down on her shoulders before pulling her close and placing his lips on hers. A slight shiver of excitement went through her. It never failed to amaze her that her body had this power over his. He groaned as she closed her hands over his hardness, then gasped as he turned her over and plunged into her from behind. With her face in the pillow muffling her soft cries, he rode her till he was spent. Then he pulled out of her and placed a soft kiss on her neck.

"You are so beautiful, my Radhu," he whispered, turning her back around to face him.

She smiled at him, shyly, before reaching up to kiss his dimple.

He laughed and took her into his arms, falling asleep moments later. She watched his face as he slept, remembering how she had thought of him as a middle-aged man only hours earlier. It seemed like a betrayal now. This was her young and virile husband, and they had years to enjoy each other and their youth together.

Old age could wait.

That Sunday, the traffic was terrible as they drove towards Delhi and the traffic jam at the border checkpoint took them over an hour to negotiate.

Radha rolled down the window of the car.

"Why are you doing that?" Shyam said with a frown. "It's letting all the air conditioning out."

"I'm tired of sitting in the cold. I need a bit of fresh air."

"Are you crazy? What fresh air? There's just pollution and exhaust fumes. Roll up that window now."

Radha complied, then turned towards him.

"Why is it always us going to them? Could they not come to us for a change? I could prepare lunch, and for once, we could have a Sunday at home."

"Radha, my parents are too old to drive all the way to Gurgaon. Besides which, it is my duty as a son to visit them. Why are you complaining? I'm the one doing the driving and they don't expect you to cook. In fact, it's a break from the kitchen for you."

Radha kept her face neutral as she looked out of the window. She had dressed in a green and gold saree from her trousseau today, put on her gold bangles, worn her *mangalsutra* and applied *sindoor* in the centre parting of her hair after coiling it into a bun. She fidgeted, feeling uncomfortable, envying Shyam his T-shirt and jeans. As a relatively new bride, less than a year into marriage, she was expected to dress up every time she visited her in-laws. She didn't dare object as they were traditional people who expected a certain conformity from their daughter-in-law.

"Will Sangita be there?"

"I'm not sure. She may not be back from the school trip."

Lucky Sangita! On a trip to Darjeeling with her students. How she had stayed unmarried at twenty-two was something that constantly mystified Radha.

"Are they still looking for a boy for her?"

"Maa and Baba? Of course they are, but Sangita is as stubborn as a mule. She won't agree to marry anyone unless he ticks all her boxes. You know what she's like."

The traffic had finally started to move and as their car inched forward, Radha wondered what would have happened if she had been equally stubborn with her parents. What if she had said that she didn't want to marry just then? What if she had asked to do her master's? Or work?

She looked at Shyam from under her lashes. She would have lost him for sure. Such an eligible man would not have lasted long on the marriage market. And she could just imagine the furore at home. Mummy would have been horrified and Papa would have insisted it was all thanks to her B.A. degree that she was getting these strange ideas. Women were meant to get married, keep home and have babies. Work was for men.

When they finally arrived two hours later, it was well past lunchtime.

"Sorry Maa," Shyam planted a kiss on his mother's head, "the traffic was murder."

Radha kept her head covered with her saree *pallav* as she bent to touch her mother-in-law's feet.

"You should have left earlier then, *na*?" her mother-in-law chided her. "You know Baba needs to eat by a certain time after his insulin injection."

"Sorry, Maa," Radha murmured, following them indoors. Baba was sitting in his usual place watching cricket on the television, and he grunted as she touched his feet.

"*Bahu,*" he said to her, "bring me my *supaari* from the table."

His incisors were almost entirely black, and Radha suppressed her shudder as she fetched him the betel nuts and *paan masala* from the table. She hoped Shyam wouldn't turn to these addictive stimulants later in life. It was ironic that the very same people who frowned upon smoking and drinking didn't bat an eyelid when it came to these substances.

"Come," her mother-in-law called out, "I'm serving lunch. We ate earlier as we didn't know how long you would be."

Sitting at the table, Radha added little to the conversation. Lunch was an elaborate affair of three vegetables, a daal, raita, *papads, puris* and *achaar,* followed by carrot *halwa.* She made a great show of complimenting her mother-in-law on everything. One time, she had accidentally said how she disliked *karela,* the bitter gourd vegetable that she could not stomach, and hadn't heard the end of how much she had offended her in-laws. Only profuse apologies had amended the situation.

It still baffled her that such domineering and orthodox people had produced two kind, gentle and thoughtful people like Shyam and Sangita. Not that Shyam did not have his faults, but at least he was willing to listen. Anyway, as her mother had pointed out, she was lucky to be living separately from the in-laws. She had her independence, and could live, eat and dress near enough as she chose. Her mother had lived her entire married life under her in-laws' roof, and it wasn't until they had passed away that she had been able to assert herself or place her own stamp on her home. Times were changing, and Radha was the lucky beneficiary of the changes. Although, sometimes, Radha wondered whether freedom was a word that could apply to her existence. Then she would shoo these rogue thoughts away and apply herself to being the very best version of herself that she could.

"Did you hear about Rohini?" Her mother-in-law asked Shyam as she placed another *puri* on his plate.

"Who, Mrs Bhola's daughter? The one who went to America to study?"

"Yes. She brought home a *gora* boyfriend, an *Amreeki*!"

Shyam guffawed.

"That skinny brown thing with spectacles? She has a boyfriend?"

"Oho, she has turned all hep now. Wears these tight-tight clothes and walks around holding hands with him."

"What did the Bholas say?"

"What can they say? They have to pretend it is all okay, that she is getting married to him next year. How else are they going to shut everyone up? The whole locality is scandalised!"

Her father-in-law grunted from his corner, and let out a gentle fart before turning his attention back to the screen.

❖

"Want to stop over at your parents' before heading home?" Shyam asked as he was starting the engine in the car.

"Really?" Radha couldn't suppress her excitement at this unexpected development.

"Well, why not? It's been over a month since you saw them, *na*?"

She leaned over and gave him a hug. He really was a wonderful husband.

The distance from Jangpura to Lajpat Nagar was a mere 3-4 kilometres, and with the traffic having thinned out, they made it there in less than ten minutes.

Papa opened the door and let out a yelp of delight upon spotting Shyam.

"*Arey beta*, why didn't you call? We would have ordered some food in. How are you? Come in, come in. So nice to see you."

Radha gave her father a tight hug, and he responded with a pat on her head, turning his attention back to Shyam.

"You are looking well. I hope our girl is taking good care of you? *Arey*, Mona, look who is here!"

Mummy came out of the bedroom and immediately went into a paroxysm of euphoria. Radha sighed internally. Shyam was always treated like a VIP, and she was always the afterthought. Still, it was nice to visit, and she really ought to be grateful that he had brought her here. So many husbands never gave their in-laws the time of day. At least Shyam was civil and courteous to them, even as they flapped around him, offering him *samosas* and *kachoris.*

"Radha, come in the kitchen and help me make the tea," Mummy ordered.

Together, they measured out the cups of water and put it in a metal pan to boil. Radha sliced the ginger and ground the spices while Mummy added the tea leaves and sugar to the water.

"So, how is everything?"

"Good, Mummy. How are you and Papa doing?"

"We are okay, but I want to know if all is well with you."

Puzzled, Radha looked up from grinding the spices in the mortar with the pestle.

"Why wouldn't it be?"

"Radha, *bitiya,* it's been ten months since you were married. You still haven't given us any good news."

Radha blushed and looked down.

"Is everything alright in that department?" Mummy persisted with her line of questioning.

"Of course it is, Mummy. Please!"

"Don't be silly, child. Any mother with an ounce of sense would ask these questions. I'm surprised your in-laws aren't asking you yet. I don't want people thinking there is something wrong with you and you can't conceive."

"Mummy, please," Radha's eyes filled with tears. This wasn't the welcome she had expected.

"Are you one of these modern couples who wait for a few years before having children? A bad idea, I tell you! Best way to tie a man to you is to produce his child. Then he's not likely to go wandering off."

Radha nodded her head, hoping this would shut her mother up. It wasn't like they were averse to having children, but neither of them was in a hurry either.

"And your Papa and I aren't getting any younger. We would like to play with our grandchildren before we have to bid this world goodbye."

Radha didn't have the heart to point out that they barely played with the five grandchildren they had already. She knew this was an argument she was unlikely to win, so it was best to let the words wash over her.

Later, as she poured the tea into the teacups and carried them out into the living room, she had a flashback to the first time she had served Shyam tea in this very room. The first time he had come to 'see' her officially. She had kept her eyes on the floor and carried the tray in with as much grace as she could muster.

A year later, so much had changed, and yet, so much remained the same.

CHAPTER 2

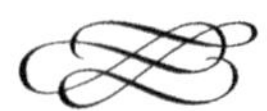

The doorbell rang repeatedly. Annoyed, Radha dropped the mop to the floor, washed her hands quickly and made her way to the door. She hoped it wasn't the maid who had called in sick for the last three days. Radha intended to give her a piece of her mind.

She yanked the door open, a scowl on her face.

"Hey, neighbour!" Mira stood there with a small box in her hands. Her hair was piled in a messy knot held together with what looked like chopsticks, and she was dressed in a silky blue kaftan. "Thought I'd bring you these. Gosh, you look rough. Everything okay?"

Stunned, Radha nodded her head, motioning for her to enter the house. It had been over a month since she had been to visit them, and since everything had been quiet on that front, her own interest in Mira Das had ebbed naturally. Now, here she was, bearing who-knew-what in her hands, acting all chummy. What did this signify?

"These are some cupcakes I'd baked over the weekend. Coffee and cardamom flavoured. They are so yummy, and I figured I'd bring some over to you."

"Thank you, that's really kind. Can I make you a tea or coffee?"

"A coffee would be great, thanks. Shall I bring these into the kitchen?" Mira followed her in, placing the box on a side. "Everything is so tidy... and masculine. You do like your chrome, don't you?"

"Shyam does. It was his idea to decorate the house in this manner."

"Very minimalistic. Black and chrome is every man's wet dream, isn't it?"

Radha blushed and nodded. Mira's choice of words had shocked her, but she didn't want her laughing at her again, so she turned her back to reach into the fridge for the milk.

"Would you like some biscuits with your coffee?" She asked over her shoulder.

"Sure, why not? Hey! I forgot to ask if this is a good time for you. If it's not," Mira glanced at the abandoned mop, "I could come back another time..."

Radha followed her glance.

"Oh, no. Don't worry about it. And sorry about the mess. The maid has been playing hooky the last three days, and I was just cleaning up."

"My goodness, you are a little star! If anything happened to Tilo, I would be lost."

"Tilo?"

"Tilottama, our live-in maid. You know. You met her when you popped in."

"Oh, yes." Radha brought out the coffee and biscuits, wishing she had worn something smarter than the old *salwar-kameez* she wore to do housework. Not that Mira's kaftan was particularly formal, but she just looked so stylish that Radha felt gauche and awkward next to her.

"Is this your wedding photograph?" Mira picked up the framed photo from the side cabinet. "How stunning you are! You really don't need all that makeup, though. It never ceases to amaze me that brides are tarted up to this extent. I mean, you are naturally beautiful. What was the need for all that?" She waved her hand around her face.

Radha felt annoyed and relieved at the same time. She remembered looking at herself in the mirror shortly after the makeup artist had finished with her, and wondering at the face staring back at her. The red lips, the acres of rouge, the false lashes felt like they belonged on some other girl. But Mummy had insisted that all brides had to look a certain way, so she had gone along with it.

"Hey, you've gone really quiet. I hope I haven't offended you?" Mira said, placing the photograph down.

"No," Radha found herself laughing, "I was just thinking that I agree with you. I didn't feel like myself on my wedding day, but I thought that's how you were meant to look and feel. It isn't like any other day, is it?"

Mira smiled. "No, it's not. Although Monish and I just had a simple registry, and it felt like just another day to me. A quick lunch with some friends and back to normality."

"Did you not want a big wedding?"

"Not particularly. It was just a formality, anyway. We'd been living together for over two years at that point."

At Radha's sharp intake of breath, Mira said, "Have I shocked you? It's unconventional, I'll grant you, but not unheard of."

"Umm, no, no, it's okay." Radha took a big gulp of her coffee and ended up coughing and spluttering all over herself. Mira took the cup out of her hands and whacked her back a few times.

When she was back to breathing normally, she apologised, "I'm sorry, the coffee went down the wrong way."

Mira sat back in the armchair and observed her.

"You know, Radha, I don't know you at all, but I am going to say something that you may or may not appreciate." She took another sip of her coffee before placing her cup on the table, missing the coaster entirely. "Don't apologise for every little thing. You don't need to. And learn to assert yourself. Getting swept up in other people's ideas and visions might work in the short term, but long term, it will chafe on your soul."

Radha stared at her. She didn't know what to make of this strange woman sitting in front of her, imparting life advice so casually. But something about her words resonated strongly with her. It was at that moment that she decided she needed Mira Das in her life. Aside from Sangita and a few school friends, she had no other close female friendships. Mira represented freedom, choice, and independence.

None of which had been present in Radha's own life. Perhaps, little by little, she could learn to exhibit and fulfil her own desires and taste a bit of what Mira took for granted. Perhaps, under her tutelage, she could become the woman she really wanted to be.

"Mira?"

"Yeah, sorry." She grimaced. "Shouldn't have said that. I'll go now."

"No! I wanted to ask: will you stay for lunch?"

❖

"So, you've been meeting her every day?" Sangita spooned the *chaat* into her mouth as she spoke.

"Not every day. Every other day. We go for a walk in the locality some days. Sometimes she comes over for lunch and sometimes I go over." Radha took a bite of her *kachori* after blowing on it to cool it down.

"And Shyam is okay with this?" Sangita raised an eyebrow.

"Yes, he's happy I've got a friend in the colony now." What Radha omitted was that he was not aware of how frequently she was meeting up with Mira. Her friendship was too new and too special to let him in just yet. Eventually, she hoped he would get to meet and like Mira as much as she did, her initial reservations notwithstanding. For now, though, she wanted the friendship to grow as organically as possible with no interference from the outside.

"Wasn't this the same woman you'd said was odd?"

"Yes, but that was before I really got to know her. She's not like most women, that's for sure. But she's quirky and very much her own person. I think you'd like her, Sangi." Radha resorted to the college nickname she had had for Sangita.

"Hmmm. T, I just think you should be careful about who you let in. Remember when that strange bird latched on to you in the first year of college? Rita, Gita something..."

"Reena."

"Yes, her. One minute you were feeling sorry for her, the next minute she was stuck to you like glue. It took close to six months to dislodge her."

"I still feel bad about that. She had no other friends, and when we dropped her, she was so lonely."

"I recall all those lovelorn looks she'd give you as you walked past."

"I'm glad she found her own group, eventually."

"Of other odd bods."

Radha shook her head.

"No, this isn't like that at all. If anything, I think she feels sorry for me."

"For you? Why on earth?"

"Because all she sees is a lonely young woman who has no other purpose in life other than taking care of her husband and home."

"Nothing wrong with that. Both our mothers are housewives and perfectly content being so."

"Are they really? Have we ever asked them how they really feel about it?"

Sangita leaned forward and put her palm on Radha's forehead. "Are you running a temperature? Why all these doubts suddenly? Is Shyam not treating you well?"

Radha swiped her hand off with a grin.

"Of course he's treating me well. You'd be the first person I'd complain to if he wasn't!"

Sangita set her spoon down and looked at Radha.

"Promise me you would. He's my brother and I love him dearly, but I will not have him treating you unkindly."

"Don't be silly, Sangi. He's a wonderful husband."

"I'm glad to hear that, but I still feel that you rushed into marriage. You could have waited, you know?"

Could she have? Sangita did not understand the subtle pressure she had lived under her entire life. Conformity was second nature to her. How could she have resisted? What could she have said to her parents?

Sangita waved the waiter over.

"Okay, so we'll have one *chana bhatura,* and one *Amritsari thali* as well."

"Are you sure we can manage that much more food?" Radha asked.

"Listen, we used to eat twice as much in college. Don't know about you, but I'm starving!"

They were at their old college hangout, Bengali Sweet House, in South Extension. This was where they retreated to at the beginning and end of every term, gorging themselves on delicious street food from *golgappas* to *tikkis* to *jalebis*. It was here they had fought over who was more desirable as a crush, Aamir Khan or Shahrukh Khan. It was at their own little table in the corner that they had revised for their exams while wolfing down plates of vegetarian Hakka noodles. This was where Sangita had told her that Shyam had been bowled over by Radha at their first meeting. This place held many memories for them.

"So, how's school?"

"Not bad. Not bad at all."

"And the school trip?"

"Was great!" Sangita blushed a little as she said this.

"Anything you want to tell me?"

Sangita stared at her hands before looking up. Her eyes were shining as she said, "Actually..."

Marriage had never been the destination. Not at first. Somewhere within her, though, Radha had always known that's where she would end up. At twenty-one, however, she was still enjoying her college life, gratified that higher education had not been withheld from her. Even if the condition had been that she would attend an all-girls college.

Having gone to a co-ed school with boys, it had been a bit of a shock to her system to be surrounded by only girls. In the first few days, she had tentatively felt her way through, trying to ascertain who she would get along with, and who was just not her type of person. It was then that she had started a conversation with Reena, a fellow first-year student like herself.

Reena had been awkward and shy, with fidgety movements, short curly hair and a five o'clock shadow that hinted at a hormonal issue. Radha had felt sorry for her and taken her under her wing, not entirely sure whether this friendship would develop long-term. Within a week, she had figured out that they were not a good fit, but hadn't had the heart to break it off. Friendships, she realised, were just as fraught with heartbreak as any other relationship.

It wasn't until Sangita had marched into college four days later, taken one look at Radha, and decided she wanted to be friends with her that Reena had been relegated to playing third wheel in their friendship group. It had taken nearly six months of heavy hint-dropping by Sangita, furtive plans that didn't involve Reena, and the picking of silly fights, for her to finally get the hint and wander away from them. Even though Radha had never been entirely comfortable with what had transpired, she had also felt curiously relieved at Sangita taking charge of the situation.

In the following years, she had grown so close to Sangita that she had started considering her a sister. There was also a healthy rivalry between them to claim the second and the third spots in their exams results, the first spot being permanently allocated to an *uber*-intelligent and studious girl called Vanita.

They had many crushes that ranged from American pop stars to Hindi film stars, but never on anyone 'real'. They would not allow their minds or hearts to go there. As girls who belonged to relatively conservative families, they had always known that their husbands would be chosen for them by their parents. Both of them hoped that within the arranged marriage set-up, they would also find love and companionship.

Of the two of them, Sangita was the bolder and more stubborn one. She knew just how to get what she wanted from her father, who had a soft spot for his younger child. Radha had no such leeway with her parents, who, after having their two sons, had been surprised to discover they were pregnant with another child in their forties. While they weren't over the moon at the news, they had accepted it graciously enough and started setting aside enough money for her dowry from the day she was born. The only allowance they had made was to permit her to do a psychology degree, with the proviso that as soon as she had graduated, they would start looking for a husband for her.

Any dreams she had had of finding a job and working for a while before marriage were just that. How Sangita had convinced her parents to let her work she never found out. Her own life had taken a strange and unexpected turn in her final year at college.

Radha had gone over to Sangita's house to pick up some notes when she had run into Shyam for the first time. She had only had a moment to say a shy hello before leaving, but as Sangita related it, it had been enough to leave quite an impression on the young and very marriageable Mr Misra. He hadn't stopped haranguing his sister for her details, and once the parents had found out about his interest, it had set the ball rolling. This would see Sangita's parents reach out to hers and put forward a *rishta* for her; a formal request for her hand in marriage for their eligible, well-educated, well-placed and handsome *Khatri* son. Of course, that they came from the same caste had gone a long way in convincing the elder Misras that Radha would be a good match for their son. They had even agreed to waive the dowry, in lieu of a new car and a contribution towards the young couples' honeymoon.

At first, Radha had been flattered. This was the first time that a man had evinced this much of an interest in her. Then she had developed cold feet. She was not ready for marriage, regardless of how handsome and eligible Shyam was; regardless that he was her best friend's brother. There was also the fact that she had never completely warmed to Sangita's parents, finding them orthodox and judgemental, albeit no less than her parents. She couldn't share these reservations with anyone, so she had demurred, asking for a bit of time. Time enough to complete her degree, at least. Hoping that if she played her cards right, her parents would allow her to work awhile before settling down.

That's when Mummy had taken to the bed with a mysterious ailment. Convinced she was dying, she had extracted oaths from her daughter that she would see her married before meeting her Maker. Partially afraid that this was true, Radha had agreed to getting married, as long as she could sit her exams after marriage. Furious at her mother's equally rapid recovery, she had felt like baggage being disposed of, while also realising that it could have been much worse. Whatever little she had seen of Shyam, she had liked. Having Sangita as a sister-in-law had felt like fate too.

Meanwhile, Sangita had not just secured herself a job, but had also fallen for the Taekwondo teacher at the school. Radha knew that this would go down like a tonne of bricks with her in-laws. How would Sangita wiggle out of this one?

❖

Mira stopped short in front of the *peepal* tree.

"You can't be serious!"

Radha twisted her *dupatta* in her hands and nodded again. They had been friends for nearly four months, and nervous though she was, she also felt it was time to come clean to her friend.

"I am serious."

"And you allowed them to do this?"

"I didn't have a choice."

"What?" Mira ran her fingers through her hair, exasperation written all over her face. "You *always* have a choice."

"Not where I come from. Your parents..."

"Mother."

"Yes, mother. She seems quite...uhh...bohemian?"

"She's a sixties child."

"Well, my folks aren't like that at all. If anything, it's like they are still living in the previous century."

"So, they allowed your in-laws to change your name?!"

"Mmm-hmm."

"I did think Radha was such an old-fashioned name... Sorry, no offence!"

"They chose it because they thought it went well with Shyam."

"Like the whole Radha Krishna thing?"

"Yes, well, Shyam is another name for Lord Krishna, so Radha was the name they picked for me."

"What is your real name? The one your parents gave you?"

"Tina."

"That's a pretty name, and it suits you! Why on earth did they want to change it?"

"They said it was too modern and westernised."

"Wow! They sound like a charming lot."

"You have no idea."

"And your husband? He was okay with this?"

"I don't think he had an opinion on it one way or another."

"Well, it's a good thing they haven't encountered me. I'd have a thing or two to say to them about this!"

"Please, Mira! I've told you this in the strictest confidence. Please don't say anything to anyone about this. Not even to Monish. Please?"

"Very well, if you insist."

They were on their third round around the block when Mira said, "Since we are in the mood for confessions, I have one to make too."

"Oh?"

"I didn't want to change my surname to Das, but bowed to pressure from friends and colleagues."

"What kind of pressure?"

"They said it would be easier in the long run to have the same surname. Especially when applying for EMIs for the house or visas to travel abroad. I guess I got lazy and figured, why not?"

"Most women change their surnames to their husbands' after marriage. I don't think it's that big of a deal." Radha said.

"Let's sit here for a bit." Mira sat on a bench, patting the spot next to her. "Yes, it's true that our surnames belong to our fathers or our husbands, but I think our names are so closely tied to our identities. For instance, you've told me your name was Tina, but I can't think of you as anything else but Radha anymore. You can think I'm nuts, but I do believe that we become our names. Everything has a vibration, and the sound of one's name becomes the vibration of one's personality. A strong name will nearly always have a strong personality attached to it, and vice versa."

"But who is to say which name is strong and which is weak?" Radha interjected. "It's perception, isn't it? Maybe you think of Radha as a weak name because you think I'm not strong; that I don't think for myself and am easily led. But I was Tina when I submitted to it all, and had I still been called Tina, my life would be no different."

Mira was silent for a moment. Then she placed her hand on Radha's.

"I don't think of you as weak at all. I think you are a very smart young woman who has yet to discover all that she has to offer to the world. Sometimes I forget we live in such a patriarchal country where a woman has to choose which battles are worth fighting."

Radha squeezed her hand in return.

"I'm sorry. I didn't mean to project my insecurities onto you. I am happy in my marriage despite everything. He is a good man who cares for me. Do I want more? Of course I do. But I also realise that the grass is nearly always greener on the other side."

"Say," Mira said with a smile, "Don't you think it's time our husbands met?"

"Tilo?" Radha had been hoping it would be Mira who answered the phone, but it was her maid instead. In all these months, she had still not deciphered her accent. "*Memsahib kidhar?*"

"*Memsahib soi raha hai.*"

It was 10am and Mira was still asleep. Radha felt a pang of envy. She had woken at 6:30am to pack Shyam's lunch, then she had woken him, ironed his shirt while he showered, laid out his tie and briefcase, and prepared breakfast for him. Only after she had seen him off to work did she have her first cup of tea, before letting the maid in to do the sweeping-swabbing and the dishes. By the time 10am came around, she felt like half a day had gone by.

"Hallooo?" Tilo sounded puzzled at the long pause.

"Please tell Mira *memsahib* that I won't be able to go for a walk with her today. I'm going to Delhi for our festival."

Tilo's garbled answer sounded like a yes and Radha rung off, hoping the message would reach Mira intact. Sometimes she felt that Tilo wasn't the full ticket, but what did she know? The Das' functioned perfectly well with her, and her own shrewish maid was far more trouble than Tilo had ever been.

Radha pulled out the little case from under the bed and started packing her clothes for the next few days. While she was excited about seeing Sangita, she was also dreading spending the next two nights at her in-laws. But there was no escaping it. Her first *Karva Chauth* had to be spent in the company of her mother-in-law, following the rituals to the letter, and receiving her blessings. Shyam had told her to take a taxi and that he would get there directly after work.

She made sure to take her heaviest saree, the red silk with the gold *gota patti.* She packed a cerise *salwar kameez,* her gold jewellery, lipsticks and *bindis* to match. Radha wasn't much of a makeup enthusiast, but on an occasion like this it was expected, and she didn't want to run afoul of Shyam's mother.

She showered, wore a simple pink *kurti* and her mangalsutra, and tied her hair in a plait. As she was travelling by public transport, she didn't want to appear conspicuous. Daytime robberies were rare but not unheard of.

The taxi arrived promptly at 2pm. She carried her case downstairs and placed it in the boot before casting a quick glance at Mira's house. There was no movement, so she shrugged and got into the taxi. She was sure Mira would have lots of opinions about the festival, but it was one she was looking forward to celebrating.

All her life she had seen her mother fast for her father's well-being and long life. As a young girl, she had asked if she could take part too, but had been told it was only for married women. There was something so special and beautiful about performing a ritual such as this for your husband. She couldn't wait to start fasting tomorrow.

When she arrived at her in-laws in the afternoon, Sangita was still not back from school. She paid the driver and hauled her case inside. Her mother-in-law gave her the once over as she bent to touch her feet.

"Where's Shyam?"

"He'll be here in the evening."

"Okay, take your things into his bedroom. I've set it up for you."

Being back in the room brought back memories of her early days of marriage. Shortly after the wedding, she had moved in with Shyam's family. Right from the start, she had been expected to get up at dawn and start work in the kitchen. Shyam's mother did not believe in hiring full-time or part-time help. In a way, it was a test to see if Radha would fit in with the family. She must have passed because even though her mother-in-law grumbled out of habit, there were no direct complaints to her parents about her being lazy or insolent. Her mother had taught her well.

Radha unpacked her case and hung her clothes next to the many shirts and trousers that Shyam had left behind. It was so easy for him to come back here and fit right in; this was his home, after all. Despite living here for the first four months of their marriage, it had never felt like hers.

In the evening, as she was making tea for everyone, the doorbell rang.

"*Haan,* your mother has sent the *baya.* Come," her mother-in-law instructed.

Heart pounding, Radha took the box out of the courier's hand, hoping everything was as it should be. Unwrapping it she found two boxes of *mithai,* a coconut, one silver *thali* filled with dried fruits, a dark green *saree* shot through with gold thread for her mother-in-law, a *rani* pink *dupatta* for Sangita, a silk shirt for Shyam, a *khaadi kurta-pyjama* for her father-in-law, and finally, a red and yellow *band-hani* print *saree* for her. There were bangles and assorted pieces of costume jewellery alongside a small pot of *sindoor,* the traditional vermillion all married women wore in the centre parting of their hair.

"Very nice," her mother-in-law uttered, clearly satisfied.

Radha presented it all to her formally, covering her head and touching her feet again for her blessings.

"*Sada suhaagan raho.*" A blessing to remain wedded forever.

Radha thanked her and went back to the kitchen to finish making the tea. When Sangita arrived, she saw Radha standing at the kitchen window staring out into the street.

"Hey T, what are you looking at?"

Radha turned and smiled before hugging Sangita. "Nothing, I was just lost in my thoughts. I was thinking we have such lovely traditions, don't we? I can't wait to fast for Shyam."

"Is he fasting for you?"

"What? Don't be silly! Men don't fast."

Sangita lowered her voice. "Mine is. And I will, as well."

"But you're not married..."

"Shhh. It's okay. Maa allows it. She thinks it will help with finding a good husband. She doesn't know I've found one already!"

Sangita giggled, then composed her face promptly as her mother walked into the kitchen.

The women woke before dawn the next day, and Shyam's mother served them *sargi* which comprised fresh fruit, dry fruits, a small bowl of halwa, a plain *roti* and some vegetables cooked with a light *tarka.* As they wouldn't be eating any food or drinking any water for the rest of the day, this had to sustain them until sunset.

When Shyam woke at 7am, Radha had already prepared breakfast and helped Sangita with the laundry and ironing. Sangita had taken the day off from work, and Radha hoped Shyam would consider it too.

"Nonsense, Radha. Try explaining that to my American boss: Sir, I can't come into work because my wife is not eating all day long. He'll laugh in my face."

"But..."

"No buts. I'll try to finish early. That's all I can do."

He gave her a quick peck on her cheek before leaving the room. Any displays of physical affection were strictly forbidden in front of the elders. She thought back to her childhood. She didn't recall her parents ever holding hands even.

After the household chores were completed, the women lay down for a siesta. Sangita came and lay on the bed with her.

"How are you feeling?"

"A bit faint, to be honest. It's not the food I'm missing, it's not being able to drink any water."

"I know," Sangita groaned. "This is torture. I hope Hari is suffering too."

"Have you spoken to him?"

"How? Maa knows exactly how many phone calls are being made, and she watches everyone like a hawk. There is no way I'd get away with it."

"Sangita?"

"Hmmm?"

"You think your parents will agree to this match? He's a South Indian, and you said he's a non-vegetarian too. I'm not sure they are going to like this."

"I know they aren't, but don't worry, I'll figure a way out."

Radha stayed silent. She couldn't imagine standing up to her parents, let alone hoodwinking them in this way. But she hoped it would turn out alright for her friend. If marrying this man made her happy, what did it matter if he was from another state, or ate meat, or wasn't of their caste?

"Radha?" Sangita whispered.

"Yes?"

"Still find our traditional festivals amazing and beautiful?"

"Don't be horrid! We just have to get through the next few hours, and then it will be amazing."

They slept fitfully for an hour before Sangita's mother woke them and told them to get ready.

Dressed in their finery, they put fragrant *gajras* in their hair, behaving like teenage girls, laughing and teasing each other, momentarily forgetting their hunger and thirst. Soon they made their way up to the terrace where the neighbourhood women had congregated and were sitting in a circle. They had brought their respective *thaalis,* which contained coconut, fruits, a small *diya,* a glass of *kachi lassi,* and sweets. They sat together and listened to an old woman who conducted the *puja* and sang devotional songs. The women then rotated the *thaalis* around the circle seven times. After the prayer was completed, they touched the feet of their mothers-in-law again before departing for their respective homes.

Later, when the moon was high in the sky, Radha went up to the terrace again and viewed the orb through a sieve while offering it the milk and water of the *kachi lassi.* Shyam waited for her to finish before taking the glass out of her hand and tenderly placing it at her lips. She took her first sip from him and broke her fast, while praying that he would have a long and healthy life.

Downstairs, they touched Shyam's father's feet as well, receiving blessings from him and then proceeding to feast on the delicious meal that the womenfolk had prepared earlier in the day.

As she curled into Shyam at night while he slept, Radha wondered if he had prayed for her long life just as she had for his.

CHAPTER 3

"Well, all of that sounds absolutely wonderful," Mira said, "except I don't get how your sister-in-law broke her fast. Her boyfriend wasn't there to feed her tenderly."

Radha ignored the sarcasm.

"She was smart about that. She kept his photograph in front of her after she had seen the moon, and she fed herself as if it was him feeding her."

"Very clever. Mark my words, this will end in tears."

Mira had all but scoffed at *Karva Chauth,* just as Radha had expected. Instead of feeling annoyed, though, Radha was curious. How could someone be so dismissive of one's culture and tradition?

"Tradition? If we were still following all that tradition, we would be burning widows at their husbands' pyres! What about common sense and logic? And why is it always the woman who is expected to make the sacrifice, while the man gets away scot-free? Trust me, if there was a festival where a man had to starve, it would be abolished in no time."

"Perhaps. But I felt like a part of something that was bigger than me, a history, a kinship with my ancestors and a sisterhood with the other women of the community. You cannot tell me I imagined all of that."

"No, I'm not saying that. There are so many beautiful festivals that we celebrate in this country and I'm not anti-those. It's the regressive ones that I cannot abide. As an educated girl, don't you want to question these practices?"

"Let's not argue, Mira." Radha sighed. She had wanted to have a pleasant walk around the neighbourhood, not get into a debate with her neighbour. One that she was bound to lose.

"It's not an argument, it's a discussion. Why do you shy away from confrontation? It's good to disagree, to expose other points of view."

"Gosh, you must be so exhausting to be married to!" Radha blurted out. Then she bit her lip, realising she had vocalised her exasperation unwittingly. She looked up at Mira's astonished face, not sure whether she would give her a lambasting or cut her cold. Instead, she started laughing, a long, loud belly laugh which had tears streaming down her face. Radha smiled, self-conscious, confused by Mira's reaction. She had not said anything that funny.

When she had finally caught her breath, Mira spoke.

"Two things. You are absolutely right! I am exhausting to be married to, and Monish tells me often enough. But I'll tell you what I found funny. Underneath that prim and proper exterior, you, my little kitten, have very sharp claws. And I love it!"

Mira reached over and slung her arm over Radha's shoulder.

"Hang around with me, and I'll make you into an exhausting wife, too. In the best possible manner!"

"*Na re baba*!" Radha shuddered dramatically. "I want to stay sane and stay married."

Something of the last bit of formality between them evaporated at that moment. They were so unlike one another, but a cord of liking bound them to each other. A liking that transcended age, background, upbringing, political and religious leanings, and all the things that divided people the world over.

If either of them were to be asked later what had drawn them to the other, they would not have been able to give a definitive reply. Yet, in the months that followed, they would become each other's confidantes and champions, challenging the other's thought processes, making them view life through another lens, and offering one another something invaluable—a genuine friendship.

❖

"Come and look at this, Radha," Shyam called out to her.

He was sitting at his laptop, his usual beer by his side. This was the first free half hour she had had to paint her nails, so she bit back her irritation as she placed the nail polish bottle on the table and walked over to him.

Shyam pointed to a photo on his laptop of a young man with spectacles and a serious face.

"What do you think?"

Radha looked at the photo again.

"What am I supposed to think? Who is this?"

"Oof oh! Sit next to me." Shyam scrolled down the page. "Look, this is his bio-data. He's twenty-seven, works in a bank, and is the same caste as us. His sister, who is a colleague, sent this across to me. I think he's quite smart, don't you?"

It slowly dawned on Radha that this was a prospective match for Sangita.

"Hmmm, have you consulted Sangita yet?"

"Consulted Sangita?" Shyam guffawed. "I'll show this to Maa and Baba first. Sangita will only get to see this once they've approved."

Radha bit her lip. It wasn't her place to object, but she had to say something.

"Shyam, if she is the one getting married, isn't it important that she approves?"

"What's gotten into you, Radha? This is how matchmaking has been done for generations. We, as the elders, know best what will work for the girl. We look into everything—family, background, education, prospects—everything. You think Sangita, with her twenty-two-year-old brain, will focus on any of that? She'll just want a handsome guy, end of story. It's our job to see that she finds someone who will provide for her, and be there for her in the good times and the bad."

Radha nodded. She knew all this to be true, but Sangita's secret weighed heavily on her. She decided she would have a quiet word with her warning her of the imminent end to her freedom.

"You're right, of course. I was just thinking as her friend..."

"Don't. You need to start thinking as her sister-in-law now."

Shyam sounded annoyed, and to distract him, she changed the topic.

"By the way, we've been invited next door to Mira's birthday party next Friday evening. Is it okay to go?"

"Mira, the woman you go on walks with?"

And had coffees and lunches, and watched movies with, but Radha had not divulged the extent of their friendship yet, fearful that Shyam would not approve of all the time she was spending with her.

"Yes. Her husband wants to meet you too, and her mother is coming from Bombay as well. It would be nice to go to a social occasion, *na*?"

In the past year, the only socialising they had done had been with Shyam's family, and occasionally, her own. He never took her to his office events, saying that she would feel out of place there. Also, he didn't want to expose his private life to his work colleagues and become the subject of gossip. Radha didn't mind, but sometimes wished she had other people she could mingle with as well. Hence, her friendship with Mira had become so precious to her. She waited with bated breath for his response.

"They are Bengalis, you said?"

"Monish is. Her husband, that is. Mira is a Maharashtrian. She grew up in Bombay and moved to Delhi around nine or ten years ago."

Shyam took a gulp of his beer.

"No children?"

"No, they are both working hard at their careers. He is a professor at some college in Delhi University, and she is on a hiatus..."

"Yeah, yeah, writing a book. You said." Shyam shrugged. "Okay, why not? But if I'm bored, we're leaving early."

Radha hadn't realised she had been holding her breath, and she exhaled quietly. She hoped that taking him along to a party where there were plenty of other guests would gently expose him to a different mindset. She knew if he found out just how liberal Mira and Monish were, he wouldn't be happy about their friendship. In this manner, the exposure would be minimal, and not lead to too much analysis on his part. She hoped.

That night, as Radha brushed her teeth, she felt a sudden trickle of blood between her legs. She spat the paste out and looked at herself in the mirror. Another month had gone by without her conceiving. She was sure to hear some harsh words from Mummy about this. It wasn't as if they were not making love frequently or even using birth control. Right from the start, Shyam had said that he did not wish to use condoms. She was welcome to take birth control pills, but as they were expected to have babies as quickly as possible, she had decided not to. Yet they had been unsuccessful at conception within the first year of marriage. Eyebrows were being raised within the family circles, and soon the whispers would start. She knew as she had seen this happen to other new brides.

As she applied a pad to her panty, she wondered if it was worth visiting a doctor to find out if there was anything wrong with her.

"Radha! How long are you going to be?" Shyam called out from the bedroom.

"Nearly done." She washed her hands quickly, patting them dry on the towel before leaving the bathroom.

He was waiting for her in bed, an expectant grin on his face.

"Not tonight, Shyam. I've just started my period."

"Oh."

His face showed his distaste. He hated talking about her monthlies, and invariably changed the topic if she ever spoke about her cramps, or the occasional stained nightie.

"Right, goodnight then."

He turned his back on her and went to sleep. Radha lay there in the dark, her mind in turmoil. Who could she speak to? Sangita had no experience of such matters. Mummy would just take her to some quack, and Maa would most definitely blame her. Mira? But she had never displayed the slightest interest in babies. Her mind kept churning out thought after thought until she finally fell into a fitful slumber.

❖

"So, I wanted to tell you that you need to figure a way out soon. Either tell them now, or be prepared for that boy and his family to visit."

"But how can I tell them? They'll kill me!"

"Don't be so dramatic, Sangi! They won't kill you."

"Okay T, so they won't kill me. But they'll make me quit my job and cut off all contact with Hari. Is that what you want?"

Radha sighed. This phone call wasn't going well.

"It's not about what I want. It's about what you want. You told me you had a plan, so I'm warning you that it's time to implement the plan. Get Hari's parents to approach Maa and Baba before Shyam gets the ball rolling on this *rishta*."

"T, you have to help me!" Sangita sounded panicked on the other side.

"I'll help you, but how? What do you need me to do?"

"Talk to Shyam. He'll listen to you. Just get him to stop with this *rishta* business."

"You must be joking! Your brother never listens to me." Even as she said this, Radha realised how true it was. In their home, Shyam's word was law. She had never crossed him, and she wondered idly what would happen if she did.

"Please T, you have to try! I'll speak to Hari in the meantime, and figure out how to proceed."

"Okay, okay, I'll try." As she hung up, Radha wondered just what she'd gotten herself into. She knew her in-laws. Everything had to come through the proper channels and be rigorously checked. To consider a Taekwondo instructor at school, a South Indian man who ate meat and was from a different caste, would be like marrying their daughter off to an alien! Still, she realised she had to try. She owed it to Sangita.

It was a Tuesday, and Radha knew that if she said anything to Shyam before Friday, he would refuse to go to the party. So she said an internal prayer and decided to hold off any discussions until after the party. It was slightly selfish of her, but she had been so looking forward to it she couldn't bear to ruin it in any way.

Radha had already decided that she would wear her pale blue silk saree, with the navy blue border. It had been a part of her trousseau and she had only worn it once before. If Shyam wore his blue suit and navy blue tie, they would look good together. People often commented on what a handsome couple they were. She wanted them to look their best as they mingled with Mira's guests.

Perhaps it was her own insecurities, but she knew that a lot of the people at this party were likely to be highly educated, well spoken and well travelled. She didn't want to appear a *behenji*, a pejorative term that a lot of posh South Delhi girls used towards girls from other socio-economic backgrounds.

Sangita and she were not like the Greater Kailash or Vasant Vihar girls, who dressed fashionably and spoke with an upper crust accent, but she refused to conform to the stereotype of a *behenji* either. She was educated and, whilst she had abandoned all western wear after marriage, she had known how to rock a pair of jeans and a T-shirt like any other South Delhi girl back in her teenage years.

As she cooked the evening meal, Radha let her mind wander to her childhood. Growing up in the shadow of her two rambunctious brothers, she had always remained silent and inconspicuous. It hadn't helped that Mummy had never really wanted a girl, and most days had treated her as an afterthought. Neither of her brothers were close to her, either.

When their wives were chosen for them, Mummy had expected that they would all live together under one roof. But one by one, her brothers had moved away at the behest of their wives, citing the lack of space as a reason. It was true that they only had three bedrooms, and growing up, her brothers had shared a room. As soon as they had gotten married, she had had to give up her room and move into the living area. When they left, she had reclaimed her room, but been acutely aware that her mother had turned even more acerbic at this turn of events. Papa had never said a word to the boys, but his disappointment was evident in the way his words dripped sorrow. Their generation had lived with and taken care of their parents in joint families. The new generation wished to live in nuclear families and independent quarters.

When Shyam had proposed moving to Gurgaon, her own knee-jerk reaction had been to think of her in-laws. Would they see this as a betrayal? Would they see her as the perpetrator? In the end, the decision had never been in her hands, anyway. Shyam's commute had been awful, and his parents had agreed to the move as long as he visited them every weekend.

Mira had once asked her about agency. Radha hadn't been sure what she meant, and she had explained that agency was having power over one's own actions and determining one's own course in life. What agency had Radha had? As far as she could tell, very little. But then she thought about her mother's life. She had had even less.

Mummy's education had been cut short at sixteen. She had been married at seventeen, and had moved to Delhi with her new husband at the age of nineteen, heavily pregnant with her first son. Her life had been dedicated to her family, and that became her only zone of control. She could not recall a single moment that Mummy had made a decision without either consulting her husband or his parents first. Not even when she had to return to her town for her father's cremation. Mummy had always said that once she had gotten married, she had become a stranger to her own parents.

Growing up in the shadow of such beginnings, was it any wonder that Radha had no idea what agency meant?

❖

On Friday, Radha pleaded with Shyam to return early. He had taken to going out for drinks with his colleagues on Fridays, and she wanted to make sure he remembered they had a party to attend.

"So, *jaan,* you'll be back by six? I don't want us to be late..."

She only called him *jaan,* her 'life', when she was desperate. It worked every single time. Radha supposed it appealed to his ego that he was her very 'life'. Lately, she had taken to questioning everything internally. It was the 'Mira effect', but she knew that her marriage was nothing like the Das' marriage. Theirs, as Mira had said, was a meeting of minds. Monish was eight years older than Mira, which was almost a generation, but it also made him patient with her outbursts and tolerant of her foibles. Even though Radha had spent little time in their company as a couple, she felt she knew Monish from the tales that Mira narrated to her daily.

He was a pacifist, a believer in the feminist ideology, and a superb cook. To Radha, these qualities were unimaginable. She had never met a man like him before, and the more she heard about him, the more intrigued she became. Yes, he wasn't much in the looks department, but Mira seemed happy with him. There was so much more to a person than their packaging, anyway.

That evening, as she dressed with care, she wondered what Mira would wear to her own party. She had only ever seen her casual outfits of *khaadi kurtas,* jeans, and kaftans. Regardless, Mira was a gorgeous woman, even more so because she never flaunted it and made so little of her looks.

For Radha, being passably pretty had been enough until she married Shyam. He was the one who insisted they always stepped out in coordinated outfits, the one who paid her an allowance to go to the beauty parlour every fortnight, and chided her if she had chipped nail polish. She wondered where his vanity came from. Maa and Baba were simple people who were not interested in fashion or expensive accessories, deeming them frivolous expenses. Sangita lived in cotton sarees and oxidised silver jewellery, her only concession to makeup being the kohl she applied in her eyes. As for Radha, she had shared one lurid red lipstick with her mother before marriage, applied only on special occasions.

Over the past year, however, she had slowly embraced the sleek polish Shyam demanded of her. She kept it subtle because of her aversion to bright colours, but she made sure her hair was shampooed and conditioned, her nails always painted, and every day, she spritzed on the perfume 'Charlie' that Shyam had bought her.

Years ago, when Radha was in her first year of college, she had gone to another college for a quiz competition as a part of a team. It was a hot summer's day and the trek over to the North Campus of Delhi University hadn't been easy. Public buses were her least favourite mode of transportation, but as it was a university bus, she and her team had sat together for most of the journey.

Upon reaching the college, she had rushed to the toilets to relieve herself. Inside the cubicle, she had overheard one of the college students say to another, "I don't understand these *behenjis*. You would think on a day like this at least, they would apply a deo. Gosh, the stench!"

Radha knew they were talking about her as she was the only other person in the toilets apart from the two girls. What Radha didn't know was what a deo was and how to procure it. She had never previously noticed that she had body odour, but as she sniffed at her armpits whilst still in the cubicle, she realised she was emanating a pungent whiff. From that day on, she became obsessed with cleanliness, waxing her armpits and hoarding anti-perspirants.

Grooming had never been high on her parents' list of priorities, but it became sacred to Radha. Shyam, however, took it to another level altogether. His products took up more bathroom space than hers did. She didn't mind. Her husband was a handsome man, and a little vanity was par for the course.

. . .

❖

In the end they were half an hour late, which by Indian standards was early. When Radha rang the doorbell, she expected that there would be many more guests than there were. Mira had said they had invited at least twenty people. When Tilo led them into the living room, she saw Monish at the bar, Mira chatting to a couple seated on the loveseat, and an older lady standing by the gramophone player looking through the records.

Radha swallowed convulsively. This was not the gentle introduction she had been planning for Shyam. She crossed her fingers and said a brief prayer that all would go well tonight. The last thing she wanted was to lose the only friend she had in the locality.

Mira jumped up as soon as she spotted Radha.

"Kitten, you made it!"

Ever since her first faux pas with Mira, she had taken to calling Radha 'Kitten'. It was a joke between them, but now Radha looked at Shyam nervously. She need not have worried. He had his most charming face on, and as he shook hands with Mira, she could tell that he was impressed by the glamorous woman standing in front of him.

Mira had pulled out all the stops. She was wearing a backless red and black *choli,* embellished with multiple mirrors and held together with two strings, leaving most of the expanse of her back bare. Paired with black jeans and high heels, she towered over Radha as she bent down to place a kiss on her cheek. A heady perfume enveloped Radha as she drew away and appraised her.

"You look beautiful, darling!"

Speechless, Radha shook her head. "No... you...you..."

"Shhh, come meet my mum."

Mira led them over to the older lady by the gramophone.

"Mater, this is my friend from next door, the one I told you about. Radha. And this is her husband, Shyam."

Radha folded her hands together in a *namaste,* but the lady reached over and pulled her into a hug.

"Hello!" she said in a husky voice. "You can call me Nisha."

Radha hesitated. She had never called an older person by their first name before. It had always been 'aunty' or 'uncle', regardless of whether they were related or not. It was the Indian way.

She observed Shyam pull out a lighter as Nisha put a cigarette to her lips. This was like no 'aunty' she had ever met. Dressed in black leather trousers and a burgundy sweater, her hair wild and grey, she looked like the very antithesis of a sedate, older woman. Mira had told her something of her mother's history, but nothing had prepared her for this. She also wondered why Shyam was carrying a lighter. It wasn't like he smoked. Or did he?

"Tell me, Nisha," he asked her with his 1000 watt smile, "where are you from?"

As they chatted convivially, Radha wandered towards the bar where Monish was mixing drinks. She was feeling a bit out of sorts. Everyone was so different and strange tonight, and she felt like she had wandered onto the set of a play and didn't know her lines.

"What's your poison, Radha?" Monish asked, squeezing lime into two tall drinks.

"Pardon me?"

"What would you like to drink?"

"Oh…I…I don't drink alcohol. Can I have a Coke, please?"

"Of course." He handed the drinks over to Tilo, who placed them on a silver tray and took them to the seated couple. Then he wiped his hands on a towel and pulled out a bottle of Coca Cola.

"Ice?"

"Yes. Thank you."

He handed her his drink and then took a sip of his own.

"So. How are you doing?"

"Yes, fine. I'm doing good. You?"

Monish ran his fingers through the scant hair on his head.

"To be honest, I'm petrified. I'm hiding out at the bar because being around too many people makes me nervous."

Radha stared at him, not sure if he was joking or saying this to put her at ease.

"But you're a professor! How can people make you nervous?"

"Not students. Teaching is an escape for me, and I love the subject, so that helps. It's social situations like these. I have no idea what to say or do. Mira thrives in social settings." He looked over to where his wife was hugging the latest entrants. "I detest them."

"Oh." Radha looked at him with fresh eyes. "I'm socially awkward, too. You don't mind if I stay here with you?"

"Not at all. But Mira might think I'm monopolising you, and your husband, I haven't met him yet. What will he think?"

"Actually, I've been meaning to introduce him to you. Excuse me, I'll bring him over now."

Radha went over to Shyam and Nisha just as a horde of people entered the room, distracting Nisha.

"I want you to meet Monish, Mira's husband."

"M and M, eh?" Shyam grinned, allowing her to lead him to the bar.

After introductions had been made, and Monish had given Shyam his first double whisky, Mira clapped her hands.

"Hey, everyone! Hey!"

There was a lull in the conversation as everyone turned to stare at her. Radha observed the crowd discreetly, noting that no one else had worn a saree. Most of the women were in little black dresses and the men were in jeans and shirts. She felt like an overdressed fool.

"I just wanted to say a BIG thank you to everyone for coming over today! I know I've been terrible at keeping in touch. First the move, and then the book, have consumed me whole. The only person keeping my sanity intact, apart from my beloved husband," Mira blew a kiss at Monish, "is my new friend, Radha." She pointed in Radha's direction and raised her glass. Everyone turned and looked. Discomfited, Radha managed a smile.

"This has been a year of changes, nearly all good ones. But, as we are almost at the end of 1996, and I'm turning 33 tomorrow, I'm hoping that 1997 will be EPIC! So, grab your drinks, and let's boogie the night away…!"

Music spilled out of the gramophone. Rock and roll from the sixties, as people laughed and clinked their glasses together. Tilo brought out platters of chicken and paneer *tikkas.* Someone yelled out, "Epic, man, epic." Another opened the French doors and stepped out, before stepping back inside saying, "There's a ferocious dog outside." Mira laughed, "That's only Batman."

CHAPTER 4

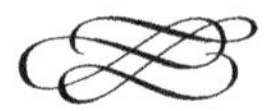

"Well, that was some party!"

They had wandered back home at 2am, and now, Shyam sat on the sofa, his feet propped up on the table drinking the last of his beer. Radha had made herself a cup of tea and she sat with him.

"My feet hurt." She said, kicking off her sandals.

"I have never seen you dance like that." Shyam grinned at her.

"I wasn't planning on it, but then Mira's mother pulled me onto the floor and..."

"No, it was fantastic, but maybe, next time wear something else? You couldn't move freely in that saree."

Next time? There would be a next time? Radha suppressed her excitement, schooling her face into polite acceptance.

"I don't have dresses like that..."

"Not dresses." Shyam frowned. "Thirty-year-old women dressed in minis isn't appropriate. But maybe you could get some nice jeans like Mira, no?"

She had watched Shyam dancing with those thirty-year-olds, and he hadn't objected to their dresses then. Still, she had to take her small victories wherever she could find them.

"So, what did you think of them?"

"The Das family?"

"Yes."

"Interesting lot. Nisha, obviously, is the most fascinating one. Did you know she rides a scooter everywhere in Bombay?"

Radha nodded. She had been equally fascinated by Nisha. A divorcee who lived life on her terms, she was like no one Radha had ever encountered in her life before.

"Anyway, I'm glad you've made friends with them. They are really interesting people, very warm and kind. I like them."

This was unexpected. Radha had expected that Shyam would complain, say that they were too much, and that she didn't need to spend quite as much time in Mira's company. Instead, here he was, giving her his stamp of approval.

The wilder the party had gotten, the more he had seemed to enjoy it. He had thrown his jacket to a side and gulped down one whisky after another, getting friendlier and more tactile with each drink. She had seen one of Mira's friends leaning away from him as he leaned towards her, jabbing his finger in the air, emphasising a point. But there had also been the few who had completely ignored Radha, choosing to concentrate on the handsome young man in their midst.

For most of the party she had stayed by Monish's side, chuckling at his droll observations, warming to him even more as he watched her watching her husband and said, "They are all in a party mood tonight. Nobody will remember any of this tomorrow, and they will have the worst hangovers after mixing their drinks. You, my dear, will be the only one who will wake up bright-eyed and bushy-tailed."

Nisha had played record after record on the gramophone. Music from three decades ago that seemed to work its magic on everyone. Radha had observed this unusual woman from a distance. She was a lot smaller and slighter than Mira, but moved with the same confidence and self-assuredness that Radha envied. Her grey hair was just as much of a statement as her outfit and life choices. This was agency. This was a woman who hadn't caved to society's expectations of her.

She had lived life on her own terms, and it showed in the space she occupied in life and in that room.

Suddenly, Nisha had looked up and caught Radha's eye. Radha had looked away hurriedly, but Nisha had come straight up to her and said, "Enough of being a wallflower. Come on! Let's dance."

They had danced together to "I Want to Hold Your Hand" by the Beatles. Something inside Radha had loosened even while her throat constricted. She could not imagine a moment like this with her own mother. How lucky Mira was! An adoring husband, an enviable life, a gaggle of good friends, and a mother who loved and supported her daughter. What more could a person want?

CHAPTER 5

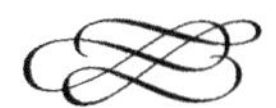

Radha fidgeted in the seat. She was early, and it had taken some convincing to get a table for four when she had walked into the heaving restaurant. This was Bengali Sweet House. Their *adda*, their hangout, their place of comfort. Is that why Sangita had insisted they meet here?

The restaurant buzzed with activity, its interior a kaleidoscope of colours and movement. The clinking of cutlery, the chatter of the diners, and the servers darting from table to table created a harmonious cacophony that echoed off the walls.

She sat at the corner table watching everyone, her heart beating unevenly. How would this pan out? She knew that this wasn't exactly what Sangita had asked of her, but in Radha's mind, if they could convince Shyam, then they had a fighting chance of convincing his parents. Therefore, she had engineered this evening.

As far as Shyam knew, they were meeting to discuss an anniversary dinner for his parents. He didn't know that they were in fact meeting Sangita and Hari today. He had grumbled a bit, but knowing he would be in Delhi all day for meetings, Radha had insisted on this specific evening.

Now, as she tapped her foot nervously, she prayed once again that everything would turn out alright. Shyam had shown his liberal side by embracing her friendship with Mira, even going so far as encouraging it now. Maybe he would surprise them again? Work had been going well for him, and he had been in an expansive mood. There was no better time to introduce Hari than at this juncture.

Just then Sangita walked in, a tall, well-built man following her. Radha recognised Hari from the photo Sangita had shown her. He was dark-skinned with a thick moustache, and tall and muscular with sharp features and a magnetism about his person. Panther-like in his gait, he moved with a suppleness that belied his height and size. She could see what had attracted Sangita to him.

"Hi," a breathless Sangita reached her first, then turned to Hari, "This is T. We call her Radha now. T, this is Hari."

He smiled the whitest smile she had seen, his features softening perceptibly.

"Hello, T. Nice to meet you."

Radha folded her hands together in a *namaste,* returning his greeting.

"Thank you for doing this for us," Hari said as he took a seat next to Sangita.

"What time is Shyam coming? Should we order? I'm so hungry, my stomach is rumbling. I've barely eaten all day out of anxiety," Sangita said while perusing the menu.

Radha didn't mention that she had barely eaten too. She nodded and took another sip of her *chai.*

"I did tell him 5pm, but you know what your brother is like. He'll get here when he gets here."

"As long as he gets here." Sangita bleated out a laugh. "So, he hasn't a clue?"

"Not really. I'm sorry, Sangi, I couldn't find a way to introduce the topic. Besides, having never met Hari before," Radha threw him an apologetic glance, "I didn't know how to vouch for him."

Hari smiled at her. "I understand. Hopefully, I will be able to persuade Shyam that I'm not an axe murderer. I come from a respectable family and even though they live in Madras, sorry,

Chennai—I keep forgetting the new name—they will have no objections to my marrying a North Indian girl. After all, my father is a Malayali while my mother is Tamilian. So, we are very accepting of mixed marriages."

Sangita nodded enthusiastically. "I've already spoken to his sister over the phone, and his parents know about us."

They held hands and gazed into each other's eyes, their tenderness palpable, their affection for each other spilling over in their words and their gestures. Radha couldn't help but be infected by their excitement. They were very much in love, and she hoped Shyam would see this and be understanding, too.

Just as his name entered her mind, she looked up to see him standing a foot away, watching them, his face blank.

"Shyam, hi! Over here." Radha swallowed as she beckoned him over.

He walked slowly to their table, his eyes on Sangita, his expression unreadable. Hari stood up as he reached their table, holding out his hand.

"Hi, I'm Hari."

Shyam ignored the proffered hand and stared at Sangita.

"So, this is what you've been doing with all the freedom Maa and Baba granted you?"

Sangita regarded her brother

"Shyam, please sit down. Let's talk."

There was ice in his voice as he said, "I'd told them to get you married after school, but Baba allowed you to go to college. Then he allowed you to teach. For what? This?" He threw Hari a dirty look. "The girls in our house don't prostitute themselves by wandering about holding hands with strange men!"

Sangita looked close to tears, and Hari's head swung around as he absorbed the import of his words.

"Look, man, there's no need..."

But Radha spoke up first, fury in her voice.

"No one is *prostituting* themselves here! If anything, your sister is involving you in her life decision. She is asking for your counsel and your help. Shyam, the least you could do is give her the consideration of listening to her without throwing abuse."

Startled, Shyam sat down without a word.

"Let's start again, shall we?" Radha said, "This is Hari. He teaches at the same school as Sangita. They have been seeing each other for, what, nearly seven months now? They would like to get married, and they would like your help in persuading Maa and Baba."

Shyam sat there, a truculent look on his face. He refused to participate in the conversation, allowing Radha to fill in the blanks of an increasingly stilted conference. Sangita kept casting desperate looks at her brother, trying to involve him by asking questions and directing remarks at him, but he stayed stubbornly silent.

When they finally left an hour later, Radha knew that the outcome of this meeting was not likely to be positive. A keen sense of injustice pervaded her being. Neither Sangita nor Hari had deserved the treatment meted out to them by Shyam. They had been polite and respectful, their only 'crime' being that they were in love. Why could Shyam not see that? More importantly, what was he going to do now?

Shyam's silent treatment of her continued all week. He was angry, and he was sulking, and this was another side to him she had not seen before. She tried behaving normally with him, cooking his favourite dishes, making sure she saw him off every morning with his packed lunch, and greeting him every evening with his chilled beer while she took his jacket and briefcase off him. He remained unyielding.

Radha had not tried to broach the subject of Sangita and Hari with him again. She hoped that time would smoothen over the incident and Shyam would come around. There was a lot of affection in his heart towards his sister, and if he allowed that to guide him, instead of his wounded pride, she could imagine the outcome being favourable to all.

He still hadn't said a word to his parents, which was a positive sign. She had reassured Sangita over the phone, telling her to stay calm and keep praying. That was all they could do.

"I can't stop looking over my shoulder now. I feel like there could be a calamity any minute," Sangita cried over the payphone.

"Don't be silly, Sangi! There won't be a calamity. We just need to give Shyam his space and allow better sense to prevail. I'm sure he'll see how much kinder it would be for you to marry someone you know and love, rather than a stranger picked out by him."

"Has he said anything to you?"

"No, he's still not speaking to me. I think he's annoyed that we ambushed him and that I was party to it all."

"Thank you for standing up for me."

"Sangi, I had to. He had no business saying those things to you."

"T, we come from such a conservative background. I knew I wouldn't have a choice in who I married, but I never thought I'd fall in love. I didn't plan this, it just happened."

"Of course. You don't need to explain any of it to me."

Yet, privately, Radha thought that despite their conservative background, Shyam had had a choice. He had seen her, liked her, and told his parents he wanted to marry her. What choice had she had in the matter?

Was it only the men who got to choose?

Mira had been conspicuous by her absence. Radha knew she was deep in the throes of editing her book, so didn't wish to disturb her. Besides, with her mother being in town, whatever spare time she had, she was likely spending it with her.

So she was surprised to receive a call on Monday morning.

"Mum wants you to join us for lunch today," Mira said as soon as she answered the phone.

"Your mum?"

"No, Number 17's mum!" Mira laughed. "Honestly Kitten, you can be so dim sometimes."

"Sorry, my mind was elsewhere. Yes, I'd love to come. What time?"

Radha carried a pot of vermicelli *kheer* she had made the previous day. If there was one thing her mother had drummed into her, it was never to visit anyone empty-handed, or to return a food container without a piece of fruit or some kind of food item in it. Shyam often laughed at her when she put an apple or a banana in a Tupperware container to take back to his parents, and she had given up on trying to explain this custom to him. In truth, she did not understand the origin of it either, but it always felt good to give, so she did.

Now, as she stood outside waiting for Tilo to restrain Batman, she wondered why Nisha wanted to have lunch with her. They had barely spoken on the night of the party, and aside from their dance, they had had nothing to do with one another. Radha was curious about what they might have in common. Then again, she had so little in common with Mira, and yet, they had become such fast friends.

"There you are!" Mira greeted her effusively, pulling her towards the dining table. There were lots of little dishes with various condiments like chopped ginger, fried garlic, green chillies, boiled eggs, and sliced onions in them. Confused, Radha looked at Mira for direction. It appeared as though they were about to start cooking at the table. Just then, Nisha emerged from the kitchen carrying a large pot, which she placed in the centre of the condiments.

"Hello, Radha. You're just in time. Have you ever eaten Khow Suey?"

Radha shook her head. She had no idea what Nisha was talking about.

"Right. Sit here and I'll explain. It's a Burmese noodle soup, and as you're vegetarian, I left the meat out. You can add whichever condiments you like. Do you eat egg? No matter. Add the groundnuts instead. It's delicious and just right for a cold December day like today."

Radha followed her instructions, watching as they ladled soup into their bowls and added all the other ingredients. When she spooned the first mouthful in, her eyes widened in surprise. This was good! She had never tasted flavours like these before. Her repertoire only extended to North Indian dishes, with the occasional foray into Chinese food. Whenever Shyam talked about the new cuisine he had tried, it rarely piqued her interest. Her palate was so accustomed to the spicy goodness of her native dishes that rarely anything else tempted her.

"I called you over today," Nisha said, looking up from her bowl, "as Mira has been telling me how kind you have been to her by feeding her and putting up with all her crazy demands for walks at odd times. My daughter is quite a handful, and you have the patience of a saint. So, this is my way of saying thank you to you."

"No, Aunty… I'm sorry Nisha," Radha paused, "actually, please may I call you 'Aunty'? I am not comfortable using your name…"

"You can call me anything you like," Nisha smiled at her.

"Okay, Aunty," Radha smiled back. "There is no need to thank me. I enjoy Mira's company and I've learned so much from her as well. So, honestly, it's a pleasure for me to spend time with your daughter."

"Well then, I am relieved." Nisha wiped her lips on the paper napkin before setting it down on the table with a contented sigh. "Did you enjoy that?"

"Mum!" Mira said, "You make me sound like some kind of diva!"

"Not a diva, no, but you, my child, have always been a little high maintenance."

"High maintenance? Just because I'm an only child! That's not fair…"

Radha listened to their loving banter and thought of her own sterile interactions with her mother. She resolved internally that this would be the sort of relationship she would have with her children. An open, positive closeness, free from expectation and judgement.

"What are you doing on New Year's Eve, Radha?"

"Oh," Radha was startled out of her thoughts. "Nothing. We'll just watch some television and go to sleep by 10pm."

"God! What are you, fifty?" Mira groaned. "Look, come over to us. Mum's here. We can spend the evening together. We'll pop some champagne at midnight, you can have your Coca Cola, and we can at least bring in the new year in a joyous fashion. 1997, baby! Three years away from the millennium. I have a good feeling about this year. What do you think?"

"I'll…umm… have to ask Shyam. He's not been in the best of moods lately."

"Really? Why?"

Radha had not wanted to talk about it, but suddenly the entire story spilled out of her. From Sangita's entanglement with Hari to her own problems with conceiving, every concern and worry poured out of her. To their credit, both Nisha and Mira listened without interrupting. When she had finished, she took a shaky breath and looked at them.

"You did absolutely the right thing by standing up to him!" Mira was incensed. "How dare he talk to his sister like that? And it's her choice who she marries! How dare he force his own opinions on her?"

Nisha turned and called out to Tilo, "Bring some *chai* and that lovely *kheer* Radha brought us."

Then she put her hand on Mira's arm, stilling her torrent.

"Radha, oftentimes marriage is a minefield. And this time, I think you might have stepped on a mine. But all is not lost. Communication is key. Talk to your husband, try to understand where he is coming from, and that will give him the impetus to understand you." Nisha brushed the hair back from her face. "As far as having a baby goes, you are still very young and our bodies work in mysterious ways. I'm sure it will happen for you when the time is right. What you need right now, though, is to foster an understanding between the two of you. There is no point in bringing a child into this until you are both on the same page. I made that mistake, and it did not turn out well for my marriage."

At Mira's sharp intake of breath, Radha blanched and glanced at her friend.

Nisha carried on, seemingly oblivious. "Mira was not the mistake.

The mistake was assuming a baby would paper over the cracks in my marriage. If anything, it drove us further apart. So, heed my words. Work on your marriage first. Babies can wait. As far as your sister-in-law's situation goes, she needs to be honest with her parents. It isn't your job or your husband's to speak for her. She needs to speak for herself."

❖

Over the next few days, Radha mulled over Nisha's advice. Never before had anyone been so forthright and upfront with her. So much of what she had said made sense. What was the point of bringing a child into a marriage that was still in its infancy? If Shyam and Radha still didn't understand one another fully, a baby would hardly solve all their problems.

She resolved to build bridges with her husband. She loved him deeply despite all his flaws, and whilst all her sympathies lay with Sangita, ultimately Radha had to focus on her own marriage.

That night, when Shyam turned his back on her in bed, she reached over and turned him towards her. Then she slipped off her nightie and took his hand and placed it over her breast. She leaned forward and kissed him before sliding his shorts off and climbing atop him. She rode him with a wild abandon she had never felt before, clenching herself around him as she felt him spurt inside of her.

Later, he kissed her and said, "I'm sorry", before holding her tight and falling asleep in her arms.

Radha brushed his damp hair back from his forehead and breathed in his sweet smell. She knew that in some mysterious way, the Universe had conspired to bring this man into her life. She may have wanted a bit more time, a bit more freedom, but maybe if she had got that, she would have lost him. Would it have been worth it? She knew the answer was a no.

Shyam and Radha were two halves of a whole, meant to be together in life and in marriage. If they were lucky, in time, they would have a brood of their own. A family they could pass on their values and traditions to. They would be a modern couple, but be grounded in their heritage. They would treasure each other with devotion, but they would change and adapt to the times, learning together, growing together.

With these thoughts passing through her mind, Radha felt pleasantly content for the first time in a long time. She was glad she had spoken out in front of Nisha, for she had received the sort of advice her own mother would likely not have imparted. Sometimes, when it was someone who was divorced from your own life, an impartial bystander, it was so much easier to accept what they said, as it wasn't tainted by bias and decades of conditioning and prejudice.

The last week of December brought the sort of sweet winter sunshine that Radha had always loved. Growing up, her mornings would be spent in front of the electric heater, but by the afternoon she would be sitting on the terrace of her house, shelling and munching peanuts, while enjoying the warmth of the December sun. It was, hands down, her favourite month of the year.

After their night of lovemaking, Shyam had gone back to being his normal self. They had not spoken about Sangita and Hari again, and for the moment, Radha decided it was best to leave it be. A new year would bring fresh energy into their lives, and when Shyam was in a mellow mood, she would bring it up with him again. The fact that he had not said a word to his parents meant he had, in some small way, decided to give his sister's love life a chance.

Meanwhile, Mira was buried deep in the edits of her book, so Radha decided to invite Nisha out for a coffee.

"I hope you don't think I'm being forward, but I thought you might want to get out of the house for a while," Radha said, while setting down a cup of coffee in front of her.

They had gone to Café Coffee Day, a new coffee place that had opened in the neighbourhood. It had taken them a while to decide on a coffee, as there were so many varieties on offer. Ultimately, they had settled on a cappuccino each. Radha was impressed with the steaming concoction, a pretty design etched on top of the foam. This was coffee as she had never seen or drunk before.

"Actually, I am glad to get out. Mira is like a grizzly bear these days. She works well into the night and only emerges at noon, growls at everybody and heads back into her study after lunch, not to be seen until dinnertime." Nisha laughed as she described her daughter.

Radha grimaced. "That can't be fun for you. I remember interrupting a writing session of hers once and she nearly bit my head off! I learned early on that unsolicited calls were not welcome in the Das household."

"Poor you! I hope you know it's not personal. She's like that with everyone, especially poor Monish. I don't know how he puts up with it."

"Aunty, I..." Radha bit her lip before continuing, "I'm sorry about my outburst the other day. I just wanted to tell you that your advice really helped."

Nisha leaned back in her chair and observed her.

"I'm very glad it did. My wisdom, such as it is, comes from my own painful experiences. So, I like to think of it as hard-won."

"If you don't mind me asking, what happened?"

"With my marriage?" Nisha raised her brow. Radha nodded a yes.

"Well, it was a case of too much too soon, with too little caution. Mira's father, Keshav, was my father's best friend's son. They lived in the UK, and we met up with them every time they visited India. Over the years, it became a standing joke that I would end up marrying Keshav, and I suppose, in a way, we started to view each other as potential mates too."

Nisha took a sip of her coffee, set her cup down, and examined her nails.

"We started writing each other letters, and I had my first kiss with him on one of his visits to Bombay. In many ways, you could have called it a love marriage. I certainly thought it was. I was twenty-three when we tied the knot, and he was twenty-six, and we were like a childhood romance come true. Everyone was overjoyed at the outcome. I was excited about moving to London and starting a new life with my husband." Nisha stopped, a faraway look on her face.

"And then?"

"The trouble started as soon as I moved to London. In actual fact, it was a place called Hounslow, which is a suburb quite far away from London. I was a Bombay girl, and I had grown up in very liberal surroundings. Suddenly I was thrust into a stifling environment with people I didn't understand, and who didn't understand me. Making adjustments was hard enough, but the worst bit was that the man I thought I knew, the man I was in love with, the man I had married, was a complete stranger to me."

"Oh," Radha said, not knowing what else to say.

"Yes, I know that's how arranged marriages work, and in retrospect, that's what my marriage was. Except that all the things my parents had taken at face value—the background, the education, the liberal values—were completely at odds with reality. For instance, my husband was vehemently opposed to my working. He wanted a stay-at-home wife. But he never had the time for me and never tried making the transition easy for someone new to his country and his family. He came home late from work, and stayed out with his friends on the weekends, while I was miserable and cooped up in a three bedroom semi-detached house with his mother and father."

Nisha took another sip of her coffee.

"So, when I tried to complain, I was told to have a baby. Babies make a family, was what my mother-in-law said. And I listened. I fell pregnant with Mira, but instead of things getting better, they got worse. Mira was a colicky baby, and Keshav, fed up with getting no sleep, started staying out nights. Eventually, it got to the point where I confronted him and found out that he had only married me out of pressure from his parents. He had not been ready for marriage. Not to me, and quite frankly, not to any woman at all."

Radha pondered her words.

"Do you mean...?"

"Yes. My husband had no interest in women. However, just to conform to our Indian society's expectations, he had allowed himself to be pushed into marriage."

"So you left him?"

"Not straight away. I was naïve enough to believe if I stuck it out, he would come around. Of course, that didn't happen. Mira was nearly two when I returned to India with her."

"Did he…does he…stay in touch with Mira?"

"A little, now and again. He's helped financially with her education, but all the main parenting has had to come from me."

"I'm sorry. I realise I've been unnecessarily inquisitive. It was none of my business."

"None of this is top secret. I am very open about my life, and if my story can help you see that babies are not the answer to marital troubles, then I'm glad you asked."

"Can I ask another nosy question?"

"Sure."

"Is that why Mira hasn't had any children?"

Nisha pierced her with a look.

"Don't you think that's a question you should ask her?"

On the night of 31st December, Radha took extra care with her outfit. She wanted to surprise Shyam by wearing the jeans she had picked up at the new mall. Along with a mint-green satin top with a scooped neck and long sleeves, and diamante earrings, she put on a pair of silver slingback sandals.

She looked at herself in the mirror and sighed with happiness. Something about how she had dressed reminded her of her carefree teenage years, although she hadn't dared to wear satin and diamantes back then. She hoped Shyam would be impressed. Things had been good between them lately, and as long as they continued to avoid contentious topics, they could carry on as if nothing untoward had occurred. Although from time to time, Radha wondered—why could a man revert to being such a baby while being a fully grown, fully functioning adult, whereas a woman had to leave all traces of her immaturity behind the moment she tied the knot?

They had both been looking forward to this evening. It was likely to be a more intimate affair as Mira and Monish had invited just a handful of people over to celebrate the start of the new year and the completion of Mira's book.

"What was she writing about?" Shyam called out from the other side of the door while she applied the finishing touches to her makeup.

"I'm not sure. It was some kind of academic text to do with English literature."

"High brow stuff, then?"

"I guess," Radha said as she walked out of the bathroom. Shyam was spraying on his cologne and she took a moment to appreciate how handsome he looked in his navy roll-neck sweater and black jeans. He turned around and let out a low whistle.

"*Wah,* Radha! You look smashing." His eyes gleamed as he took in the transformation.

She did a little twirl for him.

"I won't look out-of-place tonight, will I?"

"Not a chance. They will all be looking at you and saying what a lucky guy I am!"

Radha fidgeted. That was not what she wanted at all. She just wanted Shyam to be proud of her.

"Here, look what I got you." Shyam placed a gift-wrapped box on the bed.

"What is it?" Radha approached the bed slowly. Shyam was not the sort of man to give presents. He barely acknowledged birthdays, so she was stunned he had bought her anything at all.

"Open it and see."

Radha unwrapped it carefully, pulling out a long thin box with 'Organza' written on it. Inside it was a beautiful bottle of perfume by Givenchy.

"I thought it was high time you left the girlie stuff like 'Charlie' behind. You are a woman now, and you need to smell like one."

Radha sprayed some on herself and inhaled the heady notes of honeysuckle, gardenia, and vanilla.

"This is beautiful!" She hugged Shyam. "Thank you."

Privately, she wondered whether this upgrade was a consequence of being amongst women who smelled expensive. 'Charlie' had never bothered Shyam before, and while he had always chosen upscale colognes for himself, it had never occurred to him to buy her a designer perfume. Not until today. Still, she was gratified that he had thought of her at all. Many men wouldn't bother, happy to bask in the attention while their wives got sidelined. At least here, Shyam wanted her to look and smell as good as any other woman at the party.

They walked in at 9pm, and found the Das' living room lit with soft candlelight, and with *ghazals* playing in the background, the vibe so low-key, it was impossible to tell it was a party.

"Hello!" Monish came up to them and took their coats. "So glad you could both make it. What would you like to drink?"

Radha looked around at the few guests who were lounging on the sofas, recognising some faces from the previous party. She smiled at them shyly, and one woman waved her over.

"Hi! Radha, isn't it? Come, join us. Would you like a joint?"

Radha shook her head, turning down the rather offensive smelling cigarette. Where were Mira and Nisha?

"They'll be out soon. Some kind of wardrobe crisis for Mira." The woman looked at her up and down. "You look lovely. Very different from last time. Younger, fresher. Don't you think, Sid?"

The sleepy-eyed man next to her nodded without really looking at her.

"I'm Salome, Mira's friend from her MH days."

"MH?" Radha said, perplexed.

"Miranda House. We were in the same dorm. She did her Masters there after her graduation. Did she not tell you this?"

Radha shook her head again. There was much she still didn't know about Mira. They spent a lot of their time together, but rarely delved into each other's backgrounds or histories, preferring instead to talk about life as it was now. She resolved to get to know her new friend better, to ask her questions about what mattered to her. Wasn't friendship founded on transparency and reciprocity? Perhaps she had hogged too much of the attention for herself, not giving enough in return to Mira.

Just then, Mira walked in behind her mother. She was wearing a long sheath of a coral dress with blue beads at the neck and hemline. Nisha was in a sparkling grey poncho and black jeans.

"God, this mother-daughter duo makes me sick. They're so damn gorgeous!" Salome made mock gagging gestures before making her way towards them.

"What was the wardrobe crisis?" Radha asked Mira later as they exchanged greetings.

"Original dress didn't bloody fit! I've put on weight with all this sitting around and writing. Need to get back to the gym."

"Oh, but Mira, you are so stunning just as you are! You don't need the gym."

"Says someone naturally slender. Listen, sweetie, I have my father's genes, and if I let myself go, I could become a barrel!"

This was the first time she had ever heard Mira voice an insecurity, and it took her by surprise. Radha had never judged people adversely based on their size, but she supposed in the world that Mira inhabited, looking a certain way was important. After all, hadn't Radha seen the censure in the eyes of the well-heeled at her saree-clad look?

"Tonight you are going to try some champagne!" Mira returned with a glass filled with a fizzy amber liquid in it. "And I'm not taking no for an answer. Listen, champagne is just bubbles and happiness. How can you go through a lifetime without it?"

Radha took the glass without protest, took a sip, hid her grimace and vowed to chuck it into a potted plant as soon as she got a moment.

Meanwhile, she looked around to see Shyam deep in conversation with Monish. She was happy they were getting along. She had so wanted them to like each other. Mira wanted them to be the sort of 'couple friends' she had seen on television, the men being buddies, drinking beer and watching sports together while the women shared confidences and recipes.

In many ways, she also aspired to the relationship that Mira and Monish shared. Someday, she hoped, Shyam and she would also have the same openness and equality in their marriage.

"How are you, my dear?" Nisha asked, handing her a plate with several round disc-shaped snacks with a blob of ketchup on the side.

"Hello Aunty. I...I'm sorry I don't eat meat."

"I remember, child. These are corn fritters and I made them myself. Try them."

Radha popped one into her mouth.

"Gosh, these are delicious!"

"I know," Nisha smiled before taking the champagne glass from her. "I could see you struggling with this. Don't worry, Mira won't even notice. Like a cup of tea instead?"

The countdown to midnight was mellower than she had expected. At home, her parents had never allowed her to go to parties, and after marriage, Shyam had been quite content to watch television and turn in early. But judging by the Das' last party, she had expected this one to be an equally rambunctious affair and had been looking forward to letting her hair down, albeit sans alcohol. Therefore, this quiescent atmosphere was unexpected.

Shyam was on his umpteenth whisky and regaling Salome with some story from work, while Monish regularly changed the record, alternating between Jagjit and Chitra Singh's mellifluous vocals to the soul-stirring performances of Ghulam Ali.

"I didn't know Monish was such a big fan of *ghazals*?"

"Boring," Mira yawned, "that should be his middle name."

Radha stared. Mira had been slurring her words a bit. Maybe it was the champagne speaking?

"No, I mean it. He is so boring that I feel like slapping him some days."

"Mira!"

"What? Don't act so shocked. Doesn't Shyam bore you occasionally?"

"No."

"Ah, that's because you are still newly married," she wagged her finger at Radha. "Give it seven, no, eight," Mira pretended to count her fingers, "yes, eight years, and you'll see. They all get so boring in the end."

Dismayed, Radha retreated to a corner of the sofa. What had gotten into Mira tonight?

At a minute to midnight, suddenly everyone seemed to wake up from their stupors and start a discordant countdown. Radha joined in, looking for Shyam who was shouting along, a smelly cigarette in one hand and a glass of whisky in the other. She moved across the room towards him, but just as she reached him, he turned away and grabbed Salome, putting his arm around her waist and shouting out, "Happy New Year!"

Mira clinked glasses with them and yelled, "Here's to the best one yet!"

CHAPTER 6

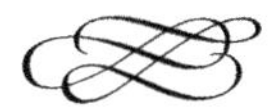

As a child, Radha had taken fidelity for granted. Her parents had never shown the slightest interest in any other man or woman, quite content in each other's company. Even amongst her relatives, the only scandal she had ever heard was of a widowed aunt falling in love with her young tenant. An affair that had been put to an end swiftly by despatching her to Benares, and frightening her paramour away with threats of bodily harm.

She had always assumed that men and women stayed loyal to each other once they married. So, she had no way of making sense of Shyam's behaviour. When she had called him out on it, he had retaliated by saying that she was overreacting. That if there had been anything clandestine about his actions, he would not have done it in front of everyone.

"You know what your problem is, Radha," he had said, "your thinking is so provincial. You take everything literally. A hug between a man and a woman is just that. It's not an affair, okay?"

Mortified, Radha had withdrawn from the argument. Yes, it was true that Shyam had not done any more than give Salome a hug, but while Radha was standing next to him? Shouldn't he have hugged her instead? Then again, she had not seen Monish hug Mira either. She did not know what to make of that night except that it had left a bitter taste in her mouth.

She withdrew from everyone. From Mira and Nisha, from Sangita and her daily dramas, from her parents and in-laws, and especially from Shyam. She spent her days cleaning the house, cooking and watching mind-numbing television serials in which all the characters looked and behaved in the same predictable way. It was comforting in the way life had not been lately. All she wanted was the rhythm of regularity, with no sudden surprises and unexpected revelations.

On the day Nisha left, she rang to say goodbye, but Radha let it go to the answering machine. She was in no mood to speak to anyone. It was mid-January, and the days were bitterly cold, so she was lying in bed, with a quilt and a blanket on her, when she heard Nisha's voice on the answering machine.

"Radha, I was calling to say bye, but I guess you must be out. It's a shame we haven't seen you in the last two weeks. Mira seems to think she's upset you in some way. If that's the case, please talk it out. It's not worth letting things fester. Life is much too short. Anyway, bye for now. I'll try to visit again later in the year. Stay well, my dear, and stay happy."

The phone clicked off and Radha remained where she was, the quilt still over her head.

January turned to February, and with it a mild sunshine returned to Gurgaon. The children returned to the parks to play cricket, and *ayahs* with prams wandered in groups of twos and threes, gossiping about their households.

Radha had not bothered to reach out to Mira. She knew she was behaving churlishly, but could not help herself. Mira's strange behaviour at the party, followed by Shyam's flirtation with Salome, had left her feeling irked enough to keep her distance.

Instead, she had reconnected with a few school friends who had asked to meet for lunch in Connaught Place.

As school girls, when they were given permission, they would take the DTC bus and head to Janpath, adjacent to Connaught Place. They would wander down the long street lined with stalls selling export-rejected clothes like slogan T-shirts, harem pants, tie-dye skirts and other such reasonably priced merchandise. Radha found it fascinating to watch the hippie foreigners try to bargain with the stallholders, invariably losing to the wiles of these multi-lingual, canny merchants.

Today, though, they were nowhere near Janpath, choosing instead to lunch at Berco's in CP's inner circle. The taxi dropped her off just as she saw Archana and Mamta stepping out of an auto-rickshaw.

"Hey, Tina!" they squealed as they saw her. "Look at you! You haven't changed at all."

Hugging, they exchanged quick compliments before making their way up to the restaurant.

"By the way, I'm not called Tina anymore. I'm Radha now."

"*Theek hai*, you will always be Tina to us, *na*. So, how are you anyway? You *toh* just disappeared after marriage. He's keeping you that busy, huh?" Archana raised her brow at her.

Mamta chimed in. "Don't listen to her. She's just jealous! She keeps telling everyone what a handsome man you've married. So lucky, arranged marriage and all..."

"It's always the quiet ones who get ahead. Tell us, was it really arranged or was there some *chakkar* between the two of you from before?"

As Radha deflected their questions and listened to them talk about their own lives, she came to the realisation that she had long outgrown these friendships. She had literally nothing in common with these girls anymore. Archana had married a lawyer her parents had selected for her, had already had a child, and was interested in having at least three more. Mamta had sat her IAS exams twice, been unsuccessful, and joined a travel agency instead. Now, she organised tours to all the hill stations in India.

"And what about you? Are you working?"

"No, I...my husband doesn't want me to."

"Starting a family then?"

"Yes, soon, hopefully."

They judged her without seeming to judge her, and she felt it in the very core of her being. Unlike Mira's sharp observations or Sangita's self-obsessed rants, these friends had known her when they had only been children and life had stretched out before them like blank canvases waiting to be filled in. But they did not really know her in the present, only the version she had once been. Did they even care to find out how she had changed or how much?

All she saw in their eyes were questions about what she had done in the interim. What did she have to show for all the years they had spent preparing for 'life'? So little, and it was obvious that they knew this and judged her harshly, albeit silently.

Their quiet indictment hurt.

It hurt so much more than she let on. So, she put on a brave face, and carried on chatting and laughing and eating, knowing full well that she would never meet them again.

Mid-March, Radha got a viral infection. Shivering and sweating, she took to the bed with barely any energy to cook or eat. Mummy came to stay with her and take care of the house.

Shyam was sympathetic, but distant. Work had gotten even busier in the new year, and he had put so much of his energy into it that any outside distractions only irritated him.

Mummy cooked and cleaned for him, taking care of him like the sons she had lost to their wives. She tutted her way through Radha's kitchen shelves, rearranging all her *masalas*, labelling the containers and topping them up from the store. She stitched missing buttons, darned shirts, knitted a winter cap that Shyam pretended to like, and dusted everything to within an inch of its life.

Meanwhile, Radha watched her with a detached interest. Her mother seemed to come alive in front of her very eyes. Taking care of her son-in-law and daughter reinvigorated her, and she hummed her way through making *khichdi* and doing the laundry.

On the fifth day of staying over, when Radha still felt too ill to keep too much food down, her mother looked at her and frowned.

"Are you sure this is a viral?"

"That's what the doctor said," Radha responded weakly from the bed.

"These new-fangled doctors don't know what they are doing most of the time. Tomorrow you come with me to Dr Joshi and we'll get you a blood test."

"A blood test? What for, Mummy? I'll recover in a few days..."

"So you will. But you will come with me tomorrow for a blood test."

The next morning, Radha showered and changed and slowly made her way down the stairs where her mother was waiting by the taxi she had ordered the previous evening. Just then, Mira emerged from her house, and when she saw Radha, she rushed over.

"Hey, you! Where have you been? God, you look terrible. Everything okay?"

Radha nodded her head feebly and made the introductions between her mother and her neighbour.

"So nice to meet you!" Mira pushed her hair back from her eyes and grinned at Radha's mother. She was in tight black leggings and a voluminous man's sweatshirt.

Radha's mother gave her a curt *namaste* and ushered Radha into the taxi.

"Call me!" Mira held her hand to her ear and waved as they drove away.

"Who is that woman?" Mummy asked.

"Our neighbour."

"Are you friendly with her?"

"Sort of, but I haven't seen much of her lately.."

"Good. I don't like the look of her. Very forward."

While they waited for the results at the doctor's, Radha felt faint and leaned her head back against the wall.

"Dr Joshi is expediting this just for us. He's been our family doctor for years and you should have come to him in the first place."

Radha closed her eyes. When she opened them next, the elderly doctor was standing in front of her mother saying, "Congratulations, Mona*ji*, you are going to be a grandmother."

At those words, Radha shut her eyes and promptly passed out.

❖

Shyam had to sit down when he was given the news.

"Are you sure?" He kept asking, looking between Radha and her mother.

"Of course we are sure, *beta*! You are going to be a father."

Radha watched the various expressions that flickered on his face. Confusion, happiness, fear. For once, she felt exactly the same as him. Ambivalence was not something she had expected, but here it was, and it refused to leave. Did they really want a baby so soon into their marriage? Especially now, when they were going through this strange rocky patch?

"Isn't it wonderful news?" Mummy crowed with delight. "Now, let's hope it is a boy who can carry forward your name."

"And if it's a girl?" Radha asked.

"Then there will be plenty more opportunities to have a boy. You are only in your early twenties. Lots of time."

Radha caught Shyam's eye, and he looked so completely baffled by her mother's enthusiasm for babies that she had to suppress a giggle.

"Yes," he jumped up suddenly. "It is great news! No cooking tonight. I'm going to order food to celebrate this. When should we tell Maa and Baba? Over this weekend? Mummy, are you staying for the rest of the week? Radha is still too weak and we could use the help."

A frenetic energy seemed to possess Shyam as he wandered around the room, gabbing away, picking up items from shelves and setting them down aimlessly.

"He's adjusting to the idea," her mother whispered. "It's quite a shock to the system."

Radha watched him, wondering how long it would take for the shock to wear off. She still had several months of growing a baby to contend with.

"Men," her mother sighed next to her, "need all the reassurance in the world when the baby arrives. They need to know that they are still number one in your life and that the baby won't take over all your love. Remember that, Radha. You will have to be a mother to your baby, *and* to your husband in the initial months."

Mummy left on Friday evening saying she wanted to give Papa the news in person. She made Shyam promise they would visit after they had been to his parents' house on Sunday.

Saturday was the only day they had together for them to talk about the implications of the news.

"Are you happy, Shyam? You don't look it," Radha said when he brought her a cup of tea in bed. He had been unusually solicitous all day long.

"What makes you say that? I am happy! I'm overjoyed." Shyam gave her a smile which didn't reach his eyes.

"Okay." She slumped back into bed. Something didn't feel right, but she could not put her finger on it.

"Is work really busy?" She said, sitting upright again.

"Awfully busy." Shyam ran his fingers through his hair. "I might have to go away for a few days in late June."

"Oh, really? Where to?"

"There's a conference in Delhi. Lots of bigwigs coming down from America and England. There will be lots of wining and dining, and we will all just stay in the hotel to make it easier for everyone."

Radha nodded.

"Do you want Sangita to come and stay with you while I'm away?"

"That would be nice. I haven't spent much time with her lately."

"I'll tell her. Also..." Shyam cleared his throat. "I've been thinking.

After we've given Maa and Baba the good news, I could try to introduce the topic of that chap she's seeing. They will be in a good mood, and might take it well."

"Thank you, Shyam." Radha felt a knot loosen in her chest. Maybe all was not lost. This had been a bone of contention between them for so long that it had subtly soured everything. Now, they could move on.

"Listen, I am sorry about accusing you that night. I wasn't in the right frame of mind and blew things out of proportion."

"It's okay, Radha. I stepped out of line too. Let's forget about it."

He sat on the bed and pulled her towards him, placing a gentle kiss on her lips. The smell of the garlic bread he had eaten was so strong that Radha pushed him away and ran to the bathroom to throw up. When she came back out, he was nowhere to be seen. There was a note on the table saying, "Gone for a walk. Will be back soon."

Radha lay down again, relieved. She had seen the look in his eyes as he had leaned in for the kiss. The very thought of physical intimacy made her stomach heave. She hoped the sickness would pass soon. Shyam asserted his conjugal rights regularly, and he wouldn't be pleased if she didn't comply.

On Sunday, they prepared to visit her in-laws in Jangpura. Shyam had bought a box of *mithai,* the Indian sweetmeats her in-laws favoured from Haldiram's, in order to give them the good news and congratulate them, too. They battled the heavy traffic in their car, making slow progress behind other cars and lorries, also heading towards Delhi. Radha sucked on fennel seeds to ward off her pregnancy nausea and kept turning down the sound on the cassette player every time Shyam increased the volume on the latest *filmi* song he was obsessed with.

They got there just shy of 1pm and Radha felt relieved they were in time for lunch, but not too early, either. It was always a gamble calculating what time to leave to get there. Too early and she was stuck making pointless conversation with her father-in-law, or helplessly following her mother-in-law in the kitchen. Too late and she would be chided for missing lunch and making extra work for them.

Shyam helped her out of the car, and she held up the pleats of her saree as she walked up the few stairs that led to the main door. Radha hoped she would be allowed to wear the more forgiving *salwar kameez* as her pregnancy progressed.

The moment they entered the living room, she knew something was amiss. An air of gloom pervaded the area. Her in-laws were sitting across from each other, staring into space.

"Maa! Baba! What happened?" Shyam's panicked voice seemed to come from far away as Radha noticed the letter in Maa's hand. Baba looked up, his face a picture of misery.

"Our Sangita has eloped with a man."

❖

"Did you know about this?" Shyam turned to her, his eyes flaming.

"I...what? No!" Radha took a step back.

Her in-laws looked up at them.

"Why would Radha...?" Baba stuttered as he stood up.

"Because she has been in on it from the beginning!" Shyam shouted, spittle collecting at the corners of his mouth. Radha looked away.

Maa thrust the letter at Shyam and came up to her.

"What do you know about this? Who is this man?"

"Maa, I swear on *Vaishno Devi*, I know nothing about this. Yes, I knew she was seeing someone. He is a teacher at the same school as her. Shyam has met him, too. They are very much in love and want to get married. That is all I know. This...this..." She pointed to the letter. "I know nothing about this."

Maa narrowed her eyes.

"You have known all along and said nothing to us?"

Radha looked towards Shyam for support, but he was shaking with rage.

"The shame this has brought upon our family!" Maa sat down again and put her head in her hands.

Shyam sat next to her and put his arm around her.

"Maa, don't worry. I'll find the guy and break his legs. Then I'll drag Sangita home by her hair."

"What for? Who will want her after this? She will always be known as the girl who ran away. Damaged goods. Let her go! If this is how she repays our love and nurturing, then let her be. Ungrateful wretch!"

Then she broke into great wracking sobs. Shyam held on to her as she cried. Baba clenched and unclenched his fists, refusing to look at anyone. Radha inched her way towards the letter and picked it up.

Maa and Baba,

Please believe me when I say I never intended to hurt you, but I know I am hurting you by leaving in this manner.

I have met someone who I know you will never accept as my husband. We have decided that the best course of action would be to leave and get married in a temple. As we are both adults, we are well within our rights to do this.

I had hoped for your blessings, but now I can only hope for your forgiveness.

With utmost respect and love,

Sangita.

Radha set the letter down and exhaled slowly. How had she not picked up on the signs? The panicked phone calls, the paranoia that her parents would find out, and the fear that Shyam would push ahead with the marriage proposal were all topics Sangita and she had discussed over and over in the past few months. At the time, Radha had allayed her fears by constantly repeating the mantra that everything would turn out all right. How could she not have guessed that for Sangita this only exacerbated her anxiety?

"Maybe she'll call me?" Radha offered tentatively. "If she does, I could talk some sense into her; get her to return..."

"Sense?" Shyam sneered. "You should have talked sense into her ages ago! Instead, you encouraged this nonsense. Now, look what it's brought upon us."

"I don't want anyone talking to her from this point on!" Maa snarled. "As far as we are concerned, she is dead to us."

"Maa..." Radha said, "isn't that too harsh? Maybe if you give her a chance to explain, if you meet Hari..."

Maa put her hands over her ears and shook her head.

"Don't mention their names in front of me ever again!"

Baba slumped into his armchair, his shoulders shaking as he suppressed his sobs. Sangita had been the apple of his eye, and now, he had lost his child forever.

In the end, they returned home without stopping off at her parents. The journey home was a silent one. Neither Shyam nor Radha had spoken of the pregnancy, the news having taken a backseat to what had transpired. Radha kept going over her conversations with Sangita in her mind. Had Sangita dropped any hints as to her plans? Could Radha have stopped her?

The phone was ringing when they got home. Shyam answered it with a curt "hello" then thrust the receiver towards her.

"It's your mother."

Mummy sounded concerned.

"What happened? We were waiting for you all evening."

"Can I call you tomorrow, Mummy? Something has happened, but," Radha looked up at Shyam as he poured himself a glass of whisky, "I can't talk about it right now. Yes, I'm fine. I'll call you tomorrow. Okay, bye."

She hung up and turned to face him.

"You know that it's not my fault that Sangita eloped. She never said a word to me..."

Shyam held up his hand.

"I don't want to hear it."

"But..."

"I said, shut up!"

Shocked, Radha stopped mid-sentence. She picked up her handbag and went into the bedroom. Unwrapping her saree, she flung it on the floor before changing into her nightie. In the bathroom, she splashed cold water on her face and waited for her nausea to subside. She looked at her face in the mirror. Her cheeks were flushed and her eyes looked unnaturally bright.

I will not cry. I will not cry.

She got into bed and waited for Shyam. When half an hour turned into an hour, she switched off the light and closed her eyes. He stumbled into the room two hours later. Lying next to her, she heard him mumble something, but ignored him. Then he turned his back on her and fell asleep immediately, snoring loudly. She lay next to him ramrod straight, willing herself not to give in to her tears.

The next morning, she rang her mother and filled her in on everything.

"Oho! So that's why they are not returning my calls. But Radha, you should never have covered up for her. It was your duty to tell her parents everything. Now look at what you've done."

"I'm tired, Mummy. Can I call you later?"

"Yes, yes. You rest. All this is too much for the baby. A happy mother will lead to a healthy baby. Yes, go and rest."

After she had hung up on her mother, Radha slipped on her sandals, went down the stairs, and walked straight over to Mira's house.

Tilo was taking Batman for a walk and as she saw Radha approaching, she grinned, "*Memsahib khoos hoiga.*"

Would Mira really be happy to see her? Radha did not know, but at this point, she was beyond caring. She needed a friend, someone who would be on her side, for once. Mira, for all her faults, was the one person she could rely on to give her the sort of support she needed.

She marched in, walked straight up to her, and collapsed into a heap in her arms.

"Hey, hey, Kitten! What's up? Shhh. Hush, hush child." Mira held her and rocked her back and forth, saying soothing words in her ears that made little sense, but gave her the comfort she had been craving.

When her tears finally dried up and all she had left in her were a few hiccups, Mira asked Tilo to bring them both a cup of tea.

"What's happened?" She asked, her voice soft, her eyes gentle.

Everything tumbled out of Radha. Sangita's elopement, her in-laws' grief, Shyam's volte face, her mother's censure and her own burden of guilt.

"No, Kitten, no. I will not allow it! You cannot control what other people think or say, but you do have control over your own feelings. You know you've done nothing wrong. Sangita did not consult with you before taking such a drastic step. And bloody hell, who can blame her? Clearly, her parents would never have allowed that marriage. Listen to me, let them rave and rant and do whatever else. You stay out of it. As far as Shyam is concerned, if he's being such a dick, you need to stand up to him! No more of this shutting up and putting up."

Radha shook her head.

"There is another thing. I... I'm pregnant."

"What?!" Mira jumped up. "Damn! Does he know?"

"Yes. We were going to tell his parents yesterday, but then all this happened."

"How long...?" Mira waved at her stomach.

"The doctor thinks around ten weeks, but I have an ultrasound scheduled next week and we'll know for sure then."

"Damn! Right in the middle of this shitstorm."

Radha started to sob again.

"Oh no, I didn't mean that. Look, it will all be fine. Just let things settle down, okay? Here, I have an idea. Why don't we go away for the weekend somewhere nearby? Like a mini vacation. We can leave these stupid men behind and just enjoy each other's company."

"I've never done anything like that before. I would need to ask Shyam…"

"No, you wouldn't. This is my treat, and you don't need anything except some clothes. You will inform him, not ask him, okay?"

Radha nodded again. Right now, she really didn't care what Shyam thought. She had had enough of him and of his entire family. She needed this break.

❖

Shyam just shrugged when she told him she was going away for the weekend. Didn't he care just a jot for her? Where was the loving and caring man she had married? Or, was the love and care only present when everything went his way?

"So?" Mira asked, slipping on her sunglasses. "Was he annoyed?"

"No. He was indifferent," Radha said, feeling miserable.

"Good. Let him pretend it doesn't matter. Believe me, a brief absence will make his heart grow much fonder for you."

Mira's driving was as erratic as her moods. Radha held on to the sides of her car seat, forgetting all about her nausea as they drove out of Gurgaon. The days were already getting warmer, and Radha was dreading the heat of the summer, when she would most likely be in her second trimester.

"Where are we going?"

Mira looked at her and smiled, narrowly missing a cyclist. At Radha's gasp, she rolled her window down and yelled, *"Andha hai kya?"*

Radha felt sorry for the poor cyclist who had been pedalling away sedately till Mira came barrelling down the road.

"Well," Mira carried on, as if nothing had happened, "I am taking you to my favourite Ayurvedic Spa. It's got the best treatments in Delhi, and only those in the know know where it is."

"Are we going for a treatment?" Radha asked, puzzled.

"Yes, a spa treatment. Have you never been?"

Radha shook her head. The only thing she ever had done was her monthly waxing and eyebrows threading appointment.

"Kitten, you are in for the time of your life. A massage, a manicure and pedicure is just what the doctor ordered."

For the first time in days, Radha giggled. She had had a sudden vision of their family doctor, Dr Joshi, commanding her to get her nails painted.

"See! You're already feeling better. I just know this is what you need."

"Mira, can I ask you something?"

"Anything, pet."

"What is your book about?"

Mira braked suddenly at the red light, sending them lunging forward.

"The book I've been working on? Why, I didn't know you were interested or I would've bored your socks off."

The light turned green, and the car lurched forward again.

"It's about queer theory, and its representation in literature."

"Sorry, what does that mean?"

"Well, I examine how queerness has always existed in literature and that it's not necessarily restricted to homosexuality. There is a spectrum of queerness that can be unearthed if one chooses to discard the heteronormative lens through which literature has traditionally been analysed. My area of interest lies in the portrayal of homoeroticism in Elizabethan literature."

"Oh." Radha bit her lip and looked outside the window. She didn't understand any of it. Sometimes life itself seemed beyond comprehension. What was she doing in the company of this bright and beautiful woman? Did she deserve to be here? Would Mira see her for the *gawar* she was? An unrefined, undeserving, uncultured girl from a lower middle class background.

"Radha, you are frowning again. Stop worrying about things that are out of your control. I've seen that life balances things out. Give it a few years and all of this will just seem like a bad dream."

Radha turned to her and gave her a half-smile.

"May I ask you something else?"

"My, you are full of questions today. Shoot!"

"Why did you say all that about Monish at your New Year's Eve party?"

Mira crinkled her brow.

"What did I say?"

"That he was boring, and that you wanted to slap him..."

"Oh, that. I must have been annoyed with him over something."

"So, you weren't serious?" Radha felt the tiniest bit of relief creep into her.

"Likely was. There are many times I could slap him, but don't." Mira shrugged. "I just have anger issues towards most men. Mum told you about my dad, didn't she?"

Radha nodded an affirmative, then realised Mira had not seen her, so said, "Yes, yes, she did."

"There's a part of me that feels like every man is capable of abandonment. That for men, leaving behind someone they love is easy. They don't really care what happens afterwards. And that is why I want to keep the upper hand in every relationship I have with them. You're the one who studied psychology. Go on, unravel that for me."

Radha stayed silent.

"Anyway, why are we talking about men? This weekend is about us. And here we are."

She parked in front of an unobtrusive white block of flats behind Defence Colony Market. Only a street away was a buzzing market filled with a variety of stores and restaurants. Yet this tree-lined street was quiet and sleepy, a world away from the busyness of the market.

There was no board at the front of the building advertising treatments or spa facilities. Radha wondered what she would find inside. As soon as they walked in, she felt transported to another land. An intoxicating smell of incense hung in the air. The walls were plain white, with pictures of waterfalls and pebbles dotted around. A large green plant dominated the reception, and a woman clad in a white-and-gold Kerala sari was checking off names against a register. She looked up and beamed at Mira.

"Mrs Das, so good to have you back. It has been a while?"

"I was busy with the final edits of my book, Kamala. How are you? Oh, this is Mrs Radha Misra. I've brought her as my guest and will take care of all the charges for her."

As they chatted, Radha let her eyes roam over the room. In the corner there was a large bronze statue of Nataraj, the God of Dance. On the other side lay a large silver container filled with water topped with floating rose petals. The ambience of the place filled her with serenity, probably the very effect they were after.

"*Shirodhara*, then?" Mira asked her.

"Sorry?"

"I've filled them in on your condition, and they will avoid the stomach area, but they recommend *Shirodhara*."

"Okay." Radha had no idea what that meant, but as she was here, she was willing to go along with whatever Mira introduced her to.

As she stripped out of her clothes and lay on the bed, she felt self-conscious about her body. No one, aside from Shyam, had seen her naked. The two women bustling around in the room barely noticed. One of them covered her with a thin sheet while the other moved her up on the bed so that her head was hanging off the bed slightly. Then the second woman started to pour warm oil on her forehead, which ran through her hair and dripped into a bowl below. The first woman took some of the warm, fragrant oil and started massaging her limbs gently. In a matter of minutes, Radha entered a stupor, a delicious lassitude filling every pore of her being. Her anxieties floated away as she gave herself over to their ministrations. This was bliss. She had never experienced anything like it before, and it was just what she needed.

Later, in their hotel room, as they sat on the bed in their dressing gowns and waited for their room service order to arrive, Radha said, "You've been so kind to me, Mira. How can I repay you?"

"Pah, I don't need to be repaid. But you can tell me why you withdrew after the party. Was it something I said?"

Radha looked down at her nails. They had been painted a deep purple. Her hands felt so soft that she didn't feel like doing anything with them.

"I've never known anyone like you, Mira. This may sound strange, but I had started to idolise you, and that evening, all that stuff you said… it made me realise that you are only human. It kind of…uhh… disappointed me, to be honest."

"So, you discovered that your idol had clay feet, and you withdrew your devotion," Mira responded.

Radha looked up to find that she was laughing, and she joined in somewhat shamefacedly.

"Don't put people on pedestals, Radha. No one needs that kind of adulation or pressure."

CHAPTER 7

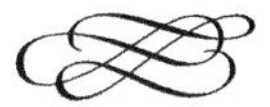

As Mira had predicted, things blew over in time. It took a few weeks for Shyam to calm down enough to talk to her properly, but in the end, he came around. They never spoke of Sangita. It was as if she had never existed. Since her elopement, she hadn't heard from Sangita either, so Radha assumed she had well and truly cut off all ties with her family, leaving her past behind.

It hurt to think that her best friend hadn't trusted her enough to confide in her, but at the same time Radha felt relieved that she could be honest and say that she truly did not know where Hari and Sangita had gone. They had both tendered their resignations a month prior to leaving, so it had all been well thought out.

Radha felt disappointed in Hari. She had assumed that he was made of stronger moral fibre and would have tried to do the right thing. Then again, she had seen how her in-laws had reacted. If Hari had asked for Sangita's hand in marriage, would they have even entertained the thought? Perhaps it was just as well that they had been blindsided, or it most certainly would not have gone in Sangita and Hari's favour.

Her in-laws were not as quick to forgive her. For over two months, she had not visited, knowing full well that she was not welcome. The news of her pregnancy had not cheered them up as she had hoped, and all she had received was a brief congratulations conveyed through Shyam.

Radha looked at herself in the mirror. She had started to show just a tiny bit at four months. Her normally flat stomach had rounded out, and she put her hand over the swell protectively. These strong maternal feelings had ambushed her unexpectedly. Her ambivalence had retreated and in its place was a tenderness she had never felt towards anyone before. She was going to have a baby. Her baby. A person who would belong to her entirely. She stroked her stomach, filled with a love she could not articulate.

Her mother had told her that babies brought people together. Perhaps this baby would fill the gap that Sangita had left in their lives. Perhaps her in-laws would focus on this new life and be able to move on from the child who, in their minds, had betrayed them in a horrible and diabolical manner. Perhaps.

Meanwhile, she carried on doing her yoga, adapting the *asanas* to her changing body. She had resumed her walks with Mira, and Shyam, no longer upset with her, had occasionally visited Monish and Mira with her for dinner or a coffee.

Radha no longer wished to be like her neighbours. She understood they were different people with a different dynamic between them. All she wanted was peace in her marriage, and an empathy between herself and Shyam.

Mira had started out being quite cold towards Shyam but had thawed slowly, noticing the small ways he was trying to make amends towards Radha. He was quiet and considerate, taking over the heavier tasks in the house. He took her to her parents every weekend while he visited his own, and as per what he told her, he was constantly advocating for her in front of them.

"They need time, Radha," he said on one of their drives back from Delhi. "They are heartbroken and they have no one else to blame."

"But you knew too," Radha stated flatly. "Why don't they blame you?"

"I'm their son. If they blame me, they will have no one left."

So she carried on as she always had, trying to extend her understanding and hoping that forgiveness would come sooner rather than later. But it rankled. Life was not fair if it allowed Shyam to get away scot-free while she bore the brunt of her in-laws' anger. She had tried, and she kept trying, to be the ideal daughter-in-law, the ideal wife, the ideal daughter. She was exhausted from all the trying. There were days she wanted to throw up her hands and say, "To hell with it!" That sounded so much like Mira that she suppressed a giggle at the thought and immediately wondered whether Mira would have ever put up with any of it.

As June arrived, the days got so hot that they were unbearable. Shyam installed an air conditioner in the bedroom, and most afternoons Radha took her siestas there. Walks with Mira had ground to a halt because of the heat, but she felt guilty for the number of times they had visited and not reciprocated the Das' hospitality.

"Can we call them over this weekend?" Radha asked Shyam as he handed him his lunch and briefcase before work.

"It's your home too, Radha. Call whoever you like." Shyam placed a soft kiss on her forehead before leaving.

She rang Mira immediately.

"Please say you will come!"

"Only if you make that delicious *kadhi chawal* again."

"Oh, but I wanted to prepare something more elaborate..."

"Then we aren't coming!"

"Okay, okay. *Kadhi chawal* it is."

Radha knew Mira had only said this to spare her the effort of preparing an extensive meal. Still, she intended to make a few extra curries. Shyam and Radha had so many lunches and dinners to repay the Das's that simple fare would just not suffice.

She phoned her local grocery store and gave them a long list of ingredients she needed for the Friday soiree. All of Wednesday and Thursday, she cooked the many dishes she had planned, including the *kadhi chawal* Mira had requested. She took frequent breaks between cooking to put her feet up.

Even as the nausea had abated, the swelling had begun. Radha had removed her wedding and engagement rings from her fingers because they were so swollen. Her feet would no longer fit in her strappy sandals, so she had taken to wearing *kolhapuri chappals* everywhere. Her *saree* blouses had been retired to make way for floaty *kameezes* worn over *salwars* that could be loosened at will. A strong dark line had developed on her abdomen and, alarmed, she had asked the nurse what it was, only to be told that it was completely natural hyperpigmentation caused by an increase in hormones.

The other consequence of this increase in hormones was Radha's heightened sex drive. She had felt herself desiring Shyam more frequently and initiating sex more often. At first, Shyam had been pleased with the development, but as her girth had increased, he had slowly started withdrawing, claiming he didn't want to hurt her or the baby.

Frustrated, Radha had taken to rereading the Harold Robbins books Sangita had gifted her when they were in college together. The innocent covers often belied the sexual content that lay within. At first these books had been an education, now they were a release.

❖

On Friday evening, Radha laid the table with her favourite *ikkat* print table mats and coasters. She put a vase of fresh flowers in the centre and lit jasmine-scented incense sticks in a corner of the room.

It wasn't as if Mira had never visited before, but this time it felt more formal, inviting Mira and Monish over as a couple. Radha wondered how they were doing. When she had confided her problems with how disinterested Shyam was in the bedroom lately, Mira had sighed and said, "Story of my life..." She hadn't pressed her any further to explain, but had wondered if that was why Mira had labelled Monish as 'boring'.

Shyam arrived ten minutes later than expected, even so, well in time to help with putting the heavier dishes on the hob to heat. Then he went for a quick shower while she added the finishing touches to the room.

The doorbell rang exactly at 8pm. Mira stood there with a bottle of wine in one hand and an enormous bunch of flowers in the other. Radha took the flowers and led her indoors.

"Where's Monish?"

"Not sure," Mira shrugged before placing the bottle on the sideboard. She had a brittle smile on her face, and Radha could tell that she was just about holding it together.

"Is everything okay?"

"Nope." Mira frowned. "We had a huge fight this morning over something silly, and I haven't heard from him all day. Normally, he rings at least once. I tried calling his work this evening, but they said he'd already left. He should have been home for seven. I waited and waited, then thought, what the hell! So, I just came over."

"Maybe something's happened? Has he ever behaved like this before?"

"No, but I was pretty vile to him, and he's probably pissed off."

Just then Shyam came out, dressed in a light blue *kurta* and jeans, smelling fresh and of his favourite aquatic cologne.

"Hi Mira! Welcome to ours. Where's Monish?"

Before she could answer, the doorbell rang again, this time insistently.

Shyam hurried to open the door. Tilo was standing outside, "*Memsahib, sahib foon aaya ki tyre poonkchur hai. Aapko boolaya auto mein.*"

Radha looked between Tilo and Mira to decipher what she had meant.

Mira sprung to her feet.

"Damn! Now I have to find an auto rickshaw and go fetch the man. His car's got a puncture."

Radha looked over at Shyam, who nodded subtly.

"No, don't worry Mira. I'll take you. Just let me put some shoes on and grab my wallet. Where is he stranded?"

After speaking with Tilo again, Mira said, "In Munirka, not far from JNU. I'll show you." She turned to Radha. "I'm so sorry, Kitten. This might take a while, but I promise we will come back and enjoy your delicious *khaana*. I could smell the wonderful aromas all the way from my house..."

They left within ten minutes and Radha decided to lie down and rest her legs until they got back. At 10pm when she woke up, there was still no sign of them. She went and checked on her food. A thin film of butter had coagulated over the *daal* and the rice had turned cold, but the rest of the food looked fine.

At 10:20pm the doorbell rang again and she let a visibly flustered Mira in followed by Shyam and Monish.

"I apologise for my tardiness," Monish said, mopping his brow. "It was impossible to find a payphone to call home. I had to walk miles before I found a serviceable one."

"And your car?" Radha asked.

"I've left it there with a sign on it. The mechanic will tow it to the repair centre tomorrow."

"Well, as long as you are okay..."

Mira glared at him. "We have ruined Radha's evening. It's half past ten!"

"Mira, I didn't plan this..."

While they squabbled, Radha went back into the kitchen to heat the food. Shyam followed her.

"I need to go to the bathroom, but I'll come and help you in a minute."

"Was she okay on the drive?" Radha tilted her head towards the living room.

"Yeah, yeah. Why do you ask?"

"She just seems really upset."

"She's fine. I'll be back in a sec."

They finally ate at 11pm. Monish would not stop apologising to her, alternating between that and complimenting her on the food. Mira played with the *kadhi chawal* on her plate, eyes downcast, saying little.

Shyam ate his fill and tried to talk about various topics without getting much of a response from either party. Radha observed sadly that one could cut the tension with a knife. Whatever had happened, it had turned her much-awaited dinner into an unmitigated disaster.

❖

Years later, Radha would look back and wonder if that was the turning point. But a few days after that disastrous dinner, she kept her distance from the couple, not because she was annoyed but because she could tell that all was not well between Monish and Mira, and assumed that giving them the space they required would be the wisest course of action.

She had not heard from Mira after that evening, and rather than take it as a sign of rudeness, she took it to mean that Mira was focussing on what was important to her in that moment, which was no doubt healing the rift between herself and her husband.

Meanwhile, life carried on at the same languid pace as before. Having had some spotting of blood now and again, the doctor had advised Radha to take it easy and not do too much housework. Shyam had hired a cook besides the maid, and now she had little to do except direct them and spend her days planning the nursery or reading books on babies.

Shyam was preoccupied with work, and was often home late. So, Radha pulled out her old psychology books from college and pored over them, realising how much she had enjoyed the subject. In another life, she might have pursued the study of psychology and tried to carve out a career of sorts. Could she have become a clinical psychologist or worked in social welfare? She would never find out. The women in her family did not work. That was a man's domain, had always been and would always be. No matter how much it grated, she knew she was in no position to change the status quo.

Her thoughts still wandered to Sangita often. Where was she? How was she? Had they gotten married? Were they still in Delhi? The hurt had receded somewhat and in its place was the pragmatism she had always prided herself on. People chose what was right for them. Sangita had chosen Hari and in doing so, she had turned her back on anyone who might have kept him from her. Right or wrong, it was her life and her decision. In time, Radha hoped, Sangita would find her way back to her family and to her.

The truth was that she missed her friends. Both Mira and Sangita had been important influences in her life. Sangita in her carefree optimism, her innate ability to understand and shield Radha, and her courage in trying to live the life she wanted, had been the solid ally she had taken for granted for the better part of five years.

Mira was her hero and her mentor, a woman whose thought processes were so removed and alien from her own, yet one who inspired and guided by being true to who she was. One whose perceptive dissections of Radha's own complexes and insecurities allowed Radha to examine and shed those that did not serve her.

Yes, she missed her friends, and wished life had been kinder to them, and to her.

Mummy came over one morning when Radha was lying in bed, reading the newspaper. Radha called out to the maid to open the door, expecting it to be the *presswallah* delivering Shyam's ironed shirts. Instead, Mummy marched in.

"Come on, get dressed, we are going to the *mandir.*"

Radha sat up hurriedly.

"Why?"

"I have fasted for ten days for you to have a boy. Today I have to give some money and *prasad* and you have to receive the priest's blessings."

Radha changed without a word. Mummy had insisted she hang a gaudy calendar with a plump, rosy-cheeked infant on her wall so that her baby boy turned out fair-skinned. She had also asserted that Radha drank two glasses of milk daily to help with the colour of the child's skin. When she had told Mira on one of their walks, she had guffawed so loudly, the locality aunties had turned to stare.

"Your mother truly believes that drinking milk affects the baby's skin colour? Hasn't she heard of genetics?"

Radha had shrugged.

"Look at me," Mira had stopped and faced her. "I'm dark-skinned. Does that make me ugly?"

"No," Radha had murmured. "I can't change the way she thinks, and to keep the peace, I go along with it."

"If our generation doesn't speak up, these ridiculous myths will just keep being perpetuated!"

As Radha brushed her hair while Mummy chatted to the cook, she wondered if it was worth saying anything. Then she shook her head and figured the path of least resistance was best with her mother. She had never won an argument against her, nor had Papa. So, why start now?

She tied her hair in a bun and stuck a few *jooda* pins to hold it in place. Maybe that is why her sisters-in-law had moved away, too. Who could bear to live in a house where one person's word was law? Just before she had left, Radha had overheard her older *bhabhi* say to her brother, "I want my own kitchen. With your mother, we have no choice in the food we eat."

Radha thought of her own time in her in-laws' home. She had never had the ability to question any of their decisions either, whether in the kitchen or in their living arrangements. Although she had not realised it at the time, Shyam's new job had been a blessing in disguise. In her own home, she could live and eat as she pleased.

The taxi took them to the Sheetla Mata Mandir, a prominent temple in Gurgaon. She was known as the goddess of healing and protection who treated smallpox, sores, pustules and other diseases, and people from all over the world came to seek Sheetla Mata's blessings.

"Why here, Mummy?"

"*Arey*, what does it matter where we go? The goddess is an incarnation of Durga and will bless you no matter what."

Radha had always found it interesting how Mummy bent her beliefs to suit her convenience.

"Come on now, don't daydream. We have to join the queue."

Radha used her *dupatta* as a fan as they joined the long, snaking queue that led to the idol of the goddess. The heat was making her queasy, and she sipped on the water bottle she had brought along. Mummy had covered her head and was chanting prayers as they moved along. They finally got to the idol, prostrated themselves before it and offered the fruits, money and *prasad* that Mummy had brought with her.

After receiving the priest's blessings, they went to sit in a cool corner of the temple. Radha closed her eyes and breathed in the smell of the incense. The tranquil surroundings, the many worshippers, and the feeling of being in the presence of the divine allowed a certain peace to saturate her being. All at once she felt she was only a tiny part of a grand design, and that no matter what happened, everything would turn out well in the end.

On Monday morning, when the phone rang, Radha answered thinking it was another one of her mother's phone calls. Mummy had brokered peace between her in-laws and Radha, and had not stopped crowing about her success since then. Radha had swallowed her resentment and resumed visiting them every weekend as a result.

"Radha?"

Sangita's voice took her by surprise and she nearly dropped the receiver.

"Sangi? Is it really you? How are you? Where are you? Why haven't we heard from you in two months?!"

"I know," Sangita groaned. "I'm sorry. I know you have a thousand questions, but first, how is everyone? Are Maa and Baba still angry?"

Radha stayed quiet. What could she say? They had still not spoken of Sangita to her, and the fragile peace that existed between them could potentially implode if she mentioned this phone call.

"Hello?" Sangita's voice sounded so far away.

"Yes, Sangi, they are still furious. What you did..."

"I know, T! I am sorry, but I had no choice. They had started talking about *rishtas* and marriage again, and Shyam... I wasn't sure what he was going to do."

"You could have talked to him, or to me. But this..."

"Are you going to keep accusing me, or do you want to hear my side?"

"Okay, tell me your side."

"Hari had this job offer, which would have meant leaving Delhi. So, the choice was that either he approached Maa and Baba, or that I left with him."

"Where did you go? And if you had it all planned, why didn't you speak to me about it?"

"And put you in the middle of it all? You saw how Shyam behaved the first time. I didn't want you caught up in my mess again. Listen, you may think I was unnecessarily secretive, but I was only trying to protect you."

Radha bit her lip. She could not dispute the fact that not knowing had helped her case with her in-laws. She had been damned for much less, and if she had been complicit in Sangita's elopement, she could only imagine the horror of the consequences to that.

"Where are you now?"

"In Chennai, with his parents."

"Married?"

"Of course. I refused to go anywhere with him until we tied the knot. Just a small ceremony in a temple in Delhi, and then we had it registered here."

"Are you happy?"

"Beyond happy! His family is so loving. They have no hang ups like Maa and Baba."

"What about Hari?"

"He's great! He calls every weekend..."

"Wait! What? He's not in Chennai with you?"

"No," Sangita laughed, "that's what I've been trying to tell you. He's gone to the US. We are waiting for my visa to come through, and then I will join him there, too."

That evening, as Radha stirred the *channa daal* the cook had prepared for dinner, she wondered whether it was worth saying anything to Shyam about the call. Sangita had promised to write a long letter to her parents before she moved to the US. She wanted to explain and apologise, and insisted that Radha say nothing to any of them.

Each time Radha had tried to help Sangita, it had backfired on her. Now she oscillated between coming clean to Shyam, or letting events take their natural course.

Why, oh why, could she not have a simple life in which she could enjoy her pregnancy and look forward to having her baby in peace? Why did she always have to worry about where Shyam was and what he was thinking? Or how to appease her in-laws? Or keep being the dutiful daughter her parents expected her to be? Or why Mira still had not called her ten days later?

Other people's expectations weighed heavily on her. She stroked her stomach and vowed that her baby—boy or girl—would never have to live out other people's dreams and desires. They would have the freedom to live out their own.

June 21st was the longest day of the year. It was also one of the hottest. The mercury had been hovering around 45 degrees celsius, and the heat was sapping Radha of all her energy. Shyam's conference was two days away, and as she made sure all his shirts were ironed, his underwear folded, his socks matched and his shoes polished, she yearned for the coolness of December.

After she had finished packing his case, she went and lay down in her air-conditioned room. She felt restless today, her mood changeable. Shyam had been so distant lately that she also felt alone. Her only company the last few days had been the maid, Tapeshwari, and the cook, Sarla, who regaled her with vicious stories about the vegetable seller's wife getting caught in an affair with his rival. Radha only half-listened, her mind flitting from one topic to another.

Now, as she lay on her bed, resting her swollen feet, she wondered if Sangita had written her apology letter. Had her visa come through? There had been no further contact between them, and Radha had not asked for her number. Much as she loved her friend, she intended to focus on herself this time. Her baby needed her to remain calm and happy, and she wanted to avoid any more upheavals.

A part of her had started to feel irritated at Mira's continued silence. It had been over two weeks now and her friend had not called or initiated any contact. What was going on with her? Surely by now Monish and she would have resolved the spat between them?

Radha closed her eyes and decided she would wait another week before checking in on her. Once again, she did not want to get in the middle of anything that would upset her. One of the baby books she had read said that the mother's moods greatly influenced the baby's temperament. Radha wanted to stay happy and placid for the baby's sake.

The knocking at the door woke her up, and she groggily called out, "Yes?"

"Radha *didi, khaana taiyyar hai,*" Sarla, the cook, called out, cracking the door open. Then she opened the door completely and stood there, staring down at Radha, her mouth a large O.

"*Kya hua?*" Radha asked, weariness lacing her voice.

Sarla shook her head and pointed at Radha's thighs.

Radha propped herself on her elbows and looked to where she was pointing. A deep pool of crimson had soaked the sheets beneath her, the largest patch forming an orchid-like pattern on her *salwar.*

"Call Mira *memsahib*!" Radha managed to whimper, sitting up slowly.

. . .

Who rang Shyam? Was it Mira? How did they take her to the hospital? Was she conscious when they took her?

Weeks later, all she would remember was the suffocatingly sterile smell of the hospital, a combination of antiseptics and disinfectants. The D&C the doctors performed to remove the remaining tissue from her uterus, because her miscarriage had been 'incomplete' was all but erased from her mind. The only word that lingered was 'incomplete'. Her baby had not wanted to leave her completely, but she had. She had fled her womb, leaving only traces of herself behind.

Why had she fled? Had she sensed that Radha would not be a good mother? Had she picked up on her cowardice, her timidity, and her incompetence? Had her little body wilfully rejected its housing, her soul refusing to enter a life of strictures and curtailment?

Why? Why? Why?

Her incomplete miscarriage sucked everything good out of her. Radha would never feel complete again.

For the three months that Radha stayed at her maternal home, she barely spoke. It was an effort for her to get out of bed. It was an effort to brush her teeth, take a shower or eat any food. She lost weight and stopped caring about what people thought. All she wanted to do was lie in bed and lose herself to sleep.

In her dreams, her little girl visited her. First as a baby, with bouncing brown ringlets that glinted in the sun. Then, as a toddler, her plump legs carrying her away as Radha gave chase, her giggles still reverberating in her mind when she woke.

Mummy tried taking her to the temple, Papa tried buying Radha her favourite snacks, but she turned away from them. She was grateful to be there, to be away from Shyam, who had held her hand when they had given her the news, who had tried to placate her as she had sobbed and screamed. Radha could see the disappointment in his eyes. She had failed him, just as she had failed everyone else.

Mira came to see her once. She sat in silence on the bed, waiting for Radha to speak. When she did not utter a word, Mira leaned over and gave her a hug, engulfing her in the same spicy and exotic fragrance she had always worn. She left after planting a soft kiss on her head. She had not been back since.

Her in-laws visited too. Maa cried and asked forgiveness for her cold-heartedness. She wrung her hands together, saying, "*Bitiya,* I understand your loss. I have lost my daughter, too." Baba sat in the corner chewing *paan masala* and averting his eyes from the women's misery.

Through it all, Radha felt numb. Nothing anyone said mattered anymore. Everything had changed. She knew herself to be nothing but a hollow shell, incapable of love or mirth, duty or desire.

Every evening she would slide into slumber, waiting for her little girl to come to her. On the nights she did not visit, Radha would wake up, her pillowcase soaked in tears. In the day, she remained dry-eyed and brittle. She spoke to no one and rejected all compassion. Her grief was hers alone, and she refused to share it with the world.

In early September, Mummy entered her room and yanked open the curtains.

"Enough now, Radha! Get up." She pulled the sheet off her and bundled it under her arm. "You are not the first person to have lost a baby, and you won't be the last. You've wallowed long enough, and we have allowed it, but now it's time to head home."

"This…this is my home," Radha whispered, curling herself into a foetal position.

"No, it's not. You know fully well that after marriage your *maika* is a place you visit, but it is no longer your home. You need to go back. Go to your husband, be a wife to him again, and in time, you will be blessed with a baby."

"No, please," Radha whimpered, "Please let me stay…"

Papa came in and sat by her side. He looked up at Mummy and said, "Mona, let her stay another month. What does it matter?"

"It matters a great deal. Shyam has only visited twice in two months. That is not a good sign. This distance between a husband and wife can widen into an unbridgeable chasm. Then what will she do? She needs to go home and fix her marriage, and get pregnant as quickly as possible."

Radha closed her eyes and shut out her mother's voice. She tried to reach for an image of her baby, but it was hazy and just out of grasp. She did not want to return to the emptiness of her reality, to days spent waiting for Shyam to come home, her only purpose cooking his favourite dishes and watching cricket with him. So she remained curled up in bed, taking the tiniest bit of comfort from her father's callused hand that stroked her forehead absently.

The house was exactly how she had left it. Someone had replaced the mattress and sheets on the bed, but apart from that, it looked untouched. Tapeshwari had swept and swabbed the floors and washed the dishes regularly. Sarla had cooked for Shyam. The house had carried on running in her absence, which made Radha feel even more superfluous.

Shyam had greeted the news of her arrival with a cautious note of happiness. Radha knew she had withdrawn from him, and maybe he thought she blamed him. She did not have the vocabulary to explain the storm of feelings inside of her, so she allowed him to retreat from her as she withdrew from him. Mummy had been perceptive enough to realise that this was indeed a chasm.

Yet, in all her emptiness, she still felt a flicker of happiness when her gaze fell on the wedding photograph sitting on the mantelpiece. She took a kitchen cloth to remove the film of dust that had gathered on all the photographs and ornaments dotted around the room. Then she noticed the cobweb in the corner, and the dead fly in the lamp, and before long she was in a cleaning frenzy.

The hours went by so quickly that when Shyam arrived from

work; she was balanced on a stool trying to change the bulb above the sideboard.

"Radha! What are you doing? Get down immediately. I'll fix that." Shyam marched over and held the stool as she climbed off it.

"Why didn't you say you were coming today? I would have fetched you."

"No, I... thought you would be busy at work. It was easy enough to take a taxi."

Shyam took the bulb out of her hand and set it down, his face a mask of polite blankness.

"How are you?" She asked, her eyes searching his face.

"Oh, you know. Busy. Work has been manic." He ran his hands through his hair and grimaced. "You?"

"Yes, alright, I suppose." She gave him a wan smile. "Mummy has sent some food."

"We could order pizza?"

"No, I... I'm not really hungry. I think I'll sleep early today."

"Okay."

Radha unpacked her small valise and went into the bathroom to wash her face and brush her teeth. The woman in the mirror bore a passing resemblance to the one who had lived in this house three months ago. That woman had lived in hope. This woman was just tired of life.

Later, Radha could hear the television from the bedroom as she lay in the dark. Some American movie with lots of guns and people swearing and shooting. The sort of movie Shyam had always enjoyed watching. She had hated them back then for their noise and violence, but now she didn't mind. It filled the silence that inhabited their home and their marriage.

❖

When Sangita's letter finally arrived, it set off a mini earthquake.

"She's leaving for America!" Baba cried out, a mixture of pride and disbelief in his voice.

"She's pregnant," Maa muttered, clutching the letter in her hand.

Radha felt a knife twist in her abdomen, and she schooled her face into a semblance of delight. Before she could say anything, she heard Shyam say, "Tear that letter up right now! When she left this house, she severed all connection with us. I don't care what she does or whose child she has..."

The venom in his voice startled her. Later, Maa explained that Shyam had always been the tiniest bit jealous of Sangita. Not only was she Baba's favourite, but she had accomplished that which Shyam could only dream of.

"Having a baby?" Radha asked, confused.

"Oh no, not that. That is up to you, my dear. No, no," Maa raised her hands, "there is no rush. You take your time." She stopped sifting the rice for stones and looked up at Radha, a peculiar gleam in her eyes. "He has always wanted to go to America, to live and work there. But for some reason, it has never worked out for him. So, now that Sangita has managed it..."

She had never known this about Shyam. Radha wondered how much more she did not know—and would she ever get to find out?

"Are you going to write back to her, Maa?" Radha asked, taking the platter out of her hands and working her fingers through the rice.

"She is my child," a sob caught in Maa's throat before she composed herself. "If not today, then someday, I would have forgiven her, *na*? And after losing our grandchild," she leaned forward and stroked Radha's hair, "I realised how unpredictable life can be."

Radha nodded and kept removing the tiny stones from between the rice grains. Her in-laws had softened towards her in the last few months, and while nothing could fill the emptiness inside her, their warmth had acted as a salve to her bruised soul.

On their way home, Shyam stayed silent. It was a silence filled with a suppressed anger, a simmering resentment, and Radha didn't dare broach the subject of Sangita's emigration. In the past few weeks, she had allowed silence to dominate the space between them, and now, more than ever, it seemed to be the appropriate course.

As they parked up, she noticed all the lights were on in the Das home.

"Have you heard from either of them?" She asked casually, while getting out of the car.

"Who?" Shyam was sharp, as if spoiling for a fight.

"Mira or Monish." Radha looked at him.

His lips were a tight line as he glanced towards their house.

"No." His curt monosyllabic answer cut off any further questioning, and she followed him inside quietly.

The next day, she rang the doorbell to the house. Batman started barking behind the door and Tilo came outside, shushing him as she did.

"Mira *memsahib hain?*"

Tilo shuffled her feet and looked at the floor before looking at her and looking away. Then she muttered something garbled.

"Sahib, gussha hoeegaaya kyonkar oonko patta challeegaya. Obhi buhoot noraaz hoi."

The little she could understand allowed her to believe that things were no better between the couple. Radha had been so wrapped up in her misery, she had forgotten that in all likelihood Mira was not in a good place herself. If it had not been for Mira's quick thinking, Radha would have haemorrhaged to death that day.

When memories of that afternoon ambushed her unexpectedly, she could remember Mira's hoarse commands to call for an ambulance, the way she had held her hand and said, "I'm here, I'm here. Radha, stay with me."

Where was she now? Radha needed her to know that she appreciated everything she had done for her. She wanted to be there for Mira just as much as Mira had been there for her.

. . .

❖

On October 7, 1997, Radha stood in front of the calendar her mother had given her, and observed the rosy-cheeked, plump toddler's picture. Then she took it down and tore it into several small pieces before gathering them up and putting them in the bin. She went through every baby item she had bought or knitted, the baby books, the pictures she had torn out of the magazines, and put them all in a big bag.

She dragged the bag towards the small room at the back, which had always served as a junk room where they piled all the things they did not know what to do with. They had resolved to turn it into a guest room one day, but for now, it remained filled with the odds and ends of their lives. Radha remembered vowing to herself at the start of the year that she would tackle this room, that she would enlist Shyam's help in getting rid of all that was redundant. Yet, the room had only accumulated more as the months went by.

She sighed and pushed the bag in and away from the door, ready to turn away, when a bit of handwriting caught her eye. The swirls of the t's and g's looked vaguely familiar, but she couldn't place it immediately. She pulled the sheet out from under the book and read the brief note written on it.

I hope you will be wise enough to destroy this once you have read it. This cannot carry on. We cannot carry on. No matter what you say about the state of your marriage, or know about the state of mine, this is deceit and I will no longer be a party to it.

I am leaving for my mother's tomorrow morning. Do not contact me. Fix what is broken and figure a way out of your mess.

. . .

With trembling hands, Radha set the note back on the desk, guiltily replacing it under the book.

When Shyam came home that evening, she was sitting on the sofa, her hands on her lap. As he walked in, she looked up and said, "Do you love her?"

"What?"

"I asked, do you love her?"

His body seemed to collapse into itself. He sank to his knees, his face in his palms.

"Radha, I can't lose her. I'll die without her."

She picked up the case she had packed and looked down at him. Her voice was soft but the steel in it was unmistakable.

"Then go find her."

With that, she walked out of the door and their broken marriage.

SHYAM

2008

CHAPTER 8

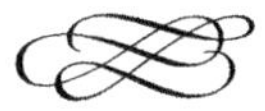

Someone had given him a paperweight once with the saying, "Be careful what you wish for, lest it come true."

It sat on his desk now, taunting him with its wisdom.

He twirled the pen between his fingers, thinking back to this morning. The noise, the chaos, and his utter helplessness in the face of it all.

"You coming?" Graham popped his head around the cubicle.

Shyam looked up. It took him a moment to decipher what Graham was talking about.

"Yeah, sorry. Was miles away."

"I could see that, mate. Everything okay with you? Been a bit quiet lately."

"Yeah, yeah, everything's great. Just preoccupied with this new project."

"Speaking of which, the lady in charge is coming down next month. We better have something good to serve her up. Apparently, she's quite the Rottweiler!"

Graham winked and left. Shyam sat still with the pen in his hand, then jumped up and grabbed his jacket. He pulled his mobile phone out and rang home.

"Hello?"

"Hi *jaan*, I'll be home late today. Don't wait up."

There was a pause on the other end.

"How late?"

"Late. It's drinks night at the pub, and you know how Graham and this lot are."

"How are you getting home?"

"I'll take a cab."

"Sleep in the guest room then. I don't want Esha waking up."

"Yes, okay, I will. How is she? Did she calm down?"

"What do you think, Shyam?" Mira's voice was cold. "Of course she calmed down. She's a baby, not a circus animal that you stare at from a distance."

He sighed quietly.

"Alright, I'll see you later. Bye."

She hung up without saying goodbye.

They had moved to their house in Osterley five years ago, but before that they had rented in Wembley, then Pinner, both areas with overwhelmingly large Indian populations. Mira had not been happy with that, but they could afford little else. At least here, in Osterley, their immediate neighbours were an elderly English couple, Jenny and Jerry. They had taken to Mira immediately, but always kept him at arm's length. He was not sure why, but it did not bother him too much, as long as Mira was happy.

He often asked himself if she was happy.

You cannot build a home on the foundation of someone else's unhappiness, Nisha had said to him when he had followed Mira to Mumbai the same year that Radha had left him. Ten years on, he wondered if that was true.

They had had some happy years. In the beginning, once they had moved past the carnage of their broken marriages, they had been happy. Mumbai had given him the breathing space he required. It was far enough from his accusing parents, far enough from his old life, yet it was still near enough that he could get on a flight and be home, if required. Not that they ever required it of him. These same parents who had sworn never to forgive Sangita had embraced her with open arms when she visited. But he had become the black sheep, the son who let them down because he divorced his wife for a *badchallan*, characterless woman. They had refused to meet Mira while taking Hari into the bosom of the family. They had all but cut off communication with him while making long international calls to their daughter in Detroit.

As for Sangita, her first words to him had been, "How could you?"

How could he? Didn't she know? Didn't she understand that love could overwhelm common sense, subsume decency, and overpower discretion? She, who had eloped with that giant of a man. She, who was well ensconced in America, enjoying all the good things that life abroad provided. She should have been on his side. Instead, she chose Radha.

As for Radha, something inside him had died the day she left. A part that knew how grievously he had wronged her; a part that understood that she, out of everyone, was the only person who had not pelted him with accusations or created any drama around their split. She had removed herself quietly and with dignity. In doing so, she had left both him and Mira with a guilt that not even a lifetime could erase.

Where was she now? Had she remarried? Was she doing okay? No one spoke to him about her. Not his parents, not Sangita. He had tried calling her parents once, but the moment he had said his name, her mother had hung up on him.

Why did he want to know? Did some small part of him still care for that sweet, innocent girl he had betrayed in so heinous a manner?

They never spoke of her at home. From being consumed with her at the beginning of their relationship, when Mira had spoken of little else but how she couldn't bear the hurt she had caused Radha, she had consigned that entire part of her life to the past the moment they had married. He wished he had the same talent for compartmentalising his life.

One day, he had tried bringing her name up. This was when Mira was still struggling with morning sickness.

"You know, Radha used to suck on limes or *saunf*. She said it helped with the nausea."

Mira had looked at him, her eyes hard.

"I can manage very well, thank you. You don't need to keep regurgitating the past."

He had stayed silent after that, never mentioning Radha's name to her again.

❖

In the pub, he sat next to Graham and Roy, his colleagues from work. They talked shop for a while.

Graham leaned forward and said, "Have you chaps been following the buzz around SOA? Shyam and I are exploring it around our project, and it seems like a game-changer."

Roy took a gulp of his lager before placing his glass on the table. "We're knee-deep in ETL processes. Business Intelligence is becoming more critical, and we're looking at ways to make our reporting more real-time."

"I've heard," Mark said, joining them at their table, "the boss lady is coming down to talk about virtualisation and the possibilities of mobile apps. What do you think, Shyam? You've been beavering away on it all long enough."

As systems analysts, a lot of their Friday evenings at the pub began with going over all that had happened at work during the week, and what was expected from them. Shyam used to find it invigorating, but now he found it tedious. Still, he responded as expected.

"Virtualisation is gaining traction in our server infrastructure. It is helping us optimise resources and reduce costs. So, yes, I think mobile apps are the way forward. In fact, I predict that in ten years, nearly everyone will be using them," Shyam responded with a shrug.

"Anyone worried she's coming to axe jobs?" Roy asked, leaning forward, a frown on his face.

"What, because of the credit crunch? We're lean enough as it is," Mark replied.

"There's a global financial crisis, mate," Graham said, his voice dipping an octave, "Just in case you hadn't noticed..."

After a while, Shyam tuned them out, nodding and laughing in enough of the right places for them to think that he was still a part of their conversation. He understood that these Friday evening pub jaunts were their opportunity to decompress. It had taken him long enough to get an invitation that he now didn't want to jeopardise his position in the group by seeming disinterested. But his mind kept wandering away from these men and their predictable chatter about work, money, cars, and football.

When he had left India for the UK, he had thought life would be so much easier. In a new country, he could be whoever he wanted. Here, the baggage of a failed marriage and his estrangement from his family wouldn't follow him around like a foul odour. Here, he would, with his affability and intelligence, make friends quickly and begin a new and exciting chapter in his life.

It had not been that easy.

In the first job he had landed, he was only one of hundreds of Indian men working in IT. The British had treated him like a robot. They had been polite and distant, unwelcoming to their own already well-formed friendship groups. As for the Indian cliques, he had quickly realised that he needed to keep his distance from them if he wanted to rise through the ranks. Otherwise, he was likely to become just another nameless, faceless, "smelling-of-curry" Indian man providing IT services. No matter how hard he worked, or how much he tried to assimilate, his place in the pecking order would not change.

So he resolved to keep himself apart from the Indians, and concentrate his efforts on making inroads into the higher echelons of the company cliques. This had been his mantra, and it had seen him rise through four job changes until he had landed at Axis & Co. as a Senior Systems Analyst.

In the early days, when he had confessed his game plan to Mira, her eyebrows had shot up.

"Didn't know you were such a snob!" She had laughed at him while pouring a glass of wine.

"Aren't you as well? You didn't want to live amongst Indians either."

"I suppose I am," she had grinned back, "but that's more because I don't want to be judged by them. And aren't we Indians the most judgemental people? Imagine if I told them about my past. How do you think that would go down?"

"Why tell anyone?"

"Because, my darling husband, Indians are naturally inquisitive. One *chai* session and they would ferret all the information out of me without me even realising what was happening."

"And the English?"

"Couldn't care less. That's true privacy. Just like you are reinventing yourself at work, I am doing the same in my private life."

How aligned they were back then, how in step with each other. Why had everything changed, and what could he do to change it back to how it was?

❖

Esha's wailing woke him up at 5am. He had only stumbled into bed two hours earlier, so he took a pillow and covered his head with it. Moments later, he heard the creak of the floorboards as Mira got up and padded towards the cot. Soon she would be rocking the baby to sleep, singing some soothing lullaby.

He turned the other way. Esha was nearly two years old, and he had asked Mira several times to move the cot into the spare room, but she had refused to listen. The baby cried all night on some nights. He couldn't sleep, he couldn't concentrate at work, so he had taken to sleeping in the spare room. Why couldn't Mira see how this was affecting their marriage? He couldn't remember the last time they had made love. Even that he was willing to sacrifice just to hold Mira's warm body and feel her arms around him.

"Esha needs me more than you do, Shyam. Why can't you see that?" Mira would ask, the ice in her voice sending an unbidden shiver down his spine.

How could he argue with that? But he needed her, too. Needed and desired. Her body had changed with pregnancy. She had filled out even more, her normally curvaceous figure now even more voluptuous. He wanted to explore this new body, rediscover the crevices, plant kisses on the domes, trail his fingers through the valleys, and breathe upon the unexpected dimples. She would not allow it.

Her body was the baby's now, to feed on, to lie upon, to crave and demand from. He was relegated to watching and resenting. Yes, he was resentful of this interloper who had taken the most precious of his possessions away from him: his wife's love.

When Esha was born, he had called home to tell Maa and Baba. By then, Baba was already debilitated and in bed. Maa had heard the news and said, "Well, all I can say is that karma comes home in the most unexpected ways."

So, this was his karma?

Sangita had been more forgiving, asking if he needed her to come down. They had recently moved to San Jose, and with two young children and the upheaval of the move, he knew it would be unfair of him to say yes. How he wanted to! He missed his family more than he realised. He missed their earthiness, their dour humour, their traditional grounding.

In marrying Mira he had given all that up willingly, but in time he had realised that his DNA could not be denied. They were a part of him just as much as he was a part of them.

"Do you think this is my karma, Sangita?" He had asked his sister on one of his infrequent calls to her.

"That's what Maa said, *na*? Don't take her words to heart, Shyam. She is so exhausted from caring for Baba that she often says cruel things without realising it. It's been very hard on them with both their children abroad and no family nearby to rely on."

He had grunted his understanding but persisted in his line of questioning.

"But what do you think?"

She had paused before responding, then said, "I think one can ascribe so much to karma, but I also think it is up to us to make the most of any situation. You need to make peace with your life as it is now, not as you had hoped it would be."

He tried making his peace. He tried bonding with the baby, but somehow, every time he looked at her, it felt as if life was mocking him. As if God himself had decided that Shyam, who had sailed through life with the bare minimum of obstacles, would now encounter something so insurmountable that it would break him into smithereens.

Nisha had come to help Mira shortly before the baby's birth. Nisha, the mother-in-law he had never seen eye to eye with. He was grateful for her help, that much he could not deny. She was hands on, taking over all the household chores, letting Mira sleep when she was exhausted, helping her pump milk so that she could take over the night feeds. In all of that, too, he had felt relegated to the background. Three generations of women conspiring to keep him on the sidelines. He knew that if he vocalised this, they would scoff and call him paranoid and misogynistic, words he had only understood after marrying Mira.

These days, he felt emasculated.

Yet, so much of him craved Mira. She had always been like a drug to him. From the day he had first laid eyes on her to the day she had succumbed to his advances, she had never been far from his thoughts. It wasn't just her beauty, although undeniably, she was beautiful to him. It was the very essence of her. Her devil-may-care attitude, her social superiority, her intellectual and verbal dexterity—all the things he had never encountered in a woman before had drawn him helplessly towards her.

When Nisha had left six months after the birth, he had tried to make his way back into Mira's orbit. She no longer had room for him there. It had become all about Esha. Her every waking moment was devoted to the baby. This baby that she had wanted so badly that she had ignored all the warnings, had decided despite being told of the consequences of falling pregnant at forty that she would have this infant, and finally, when Esha had arrived, she had readily dedicated her life to caring for this child.

Sometimes Shyam wondered whether she would ever have room for him in her life again? After all, things would never be easy for Esha. A child with Down syndrome would need constant attention and extensive therapies. Where would he fit in all of that?

❖

Shyam finally woke up at noon the following day. The rain was pelting down outside and he could tell it would be another grim, grey and slushy day. This was May! He could remember the sweltering hot summer days in Delhi when he had played cricket on the *maidan* close to their house. Rain had been welcome then. Now it was a nuisance, a constant, unrelenting dribble instead of the downpour that heralded monsoons. He missed India, even if he would never admit it, least of all to Mira.

He waited to hear the mid-morning noises he had gotten used to. Esha gurgling as Mira fed her, or the sound of the vacuum cleaner going while the radio played softly in the background. There was just silence. He sat up, alarmed. Where were they?

Outside, he found a note on the table under the bowl of pot-pourri.

Gone to the park. Will be back by 1pm.

Mira rarely signed her notes. Sometimes he wished she would show her affection in some small way. An x to indicate a kiss, an o for a hug. He had never required demonstrations of love of Radha. He had known that she loved him. With Mira, he was never sure. Yet, she had to have loved him to leave the baldy and come to him. She had to have loved him to leave India and come here.

He showered and changed, then picked up all the toys littered around the room. In the kitchen, the dishes were piled high in the sink. He loaded them into the dishwasher and turned it on. Mira had never cared for housework, calling it boring and soul-sucking. Over the years, he had taken over the bulk of it, even experimenting with cooking. Soon after they had gotten together, he had realised that Mira was no cook. Her fallback was Maggi noodles doused in ketchup. In India it had not mattered, as at first Nisha had cooked for them. Then, when they had moved in together after their wedding, they had relied on good, cheap restaurant food, the varieties of which were aplenty near their Bandra flat. It was only when they had moved to the UK that Shyam had figured that if he wanted to eat home-cooked food, he would be the one cooking it. He did not mind. After a day of working through design and model information systems, data flow and entity-relationship diagrams, cooking allowed him to switch his brain off and relax. In time, he had become a fairly good cook, experimenting with Thai and Chinese cuisines too.

He looked at the mess on the hob and sighed. A pan of porridge was congealing there while baby food was stuck to the surface of the stove. He pulled out the cleaner and started work on it. As he was finishing, he heard the door open.

Rushing out, he took the buggy out of Mira's hand and folded it while she rocked Esha in her arms.

"Look, babushka, Daddy is awake," she cooed.

Shyam looked at Mira. Her cheeks were ruddy from the outdoors, her mackintosh soaking wet, hair windblown, and she had never looked more beautiful. He leaned in for a kiss. She gave him a quick peck and handed the baby to him.

"I need to get changed. It's so cold and blustery outside. Brrrr!"

He held Esha in his arms, uncomfortable and uncertain what to do with her. She stared at him with her almond-shaped brown eyes, her thumb in her mouth. Try as he might, he had never seen any family resemblance in her. She had the typical features of a baby with Down syndrome—a flattened face, eyes that slanted upwards, a short neck and small ears. She was as alien to him as the child two houses away.

He set her down on her high chair and gave her a rattle to play with. She took it from him and put it on the table, then carried on considering him, as if he was something new and strange to her too.

"Hi." He waved at her.

She did not respond, but her little tongue stuck out of her mouth.

"Dada." He pointed to himself as he said this.

She picked up her rattle and shook it.

"Rattle," he mouthed at her.

She shook it again.

Mira came up behind him and put her arms around his neck.

"Daddy and Esha bonding session? I'll do lunch today."

"No," he jumped up. "I was going to make egg *bhurji*. You take it easy."

He fled to the kitchen, escaping the only way he knew how.

It was June when the call came through.

"Daddy has gone," Sangita sobbed at the other end.

"What?" Shocked, Shyam stopped in his tracks. Roy stopped a few feet away, looking concerned. They had been on their way to a meeting in the conference room.

After he had rung off, Shyam turned to him and said, "I have to fly to India straight away. My father has died."

They booked him on a flight leaving Heathrow the same night. Graham urged him to leave early and get packing.

"But...the meeting?"

"Sod the meeting, mate! This is your dad."

He drove home, automaton-like, and when he parked, he sat in the car in silence. Memories engulfed him. Baba carrying him on his shoulders, buying *jalebi* from the roadside vendor, teaching him cricket, taking him to watch the latest Hindi movie... When was the last time he had spoken to his father? How many years since he had last visited? Tears ran down his face as he contemplated the loss.

How easy it was to believe that one's parents were invincible, that they would live forever. How difficult to comprehend that he would never ever feel his father's hands ruffle his hair, or ask him to pass him his *paan masala.*

He wiped his face and got out of the car. As he let himself in quietly through the front door, he noticed Mira and Esha fast asleep on the sofa. With both their faces slack in sleep, he noticed Esha's resemblance to her mother. The same olive skin tone, dark brown hair, and long lashes that fluttered against their cheeks. How could he not have seen it before?

He stroked Mira's arm to wake her gently. She opened her eyes and stared at him in confusion. He put his finger to his lips and asked her to come to the bedroom. She placed a few cushions around Esha, leaving her asleep on the sofa.

"What's happening?" She whispered, following him into the room.

"Baba died this afternoon," he said, removing all traces of emotion from his voice. "I'm taking the evening flight to Delhi. The cremation will be tomorrow, and I'll have to do all the last rites."

"Oh, my God! I'm so sorry, Shyam. Do you need me to come?"

"No, that...it...yeah, no, it's okay. This is something I have to do."

"How long will you be away?"

"A couple of weeks, at least. Will you be okay?"

"Yes, of course! Is Sangita coming too?"

"The earliest flight she could get leaves tomorrow, so she will miss the cremation, but she will be there for the prayer meeting and then we will probably head to Haridwar to immerse the ashes."

Mira nodded.

"What can I do?"

"Nothing, really. I need to pack. The taxi is coming to fetch me at 5pm."

"Do you need help with the packing?"

Just then, Esha woke up and started crying.

"I'll be fine. You just take care of yourself and the baby."

Mira left the room to soothe Esha. Shyam pulled his case out from under the bed and started packing. His thoughts were scattering in a hundred different directions, but he forced himself to focus on the task at hand. He had the rest of his lifetime to mourn his father.

"Shyam?" Mira stood in the doorway with Esha on her hip.

"Yes?"

"If you need to bring Maa back with you, you know that's okay, right?"

He nodded, gulping down a sob. How could he explain that his mother would never set foot in his home, ever?

"I mean, she could do with getting away from it all. It must have been so difficult for her."

Shyam nodded again. "I'll ask her, but I think Sangita plans to stay for a while."

"Oh, that's good. Maybe my mum can come for the cremation, if you are okay with it?"

He knew she was trying, but sometimes Mira could be wilfully obtuse about the true state of affairs.

"I think," he picked his words carefully, "it might be too much to expect Nisha to go all the way from Mumbai to Delhi, especially at such short notice. Maybe later, hmm?"

"Yes, sure. I just feel so helpless. I can't imagine what you're going through."

A flash of irritation shot through him and, for the first time ever, he felt like snapping at her. No, she had no idea what he was going through. No idea what losing a parent felt like because both of hers were alive and well. She could not imagine his grief, his guilt or his self-recrimination, because all that mattered to her was that child slung over her hip. He stayed silent as he zipped his case close.

"Can I make you a sandwich?"

"No," he kissed her on the forehead. "I don't have much of an appetite right now."

On the drive to the airport, he tried remembering the last proper conversation he had had with Baba.

"Shyam," Baba had pleaded, "there has never been a divorce in our family. Please don't do this. Don't break up your home over some woman."

"She isn't some woman!" Shyam had yelled. "She is the woman I'm in love with."

His father had shaken his head sorrowfully and retreated to his armchair.

From then on, all their stilted conversations had been filled with the blank spaces of words unspoken and deliberately unheard.

How he wished he could rewind the clock and tell his father how sorry he was. Not for his love for Mira, but for his inability to explain himself, his impetuosity in leaving home to pursue her, and the distance he had put between those who had birthed and nurtured him and himself.

Maa was stoic in her white, starched cotton saree. He touched her feet first and then hugged her. She felt like a bag of bones to him. When had she aged this much? Nearly all her hair was white, and her face was heavily lined. The last time he had visited six years prior, she had still been as robust as ever. Had caring for his father taken such a hard toll on her?

Baba's body lay in the front room, a white sheet covering it. A few of the neighbourhood ladies were sitting around, also dressed in white. A large framed photograph of his father, from when he was in his forties, sat at his head. A garland of marigold flowers hung on it, and a *ghee diya* sat in front of it. The smell of sandalwood filled the room, incense sticks dotted around.

As he entered, all chatter stopped, and the women stared at him. The prodigal son returns, he thought to himself, wry in his observation, not really caring what the gossip-mongers would say later. He knelt at his father's feet and touched his forehead to them. Could Baba see him from wherever he was now? As per the Hindu customs, the soul still lingered near the body until the cremation. For the *atma* to return to the *paramatma,* the soul to rejoin the divine, all rites would have to be performed as per their customs and traditions.

"The van is coming to collect the body at 1pm. We have to be at the crematorium by 2pm for the cremation. I've laid out a white *kurta pyjama* for you on the bed. You can change into it after your bath."

Maa stated everything so matter-of-factly that Shyam had to look closely to realise how hard she was working to keep her emotions in check.

He went into the bedroom and sat on the bed. This was the same bed that he and Sangita had slept on as children, before she had moved into the smaller bedroom when she had turned ten; the same bed he had wet as a toddler and read Archie comics on as a teenager; the same bed he and Radha had once made love upon. Today, a stark white *kurta pyjama* lay on it, reminding him of all his failings as a son, a brother, and a husband.

Shyam rubbed his hands on his face. He had not slept a wink all night, plagued with memories and regrets. Could he have done more to bring his family together? Why had he allowed himself to be so swept up in love that he had discarded all those who had made him who he was?

There was a knock on the door and he glanced up to see a woman dressed in a pale lemon coloured *salwar kameez* standing at the doorway. His vision blurred for a moment and when it cleared, he realised he had not been mistaken. It was Radha. Older, thinner, even lovelier than she had ever been, but it was still her.

"Shyam, may I come in?" There was sorrow etched on her face, and he noticed now she wore wire-rimmed spectacles.

He nodded, and as she approached, he fell to the floor and grabbed at her legs. His grief flooded him in great, racking sobs that shook his entire body, and he held on to her like a drowning man. She put her hand on his head and allowed him to cry his heart out.

CHAPTER 9

One of his earliest memories was of Sangita crying and calling out for Maa. He had wet the bed again. Maa had pulled him off, stripped the sheets, shunted him into the bathroom and scrubbed him clean after giving him a smack on his bottom.

"You are nearly seven now, Shyam!" She had thrown icy water over him as he had stood naked and shivering in the cold. "When are you going to stop doing *susu* in bed?"

Sangita had slept with his parents while he had laid ramrod straight in his bed, afraid to fall asleep in case his bladder betrayed him again.

In time, he had overcome his night time incontinence, but the shame had stayed with him for a long, long time. Boys did not wet their beds, nor did they cry. The first time he had come home crying after a defeat in the locality cricket match, Baba had taken him aside and told him that crying was a sign of weakness. Women cried; they were allowed to because they were the weaker sex. But for a boy to cry, it signalled to the world that he was feeble and incapable of controlling himself. People would prey on that vulnerability if he gave them half a chance. "Be a man!" Baba had said, and Shyam had resolved that was what he would be.

He had never seen Baba cry, not even when his parents passed away. Baba was as strong as the oak tree that grew near their house. He sheltered and protected his family, never allowing his doubts or fears to percolate into their daily living.

Shyam knew that as he grew into a young man, the expectation from him was not just to be as good as his father, but to surpass him. To be more successful, richer, smarter and stronger. That is what every successive generation of men did. They took the baton handed down to them by their fathers and ran with it farther and faster until they were ready to hand it over to their own sons.

"Why did you marry me?" Radha had asked him on that day that she had visited to pay her condolences.

"Because," he had said without having to think, "it was expected of me. You were the sort of *bahu* my parents wanted, the sort of wife I needed to score to move up in life, and you were Sangita's friend, which helped."

Radha had sat next to him on the bed, absorbing his words. Then she had looked up, her eyes gleaming with unshed tears, and said, "Thank you for your honesty."

Before he could ask her more or even apologise for his behaviour, his mother had come in and scooped her up. Afterwards, much as he had tried, he had never been able to talk to her again. There was too much to do and too much to mourn.

Back in England, when Mira pressed him for details, he told her about everything except meeting Radha. It seemed a betrayal to bring her up. Not to Mira, although, undoubtedly, she wouldn't be pleased, but to Radha. There had been heartbreak in her eyes and he had realised in that moment that she was still not over him or what he had done to her.

"Will Maa stay on her own in Delhi now?" Mira asked as she ladled the baked beans onto his toast.

"For now, yes. Sangita is trying to organise a visa for her to go to the US. If they manage it, she may end up living with them long term."

"Oh, wow."

Shyam had seen the barely suppressed shudder but chose to ignore it. Inside, he felt he was letting Baba down by not housing his mother. He was the son. It was his duty. Instead, Sangita and Hari had stepped up and all he could do was be a bystander to their decisions.

After they had returned from Haridwar, he had sat with Maa, sorting through Baba's old clothes. She had taken an old Seiko automatic watch that had been his father's pride and joy, and handed it over to him.

"Baba wanted you to have this. His office gave it to him when he retired. You can keep it or throw it away, I don't care. Just don't tell me."

Maa's words had been designed to cut. Maybe she had wanted a reaction out of him, but he had refused to give it, taking the watch and putting it in his pocket.

"How long has Radha been visiting you?" He had asked instead.

"She never stopped. Just because you left her doesn't mean we did too. She became our daughter-in-law the day you married her, and she will always be our daughter-in-law until the day I die." Maa had challenged him with her flashing eyes.

"I'm glad she was here for you. What is she doing now?"

Maa had picked up the bundle of clothes she planned to donate to the school for the blind and walked out of the room.

Ten days later, he had been on the plane back to the UK, his heart heavy with grief, his mind full of unanswered questions. The physical distance that he had put between his parents and himself, and between his sister and himself, had grown into a vast and unfathomable emotional expanse that, try as he might, he could not traverse. He no longer had the language for it.

"Keshav wants a visit," Mira said as soon as he walked in through the door.

Shyam had been back at work for three weeks now, and the new project had swallowed him whole. With the boss' visit looming, the team had been working round the clock to tie up all loose ends and have a stellar presentation lined up.

"Now?" He sighed as he loosened his tie.

"Well, Shylock will always want his piece of flesh," Mira stated cryptically, her legs curled up under her, a magazine resting face down on her lap, an empty glass of red wine in her hand.

Over the years, Shyam had learned to ignore her esoteric references. He was not a literature buff and in the beginning, when he had exhibited his ignorance, she had mocked him lovingly. So, he had decided never to take the bait. Sometimes, if he could remember, he would try to Google the words. More often than not, he chose to forget.

"Does he want to come over to us?"

"No, he's planned some soiree at his and wants us all to traipse over to him."

"All the way to Windsor?"

"All the way to Windsor."

"When?"

"How does tomorrow evening sound to you?"

"Bit late notice, isn't it?"

"That's my dad."

Mira's words were thick with scorn. She so rarely called him Dad that when she did, it nearly always took Shyam by surprise. Keshav was how he had always known him, and Keshav was how they always referred to him.

Shyam had actually liked him from the very start. Keshav was personable and friendly. He was also wealthy and well-connected. Shyam owed him his new life and career, and he did not mind paying the occasional obeisance to him if that was all that was required of him. Mira resented it. She had never been happy asking her father for assistance, and now his occasional requests for visits inflamed her even further. She did not feel any filial devotion to him, and barely contained her animosity towards him.

"Yes, no problem. I'll finish work early and we can drive down. Does he mind us bringing the baby?"

"And if he did? Should we leave her here to her own devices while you prostrate yourself at his feet?"

"Mira, I know you're not happy..."

"You're bloody well right, I'm not! It's been bad enough asking him for help, but now I have to put up with seeing him nearly every month. And that boyfriend of his!"

"Listen, as someone who has just lost his father..."

"No," she put her hands up as if to ward him off. "Don't you start with that emotional bullshit! You had a relationship with your father. He brought you up, took care of the family, and never once shirked his duties. This man lied to my mother, married her under false pretences, then betrayed her horribly and had no relationship with me except for the money he flung in our direction. I owe him nothing! And if it hadn't been for your desperation to get out of India, I wouldn't have had anything to do with him, ever."

Shyam shrugged off his jacket and went to the drinks cabinet. He poured Mira another glass of red wine, and a large measure of whisky for himself.

"I know it hasn't been easy."

"Easy? I've hated every minute of it! Imagine trying to explain to Mum that I had gone behind her back to ask for help from a man she loathed? Yeah, easy isn't the word I would use."

"What's done is done, Mira. Maybe this is his way of making amends. He wants a relationship with you now, and he wants to be involved in Esha's life. Can we not give him that much after everything he's done for us?"

Mira snatched the glass out of his hand.

"All I've done is give, give, give ever since we met."

"What do you mean by that?"

"I gave up my career, my freedom, my country and now, my self-respect. All of it, just to accommodate your desires. You've always just taken, haven't you, Shyam? And the beauty of it is that you don't even realise that you've done it. You seem to think that the world owes you."

"Mira, I never asked you to give up your career. You chose..."

"How do you expect me to teach or write? I have a baby to care for!"

"Now, you're being unreasonable. You wanted this baby. You tried..."

"Don't remind me how long I tried!" She screeched at him. "Yes, I wanted this baby, but I DID NOT want this life." The glass of wine dropped out of her hand, glass shattering on the floor, the red staining the rug.

"Damn!" she sobbed, running to the kitchen.

Shyam knelt down and started gathering up the fragments of glass. A thin shard sliced through his finger and he dropped it, watching the blood ooze out.

Mira came and threw salt on the wine stain and then saw his bleeding finger.

"Oh shit! You've cut yourself." She ran back to fetch the medicine chest.

As she bandaged his finger, he sipped on his whisky and closed his eyes.

"I'm sorry, Shyam. I don't know what's come over me."

He opened his eyes to look at her. Mira looked close to tears. Her hair was in a clumsy topknot, and her shirt was stained with baby food. There were dark shadows under her eyes, and she had bitten her nails down to the nubs.

"Come here," he said, his voice soft. She sat down next to him on the sofa and snuggled into him.

"It's obvious that you are exhausted. You need a proper night's sleep and tomorrow everything will seem much better."

She leaned her head on his shoulder.

"I didn't mean the last bit about hating my life with you. I love you, Shyam."

"I know, baby, I love you too."

That night, they made love like they used to. It was tender and filled with promise. She allowed him to explore her, invited him into her, and melted into him with soft whispers and hushed promises. He held her as she slept, breathing in her warm and sensual fragrance, filling himself up with all that she had offered. It would tide him over until the next time.

Their mellow mood extended well into the next day. Even Esha, normally fractious by the evening, was happy enough to be strapped into her car seat and handed her favourite baby book to thumb through.

Mira had made an effort with her outfit, and Shyam wondered if that was her way of making further amends for the row they had had. She wore a long black skirt, a black sequin blouse and pencil heels that nearly brought her up to his height.

"You look stunning, *jaan*!" He said to her as she emerged from the bedroom.

"It's been so long since I dressed up, I'd forgotten I'm more than just a mum."

"You are so much more than that!" He leaned forward and grazed her lips, careful not to mess up her red lipstick.

He remembered placing a photograph of the two of them together —a candid shot taken in Goa—on his desk at work when he had first started the new job. Her hair had been flying in the wind and he had been looking at her as if she was the most magical thing that had ever happened to him. It was a photograph that always transported him back to their honeymoon, a time when they had loved each other freely and wantonly, finally released from the shackles of their deception. It was a photograph that made him happy. Graham had walked past his room and glanced at the photo. Then he had walked in and picked it up, looking at it for a long time.

"Lucked out here, didn't you, mate? Punching above your weight, hey?"

Shyam had put the photo away shortly after that.

Seeing Mira day in and day out, it was easy to forget what about her had dazzled him in the first place. Today she reminded him of the Mira he had first encountered. Sexy, unpredictable, even a little dangerous. A woman he had wanted to ravish and possess. Yes, he had lucked out, and he would never forget it.

The drive from Osterley to Windsor normally took them forty minutes, but the Friday evening traffic had them sitting in a gridlock for over an hour. Luckily, Esha had fallen asleep. Mira seemed lost in thought, and he was happy just to have her next to him, nearly present after being so absent for the last two years.

"Shyam?" She turned towards him. "Did your parents ever ask about Esha?"

His back stiffened immediately. This was a topic he had successfully dodged over the months, and now there was no getting away from it.

"I'd shown them photographs."

"And?"

"They said she was cute."

"But did they not want to meet her?"

"Umm..."

The traffic moved, and he was spared answering her. Yet Mira was nothing if not persistent.

"Sometimes," she said, "I've wondered what would happen to Esha if either or both of us got in an accident or something."

"Why such morbid thoughts?"

"These things happen, don't they? Aside from my mum, she has no one else. Your parents and your sister have never even met her..."

"Your dad..."

"Don't fool yourself. Keshav will never take responsibility for her. He is all about the 'image'. A disabled child does not fit into that."

"That's not entirely true, Mira. He always buys her so many gifts and has offered to pay for a nanny, too."

"Typical Keshav. Just throw money at the problem. But you have not answered my original question. Why don't your folks want a relationship with our daughter? Is it because of me? Or is it because she's a child with Down syndrome?"

"Mira," he stalled, turning off the motorway, "Baba's death has changed a lot of things within the family. Once Maa settles wherever she decides to, we can revisit this."

"So, you've talked about this with them?"

Shyam recalled the one time he had introduced the topic of bringing Mira and Esha down to Delhi with him for a vacation. The silence that had greeted his statement had been answer enough.

"I've tried. Baba and Maa never truly got over that entire episode with us."

"For God's sake! It's been ten years! How long will this vendetta against me carry on?"

"It's not a vendetta. They are...were...old-fashioned people."

"Yet they forgave your sister who ran away from home to get married?"

"Yes, well, Sangita was always Baba's favourite."

"And you were no one's favourite? Could your mother not find it in her heart to forgive you?"

"Look Mira, let's not ruin our moods. We'll talk about this when we get home, okay? I promise."

With a huff, she turned away from him.

Shyam understood her concerns, even shared them. But what could he do? The fact that Baba and Maa had reluctantly taken him back into the fold of the family was, in itself, a miracle. Their refusal to acknowledge or accept Mira was a battle he had tried fighting with patience and forbearance. It had not yielded any results. Besides, he was getting tired of trying. He had just wanted a bit of peace in the limited interactions he had had with them, and admittedly, had not brought up Mira or Esha with them in the last few years.

Now, predictably, Mira placed the blame of that on him as well.

As they turned onto the road that led to Keshav's mansion, he placed his hand on Mira's and gave it a little squeeze. He was heartened by the squeeze she gave in return. Tonight, they were a team. They would present a united front. Keshav and Hugo had always been gracious to him, but he wanted Mira to realise that they were not the enemies. If she allowed it, they could become the surrogate family that she was looking for, for Esha. If she did not allow her anger and animus against her father to reign supreme, she would realise that he was trying, in his own way, to make amends.

❖

Keshav had hidden his truth from his family for several years. It had taken a divorce, the death of his father, and his mother's stroke for him to finally acknowledge his queerness to the world.

Nowadays, he lived in a large mansion in Old Windsor and liked to boast that Elton John was his neighbour.

"We're not the only gays in the village", he would titter, and Mira had had to explain to Shyam that he was referencing some television programme called 'Little Britain'. Regardless, Shyam had always found him and Hugo endlessly entertaining, refusing to take Mira's cynical stance that they were self-involved and flamboyant to an extreme.

As they drove up the long and winding drive, Shyam wondered aloud how Keshav had made all his money.

"He comes from a business family," Mira sighed with exasperation. "He has money in his blood. It's the only language he speaks, and why do you think Hugo is with him, huh? Not for his good looks, that's for sure."

"Mira." Shyam glanced at her as he parked the car. He wanted this evening to go well.

"What? Just because you are desperate for his approval doesn't mean I am as well."

"Be nice. It's just one evening."

Mira exhaled loudly.

"Fine. Just don't expect any bowing and scraping from me."

Shyam lifted Esha out of the car seat, grateful that she had carried on sleeping. The last time they had visited, she had just started crawling and had pulled on the tablecloth, which had sent a large crystal vase crashing to the floor. While he had spent all evening apologising, Mira had been apoplectic.

"You would think they would child proof their rooms if they knew a toddler was visiting…!"

It had taken several months of placating her before she had agreed to another visit. Shyam intended to avoid all such disasters today.

"Ah, there are my favourite people!" Keshav greeted them at the door, dressed in a deep purple velvet jacket with matching trousers. The party had already begun indoors. They could hear the voices of the guests and the clinking of glasses. Soft jazz music played in the background. Diptyque candles were dotted around the room, sending a pleasant aroma of roses into the air. Mira shot him a loaded glance. This was definitely not a child-proofed home or party.

"How are you, my darling?" Keshav air-kissed Mira, who responded by rolling her eyes.

Hugo came out holding a champagne flute. He was dressed in an identical velvet suit except that it was teal.

"Well, well, well. Here you are! We thought you'd forgotten all about this evening."

"A little hard to forget when the invitation was only issued yesterday," Mira responded acerbically.

"Happy Birthday, Hugo," Shyam ventured, indicating to Mira to hand over the present he had bought earlier in the day.

"No, you shouldn't have," Hugo simpered, taking the package out of Mira's hands. "Do you want to put the bubba down in the bedroom?" He looked at Esha, fast asleep in Shyam's arms.

"Actually, I'd rather have her somewhere I can check on her regularly," Mira intervened, taking Esha from Shyam. "How about the study? You have a sofa in there, right?"

Mira marched towards the study, and Hugo pulled a face at Shyam.

"She's in a mood tonight."

Shyam smiled at him blandly and accepted the glass of champagne being handed out by the server. He had no intention of getting involved in any family politics today.

"So," Keshav put his arm around Shyam's shoulders as he led him in, "how are things at work?"

"Yes, really good. Very busy with this new project we've been working on, but I think it's turning out well. I'm pleased with it."

"Good, good. And what about the baby? Have you started any of the therapies?"

"Some. Mira has been taking her to an occupational therapist on a weekly basis. We are looking for a speech therapist, too."

"What about schooling? Have you looked at any specialist schools?"

"Isn't it too early for that? Besides, Mira wants Esha to go to a mainstream school, somewhere that she will assimilate with other children her age. She wants her to lead as normal a life as possible."

"But she isn't normal, is she?" Keshav jerked his head towards the study. "Why can't Mira accept that?"

"Why can't I accept what?" Mira had come up behind them silently.

"Oh, nothing, darling. How are you? You look rather swish today." Keshav seamlessly changed the topic, ignoring Mira's narrowed eyes, guiding them into the room and introducing them to all his guests.

They were deep in conversation with a German couple when Esha stumbled into the room, crying.

"Mama," she wailed as she made a beeline for Mira.

"Baby," Mira scooped her up and planted numerous kisses on her face, trying to calm her down. "Mama is here, don't worry. Mama is here."

Esha wailed and held on to Mira, pulling at the sequins on her blouse.

"Hush, baby, Mama is here."

As Mira rocked and soothed Esha, Shyam noticed the German couple take a few steps back. They spoke to each other in an undertone, then mumbled something indistinct as they walked away.

Mira didn't notice as she carried on rocking Esha in her arms. Shyam felt deeply embarrassed. He made a garbled excuse and fled to the garden to calm himself.

"Tough, isn't it?" Hugo called out from the shadows, the orange tip of his cigarette glowing in the dark.

"Hmm?" Shyam was unprepared for anyone noticing his discomfiture.

"To be the father of an unusual child."

"Oh," Shyam thought for a moment. "Mira doesn't think so."

"What do you think?"

"I… don't like being judged."

"You don't like people thinking any less of you."

"Yes, I suppose that is true."

"But it's not your fault is it that your child isn't the same as all the other so-called normal ones."

"I don't know. I've never thought of it that way."

Hugo stepped out of the shadows.

"Learn to love that little girl for who she is, Shyam, or you will end up losing far more than you've bargained for."

That night, as they tucked Esha into bed together, Shyam willed himself to lean in and kiss her cheek. A sudden swell of love rose in him as he breathed in her baby aroma. He blinked back his tears as he stepped away from the cot.

Mira had been watching him all along. She clasped his hand and led him into their bedroom.

If last night had been an apology, tonight was a benediction. This was Mira as a goddess. She took charge, stripping his shirt off and then shedding all her clothes in a provocative striptease. He marvelled at her body, the softness of it, the roundness, all her stretch marks just adding to the allure and mystery of her. He buried his face between her legs, grateful that he still had this. For a while there, it had been so denied to him that life had seemed strange and incomplete.

Her musky smell drove him to the edge of insanity. He buried his tongue in her, tasting her, enjoying hearing her moan. She clutched his head, pulling him closer. Then he nipped her lightly, knowing that would do it. She came in a gush, just as he knew she would. But they had always had a rhythm of their own, and as she pushed him onto the bed, he knew her tongue would give him the pleasure he had been craving for months on end. They rocked together, their erotic dance as electrically charged as it had ever been. She refused to let him come in the softness of her mouth, climbing over and straddling him instead. She took his hands and placed them over her full breasts, and as she rode him, he cried aloud his ecstasy, coming in hot, fresh spurts inside the molten core of her.

"I love you, Mira," he panted, refusing to withdraw, feeling himself shrivel but wanting the warmth of her; wanting to stay inside her forever.

"I know, babe," she whispered as she kissed him goodnight.

The day Shyam had first seen Tina, he had been struck by her delicacy and innocence. She had seemed to him like a rosebud that was slowly unfurling. He had known in an instant that if he didn't grab her, someone else surely would.

Maa and Baba had been reluctant initially to ask for her hand.

"She is still studying. Why not look for a slightly older girl in our community? There are plenty of *rishtas* coming for you, anyway."

Shyam knew he was considered an eligible match, but the girls he had been shown had just seemed so plain and ordinary to him. They were pretty, but in an everyday pedestrian manner. Tina had had something elusive about her, a mystique, an unspoiled naïveté that was so hard to find in the hardened street smart Delhi girls. He had known she would make a good wife to him, and an even better daughter-in-law to his parents.

Later, Mira had teased him that all he had wanted was a pretty little doll who did as he said, and did not have a single thought of her own. This was not entirely true. He had never told Mira or anyone else that during the course of his short-lived marriage, he had found that his young wife was made of much sterner stuff than he had suspected. She was obedient to a point; she was amenable to a point. But once that point was reached, she was completely intractable. They may have renamed her Radha, but somewhere inside her, Tina still remained.

"Have you ever wondered about our names, Shyam?" He could recall Mira saying in the early days of their marriage, as they lay on a beach in Goa.

"Wondered what?" He had pushed his sunglasses up on his forehead and crinkled his brow.

"Shyam, Radha and Mira," she had responded softly. "The eternal love triangle."

Shyam was another name for Lord Krishna, who, in his youth, had enjoyed a prolonged love affair with a cowherd's daughter by the name of Radha. Such was their passion and divine love, that for the ages ever since, their names became intertwined, so that one could not be mentioned without the other. Yet, hundreds of years later, a young girl by the name of Meera rose to prominence on the strength of her love and devotion to Krishna. Renouncing all her earthly bonds, she spent her life singing paeans to her beloved, her Lord Krishna. In time, Meera became just as much a part of Krishna's legend as Radha had been, her name just as inextricably linked to the charmingly elusive God as Radha's had been.

Every Hindu knew the story of Radha, Krishna, and Meera. But Shyam had never once considered himself in that religious context.

Mira had been watching him, assessing his expressions to gauge what he made of her statement. He laughed as he pulled her towards him, "Firstly, you are no believer, so where on earth have you come up with this comparison from? Secondly, you are no Meera*bai*. I can't imagine you wandering the streets with an *ektaara* singing songs of love for me!"

Mira had started giggling, and the moment had passed. Still, the thought had lodged itself in his mind somewhere. Was he destined not to give complete happiness to either of the women who loved him?

. . .

On Sunday morning, Shyam woke up feeling refreshed for the first time in months. It had been a strange weekend filled with highs and lows, but it had also shown him that Mira was still his, always had been and always would be. Baby Esha may have temporarily taken her attention, but as she grew, he could reclaim his wife once more.

The smell of sizzling bacon wafted into the room. He pulled on his T-shirt and walked out to be greeted by a smiling Esha sitting in her high chair.

"Dada," she said, banging the wooden ladle on her little plastic table.

He stopped in his tracks.

"What did she say?" Shyam looked between Esha and Mira.

Mira turned around and grinned at him.

"She's been saying it all morning."

As if on cue, Esha repeated, "Dada."

"Yes," he murmured, going straight up to her. "That's me. I am Dada."

"Let's go to Osterley Park today. The sun is shining and I could pack us a picnic," Mira said as she was dishing up the eggs and bacon.

Shyam needed to catch up on work, but this was too good an opportunity to pass up. Mira seemed so much happier, and he wanted to bask in the warmth of that happiness.

"Yes, let's! Maybe we can watch a nice movie tonight? I've got a DVD of '*Rab Ne Bana Di Jodi*', that new Shahrukh Khan film."

Mira pouted at him.

"You know I'm not a Bollywood fan... Another rehashed love story? Really?" Then she winked at him and laughed, and he knew she was kidding. They would have their picnic and they would watch their movie. His work would take a backseat to it all because this was way more important than some stupid office project. He felt lucky because somehow, in some very mysterious and incomprehensible way, over this weekend they had turned a corner in their floundering marriage.

CHAPTER 10

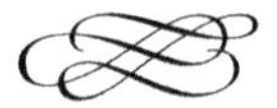

Amanda Swift arrived in mid-August. She was incredibly tall and wafer-thin, but her face had an indeterminate ageless quality thanks to the several procedures she had probably undergone. Her lips were plumped, her cheekbones prominent, and her skin as smooth and unlined as a baby's bottom. For all that, Amanda was nobody's fool. She brought with her the reputation of being razor-sharp and ruthless. The rumours swirling about before her arrival involved several jobs being axed. One look at her, and Shyam knew he would have to impress her greatly if he wanted to save his neck.

The first morning, she came into the office and set up a mid-morning meeting with several of the project managers and systems analysts. Their group was called in for 11:30am.

Amanda was already seated in the conference room, and her eyes assessed them as they filed in one by one. Graham went in first, followed by Shyam, Mark, and Roy. The tension in the room was palpable.

Amanda began with no preliminaries.

"Morning, everyone. Let's cut to the chase. How is the project faring?"

Graham cleared his throat and answered her, "Morning, Amanda. We're making progress. We've faced some challenges, but the team is pushing hard to meet the deadlines."

"Progress is good, but I need a date, and it better be soon. I'm leaving at the end of the month and I want to take something substantial back to report."

Graham nodded, his face grave, perhaps sensing just how serious she was.

"We are addressing the issues. Also, we've revised the timeline and have been putting extra hours alongside."

"Good," she smiled, a mere baring of teeth. "I hope you're not telling me what I want to hear, Graham. I expect results. This project is crucial, and I won't tolerate mediocrity."

Mark spoke up, "We understand the importance, Amanda and we're committed to delivering."

Her green eyes flicked to him, then back to Graham.

"Commitment is good, but I need more than promises. I need results. If your team can't meet expectations, I won't hesitate to make changes."

Graham took a deep breath before saying, "I've heard about the restructuring. What does this mean for us?"

Amanda leaned back and surveyed the men sitting across from her.

"It means we're cutting the fat. The company needs to be lean and mean to survive. And that means we keep the top performers. As for the rest..." She made a dismissive gesture with her right hand.

Roy's voice quivered as he asked. "What about those who've been putting in the hours?"

"Hours don't guarantee results. I need a high-performing team. If that's not what I see, changes will be made."

She picked up her cup of coffee, took a sip, made a face, and set it down. Roy jumped up to fetch her a fresh cup. She didn't thank him. Instead, she looked straight at Shyam and said, "You're the lead, aren't you, in developing the mobile apps? What's been going on there?"

"Well," Shyam tried sounding more confident than he felt, "we hit a snag a while back, but we're pivoting. Instead of tweaking existing code, we're diving into native app development. It's a bit unconventional but it gives us control over the user experience and opens up possibilities for unique features."

Amanda arched an eyebrow.

"Native app development? That's not the usual playbook. Why take the risk?"

Shyam leaned forward, his passion for the project overriding his nervousness.

"I see this as an investment. By tailoring the app specifically for our needs, we can create a more intuitive and responsive experience. Plus, it positions us well for the future as mobile usage continues to grow."

Amanda's expression softened. "Timeline concerns? Can we afford the delay?"

"We've adjusted our schedule to front-load the development phase. Yes, it might take a little longer initially, but I'm confident it'll pay off in terms of performance and user satisfaction."

"That sounds like a bold assertion, Misra. But I like it. It's forward-thinking. Keep me posted on the progress, and if you need additional support, ask."

They filed out thirty minutes later, feeling completely wrung-out.

"That, my good fellows, is what is called a ball-breaker." Graham exhaled. "I think we just about got out with ours intact."

"I need a piss," Mark said, mopping his brow. "Never thought I'd feel like a schoolboy again."

"Oh, she can spank me anytime she wants," Roy squeaked next to them. "I thought she was hot!"

"And old enough to be your mother, you wanker!" Graham mock-punched him. "What about you, Shyam? Or, Misra, as she called you in there. Bet you were always impressing the teachers at school!"

Shyam shrugged. He wasn't sure if she had been all that impressed, but he needed to prove himself, and that would only happen with hard graft, not this silly banter.

"She was eating you with her eyes, chocolate boy!" Graham ribbed him.

"What? Don't be ridiculous. She was just interested in the project."

"Yeah, yeah. You didn't see the way she was checking out your bum as you left the room."

Shyam shook his head and refused to answer. There was only so much teasing he was willing to put up with. These men often tipped over the edge, becoming salacious and jeering. He thought that maybe they didn't have happy relationships at home, but he wasn't interested enough to find out.

He shut the door behind him, took a deep breath, and got back to work.

❖

"She's tough, but fair, I think," Shyam said, while spooning the soup into his mouth. After gulping it down, he rearranged his features.

"What? You don't like it!" Mira looked at him accusingly.

"No, it's really good and very healthy, I'm sure. But, uhhh, maybe a little less salt next time? Spinach has its own natural salt so you don't need to add more..."

As Mira took a mouthful, he wondered what his mother would have made of this wife who couldn't cook, and her son who had learned to cook. How different it had been with Radha. How conventional. Here, every day was a fresh surprise.

"Oh, Shyam, it's awful! Leave it. I'll pop a pizza in the oven."

He dropped his spoon, relieved he wouldn't have to drink the rather awful soup. He appreciated Mira trying, but she just did not possess any skills in the kitchen, aside from baking. Her cakes and cookies were delicious, but a man could not survive on cakes and cookies alone.

"I've been thinking..." he called out to her. "How about if we hire a cook?"

She popped her head around.

"A cook?"

"Well, there must be some Indian lady around here willing to make some extra money. It will take the pressure off you." And me, he thought to himself.

"Mum is going to say I'm being a lazy wife. I don't work and now, I won't even cook."

"You have plenty to do with taking Esha to all the different therapy groups. Say, how is that going?"

"No, you first. You were telling me about this woman who has come from the US."

"Oh, yeah. I mean, the other guys are just saying all sorts of mean stuff about her. But if she wants results, what's wrong with that? They are running a business, not a charity."

Mira came up behind him and planted a kiss on his head before heading back to the kitchen.

"So proud of you, babe. You have come a long way from your patriarchal beginnings."

"What? How? What do you mean?"

Mira came out holding a toast with some peanut butter on it.

"Here, have this while the pizza heats." She sat next to him at the table. "What I mean is that if a man was doing the same job, no one would call him mean things. He would be respected, idolised even. Most men can't bear the fact that a woman can do the job just as well, if not better than them. I'm glad you recognise this."

"Well, I don't think Amanda is losing any sleep over what they think or say."

"I like the sound of her."

"She is a little scary," Shyam admitted. "I wouldn't want to be at the receiving end of her wrath."

"You won't be. You're good at what you do and you're hardworking. I'm sure she will recognise that."

"Okay, now tell me how Esha's therapies are going."

"Well, we started the day with physical therapy. Esha was all giggles, trying to balance on those tiny stepping stones. You should have seen her determination trying to take those little steps. It was heart-melting."

The oven beeped and Mira went and retrieved the pizza and brought it out with the pizza cutter balanced on the plate.

"The speech and music therapy are on Friday, and tomorrow we'll go in for occupational therapy. Esha has been loving finger painting. She's like a mini Picasso."

Shyam nodded. His mind was still swirling with thoughts about the meeting with Amanda, but he forced himself to concentrate on Mira's words.

"You know what, babe? Everyone comments on how sunny-natured she is. Remember how clingy she was to begin with? As she's growing and becoming more independent, her natural temperament is coming to the fore. People just love her! Maybe now is a good time to start looking for a pre-school?"

"She's not even three yet, Mira. What's the hurry?"

"No hurry, but if we look now, we'll probably settle on something by the time she turns three. Besides, I've been thinking that I would like to return to writing."

Mira's last book had been a critical success within the academic community, but she had been removed from academia for so long that he was surprised she wanted to write again.

"No," she shook her head, as if reading his mind, "not academic stuff. This time I want to write fiction."

"Fiction?"

"Yes, why not? I've always loved writing, and as a child I wrote plenty of stories. I'm sure it's not gone entirely. In fact, I've been making notes in a little diary for some months now."

"What kind of fiction would you write, then?"

"Any kind. Maybe romance, or maybe a tragedy. Why? Don't you think I'm qualified?" She laughed at his surprised expression.

"I think you, my *jaan*, are as determined as that little girl asleep in the next room. When you really want something, you always find a way to get it."

She sat in his lap and buried her head in his neck.

"Thank you, babe. I think I'm ready to return to the real world now."

❖

On Sunday, he made his monthly call to Sangita. Maa had been granted a temporary visitor's visa, and had just reached San Francisco.

"How was the journey, Maa?"

"I am exhausted. Thankfully, Hari paid for an upgrade from Frankfurt to San Francisco, otherwise I may not have survived the journey."

Shyam swallowed his resentment. From being the devil incarnate, Hari had become his parents' blue-eyed boy. A taekwondo champ who had been handpicked to coach in America, he was doing very well for himself. He had invested in a couple of Subway franchises, and was raking in the moolah, while continuing with the coaching and touring. Sangita had chosen well, Maa kept saying, conveniently forgetting the brouhaha of her elopement.

"That's wonderful. I'm glad that the rest of your journey was comfortable. Have you settled in alright?"

"The jet lag is terrible, but this country is amazing. Everything is so big. The houses, the shops, the roads... You should see Sangita's house in San Jose! Five large bedrooms and an enormous yard, too."

Once again, Shyam felt the weight of comparison. Their two bed semi-detached would probably fit into Sangita's living room.

"Yes, America is a fascinating country."

"Why don't you come for a few weeks? You haven't even met Sangita's children."

Shyam was careful with his words.

"Maa, I would like to come and meet Sangita and her family, but not without my wife and daughter. If they are welcome, then I might consider coming over."

"Oh." Maa was silent for a moment, then said, "Well, maybe we can talk about it another time."

There it was again. This wall that came up every time he tried bringing Mira into the conversation. It was not just the humiliation and embarrassment from all those years ago; it was not the fact that she was older or from a different caste; it was not even the fact that she had supplanted Radha. This was a refusal to see that his happiness lay with someone so far removed from their sphere of experience; a refusal to accept that what he needed to feel fulfilled in life, while being contrary to their expectations, wasn't just him rebelliously flouting his background and traditions. Yes, he may have outgrown the orthodoxy of his roots to a large extent, but he was still their son, and he loved them as much as he always had. His following his happiness did not negate that.

Privately he often wondered how many Indian boys and girls gave up on their own dreams to satisfy their parents' vision of what their lives ought to be? Was his reneging on this unspoken promise going to keep him and his family on the outskirts forever?

Yet, was it worth picking a fight over? Especially when Maa was still mourning his father. No, he decided to himself, finishing the conversation on a positive note, promising to call again soon. If ten years and a granddaughter had not mellowed his mother's stance, his throwing an almighty tantrum was hardly likely to.

The only person he could appeal to was Sangita. That was, if she was finally willing to forgive him for his betrayal.

Later in the evening, as they went out for a walk with Esha in the pram, Jenny from next door stopped Mira for a chat.

"My grandchildren are coming home next weekend. Would you like to bring Esha around for a play?"

Mira nodded enthusiastically. "That would be lovely. I have been wondering how to get her to socialise with her peers. I don't want pre-school to be a shock to her system."

"Then all the more reason to bring her. My grandson is three and my granddaughter is five. A few years between them, but we can let them play and keep an eye from a distance."

With promises made, they carried on walking.

"I've looked into this new pre-school they have opened in

Norwood Green. It's all brand spanking new, and the staff seems very young and eager. I'd like you to come with me when I visit."

"When have you booked this visit?"

"In two weeks' time, on Tuesday the 14th. Can you take a half-day off?"

Shyam didn't want to take any time off, what with Amanda watching them all like a hawk, but this was important to Mira and he didn't want to ruin their new found amity, so he gave her his word that he would return from work early.

As they walked around their leafy neighbourhood, Shyam recounted some of his conversation with Maa earlier in the day.

"Do you think she will settle in America with Sangita?"

"I don't know. It's definitely a possibility. Now that Sangita has three little ones, she could use the help too, especially as Hari is on the road so much."

"So, a win-win for all." Mira did not keep the sarcasm out of her voice.

"Give it time, Mira. Eventually, they will accept you."

"When? When I'm fifty? This is ridiculous, you do know that, right?" Mira frowned up at him. "Mum wasn't pleased about what happened either, but she came around. Why couldn't your parents make peace with it, too?"

Shyam shrugged. What could he say to make it better?

Just then, Esha spoke up.

"Birdie," she said as she pointed to an airplane in the sky.

"Birdie," Mira responded with a laugh, leaning down to plant a kiss on her cheek.

The word "plane" died on his lips. Sometimes the truth had to take a backseat to perception.

At first, Shyam had dismissed all the teasing, assuming it stemmed from jealousy. But now, even he had started to get a distinct impression that Amanda was developing a soft spot for him.

Whenever she came into the office, she would ask for a one-on-one with him. Then, as he outlined his progress on the project, she would circle him, often perching on the edge of the desk, uncomfortably close as she leaned to look at his notes.

He did not know what to do about any of it. This was the first time a woman had paid him attention in this manner. As a young man, he had often been at the receiving end of flirtatious looks and giggling as he walked past girls. He had been flattered by it, sometimes even returning the attention with a grin and a quip. Being a good-looking man had always worked to his advantage. Now, he was not sure.

It was Thursday morning, and Amanda had summoned him to her office again. Dressed in a bottle green suit, she barely looked up as he walked in, pointing to the chair.

He sat down and waited for her to ask about the latest on the app. Instead, she waved to the coffee machine in the corner.

"Help yourself, Misra."

He got up, made himself a cappuccino, then asked her if she wanted one.

"Espresso for me." She carried on, tapping away on her keyboard.

He placed her coffee next to her, then sat down with his own. This was odd. Normally, she attacked him with questions as soon as he walked in. Today she was behaving like he was part of the furniture.

"Are you married, Misra?" She asked while carrying on typing.

He had never worn a wedding ring. Not with Radha, not with Mira. Jewellery was not his style.

"Yes, Miss Swift."

"Ms, please."

He had never understood the difference, the nuance in pronunciation too subtle for him. Mark had explained that any woman over thirty needed to be addressed as a Ms. In Amanda's case, he had speculated, she was probably divorced and did not want to be called Mrs.

"Sorry, Ms Swift."

"Actually, why don't we dispense with it altogether? Call me Amanda."

"Uhh..." Shyam felt lost for words. He had lived in the UK for nearly seven years now, but this habit of calling people by their first names had never really sat well with him. Culturally, at home, anyone older was always given respect and addressed either as 'Sir' or 'Madam' or with a *ji* attached to their name. If that older person also happened to be your boss, you would never have the temerity of using their first name.

Amanda glanced up at him.

"Really, it's an easy name. You should try saying it with that charming Indian accent."

She smiled at him, and from somewhere an old nature programme about a praying mantis popped into his head. He blinked and smiled back. It would not do to offend her at this stage.

"Am.. Amanda."

"There! Easy enough, wasn't it?" She pulled off the glasses she was wearing and set them next to her coffee cup. Then she took a sip of her espresso and sighed. "I needed that, thanks Misra. This morning has been all sorts of crazy!"

She gulped the rest of the coffee down, then turned to face him again.

"So, you are wondering why I've called you in." She arched her eyebrows and looked at him.

"About the project."

"Yes, that is also on the agenda, but first: how do you feel about going to the States?"

"States?"

"The US of A. My country."

"M...me?"

"Yes, you." Amanda got up and came around. She positioned herself next to him, leaning against the desk, and he noticed she wasn't wearing any shoes.

"I've been watching you, and I think you show a lot of promise. There are some new openings coming up and I'm thinking of putting your name forward for an interview. We need people like you at headquarters."

"In San Francisco?"

"Where else?" She laughed. "The reason I asked if you're married is that the initial interview and familiarisation could take a week, maybe more. If your personal situation doesn't allow..."

"Oh, no! No, nothing like that. My wife would understand completely."

"Just wife? Any children?"

"A little girl who is nearly three."

"I see." She retreated to the back of her desk again. "It's just a thought I'm toying with right now. But if you do well and get selected, you could be offered a position at the headquarters. A lot of ifs, but I think you are up to it."

They chatted for a few more minutes and Shyam kept his composure by focusing on the length of Amanda's lashes every time she blinked. *Those aren't real,* he thought, *but this is.*

Shyam left the room, shaking with excitement. A lot of ifs, but *if* this happened, it could be the answer to all their conundrums. He could move to America, get closer to his family, introduce Mira and Esha to them, and finally achieve all that he had set out to do. He crossed his fingers under the desk, his legs still trembling. Shyam had never been religious, but now he prayed hard. He wanted this so badly, he could taste it.

Please God, he muttered to himself, *let this happen.*

"Guess what?" Mira called out to him from the kitchen as he walked in through the door.

"What?" He saw Esha playing with her toys on the carpet and patted her head as he walked past.

"Mum is moving to Delhi."

"What?" His surprise overtook his desire to spill his own news first. Nisha did not strike him as a Delhi person at all. She loved the freedom and anonymity that Mumbai gave her. Delhi was filled with pretentious wannabes who always wanted to know which part of the city you came from and what your lineage was. This was all that he remembered from her various rants about the capital of India.

"I know!" Mira walked out with a spoon and stuck it into his mouth. "What do you think?"

"It's delicious! What is it?"

"This new cake recipe I'm trying for Sunday. I want to take something nice over for Jenny and Jerry."

"Yeah, it's yummy. Cherry?"

"Cherry and chocolate. You like?" She went back into the kitchen. "So, I was chatting with Mum today and she just dropped this bombshell right in the middle of the conversation."

He followed her into the kitchen.

"Moving how? Bag and baggage?"

"Yep!"

"But why? And what about her flat in Bandra?"

"On sale as we speak."

"But why?"

Mira pulled a quiche out of the oven. Shyam couldn't wait for them to find a cook. He was tired of quiches and pizzas.

"So, get this. You know she's been learning pottery, right?"

Shyam nodded. He vaguely remembered a conversation about it a while ago. Nisha had always had several hobbies, from photography to painting to pottery.

"Anyway, she stumbled across this thing called Kintsugi. It's this traditional Japanese art form of repairing broken pottery with gilded lacquer. Something to do with celebrating imperfections..."

Mira tossed a salad with some olive oil and vinaigrette. He carried the quiche to the table, and she followed with the salad.

"Wine?" she asked, placing the salt on the table.

"Isn't there a bottle of Prosecco in the fridge?"

"Bubbles? Why?"

"Tell you in a minute. Carry on."

He brought the bottle out with two flutes as she spoke.

"So, apparently, there is this Kintsugi master from Japan who has been invited to Delhi to live and teach his craft to pottery enthusiasts. Mum signed up. Then she realised it was worth her while to move to Delhi as she wanted to immerse herself in his teachings. He is also quite a renowned philosopher, she tells me."

"But why sell up? She could just as easily have rented."

"I know! Sometimes Mum's decisions completely confound me. But who am I to argue? She hasn't agreed with most of mine, either."

"It's interesting," Shyam remarked, while pulling off the foil from the bottle before uncorking it with a pop, "how you allow each other the space to live and make mistakes."

"Is there any other way?" Mira said, an eyebrow raised. "Okay, what's the occasion? Why are we drinking Prosecco on a weeknight? What are we celebrating?"

"It might be premature, but I might be going to America for an interview." Shyam poured the Prosecco into the glasses and handed one over to Mira. "This could lead to permanently relocating to America, if I play my cards right." He grinned as he raised his glass.

Mira did not raise hers.

"Interview? When and how did this come about?"

"Not sure, as it's just an idea that's been floated. Nothing has happened yet, only a conversation. Why are you looking so worried?"

"Shyam, we can't move again. I've just settled Esha in with her various therapists. She's just about to start pre-school. I don't think I could cope with another upheaval."

"Hey! No one is moving just yet. I'm not even sure the interview will happen. It's only a possibility, but it's a good one. Listen, can you imagine the life we could give the baby in America?"

"Why don't you call her by her name? She is not a baby anymore!"

"Okay, okay. Esha. Our daughter. Imagine the opportunities in America."

"America is your dream, not mine. I never even wanted to move here."

"Mira, for once, can we not celebrate something good happening to me?!" Shyam slammed the table and stood up.

Esha started crying, and Mira gave him a vicious look as she picked her up.

"Now look at what you've done!"

She walked out of the room, carrying Esha in her arms.

The food and the Prosecco sat untouched on the table.

The next two days were filled with a silence that neither of them chose to break. This time, Shyam felt Mira owed him an apology. Yes, he had brought change and upheaval into her life, but it had always been for the better. Hadn't it?

He remembered the first time he had kissed her. They had been on a rescue mission to retrieve her oaf of an ex-husband. Things had not been going well between Mira and Monish, and when his car had had a puncture, Shyam had volunteered to drive her over to fetch him. They had sat in traffic for a while before he had noticed her weeping silently.

"Are you okay, Mira?" He had asked, concerned for her. He did not know her well back then. She was Radha's hot friend, and although he had been violently and rather inexplicably attracted to her from the first instance, he had filed it away as a crush, never to be acted upon. Now, this glamorous, sexy woman was sitting next to him, crying, and he did not know what to do. So he had put one hand over hers and squeezed it as if trying to impart strength. She had held on to it for dear life, her sobs getting louder.

That's when he had pulled over into a side street and switched the engine off.

"What's happened? Has something happened?" He had asked, turning towards her. When she had not answered, her sobs catching in her throat as she tried to suppress them, he had pulled her towards him to hold her in his arms. It had never been his intention for it to develop into anything else. He had not intended to stroke her hair or kiss her forehead; not intended for his lips to find her in small, sympathetic grazes that turned into a deep, passionate kiss, their tongues colliding, her salty tears mingling with the honeyed taste of her, sending an explosion of desire through him.

They had pulled away from each other in shock. Neither of them had planned this, and they had spent the rest of the drive in silence, each wondering how to undo what had just occurred.

It was a silence that stretched between them for weeks on end. Shyam had realised then that Mira would never act upon their mutual attraction. She was too stubborn, perhaps fearful as well. All he knew from that moment on was that he wanted her. Desperately, madly, with no fear of judgement or consequence.

It was sexual; he convinced himself. Radha was a sweet and pliable partner in bed, but he needed fire. He needed to feel himself burn in Mira's arms. He imagined himself plunging into the lava that lay between her legs, his erections taking him by surprise at the most inopportune moments.

Silence. That is all he was greeted by, day after day. Until the day Radha miscarried. His heart had leapt when he had heard Mira's voice on the phone, then sunk immediately as she had given him the news.

In the hospital, he had been torn between looking after Radha and looking for Mira. He no longer knew who he was and what he wanted. Radha's grief had pierced his delusion and, as Radha's parents had whisked her away to her *maika*, he had returned home to the sight of the blood-soaked sheets. Stripping the bed, he had realised that the mattress would need changing too. This was where Radha had lost their baby. This was where she had nearly bled to death. How could he have been thinking of another woman while his wife was carrying his child?

Filled with self-recrimination, he had pulled out an old bottle of whisky his father had gifted him when he turned twenty-one. Shyam had always thought he would open it on a joyous occasion. Never thought it would be today.

As he had poured himself a large measure, the doorbell had rung.

Mira had stood there, staring at him.

He had called her in, hoping he could make his apologies, hoping she would forgive his lapse in judgement, and accept his gratitude for all that she had done for Radha that day.

Instead, as she had walked in, he had set his glass of whisky aside and taken her into his arms. They hadn't said a word to each other as they had torn off their clothes. His groan as he entered her, and her panting as he rode her, were the only sounds that permeated the silence in the house.

Later, much later, they would talk of guilt and regret, of betrayal and deceit. In that moment, however, all they had wanted was to devour one another. To subdue the weeks of anticipation, to douse the fire of passion that had been building for months on end, to fool themselves into thinking that it would be just this once. That once they had had their fill of one another, they could resume the lives they had inhabited before. That it would be as easy as that.

How foolish they had been! How quickly they had realised that it wasn't lust but love, it wasn't passion, but fate that had brought them together.

Today, fate was steering them towards a different future. Once again, silence was the language they had retreated to.

CHAPTER 11

It was a beautiful Sunday in September when Mira got Esha all dressed up for her playdate in a pink frock, with satin ribbons in her hair. Once Shyam had trained himself to look past her distinctive Down syndrome features, he could see how cute she really was. He had gradually grown affectionate towards her, but had not yet found the unconditional love that came so easily to Mira.

They were still annoyed with one another, and he was in no mood to make amends. In fact, he was looking forward to having the day to himself. He wanted to finish some pending work, and then put his feet up and watch cricket on Sky Sports with a beer and Indian takeaway. For once, he wanted the house to himself.

The day passed pleasantly enough, in just the way he wanted. He wondered why he did not do this more often. Maybe once Mira made more friends with the school mothers, he could get the occasional Saturday or Sunday to himself. As he burped and scratched himself, all the things he could not do in Mira's presence, his thoughts wandered to Amanda Swift.

Everything about her was plastic. From the perpetually surprised expression on her face, the unusually plump lips to the large, obviously fake breasts contained behind the tight dresses. Yet, she knew how to command a room. Men quivered in her presence, and he could sense that she enjoyed the power she had over them. His hand wandered to the front of his sweatpants, then inside, and suddenly all he could think of was how much fun it would be to subdue a woman like that in bed. Holding himself, he closed his eyes and thought of her bending over her desk, her skinny legs akimbo, her bony bottom sticking up as those swollen breasts bounced against the surface of the desk as he pounded her from behind. He grabbed the sock off his foot and came into it in hot spurts, his imagination running wild.

A moment later, he settled back into the armchair, wondering why his psyche had presented him with that spectacle. He was most definitely not attracted to Amanda, so why this particular day dream? Then he shrugged to himself, dismissing the thought as he peeled off his soiled clothes and shoved them into the washing machine. Changing into a pair of jeans and a T-shirt, he wondered idly how long Mira would be.

It was nearly 5pm when she walked in through the door. One look at her and he could tell that the playdate had not gone as per plan. Esha looked like she had been crying. Her face was red and her eyes swollen. Mira looked close to tears herself.

"What happened?" He asked, taking Esha out of her arms.

Mira shook her head over and over, as if trying to clear it.

"I… I think I need a holiday," she said, her voice quivering.

"A holiday?" He asked, perplexed.

"I want to take Esha to Delhi. I could help Mum settle into her new place too. Please, I need this."

"O-kayy," Shyam said, trying to figure out where this was coming from. "I can look into booking some tickets for you, but why don't you sit down and tell me what happened?"

Mira took a shaky breath and sat down, asking for Esha to be placed in her lap again.

"Do you want a cup of tea?" He asked as he handed Esha over to her.

"Yes, please."

As he made the cup of tea, he worried about what may have brought this on.

"Did something happen at Jennys?"

"Oh, Shyam, it was so awful!" Now the tears came in a flood. "She tried so hard, but her grandchildren just wouldn't play with Esha. The little boy kept hitting her every time we weren't looking, and the little girl flat out refused, saying that she was ugly."

Mira hiccupped and Esha started crying alongside.

"Poor Jenny was mortified. She even tried to get them to sit and draw together, but they just wouldn't. It was horrible to watch! Esha kept going over to them and they kept rejecting her. My poor baby was trying so hard. Then the little boy pushed her, and she fell and hit her head."

They both started wailing together, and for a moment Shyam wondered if Jenny and Jerry could hear them next door.

"We had to come away. It was just too awful for words. I worry about Esha, Shyam! What will happen to her? How will she adjust? Am I making a mistake trying to put her in a mainstream school? Should I ask Keshav for help?"

"Shhh, shhh. Now, listen. You've had a shock. Of course, you are worried about her. Which parent wouldn't be? But just because this playdate didn't go well, doesn't mean everything is downhill from here. Let's go check out that pre-school and see what they say. Maybe they could guide us with the right sort of environment for Esha? Here, hand the baby over to me, and drink your tea. I'll calm her down."

As he walked around with Esha in his arms, Shyam couldn't help but wonder what life would be like for this child. He had been so wrapped up in plans for his own life that he had not considered the fact that someday both he and Mira would be gone. How would this little girl navigate the world on her own?

On the day he was meant to leave work early to accompany Mira and Esha to the pre-school, a crisis occurred. In the fragmented landscape of various operating systems, Shyam was finding it hard to make his app work seamlessly across the platforms of Symbian and Blackberry. The app had completely crashed on Symbian, and now Amanda was demanding answers.

Shyam rang home with just an hour to spare for their visit.

"Sorry, *jaan*, I don't think I'll be able to make it today."

"I don't believe this! I told you about this visit weeks ago." Mira sounded angry, but he was too caught up in work to care.

"I have to go. I need to figure this out by the end of today or my head is on the chopping block. Sorry Mira, but you will have to do this on your own."

"Pretty much what I've been doing all along..."

He hung up, his mind grappling with different fixes. Three hours later, he was still trying various strategies which involved managing memory allocation and deallocation to prevent leaks and crashes. When that didn't entirely fix the problem, he checked if the app was running on the most current version of the Symbian OS rather than the older versions, where compatibility issues were arising. In the end, it came down to something as simple as network connectivity. The mobile networks on Symbian devices varied in speed and reliability. Shyam had to implement proper error handling and timeouts for network operations to prevent the crashes from occurring.

"So, that's sorted. What about Blackberry?" Amanda was short with him, annoyed that he had not foreseen these problems.

"I'm working on that," he said, unable to look her in the face, his erotic daydream about her too recent and vivid for him to ignore.

"Well, I want it sorted today. Maybe apply the same fixes there and see if it is a similar network issue."

"I tried that. This is some other bug, but I'll get it done by the end of the day."

"Good. I'll be here if you need me."

Shyam left the room and went back to his desk, passing Graham on the way.

"All okay, mate? Need a hand?"

"No, I'll be okay."

Shyam could have done with a fresh pair of eyes, but it was important he showed Amanda that he could sort this out on his own. She had extended her stay by two weeks because of his part in the project, so he desperately wanted to get it done. Crucially, he wanted her to pick him for the interview, and that meant proving that he could deliver on all that he had promised.

All thoughts of Mira and Esha vanished from his mind as he worked well into the evening. People had already left the office and when he finally looked up, he noticed it was nearly 9pm.

Amanda was standing at the door, looking at him.

"Any luck?"

"No," he said, feeling defeated. "I feel like the answer is staring me in the face, but I just can't seem to grasp it."

"Let's go for a drink."

Shyam's eyes widened.

"I can't. I promised I'd have this done today."

"You promised me. I don't care," she enunciated each word slowly. "Look, it's obvious you will not get this sorted today. So, take a breather, come out for a drink, relax, and come back to it tomorrow."

"You don't mind?"

"Oh, for fuck's sake, just come on..."

They drove to a pub nearby, Shyam following her BMW into the car park.

"I'm not much of a drinker," Amanda said, ordering a white wine spritzer while he ordered a beer. "But today I figured we needed one. Sometimes, it's better to let the problem lie while your subconscious fixes it. It always works for me."

This was the first time he had sat with Amanda in a non-office environment, and the change in her was quite startling. She lost her usual tense and hungry manner, seeming softer and more relaxed outside of work.

"Tell me about yourself," she said as she popped some peanuts into her mouth. Shyam's stomach growled as he realised how ravenous he was. He had not eaten since breakfast.

"Would you mind if I ordered some fish and chips?" He asked, glancing at the menu.

"Be my guest."

"Would you like anything?"

"No, I don't eat after 7pm." She pushed the bowl of nuts away. "Shouldn't be munching on those, either."

He realised that her slim figure resulted from an iron-will. He couldn't imagine Mira pushing food away, despite her not knowing how to cook anything.

"What would you like to know?" Shyam asked, sitting back against the sofa.

"Everything. Start from the beginning. Where you were born, where you grew up, when you moved here. I want to know."

Amanda crossed her legs and leaned towards him.

"I find you fascinating."

❖

He walked into the house past midnight. Mira and Esha were fast asleep, and he could tell that he had been consigned to the spare room once again. For once, he didn't mind. His mind was churning with all kinds of ideas.

Amanda had proven to be a great listener, and someone he could bounce his ideas off of. She was receptive and smart, engaging and patient, qualities he had not spotted in her at first. Shyam was keen to have her as a mentor and he had nearly said it, but held back at the very last minute. He did not want to come across as try-hard and desperate.

She kept asking him all sorts of questions about India. She was a yoga practitioner, and keen to go to a yoga retreat in India. He had laughed and said that the closest he had ever come to yoga was watching Dhirendra Brahmachari on television as a young boy. He had understood none of it, least of all the thread he put in through one nostril and took out through the other. *Sutra Neti,* she had murmured in response.

Their conversation had lasted well into the night, and at 11:30pm he had jumped up, embarrassed, making his excuses, promising to be at work by 8am.

Now, his mind refused to shut off. Every time he had looked at Amanda, he had seen an opportunity. It had felt like fate had put her in his life. She was his golden passport to America, his bridge to the country he had always wanted to live in, and to his family that he could no longer live without.

The door to the room creaked open. Mira stood there watching him, but he pretended to be asleep. He was in no mood for an argument after the wonderfully stimulating evening he had had. He even allowed a little fart to escape him, knowing that would put her off entering the room. She shut the door softly and left.

Yes, a small part of him was sorry he had missed the pre-school visit, but he could not think of a single occasion that Baba had ever visited his school. Maa did all of that. From meeting the teachers to attending Sports Day, all those things were a mother's domain. He was the breadwinner. Surely, Mira could understand that work came first. Work was what put a roof over their heads and food on the table. Work was what allowed them to pay for additional therapy for Esha. How could she expect him to abandon all that to accompany her on a school visit?

The next morning, instead of recriminations, he was greeted by a note:

Visit went well. Esha will start in January. Fees £350 per term.

Short, to the point, with no room for argument. The fees would be an additional expense to add to all the others. But, of course, that did not bother Mira. Her sense of entitlement was beyond belief.

When was the last time she had worked? How much did her book royalties cover except for the weekly grocery bill? Did she realise how expensive their mortgage was, how much their utilities and council tax cost? He was just meant to cough up everything she needed, and cook, and turn up for visits!

He let them sleep as he crept into the room, gathered his clothes, and crept out. He showered in the small ensuite, thanking his stars he had left an additional set of toiletries in there. Spraying himself with Bulgari Blue, he spied Mira's old perfume in there: Opium by Yves Saint Laurent. He pulled out the bottle and sniffed it. It immediately transported him back to the early heady days of their romance, days when all that had mattered was how much time they could spend in each other's arms. Why didn't she wear this perfume anymore?

He fixed his tie, smoothed his hair with gel, then looked at himself properly in the mirror. A few streaks of grey had appeared at his temples, but he quite liked them. He wanted his boyish good looks to evolve into something more distinguished, with a certain gravitas. He wanted to play with the big boys, gain an entrée into a world he had only seen in the movies. Suddenly, it did not seem impossible. 'Where there is a will, there is a way,' his old English teacher had often quoted at the students. Now Shyam understood what he had meant.

Amanda left mid-September, satisfied to be taking back a good account of the various teams and their projects. A few jobs had been axed, and as they had predicted, Roy, despite all his schmoozing, was amongst the first to go.

After she left, Graham, Mark, and Shyam went out for their Friday night pub meet nearly five weeks later.

"Got to be said, mate—she didn't take any prisoners," Graham remarked as he bought the first round.

"Ball breaker," Mark joined in.

Shyam stayed silent.

"What's got into you, Misra? Missing the dominatrix already?" Graham narrowed his eyes.

"No, of course not. I'm just relieved none of us lost our jobs. Poor Roy! Where is he now?"

"Last I heard, he headed back to Portsmouth to lick his wounds." Mark shrugged. "He knew it was coming, so can't say it caught him by surprise."

"Still, he must have been gutted," Shyam replied, wondering how Roy was truly getting on.

"There will be other stuff," Mark said, before switching the topic to football.

It had always amazed Shyam how cavalier people in England were about their careers and livelihoods. He supposed it was because there was always a safety net to catch them if they fell. The government assisted those in need. The social fabric was such that even if you fell, you could still get a house through the council and get unemployment pay. In India, unless you belonged to the wealthiest echelons of society, there was no fallback. It was up to you to study hard, find the right job, work to progress within the company, and be willing to take the abuse doled out by your superiors until you got to where you were the one dishing it out. If you were lucky, you could retire with a decent pension, but every stage of this journey was fraught with danger. The danger of failure, of a misstep that could leave you jobless and homeless, the fear of not meeting the expectations of your family and society, and ultimately the scales with which you measured your own success and compared it against your peers. Roy would be subject to none of this. He could just dust himself off and start again. In some small way, Shyam was envious of these constant reinventions he saw around him. He had never had the luxury of that.

"So, now that the wicked witch has returned to the west, what are the plans, boys?" Graham asked, banging his empty glass on the bar countertop.

"Here, let me." Shyam called for another round.

"I'm taking the Missus to Spain," Mark said. "She's been at me for months. Says she needs a holiday. What from, I ask? Not like she's had a dragon breathing down her neck."

"These women. All they do is hoover a bit, watch loads of daytime television, and then complain they need a break!" Graham chimed in. "Does your little wifey work then, mate?"

Shyam shrugged. "She used to, but not anymore. In fact, she's been asking for a holiday too."

"There! Didn't I tell you? Although, I'd rather that than bloody scary Amanda. At least with them you know what you've got. Ms Swift was more unpredictable than our English weather!" Graham laughed, slapping his thigh.

"Where are you taking her, Shyam?" Mark asked.

"Oh, I'm not taking her. She wants to go to India to visit her mother. So, I've been looking at tickets on British Airways, but they are quite expensive."

"Why not your own airline, hey? Indian Air?"

"Air India?"

"That's the one!"

"Not that much cheaper, to be honest, and I would like her to travel in comfort."

"Why, isn't it comfortable on Air Indian?"

"No, it's not that… I want to buy her Business Class tickets. First time she's travelling with our little girl, and…" He shrugged again.

"Are you barmy? Don't be blowing up all your hard earned money this way. Won't she be wanting to spend money once she's there? Save it on the tickets and give it to her. Trust me, she'll thank you for it."

"You think?" Shyam asked, tilting his head to the left.

"Of course, mate. Business class!" Graham guffawed, and Shyam wondered if he ought not to have shared that with them. What he had left out was how unlikely Mira was to travel in Economy Class. Even when they had moved to the UK, she had insisted on paying for Business Class tickets out of the sale of her Gurgaon house. That was Mira. She had grown up in a household where her grandparents had fulfilled her every wish, trying to atone for the guilt of their daughter's sham of a marriage. Nisha had been a good mother, but by the time she came into asserting her will after her parents' demise, Mira was already set in her ways.

Shyam knew Mira had a little nest egg set aside from the inheritance her grandparents had left her. He also knew that Monish, her ex, had not fought too hard over the divorce settlement, and she was well off enough if she were ever to live in India. Of course, the rupee did not go as far as the pound sterling, and since Mira had never disclosed her bank balance, he had never asked. Still, from time to time, he wondered why the onus of supporting the entire household fell on him. Why couldn't she at least offer to make the shortfall now and again?

❖

Esha's birthday fell on the 21st September, which was a Sunday. Mira had been mulling over various options, but ultimately decided on The London Zoo. They parked the car at the Osterley tube station and took the Piccadilly line to Green Park, from where they changed to the Jubilee line towards St Johns Wood. Their entire journey was spent with Mira fussing over Esha, and Shyam scrolling through his new iPhone.

The frost between them still had not thawed entirely, and even though Mira and Esha were leaving for India in two weeks' time, Shyam still did not feel the need to clear the air. He was exhausted from pandering to all of Mira's whims, fancies, and moods. When had he become such a doormat? With Radha, he had always been firmly in control of the relationship. With Mira, he had never felt settled or in control. At first, it had not mattered. His love for her overrode all such trivial considerations. Then, over time, it had begun to grate on him.

He had given up so much for this woman. His family, his standing within his community, and what had he got in return? Scraps of attention when she chose? Never an ounce of encouragement or praise. And now, when he was this close to achieving a lifelong dream, all she could do was put obstacles in his way! He was angry, in fact, he was fuming! So, if she wanted to play it this way, he was more than happy to go along with it. Two could play the game.

As he manoeuvred the pram onto the escalator, he looked down at

Esha who had fallen asleep somewhere between the stations. Her ponytail was askew and her thumb was half in her mouth, a dribble of saliva running down it. Until you looked closely, you could not detect there was anything wrong with her. So many bystanders had smiled at her and mouthed, "How cute!" Mira had put her in a little lemon jumpsuit with a pattern of pink butterflies on it. Her hair had matching butterfly clips, and on her feet she wore little shoes with butterfly buckles.

He knew he was going to miss his little girl. All the little noises she made, her gurgling as Mira fed her porridge in the mornings, the squeaking of her various toys littered around the living room, her "Dada!" as soon as she saw him. When had she started inhabiting such a large portion of his heart?

Mira cursed behind him. He did not turn around. Whatever it was, she could figure it out for herself.

When they got to the exit, she said, "I can't find my ticket. I think I may have dropped it accidentally."

She kept rummaging through her bag as Shyam waited, tapping his foot impatiently. She could pay the fine if she didn't find it. He was tired of her messiness, her forgetfulness, her inability to pick up after herself. He was her husband, not her father.

She pulled the ticket out triumphantly.

"There it is!" She smiled at him, but her smile faded as soon as she noticed his expression.

They walked to the zoo in silence. Shyam knew he should say something to change the mood, but if he was honest with himself, he was quite happy to enjoy the sunshine and the animals without unnecessary conversation.

Esha woke up as soon as they reached the giraffe enclosure. Upon seeing such a large animal, she started screaming and banging her head against the back of her pram. Other children started to point and stare. Mira whisked her out of the pram and hurried to a quiet corner, rocking her back and forth, mumbling something into her ears.

Shyam backed away with the pram, his cheeks flaming. What a

terrible idea this was! Couldn't Mira have foreseen this happening? Esha's exposure to the world was limited to the people who provided her therapy, the few children she came in contact with, and a handful of adults. To take her so far out of her comfort zone was a foolhardy exercise.

Mira calmed Esha down, and then took out a small carton of Ribena out of her bag, punctured the carton with the attached straw and handed it to Esha to suck upon. Then she looked up at Shyam, her eyes filling with tears.

"I wasn't expecting this. Should we carry on, or leave?"

Suddenly, he felt terribly sorry for her. He could see how upset Mira was, and all his annoyance at her evaporated.

"No, let's stay. Maybe we can show her the smaller animals first. She must have gotten a fright waking up from her nap and seeing such a tall animal staring down at her."

"Yes, you're right. My poor baby." Mira pushed the hair off Esha's face and fixed her ponytail. "Come on, little princess, let's go find some butterflies."

As they took her for a walk through Butterfly Paradise, they watched her little eyes take everything in with such wonder that it was impossible not to feel awe towards these beautiful creatures themselves. When one alighted on Esha's arm, Mira's first reaction was to shoo it away, but Shyam held her back.

They watched as Esha carefully brought her hand up to her face and cooed softly to the pretty butterfly.

"Buttifly," she said, looking up at them

"Yes, butterfly," Mira smiled through her tears.

"After that, she relaxed enough for us to take her around to nearly all the enclosures, even the giraffes. But I can tell you, she's no fan of theirs." Shyam laughed as he recounted their previous week's outing to Keshav and Hugo.

They had invited them over for lunch at their home in Windsor, and Shyam was relieved that this time there were no other guests. Mira had agreed with great reluctance, and only because Keshav had played the grandfather card, asking to see his grand baby before she left for India. Although thus far, he had displayed very little interest in Esha. Mira had taken her upstairs for a nap. Now, Shyam was regaling them with stories while he waited for Mira to rejoin them on the terrace.

"Another mimosa?" Hugo offered.

"No, I'd better not. I'm driving."

"We have some non-alcoholic beer, if you like."

"Yeah, sure, why not?"

As Hugo left to fetch the beer, Keshav lit up his cigar, then sat back in his chair to observe his grounds.

"I love living here," he said. "There's just so much natural beauty around here. You two should move out here, too."

Shyam laughed in surprise.

"We can't afford the homes here! Besides, my work is in West London. This is too far out."

Keshav shook his head. "It only seems that way. Once you get used to the commute, you'll realise it isn't that bad. The quality of life will more than make up for it. Look, I could lend you some money for the down payment. Why don't you consider it?"

Shyam nodded and smiled, unsure what Keshav's motives were.

"Mira is my daughter, and as you can tell, we don't have much of a relationship. I'd like to work on that. I want to get to know her better, maybe help out with Esha's education. Try to make up for lost time."

Mira emerged from the house. Today she hadn't bothered to make an effort. Her hair was piled in its usual messy updo and she was wearing a denim shirt with khaki cargo pants.

"What are you drinking, darling girl?"

"White wine. Sauvignon Blanc if you have it." Mira was short with him, as always. Keshav never stopped trying, and she never stopped throwing his efforts back in his face.

"Come inside. I'll show you the ones I have in the wine cellar. You can choose one that you like."

Mira raised one eyebrow in disbelief but followed him in, anyway. They passed Hugo coming out with Shyam's beer. He handed it to him and said, "Glad to see father and daughter getting along for a change."

"I'm not sure about that," Shyam said, his brow creasing, "Mira really hasn't forgiven him his absence."

"Shyam, the secret to keeping your child tethered to you for a lifetime is some benign neglect."

"What do you mean?"

"On the surface of it, she might pretend to hate him, but he has been and will carry on being the biggest influence in her life. Look at the book she wrote. If that's not an ode to Daddy, I don't know what is. And your daughter…"

"What about Esha?"

"Did you pick her name, or did Mira?"

"Mira did."

"Precisely. Esha is the perfect amalgamation of Keshav and Nisha. Take the K and the v away, and what do you have?"

"Esha," Shyam responded wonderingly.

"Mira has been carrying a huge Daddy-shaped hole in her heart practically her entire life."

Shyam let out a low whistle.

"Keshav has asked me to move to Windsor because he wants to get closer to her. He even offered to lend me the down payment."

"Yes, I know. He talked about it with me. I think it may be a good idea. You see, Keshav believes he is living on borrowed time."

"In what way?"

"Don't tell him I told you, and promise not to divulge this to Mira."

"Okay."

"He is HIV positive, and has been for over a decade. And although with the medication he is on, he can expect to live a fairly long and decently healthy life, there is always the lingering fear of death in our minds. Lately, Keshav has been feeling it quite a bit more."

Shyam sat in stunned silence.

"I know this has come as quite a shock, but I wanted you to be aware. So, the next time Keshav says something out of character, you'll know where it's coming from."

CHAPTER 12

Once upon a time, they had not kept secrets from each other. They had been open and transparent, wanting their thoughts to mirror one another, their minds to meet as their bodies did, wanting to meld into each other. Now, Shyam suspected, they kept many secrets—little and large.

Hugo's confession weighed heavily on his mind, but he did not want to break his promise, so said nothing to Mira. He helped with the packing by pulling the suitcases out of the garage, fetching all the odds and ends she required, and helping her select the gifts for Nisha. In all that time, his refrain to himself was that it was none of his business. If Keshav really wanted to make up for lost time, perhaps he needed to come clean with his daughter. Shyam did not want to get in the middle of that. So he kept quiet, willing himself to park his thoughts so that they would not interfere with his daily living.

The first few days after Mira's departure, Shyam felt a little lost. At work, it did not matter, but evenings at home felt hollow and devoid of life. Then he started to enjoy himself.

He had never lived on his own. First, it had been with Maa and Baba, then with Radha. When he had moved to Mumbai, they had lived in Nisha's small two-bedroom apartment in Bandra. He had never had the luxury of an entire home to himself. He could be a slob if he wanted, eat as many takeaways as he liked, watch Sky Sports well into the night if he wished. Of course, he did none of it.

Living abroad and living with Mira had domesticated him so much that he couldn't bear untidiness and preferred eating home-cooked, healthy food. As for the charm of Sky Sports, that soon wore off when he realised he could binge-watch it with zero restrictions. Where was the fun in that?

Just before Mira's leaving, they had hired an Indian lady in her fifties to come and do the cooking. Mira had wanted her to start right away, but Shyam preferred she began when Mira and Esha returned from India. He wanted solitude to think through things. He didn't want to explain why to Mira, but strangely, she understood.

"We'll only be gone two weeks. Enough time to enjoy your own company," she had smiled as she packed Esha's little coat in the case. "It will be cold when we return."

After their lunch in Windsor, Shyam had been kinder towards Mira. He had never thought about it before, but now he could see how much of Mira's resentment of her father stemmed from a desire for his attention and approval. There was a strange push and pull between them, and much as Mira claimed to loathe Keshav, she had never once turned down an invitation to his home, despite all her grumbling.

He thought back to his own relationship with his father. Baba had never been a demonstrative man, but Shyam had known he was loved. Even though Baba had never hidden his preference for Sangita, Shyam knew that was because as a daughter he only had claim on her till she married. Then she became someone else's possession, and her visits as a daughter would be sporadic and rushed. Baba had foreseen the future by observing the plight of all the other fathers in his vicinity. Shyam was a son. A son stayed with his parents. He brought home a wife to supplement the family; he took care of them in their dotage.

Or that's how it should have been.

His mind went around in circles as he cooked the *mattar paneer*, stirring the tomatoes and letting them simmer with the rest of the *masala* mix. Amanda had been gone for nearly a month and there had been no news from her except for the occasional company email. Had she forgotten all about her offer of the job interview? Would it make sense to write and remind her? Or would that appear too brash and forward?

And what of Keshav's offer? Was it worth considering a move to Windsor now that he was privy to all this information? Yes, Hugo had said that Keshav was okay health-wise, but what if that changed? And what if he did nothing and Mira found out later that he'd known about her father's condition all along? Would she hold that against him?

With a sigh, he replaced the lid on the pan. Why did life have to be so complicated?

❖

Five days after Mira had left, his mobile phone rang with a strange caller ID. At first he thought of ignoring it, but some instinct made him answer.

"Misra?" Amanda's nasal voice was on the other end. Shyam's heart leapt then plummeted. Why was she calling him on his private phone?

"Yes, hello," Shyam croaked, suddenly feeling fearful. What if there was a problem with the project? Had she called to fire him?

"Been talking to my boss about you," she said in her usual peremptory manner. "He likes the sound of you. Wants you to come here so he can have an informal chat in lieu of a formal interview."

Shyam took a deep breath.

"When?"

"Well, as soon as you can."

"I.. I… can it be in a few weeks' time?"

"Is there a problem?"

"No, no problem. Just that my wife and daughter are away, and I want to be here to collect them from the airport."

"How long are they away?" Amanda sounded impatient now, and he wondered if he had been stupid to reveal his predicament to her.

"Another ten days."

"Ten days is long enough for you to come here and be back in time. Start packing. I'll book you a seat on the next available flight."

She hung up soon after. Shyam dropped into his chair, his heart beating unevenly. How was he going to explain this to Mira?

Graham popped his head into the office, took one look at his face, walked in, and shut the door behind him.

"You okay, mate? Look like you've seen a ghost!"

Shyam shook his head and swallowed. Then, because he couldn't hold it in any longer, said, "Amanda wants me to go to the head office for a meeting with the boss."

Graham let out a slow whistle.

"With the head honcho? Is she earmarking you for a promotion?"

"Training of some sort, I think." The lie rolled off his tongue easily. He didn't want to jinx his prospects.

Graham laughed.

"Oh, she will train you all right. Do you know what her nickname is?"

"What?" Shyam stared at him, puzzled.

"Man-eater." Graham eyed him quizzically. "You do know she's been divorced three times?"

"What's that got to do with me? She knows I'm happily married." Even as he uttered the words, he wondered if it was really true. Was he happily married? Regardless, the thought of being with Amanda made him shudder, irrespective of his racy reverie all those weeks ago.

"Mere semantics, mate. You watch your back with her. But hey, good on you! You worked damn hard on the project and deserve all the recognition."

Shyam could see that Graham was genuinely pleased for him. It still took him by surprise that the colleagues here weren't all about backbiting and sucking up to the boss, unlike his previous job in Gurgaon. While sometimes he wondered at their lack of professional jealousy, he knew it was less to do with ambition and more to do with the fact that they were secure in themselves. If only he were as secure, but his entire work ethic was underpinned by desperation and fear, even if he rarely acknowledged this to himself.

He dismissed Graham's warning, knowing full well that Amanda was not interested in him. Had she been, wouldn't she have made a move on him when they had gone out for a drink? She had been a pleasant companion and nothing more.

On Sunday, he rang Mira first thing in the morning.

"Hi *jaan*, how's it going?"

"Great! It's such lovely weather here. Mid-twenties, and I am not missing that grey and gloomy country. How are you? Are you managing okay? Not working too hard, I hope?"

"I'm good. Yeah, about that, I'm leaving for San Francisco this afternoon."

"What?"

"The big boss has called me over for that interview."

There was silence at the other end.

"Hello? Mira? Are you still there?"

"Yes. I'm here." All the warmth had left her voice. "So, you're going ahead with this."

"It's only an interview. Look, I'm not signing the dotted line until you come back and we discuss everything properly. I promise."

He could hear her sigh.

"I'm not trying to hold you back, Shyam. I hope you know that."

"Yes, I..."

"You haven't even asked how Esha is?"

"I was just about to."

"She's great, and so is Mum. They are both getting on like a house on fire. You should see her development. I mean, we've only been here a week, but already she's chatting so much more. There are such a lot of stimuli here, and she's responding so well to it all. She's also been playing with the neighbourhood kids. They've all been so lovely to her..."

As she rambled on about Esha, Shyam let his mind wander. He had never been to America, and even though he hadn't let on to Mira, he was beyond excited to be going. He had also rung Sangita and asked if he could see them all on Friday. Shyam didn't dare tell Mira and spoil the cheerful mood she was in, but he couldn't wait to get off the phone and get going. America was waiting for him.

❖

It had been a long taxi ride to the hotel, and despite the journey and the time difference, he had been wide-eyed with wonder at everything. Maa had been right. Everything was bigger and better in America.

As soon as he had checked in, he rang Sangita's home.

"Hi! I'm here."

"Welcome!" Sangita sounded genuinely happy to hear from him. "We are all waiting to see you on Friday. I hope you're staying the night with us?"

"No, I have the hotel until Saturday."

"Check out a day in advance, then. Stay with us. There's plenty of room, and Maa and the children are excited to see you. Hari too."

"What about you?"

"I," she paused before continuing, "I think it's time to let bygones be bygones. I've been talking to Maa. Mira is your wife now, and we have to let the past go and accept her as such. We want to meet your little girl as well."

"What about Radha?"

"T forgave you a long time ago. It's us who couldn't. Look, T will always be my friend, and Maa is still very fond of her. But you are our blood, and this has gone on long enough."

Shyam hung up a while later, feeling so much lighter. It had taken years to get here, but suddenly, everything seemed to be falling into place.

A wave of fatigue ambushed him, and he fell back onto the bed. The phone on the bedside table rang again, and he wondered if it was

Sangita calling back to confirm what time he would arrive on Friday. It was Amanda.

"Well, hey there Misra! Glad you made it in one piece. Your line's been busy a while."

Shyam cleared his throat and tried to sound chipper.

"Hi Amanda! How are you? Sorry, I was on the phone with my sister. She lives in San Jose."

"So you have family here. That's cool."

"Yes, I'm leaving on Friday to stay over with them. My mother is visiting as well, so..."

He realised he had wandered off track and switched back to the business at hand.

"When would you like me at the office tomorrow?"

"Yes, about that. The boss is in L.A. for a meeting and won't be back till Wednesday. So, your little chat won't happen till Thursday."

"Oh. I thought it was tomorrow."

"Yeah. Something unexpected came up and he had to reschedule. But come into the office, anyway. I can show you around."

"Right." He was too tired to process any more information, so he rung off with a promise to be in by 10am.

"You can finish early tomorrow. Believe me, it will take a while to get over the jet lag. Eight hours is no joke."

After he had unpacked and showered, Shyam got into bed and wondered what time it was in India. Was it worth calling Mira and telling her he had reached safely? Then again, he had spoken to her in the morning, even if it seemed like ages ago. He decided it was best to get as much sleep as he could before jet lag played havoc with him.

Sure enough, he was wide awake at 5am, flicking through the television channels waiting for room service to arrive. He would have to be more careful with his money as this was not an all expenses paid trip, but he figured one day of room service would not break the bank.

At 8:30am he pulled up in front of the headquarters of Axis & Co. The lobby was all glass and chrome and, in a funny sort of way, reminded him of his home in Gurgaon. How fixated he had been on chrome fittings back then. Looking back, that home had never possessed any warmth at all. In their present home, Mira had insisted on an eclectic colour palette of mustard and forest green, with magnolia walls, and decorations of different varieties and hues. There wasn't a bit of chrome to be spotted anywhere except for the bathroom taps.

The blonde blue-eyed receptionist looked up and asked, "Can I help you?"

"I'm Shyam Misra, here from the London branch. Ms Swift had called me in for 10am, but I'm early." He grinned and shrugged. She did not return his smile but indicated that he should sit on one of the straight-backed leather chairs, which was as uncomfortable as it looked.

Five minutes later, he looked up from his phone as he heard the clacking of heels on the marble floor. Amanda was walking towards him, a rictus grin on her face. He had forgotten just how startling her appearance was, but jumped up to his feet, feigning delight.

"Amanda! Nice to see you again."

He held his hand out to her, but she pulled him into a hug, squishing her chest into him.

"Misra, you're early, but a sight for sore eyes. Coffee?"

He nodded a yes while discreetly stepping away. Did she greet all her employees this way? Graham's warning flashed into his mind again, and he resolved to be wary of her. He didn't want to be swallowed whole by the "man-eater".

He need not have worried. For the rest of the day, she was as professional as she had ever been. She took him around the rather impressive offices of Axis & Co. introducing him to people in different departments. He was the colleague from London, she said, who might join them here soon. People were friendly, but he could tell that they were busy and not in the mood for a chat. He respected that, reminding himself that he wouldn't be receptive either, if a visitor interrupted his work day.

Later, as they sat in the cafeteria, eating their salads, Amanda asked, "Could you see yourself working here?"

Shyam looked up at the high ceilings, the Jackson Pollock prints on the walls, the constant thrum of activity around him, the sunshine pouring in through the floor-to-ceiling glass windows and nodded enthusiastically.

"Absolutely. If you'll have me."

❖

The next morning, Amanda asked him what he was planning for the two free days he had in San Francisco. When he said not much, she took it upon herself to become his unofficial tour guide. She took a day and a half off to show him the sights.

Their first stop was the Golden Gate Bridge, where Shyam couldn't stop taking photos of the bay and the city until Amanda told him there was so much more to see and they had to get a move on. They headed to the Golden Gate Park soon after, where they visited the Japanese Tea Garden, followed by the de Young Museum. After lunch they strolled to Alamo Square to see the famous 'Painted Ladies,' a row of colourful Victorian houses with the city skyline in the background.

When Amanda took him to Fisherman's Wharf for dinner, he asked her, "Why are you doing this for me?"

"Because no one did it for me. When I moved here from Minnesota, I was just another nameless, faceless entity in a big city, and no one took the time out to show me around. I discovered this city all on my own." She took a sip of her wine spritzer. "I've grown to love it, and I wanted to show you all my favourite spots."

"That's really kind of you."

"Not really, Misra. I am being selfish, too."

"In what way?"

"I want you to fall in love with this city and move here."

Shyam felt himself flush. Was there an invitation in those words?

"I think Axis needs people like you, and I foresee a very bright future for you here."

He exhaled gently. It was business, pure and simple, and he was relieved that he hadn't said anything untoward.

The following day Amanda took him to Chinatown and as they explored its alleys and sampled the food, Shyam thought he could envision himself here. But there was a blank space when it came to Mira and Esha. Would they fit in here too? Could he convince Mira to give it a chance?

After a cable car ride and a drive down Lombard Street, "the crookedest street in the world", as Amanda informed him, they ended the day with a delicious Italian dinner in North Beach.

"There is so much more to see, but you need extra time, and I don't want you to be exhausted for your interview tomorrow."

"Amanda, I can't thank you enough. If ever there is anything I could do in return..."

"Nonsense, Misra! It's been fun, and no thanks needed. But, yeah, if I need to call in a favour, I won't be shy."

They both laughed as they tucked into their seafood linguine. Later that night, as he brushed his teeth before going to bed, Shyam wondered exactly what kind of favour she had in mind.

His interview was unlike any interview he had ever had before. The 'boss' turned out to be a long-haired Californian named Jeff, who wore jeans, hoodies, and sneakers to work. He drawled 'dude' at the end of almost every sentence and seemed so laid back as to be practically horizontal. However, Amanda had told him that the facade was just that. Jeff was extremely smart and knew just which way to steer his company to be at the very forefront of Information Technology.

"Hey there, Shyam," Jeff began, "Good to meet you, dude. Kick back, make yourself comfortable." He took a stick of gum and put it in his mouth. "Amanda's been saying some great stuff about you. You're from the London office, right?"

"That's right," Shyam answered, clearing his throat, "I've been working in London for a few years now and I'm really excited about the possibility of joining the team in San Francisco."

"Awesome! London's got its charm, but there's nothing quite like the vibe here, dude. Now, before we dive into the formal stuff, tell me, what do you enjoy doing when you're not crushing it at work?"

"Well, I'm a big fan of hiking and exploring new places. London's been great for that, but I hear California's got some amazing trails."

Jeff grinned. "Oh, you bet! We're practically surrounded by them. You'll love it here if you're into the outdoors." He steepled his fingers and looked at Shyam intently. "So, let's get into it. What drew you to the tech scene in London, and why the shift here?"

Shyam pretended to consider the question, even though the answer was on the tip of his tongue.

"London's been fantastic, and I initially moved there as my wife's family lives in the UK. And while I can't deny that my knowledge grew a lot while there, it's the innovations happening in Silicon Valley that have always fascinated me. The opportunity to work more closely with the team here and be part of that energy is something I couldn't pass up."

"I get that, dude." Jeff nodded sagely. "Silicon Valley's got its own rhythm, for sure. Now, tell me a little more about this app you developed."

As Shyam explained the rationale and processes that went into the app development, he wondered what Jeff was thinking. His eyes were closed, his head against the headrest of his chair, and aside from the occasional smack of the gum in his mouth, he was impossible to read.

"We streamlined processes and saw a significant improvement in response time." Shyam finished, "It was a game-changer for user satisfaction."

"Nice!" Jeff nodded. "Love hearing about tangible impacts. Now, our team's pretty diverse and we value different perspectives. How do you think your international experience will bring something to the table?"

As Shyam talked, he thought back to all his years in IT. There were days he had despaired of ever getting out of India, days when he had been miserable in the companies he had worked in, but now he could see that every road had been leading him here. He already felt at home in San Francisco. In its vastness, its cutting-edge culture, and its forward thinking, this company and his future were undoubtedly intertwined.

"Alright, one last one before we wrap up," Jeff said. "If you could have dinner with anyone, dead or live, who would it be and why?"

Shyam considered this. There was no pat answer to this question.

"That's a tough one. I think I'd choose Mahatma Gandhi. His philosophy and leadership style have always fascinated me, and I believe there is so much to learn from his principles."

He could see Mira raise an eyebrow in his mind. She had always called Mother Teresa the patron saint of all Indian beauty queens, and she would see him using Gandhi as a slick move. He could see her mouthing, "Et tu, Brute?"

Jeff thought otherwise.

"Solid choice, dude! It's been a pleasure chatting with you. We'll be in touch soon. And hey, if you make it over here, we'll have to hit those trails together."

"Definitely, Jeff! Looking forward to it, and thanks for the opportunity."

When he told Amanda about what happened in the interview, she just had two words for him. "Nailed it."

The Hari he had been expecting to see was the one he had met over ten years ago. The image of this tall, well-built man had solidified in his mind over the years. He had seen plenty of photographs of Sangita's family in the interim, but somehow, his first impression of the man had remained his lasting impression of him. So, the tall, nearly bald man who opened the door took him by surprise.

"H... hi, I'm Shyam," he stuttered, as he held a box of *mithai* in one hand and his case in the other.

Hari smiled and took his case from him. "I know. Come on in."

Sangita's home was truly beautiful, and extremely large. From the high ceilings and the enormous living area, to the imposing staircase that led up to the five bedrooms, this was the house of a well-to-do couple. How could he have believed that she was marrying beneath herself all those years ago?

Sangita came rushing forward and embraced him.

"You're here!" She laughed, then called out to her children. "*Bachchas,* look, your *mamaji* has arrived."

Maa came up from behind him and said, "Shyam, you are looking well."

He bent down and touched her feet, shocked to see how old and frail she had become after Baba's death. It had only been a few months, but it seemed as though she had aged twenty years.

"How are you, Maa?"

"Very good, *beta.* Sangita has been taking good care of me."

The children came down the stairs together. Two boys and a girl, he tried recalling how old they were, but his memory failed him.

"This is Soham, Sanjiv and Heera," Sangita introduced them and asked them to touch his feet.

"No, no. They are too young for all this, and they barely know me," Shyam said.

"Have you forgotten your culture?" Maa scolded, insisting he bless them as they bent down once again to touch his feet.

Had he? Something so simple, something he himself had done all his life, seemed like an archaic practice to him now. Was this Mira's influence on him?

"Come, the table is set for dinner." Sangita steered him towards the dining room where a long oblong table with twelve place settings had seven places set up with table mats and cutlery.

"Did you do all this on your own?" Shyam looked at all the delicious Indian dishes on display and his mouth watered. It had been so long since he had eaten *ghar ka khaana* not made by his own hand.

"No, Maa helped me, but we tried to make all your favourite foods. There's *baingan bhurta, dum aloo, shahi paneer* and *vadiyaan.*"

"I can't wait to tuck in!" Shyam said, his heart swelling with love for his sister and mother. They had remembered his favourite dishes. Did Mira even know what he enjoyed eating?

Over dinner they talked about his week in San Francisco, Hari's Subway franchise and the Martial Arts training school he was planning to open, Sangita's role in the Parent Teacher Organisation (PTO), and what Maa was planning for the future.

The children ate quietly, still wary of the stranger in their midst. His eyes kept wandering towards Heera, who was nearly five years old. She looked so much like Sangita at that age, but she had a dimple in her left cheek, just like him. Had Esha been okay, would she have looked like her?

"You have a little girl?" Hari asked, noticing his gaze.

"Yes," Shyam nodded, taking another helping of the *shahi paneer*. "Her name is Esha, and she just turned three."

"You've never sent us any photographs!" Sangita narrowed her eyes and scowled. "Not even one."

"I," Shyam paused, "I didn't think you wanted to know us."

"We are family, Shyam. How could you think that?" Sangita cried out.

He pulled out his phone, scrolling to a recent picture of Esha that he had taken on her birthday. It was when the butterfly had first settled on her arm. Her expression of wonder was something that constantly wounded him with its innocence and beauty. How would they see it?

"She's so cute!" Sangita exclaimed, passing the phone to Hari, who nodded his assent. Maa looked at the photo, looked up at him and smiled, and something loosened in his chest.

Then Soham leaned over and looked at the photo.

"Why is she funny looking?" He asked his grandmother in an undertone, but his voice carried. Maa hurriedly passed the phone back and with trembling fingers, he tucked it away once again in his pocket.

Later Sangita apologised.

"He's only nine and should know better, but doesn't. I'll explain it to him later."

Shyam nodded. It hurt to think that his child would never be the way Sangita's children were, that she would never grow up with the same opportunities that they would have, that she would remain an outsider her entire life, even within his family.

"*Beta,* don't make the mistakes we made bringing you up," Maa said as she sat at the foot of his bed that night. Shyam had agreed to stay over and leave for the airport from their house the next day. "Love your child just the way she is. I know what I said all those years ago was nasty, and I really didn't mean it. Look upon this child as a blessing, not a curse."

"Do you remember why you said what you did?"

"I was angry with you."

"And you aren't anymore?"

"No, *beta.* Baba's gone, and who knows how much longer I have? What is the point of carrying all this anger within me?" Her shoulders slumped, and she shivered slightly.

Shyam scooted forward to sit next to her.

"If I bring Mira and Esha with me the next time, will you accept them, then?"

She nodded and leaned into him. They sat in silence until she patted his arm and told him to get some rest.

"So, it's as good as done?" Mira said in the car on the way home from Heathrow. He had been excited to see them, and after the first flurry of hugs and kisses, had launched into all his news. Esha had fallen asleep in the booster seat at the back, and Mira had sat in silence listening to him. This was the first question she had asked him, and from her tone, he knew he had to tread carefully.

"No, it's far from done. I'm still waiting to hear from Jeff." He deliberately kept Amanda's name out of it, not sure how Mira would take the growing friendship between them. There were days when he was quite perplexed by it, too.

"But your mind is made up?" She glanced at him, before turning her face towards the window again.

"I think," he said, choosing his words carefully, "it would make more sense for us to move to the US. The opportunities..."

"Your family is there," she interrupted.

"Yes, and they are willing to accept you now." He turned and beamed at her.

"How convenient." Her voice remained soft, but he could sense the anger behind her words. "What about my family? My mother? My father?"

"Nisha can always visit." Shyam suppressed his irritation. "Keshav too. He can afford to fly there every month, if he wanted to."

Mira stayed silent.

"Tell me what you're thinking," Shyam pleaded.

"Just that you have always been an incredibly selfish person."

Shyam turned into their drive and braked.

"What do you mean by that?"

"You've always gotten what you wanted, with no thought for anyone else's needs or desires. Have you even asked how my time in Delhi went? No! It's all been about you from the time you've picked us up."

"That's because I was excited to see you and tell you everything! Of course, I want to know how it went in India, and how Nisha is, but I thought we could talk about it properly at home." He turned off the ignition. "I know you're tired, but to call me selfish? Whatever I am doing, or thinking of doing, will benefit all of us."

"Oh, like the move to the UK benefited all of us?"

"Admit it, Mira. Esha wouldn't have had a fraction of this care in India."

"Maybe. But she would have had the love and attention of a grandmother who dotes on her, the warmth of people who accept her for who she is, and..."

"And what else, huh? What if something happened to your mother?

What then? You have no other family who could step in. At least, in America, I'll have Maa and Sangita's family."

"The same family who hasn't accepted us for years."

"Yes, the same family who have forgiven us and invited you to meet them the next time I go there."

"So, there will be a next time?"

"Well..."

"Be honest for once in your life, Shyam! You know you want this job. Not only because you've always wanted to live in America, but now you have the added incentive of your family there. What's in it for me?"

"If you can't see what's in it for you and Esha, then you are far more obtuse than I had imagined. You call me selfish? Look in the mirror. I have never come across a more selfish woman! Can't cook, can't take care of the house, barely contributes to the household expenses, is utterly absorbed in taking care of her child at the expense of her marriage. How do you define this behaviour, Mira?" He put his finger under his chin and pretended to think. "Oh, wait. I think I know. It's called selfish, right? S E L F I S H." He spelled out the letters, ignoring the look of fury on her face.

Mira wrenched the car door open, slamming it behind her as she marched to the front door of their home. Behind him, Esha woke up with a start and began crying.

"Hush, baby." Shyam twisted around to face her. "Mama's just angry because she doesn't like being told the truth."

CHAPTER 13

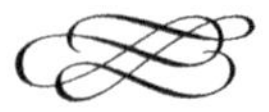

"Mira tells me you are seriously considering this job?" Keshav had called to meet for a drink after work and they were sitting in the same pub he had taken Amanda to. Shyam shifted uncomfortably in his chair. Knowing what he knew of Keshav's health, he felt guilty admitting that he was eager to move to the US.

"I am only considering it at this point," he fudged.

Keshav took another sip of his beer. "She's not happy about it."

"I know."

"How are things between the two of you?"

Shyam's eyebrows shot up. This was unexpected.

"I...I'm not sure it's any of your business, Keshav."

"Oh, but it is," Keshav said softly. "No matter how much animosity Mira holds against me, she is still my daughter. I need to know that she is happy, and from what I hear, she is not right now."

Shyam exhaled. "Mira wouldn't know what happiness was if it stared her in the face."

"You had better explain."

"She was unhappy in her first marriage because her husband refused to indulge her desire for a child, even though they had agreed they wouldn't have children before they married. I, on the other hand, agreed to having a child with her, knowing the risks, and look what happened! But hey, she got what she wanted. Was she happy then? No!" Shyam drained his glass. "Nothing makes her happy because no matter what she gets given, she only focuses on what she doesn't have."

"That's a very harsh assessment of your wife."

"And a true one. You see it too, even if you won't admit it."

Keshav's hand shook as he set his glass down.

"It's because of me, isn't it? Hugo says she has daddy issues."

"Maybe. She has never forgiven you for what you did to Nisha. But she's a forty-three-year-old woman and needs to take responsibility for her own happiness. She cannot keep blaming you, me, and the entire world!"

"Does she do that? Does she blame me?" From the stricken look on Keshav's face, Shyam realised he needed to dial things back a bit.

"Look, I'm not sure she knows where her head is at right now. She's angry because she doesn't want any more upheaval in Esha's life."

"Doesn't it bother you? All this upheaval?"

"No, because I know that it's for everyone's betterment. Look at all that is available in the US, what Esha can get in terms of therapy and schooling. I want the best for her..."

"...and yourself."

"Of course! I'm not afraid to admit it. Which man doesn't want to progress in his career? You, of all people, should understand my desire to move ahead. Didn't you do it with your business?"

"Yes," Keshav nodded his head, "yes, I do understand. But if things go south in your marriage, I want you to know that I will be here to pick up the pieces. I will provide for Mira and Esha. She will have a home with me, and she will never have to worry about anything ever again."

"What makes you think she will turn to you for help?"

. . .

With that bridge burnt, Shyam returned home with a pounding headache. He had always considered himself a pacifist, but today he had landed a low blow, one that had wounded Keshav enough that he had finished his beer in silence and left. Shyam felt rotten about it, but also angry that his life choices were being examined and questioned once again. When would people learn that he was a grown man, more than capable of making his own decisions?

Mira and Esha were nowhere to be seen. There was a note on the dining table saying,

Jacket potato in oven. Baked beans on hob. Heat and eat.

He was too exhausted to bother with any of that. So he took a quick shower, changed into his pyjamas and went to bed early. Somewhere in the middle of the night, he felt Mira's arm snake around his body. He kept his breathing even, not giving away the fact that he was awake, as he felt her body move closer to him. He had never failed to be aroused by her touch, but this time, his irritation with her overrode any desire to make love to her. So he carried on feigning sleep and gradually felt her recede as he fell into a deep slumber.

Two weeks later, Amanda's number flashed up on his phone.

"Hey Misra! How're you doing?"

"I'm doing good!" He smiled to himself as he turned into the office car park. "It's past midnight for you. Still working?"

"You know me!" she laughed. "Anyway, I have some good news for you."

"Tell me." Shyam already knew in his bones that he had landed the job, but he still needed to hear it said aloud.

"You got it!"

"I did?" His smile became even broader.

"You sure did." He sensed her smiling at the other end as well. "Now, listen, can you come back out here, end November? There are a few formalities we need to complete before we process your paperwork."

"Absolutely! When do you need me there?"

"How does the 24th of November sound to you? Jeff is taking off for L.A. on the 26th, so we can get everything sorted before he leaves."

"Yeah, sounds good to me. How long do you need me there?"

"Three days, tops."

"Great! I'll book my tickets then."

"You can stay in the same hotel again. Expense it to us, okay?"

"Okay."

"Hey Misra?"

"Yes, Amanda?"

There was a brief silence before she said, "I'm looking forward to seeing you."

"Me too, Amanda. Me, too." Shyam was surprised to find that he actually meant it.

As he walked into the office, his entire body thrummed with excitement. The first person he encountered was Graham.

"Mate, fancy a coffee?"

He was steered towards their kitchenette.

"A little bird tells me you won't be with us too long?" Graham leaned against the countertop, an eyebrow raised in question.

Shyam gave him a quick smile before making himself a cappuccino.

"Nothing's happened yet."

"Yet, hey? But it's happening. All these hush-hush trips to America..." Graham winked. "We aren't exactly blind."

Shyam shrugged noncommittally before leaving the kitchenette. Had he been wrong earlier? Had he just espied professional jealousy garbed in friendly curiosity? So, this was a world-wide affliction, not restricted to just his countrymen. Interesting! He would have to watch his back while he carried on working here, that was for sure.

Back in his office, he mulled over what Amanda's call meant for his future. Yes, he had promised Mira that he wouldn't sign anything before passing it by her, but the way things were going, it was obvious she was in complete disagreement with this move. What could soften the blow? Perhaps if he took Mira and Esha along with him to San Francisco? Perhaps if they saw how wonderful America truly was, Mira would change her mind. Also, he could introduce them to Maa, Sangita, Hari, and their children.

He started looking at flight costs, but tempered his enthusiasm with caution. Mira could be trenchant with her decisions, so he would have to introduce the entire concept carefully, with great delicacy.

Shyam had watched her struggling to write while taking care of Esha, who was getting more demanding as she got older. The cook had relieved Mira of her kitchen duties, but not enough for her to get the sort of unbroken time she needed to concentrate on the novel she was trying to write. Maybe if they moved close to his family in San Jose, she could leave Esha with Maa for a few hours daily while she focussed on her book?

Idea after idea churned in his mind. He put in for leave from the 26th of November onwards, hoping he could extend his stay in the US and really get to show them San Francisco the way Amanda had shown it to him. Then they could go to San Jose and stay with Sangita for a while. She wouldn't mind. She had all but ordered him to bring them over the next time he visited.

Under all these ideas was the looming possibility that Mira would say no. What then? What if none of this tempted her?

Then he shook his head and resolved to cross that bridge if and when he came to it. For now, he was happy to daydream of a future where he was on a fast track to success, his family by his side, his daughter well taken care of, and his wife once again giving him the love he required of her.

For the next few days, he stayed silent, trying to work out how to introduce the topic to Mira. Although things had calmed down considerably between them, they were still not back to normal. He had forgotten what their 'normal' was. Was it the way things had been before Esha came along, when they had laughed together, made love constantly, and designed a future in which they were sympathetically aligned? Or was it the time after Esha, of him being relegated to second position while she took up all of Mira's time, attention and love? At any rate, the present 'normal' was neither of those.

Right now, it felt like they were walking around a bomb on tip-toes. Neither of them knew what would set it off and just how much devastation it might cause.

Esha was meant to start pre-school in January, and Shyam knew that if he wanted to get the ball rolling on his transfer, he would have to tell Mira soon.

That night, as they tucked into the *kadhi chawal* prepared by the cook, he said, "My colleague was saying he went for dinner to 'Memories of India', the Indian restaurant close to the station."

"Mmm-hmm." Mira spooned some more *kadhi* into her plate.

"He said it was great. Shall we try it tomorrow evening? I could book us a table."

Mira kept stirring the *kadhi* into the rice, her face thoughtful.

"You know, Shyam," she murmured, "Kitten made the best *kadhi chawal* I have ever eaten."

"Kitten?" Shyam's eyebrows knit together in confusion. What on earth was she talking about?

"Radha. Your ex-wife."

"Oh." He inhaled sharply. It had been years since they had spoken of Radha. Why now? Why today?

"I've often wondered whether she could sense the demise of her marriage towards the end, whether she could sense you pulling away..."

"Mira..."

"No," she raised her palm to him, "let me finish." She pushed the plate away and put her elbows on the table. "What you and I did to her was reprehensible. In all these years, I have never been able to shake off the guilt or the fear that karma would come back around and slap me in the face. But we always think that karma will serve us our just desserts in a predictable manner. When has that ever happened?"

"Mira, what are you saying?"

"Everything and nothing."

"Can you stop being cryptic and tell me what has brought this on?"

"Keshav told me about his health."

For a second time that evening, Shyam felt his chest constrict.

"You've known for a while, haven't you?" She raised an eyebrow at him.

"Yes," he admitted, looking out of the window at the darkness outside.

"He's begged me not to go to the US with you."

"What?!" Shyam swung his head back towards her. "That's bloody unfair, Mira! He's been living with the condition for years. Just because he's going through a weird phase doesn't mean he impacts our future."

"Your future," she said, a sad smile on her face.

"Our future," he said, steel in his voice.

"Here's the problem, Shyam. Much as I love you, I love my father, too. If he does not have long to go, I want to be by his side."

"Mira, I got the job! They want me back at the end of November. I wanted to take you and Esha with me, show you around, introduce you to Maa and Sangita's family..."

She had already started shaking her head.

"I'm sorry, Shyam, that won't be happening."

"So, you're telling me that you are willing to sacrifice our marriage at the altar of your father's irrational fears?"

"They are not irrational. He's sick, and he's dying. And for once in my life, I want to do something completely unselfish."

"Like taking care of a father who abandoned your mother and you?"

Her eyes filled with tears, and she looked away. Shyam softened his tone. "Mira, Hugo told me it's just a phase. It will pass. He's probably scared that once you move away, he won't get to see you as often. Look, I'm happy to allay all his fears. Like I said before, he can visit or you can visit. I don't want to drive a wedge between the two of you, but this is about *us.* Can't you see that?"

The tears fell on the back of her hands.

"All I'm asking is for you to consider what this means."

"Have you signed the contract already?"

"No," he rubbed his hand over his face, "that's what I will do after some formalities are dealt with."

"Okay." She bent her head.

"Mira?" He reached over and put his hand on hers. "What do you mean by okay? What does this mean for our marriage?"

She stayed silent for a beat, then looked up at him, her eyes filled with sorrow. "I'm not sure we have one left."

"Fear makes people say and do strange things, Shyam." Sangita's voice on the phone had calmed him enough to actually listen to what she was saying.

He drummed his fingers on the dashboard of the car.

"What she is saying, Sangita, is that our marriage is over."

"No, what she is saying is that she needs time and space to think things over. Allow her that much."

"What if she decides she is done?"

"Then you need to figure out a way to change her mind. Listen, Shyam, I don't know Mira at all, but from what you've told me, she loves you and I don't think she would want Esha to lead a fatherless life like she did. Let her do what she has to for her father. If that means you have to shuttle between the US and the UK, do it. In time, she will see how impractical it is and how much you care for the both of them. Then watch what happens."

"How can you be sure it will work out that way?"

"I'm not sure, but from the outside, this is the only viable solution. Insisting on her moving with you would be the worst course of action..."

"Not that she would listen."

"Not that she would," Sangita echoed. "You have us here, and it will be a while before she integrates into our family. Let her have this time with her father. Maybe, if you are gracious about it, it will pay off in the long term."

"So wise, my little sister."

"*Humne bhi duniya dekhi hai, bhai.* I have grown up in the last ten years."

"How are all of you? Maa? Hari and kids?"

"We are all well. Looking forward to Thanksgiving and having you over."

"I so wanted Mira and Esha to experience this American tradition."

"There will be other years, trust me." Sangita sounded so positive, it was hard not to be infected by her energy.

"Any news of Radha?"

"I spoke to her just the other day. She's fine. Taking care of her elderly parents now. Both the brothers have buzzed off to other cities with their families, so she's the one left holding the fort. But you know what she's like. No complaints, just head down and keeping on going."

"She's brave like that. Has…" he paused, "has she met anyone?"

"T? She isn't brave when it comes to stuff like that. I cannot see her putting herself out on the market again. You burnt her for a lifetime, bro!" Sangita laughed, then checked herself. "Sorry, that came out all wrong. What I meant to say was that T is very much single and does not want to mingle."

Shyam sighed. His guilt was no less than Mira's.

"Well, the next time you speak to her, give her my best."

"I will, Shyam."

After she had rung off, he slumped back into his seat and watched the rain beat upon the car's windscreen.

Radha was wearing a blue saree, but there was a rip in the fall's hem. He was annoyed that she had not sewn it and kept trying to tell her to change into jeans. She would not listen. Every time he spoke, she turned up the volume on the car radio.

They were on the terrace of his parents' house and she said to him, "Look, there's the moon, but I ate half of it."

He looked up at the sky, and the moon was red. Then he looked at Radha's saree and the growing patch of red on her pleats. She was looking down at it, too. Amanda pointed at it with her long red fingernail and doubled up in laughter, saying, "Bye, bye, baby."

Shyam woke up, his heart juddering in his chest. What a strange dream that had been. He closed his eyes and listened to Mira's soft snores. She was turned away from him and he shifted his body closer to hers, just enough that their hips touched. Why had he dreamt of Radha? Was it because she had come up in conversation again? He thought about the dream, about the baby they had lost, and for the first time felt the ache of that loss. His daughter would have been ten years old had she lived. How different would all of their lives have been today if that had happened? He would most definitely have been tied to Radha forever then. Would that have been so bad?

Mira shifted away from him again. He let her. Letting go was a lesson life was reinforcing to him. Something good was bound to emerge from this as well.

❖

As the date of his departure approached, he noticed Mira withdrawing even further from him. He had tried talking it through with her, telling her he was willing to commute for a few years if she wished to stay on in London. The more he said, the quieter she grew. It was almost as if she had switched off from him. In the early years when he had fallen deeply in love with her, but she had been unwilling to commit to him, she had displayed a similar tendency to creating an impenetrable wall of silence around her. It was frustrating, especially when he was putting in the effort.

The night before, as he was packing the last of his toiletries, she came and stood by the door.

"How long will you be gone?"

He looked up from putting his shoes in a dust bag. Her eyes were focussed somewhere over his left shoulder.

"No more than ten days."

"Do you need me to pick you up from the airport?"

"I'll take a taxi." He put his shoes in the case and zipped it up. "Mira, I understand your wanting to stay with your father, and I'm willing to compromise. But I need you to promise me something, too."

Her gaze finally landed on him.

"Don't give up on us, will you? Marriage isn't easy, and for us it has been a tough road in many ways. I still love you, and I want us to go the distance, whatever it takes. Can you promise me you'll try?"

Mira swallowed and nodded, but did not say a word.

That night, she allowed him to hold her, and he buried his face in her hair, inhaling her scent. No matter how angry or frustrated he felt, he knew she was the only woman capable of making him happy. How he wished she could understand the depth of his feelings for her.

The next morning, she made him toast and coffee as he prepared to leave for the airport.

"Call me once you get there."

"It will be past midnight."

"Then text."

"Okay." He kissed her on the forehead and went into Esha's room. She was still asleep and because he did not want to wake her, he placed his hand on her head gently before turning away.

"I'll be back soon, little one," he whispered, once again wishing he could have taken them with him.

As Shyam turned and waved from the taxi, he watched as Mira's figure grew smaller and smaller as she receded from view. His heart lurched, and he felt a prickle of fear. He did not want to lose her, not over a job. He nearly told the taxi driver to turn around, but then quietened his fears and chastised himself for being silly. As Sangita had said, it would all turn out alright in the end.

❖

"There isn't that much, but it will take an entire day," Amanda said over the phone. "So, come in early and I'll take you over to HR."

"Thank you for everything, Amanda." He meant it. She had guided him without him needing to ask for the help, and he was grateful. "Can I take you out to dinner afterwards?"

"Why, thank *you* Misra! I thought you'd never ask," she laughed, and before he could say any more she had rung off.

He sat in his hotel room looking at the receiver. Every so often he thought he picked up a signal from her, but he wasn't sure. Amanda knew he was married. She knew he wanted to bring his family over with him. She couldn't be hitting on him, could she? He hung up and lay back down on the bed. What a silly thought. Of course she wasn't. She had recruited him because she thought he was capable, not because she wanted to climb into bed with him.

The next morning, she shook his hand professionally, dispelling all his doubts. He followed her to the Human Resources department, where she handed him over to a young, dreadlocked man by the name of Elijah.

"Find me once you're done here, Misra," she said as she walked away.

"Now, that's a fine piece of ass," Elijah drawled, watching her leave.

"Pardon me?" Shyam stuttered, unsure if he had heard right.

"Hey, it's okay, bro. She knows it, and she's happy we think so." Elijah winked at him, pulling out a file with Shyam's name emblazoned on it. "Now, let's get down to business."

They went through the internal transfer process, his new role, responsibilities, compensation and changes to benefits. Then they examined the visa and work authorisation considerations.

"Our legal department will guide you through the necessary steps and documentation regarding your application."

"How long do you think it will take? I just want to get a sense of when I will be moving here."

"Three to six months is pretty normal, I would say. We will give you relocation assistance as in moving expenses, temporary housing and any other logistical support you might require."

"And when will the team in London be told?"

"As soon as we set the ball rolling." Elijah cocked his head to a side. "HR to HR, they already know, but formally not until we get this paperwork sorted."

He put some reading material down in front of Shyam.

"I'd like you to have a look at this. Read it, take your time. It's the transition of your health insurance and other benefits. Once you've made your selections, we can get you to sign the paperwork and documentation related to the transfer."

"You want me to do this today?"

"Ideally overnight. Then you can come back in tomorrow and meet Jeff before he leaves for LA."

"Okay, yeah, that's do-able."

"Great!" Elijah stood up and held out his hand. "Welcome to the mothership, Shyam. We look forward to your joining the team."

Shyam shook his hand and smiled. "Thank you. I'm excited at the prospect."

"Axis is a great company to work for, but you know that already! See you tomorrow."

"I think we need something stronger today, to celebrate." Amanda swung her slim legs out and walked to the bar. She really did have a fantastic figure, and he flushed remembering his raunchy daydream. She came back with two martini glasses in her hands.

"I'm such a lightweight when it comes to alcohol, but today I'm breaking my rule for you, Misra." She handed him a glass.

"Sorry, what is this?" He looked at the pink liquid sloshing in the glass.

"A cosmopolitan. Cheers!" She brought her glass forward to clink his. "Come on, drink up."

He sipped the sweet concoction and hid his grimace. It was not a drink he would have chosen, but as she had paid, he did not want to appear ungrateful.

"I thought I was treating you to dinner."

"You are, but a few drinks aren't going to mess up our appetites, are they?"

They were sitting in the hotel bar, which was slowly filling up with people leaving their offices and heading out for post-work drinks.

"Besides," she slipped a coaster under her glass, "it's happy hour. We're celebrating a happy occasion, aren't we?"

He took another sip, thinking of the long and winding road that had led to the culmination of his dream. Yes, it was a happy occasion and despite his doubts, despite Mira's intransigence, despite the thought of his future commute, he was excited.

Two cosmopolitans in, his head started feeling woozy. Shyam had only had a sandwich mid-morning, and the alcohol was making its effects known.

"I think I need some food, Amanda."

"Sure." She sprung up, looking none the worse for wear. "There's a Thai place round the corner. You like Thai food?"

"I'm Indian," he grinned. "I like anything spicy."

They walked a block down to the small restaurant, and he was happy to see there were tables available.

"Never full on a weekday, but weekends, phew!" Amanda whispered as the server led them to a small table tucked away in the corner.

Amanda ordered for them, and he let her. Shyam did like Thai food, but his repertoire had been limited to the green and red curries.

Here she was ordering fishcakes and papaya salad, something called pad see ew and massaman curry with sticky rice.

"Wine?" she asked, perusing the drinks menu.

"Yeah," he nodded against his better judgement.

"Don't worry," she said, "the food will soak up the alcohol."

They talked about the contract and the visa application, the health insurance and what he needed to look out for, the place he should ask to stay to be within commutable distance to the office yet have a pleasant neighbourhood to live in.

"Will your family come along with you?" Amanda asked as she crunched down on the salad.

"Not straight away," he fudged. "Maybe a few months later."

"That's good. You can get familiar with living here before they move. It makes sense."

They chatted about their favourite places to travel, her yoga and the trip she still wanted to make to India, their boss Jeff, and how his genius was bound to change the world.

When he looked at his watch, it was nearly 9pm.

"Gosh! I didn't realise how late it had gotten. I was meant to read through the paperwork tonight."

Amanda waved her hand.

"That's just a formality. I can help you with all the salient points, if you like?"

He nodded again before calling for the bill. Jet lag, fatigue and alcohol were not a good mix for examining paperwork that would determine his future.

In the lift on the way to his room, he asked Amanda, "Say, will you be okay driving after all that alcohol?" Shyam knew she had parked her car in the hotel car park.

"Who said I would be driving?" She raised an eyebrow at him, then laughed at the look on his face. "I was planning to take a cab back."

Inside the room, he shrugged off his jacket, then helped her off with hers. They sat next to each other on the small settee as she flicked through the folder, underlining the bits that were important. Her dress had ridden up to her thigh and as she leaned forward to turn a page, he took in her cleavage. Shyam stood up abruptly, trying to hide his erection.

"I..." he muttered, "I just need the bathroom. One minute."

He locked the door behind him and sat on the pot, allowing a thin stream of urine to escape him as he tried to subdue the organ that was intent on betraying him. He took a cold flannel and rubbed it over his face, then thought of the most boring documentary he had ever watched–one about famous bridges in the world and how they had been constructed. It was not until Radha's face popped into his mind suddenly that he felt himself go limp.

When he emerged from the toilet, he found Amanda still going through the folder. Thank goodness she had not noticed his discomfiture. He sat back down next to her and they resumed flicking through the remaining pages. Once they had finished, she looked up at him, "There, Misra! All done."

He looked at her in amazement.

"You are extraordinary, Amanda! Thank you so much. I would never have been able to make sense of all the terminology."

"I know," her eyes gleamed, and then, suddenly, her lips were on his and his hands were tangled in her hair as she reached for his zipper. His pants were around his knees and her dress was pushed up to her waist, and they were on the bed when he gasped and pulled away from her.

"No!" He stumbled back. "Sorry, Amanda. I'm married. This isn't right."

She stood up, pulled her dress down and smoothened her hair. Then she reached over and planted a soft kiss on his cheek.

"It's okay, Misra, nothing really happened. See you in the office tomorrow."

After she had left, he put his head in his hands and sighed a deep, long, and unhappy sigh.

❖

In the evening, in the cab to San Jose, he went over the day in his mind. Elijah had been pleased that all the i's were dotted and the t's crossed, thumping his back and wishing him a happy Thanksgiving. Jeff had looked at him in surprise, as if he had forgotten all about his existence, but once reminded, had bumped fists with him and said, "Cool, dude!"

It was Amanda he had been worried about, but she had behaved totally normally with him, as if last night's aberration was just that. There had been no coldness, no hurt looks flung in his direction. If anything, she had been even more helpful than usual, ordering him the taxi that was taking him towards Sangita's house.

"Have a happy Thanksgiving with your folks, Misra!" She had hugged him before he got into the cab. He had felt a familiar stirring in his loins and cleared his throat, holding his jacket in front of him as he asked her, "What are your plans for the holiday, Amanda?"

"Sleep." She had grinned. "I plan to sleep all day. It's my present to myself."

She had waved to him and gone back inside the office. Now he leaned his head back against the seat and closed his eyes. Things could have been so awkward between them, just as he was about to start his new job, but she had spared him. One more thing to add to the long list of things he was grateful to her for. He wondered what Mira would make of her? More interestingly, what would Nisha make of her? Amanda was the sort of independent and liberated woman that Nisha purported to be. Only where Nisha had forsworn all men after her marriage, Amanda could pick and choose whomsoever she wanted. And if it didn't work out, there were no hard feelings. Which was more independent and liberated?

He could hear Nisha's mocking laughter in his mind. "The entire world does not revolve around men, Shyam." Or her usual, "get over yourself". He shook his head to clear all thoughts of his mother-in-law. Right now, he just wanted to enjoy his promotion and his family.

. . .

On Thanksgiving day, he could not believe the amount of food Sangita had prepared. There was roast turkey, which he had never eaten, and was surprised that his purely vegetarian mother wasn't throwing a fit over. There was stuffing, mashed potatoes, gravy, cranberry sauce, green beans, sweet potatoes, cornbread and pumpkin pie.

Later, as he let out burp after burp, Hari handed him a bottle of *Hajmola*.

"Here, this will help you digest it all." He sat down next to him. "You must be used to all this food? Don't you do the same at Christmas in the UK?"

Shyam thought back to all the Christmases he had spent, and the readymade Marks and Spencer's meals he had heated in the oven, and shrugged. "Mira isn't much of a cook."

Maa overheard and came to sit on his other side.

"She doesn't cook?" He looked at the horrified expression on her face and decided to wind her up a bit more.

"Actually, I'm the one who has been doing the cooking all these years."

"What?!"

"It's okay, Maa," Sangita said, coming down the stairs. "Men should know how to cook. It's a basic life skill."

"But, but," Maa spluttered, "Hari doesn't cook, and your Baba never entered the kitchen."

"Hari can cook. He just chooses not to. Shyam is being a progressive man by taking on the onus of cooking. Look, whoever said that only women were meant to cook? All the famous chefs in the world are men!" Sangita finished triumphantly.

Maa carried on tutting. "Never heard of such a thing! Anyway, why didn't you bring them over with you? I thought you were planning a family holiday?"

"Thanks for rescuing me last night." Shyam reached over and

ruffled Sangita's hair. She was driving him to San Francisco to avail of the Black Friday deals.

She looked at him and grinned, before turning her attention back to the road. "It's alright, *bhai*. I don't think Maa could have handled any more shocks after learning that you cook."

"Hmm. Do you think it will upset her greatly if she knows Mira won't be moving with me?"

"What do you think?" She chewed her lip as she turned right. "Maa is still very conventional in many ways. Look at how much she's had to accept in her lifetime. My elopement, your divorce... It can't have been easy. She's a product of her time and circumstances, and at nearly seventy years of age, we need to honour her capacity for change."

"You're right, of course. I just hope that when she meets Mira, she can set aside her anger and welcome her into the family."

"I don't think she's angry anymore, Shyam, just tired. She wants to see us all happy. She knows I am, and just wants to be reassured that you are, too."

"Sangita?"

"Hmm?"

"I want to apologise to you."

"For what?"

"For the horrible brother I was when you first met Hari. I was really awful about it all. Hari's a really good man, and I can see why you fell in love with him."

"He is, isn't he? And I'm sure Mira is a lovely person, too. Now, what is it you wanted to buy her? I'll pick the right place to park accordingly."

"I was thinking some kind of designer bag and perfume. Also, a doll for Esha. Maybe some more toys for your kids?"

"No, no. You've spoiled them enough as it is. But I have just the right spot. Let's go to Westfield Mall in Union Square. I think you'll find what you need there."

"You'll guide me, *na*? I am a little out of touch with all the trending stuff these days."

"My brother, the workaholic! You used to be so in the loop. I remember T telling me she was terrified she would get it wrong wearing the wrong outfit when she was married to you."

"She said that?"

"You were quite an ogre to her, you know."

"I must have been. So young and misguided." Shyam shook his head. "I wish I could make amends to her."

"Don't." Sangita parked the car. "She has finally moved on with her life. Don't go barging in and ruining it for everyone."

He felt slapped, and his cheeks reddened in response. Sangita looked at him and put a hand on his shoulder.

"I'm sorry if that came out harsh. What I meant was: leave the past where it belongs, and focus on the future. There is a lot to look forward to; you are starting a new chapter in your life."

Three hours later, they walked out laden with packages.

"Mira is a lucky woman!" Sangita laughed, walking towards the underground parking garage. "Say, there's a fantastic Indian restaurant around here. Hari loves their lamb curry. It is to die for! Let me google the location. Ah, there it is! Shalimar on Jones Street. You don't mind if we go there first?"

"Only if you let me pay." Shyam stood there, packages in hand, stubbornly refusing to move forward until she agreed.

"Oh, very well! Come on, it's getting dark. Some blocks here aren't very safe."

"Yeah, Amanda was saying something about that the other day," Shyam said as they followed the directions on Sangita's phone.

"Amanda?"

"A...a colleague."

Sangita glanced up at his face. "Shyam, what's going on?"

"N.. nothing. Just... I, umm, nearly kissed her accidentally the other evening."

"Nearly? Accidentally?"

"We'd had a lot to drink."

"Oh, for Heavens' sake! Don't screw up your life again!" Sangita sounded angry, and he peered at her in the dim light.

"I have no intention to. I love Mira, and Amanda knows that. It will never happen again."

"It better not!" Sangita growled.

They walked briskly in the fading light, and he noticed groups of men loitering near doorways. The area had a seedy and dangerous feel to it, ironic as it was just a few blocks away from Union Square, which was clearly wealthy and upmarket. Amanda had told him about the Tenderloin neighbourhood, which was known for its vibrant diversity but was also grappling with socio-economic challenges like homelessness and drug abuse.

"Are we okay around here?"

"As long as we hurry."

They entered Shalimar, and all at once, he felt safe again. This wasn't an upscale restaurant, it wasn't even like the Thai place he had gone to with Amanda. This was all plain white walls, bright lights, formica laminated floors and basic tables and chairs, but the aroma of food that emanated from the kitchen took him right back to India.

Sangita ordered, and he paid. They sat down to wait for their order and the server brought over two cups of *chai* for them.

"While you wait," he said and left.

"That's nice of him," Sangita remarked. "First time they've done this. You must be the lucky charm!"

Shyam laughed. "Hang around with me, sis, and my luck will rub off on you as well."

Sangita laughed along before she said, "You know, Shyam, on a more serious note, I am really happy you are moving here. Our family may not be identical to the one we started out with, but family is family. A continent away from our birthplace, we will finally be together again."

Shyam blinked his tears away. This was exactly what he had been thinking in the lead up to his visit. He just wished Mira could see it the same way. Give her time, Sangita had advised, but how much time would be enough? He wanted them all to be together. Maa,

Sangita, Hari, their children, Mira and Esha. Was he asking for too much?

Their food was brought out in white plastic bags, and as they juggled what to carry, he handed Sangita the lighter packages and took the heavier ones for himself to carry.

Outside, it had gotten dark quickly. They strode with their heads down, avoiding looking at the men, eyeing them as they walked past.

"How long will it take to get back?" He asked Sangita.

"The worst bit is getting out of here. The traffic can be terrible. Once we're on the freeway, we should be home within an hour."

"That's good. Listen, is Maa okay with all of us having turned non vegetarian?"

"Okay? I don't think so. But like so much else, she's just had to accept it. Poor Maa!"

He heard Sangita chuckle, and he smiled. It was true that Maa had taken so much in her stride. She was really quite remarkable.

They had just turned the block when a tall, burly man blocked their path.

"Hand it over," he said to Sangita, the menace in his voice unmistakable. The pungent odour of marijuana and unwashed clothes radiated off him. He lunged at Sangita.

Shyam pushed in front and said, "Leave us alone!"

Sangita cried out, "Shyam, don't! Just give him what he wants." She held out the bags and said, "Take them!"

Shyam pushed her back, squaring off to face their attacker.

"Shyam!" Sangita screamed, pulling him towards her. "Please!"

She thrust the packages at the man, saying, "Take them, just take them. Please let us go!"

In the confusion of the moment, the bag containing Esha's doll fell to the floor and as Sangita bent down to pick it up; the man reached inside his coat, a crazed look in his eyes.

Shyam barely had time to register the glint of metal as he whipped out a gun, pointing it at Sangita. A shot rang out, slicing the evening noises with what sounded like a car backfiring. Then he turned it towards Shyam.

No, no, no, no!

Shyam's scream gurgled in his throat as he saw Sangita falling to the ground before he felt the impact of the bullet hitting his chest.

Then all he heard was the distant wail of a siren and the grunt of the man as he wrenched the watch off his wrist. The sour smell of his perspiration covered Shyam as he leaned over to pick up the strewn packages. He tried turning his head to look at Sangita, but it was too much of an effort. The pain in his chest was overpowering, and he closed his eyes to rest for a moment, to let the pain recede.

Velvet soft darkness invited him into her warm embrace. Mira's face floated before him, her eyes filled with reproach. Then he saw Esha holding up the doll he had bought her, her little face filled with joy. He felt a mild desire to resurface before the feeling faded. There was a heaviness in his chest, like an elephant had planted its foot on him. Radha called out to him and he tried to listen, but all he could hear was the roar of his blood pounding a manic beat in his eardrums, da-Dum, da-Dum, da-Dum. Maa sat at the foot of his bed, telling him he needed to stay. There was still much to be done. He tried to open his eyes again, but they remained stubbornly shut; a metallic taste filled his mouth, and he almost laughed. He had so badly wanted to try the famous lamb curry. *To die for,* Sangita had said, and here he was, literally dying for it. Then that thought skittered away, too.

In what seemed to be hours, but in reality was only a few minutes, Shyam felt himself gradually loosening his resolute grip on life, as he first, reluctantly, and then, with a strange sense of relief, yielded to the calm silence of oblivion.

MIRA

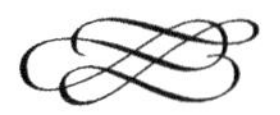

2018

CHAPTER 14

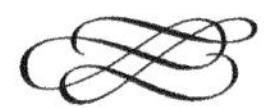

"There's a lot of anger in here." Bhumi tapped her fingers on the thick manuscript lying before her.

Mira's attention had wandered to the young couple who had walked in hand-in-hand.

"Hello? Mira? You listening?"

She turned back to Bhumi and nodded. "Yes, there is." She shrugged. "I've moved past the shock and denial, I suppose."

"It is beautifully written, but maybe we need to downplay the rage a bit?"

"Whatever. You're the editor. Just tell me what to do." Mira's gaze wandered back to the couple. The girl seemed to be in her early twenties, the man not that much older. They sat across from each other, still clasping hands, leaning towards each other, so intent on one another that nobody else existed for them.

Bhumi followed her gaze. "Young love, eh? Listen, I'm peckish. Want to share a pizza and some of their bacon fries?"

"Sure, why not?"

Bhumi left to order, and Mira leaned back in her chair, wiggling her toes in her sandals and closing her eyes, feeling the warmth of the

January sun on her face. Blue Tokai in Khan Market had been Bhumi's suggestion, and she was glad they had managed a table outside before it got busy, as it invariably did on a Saturday afternoon.

"It'll be twenty minutes," Bhumi said as she returned to the table. "So, how are things at home?"

Mira wound her hair and clipped it into a bun. "Not great, actually. Esha's been struggling at school, and Mum keeps droning on about homeschooling her."

"Why is that a bad thing?"

"Bhumi, I want her to assimilate into normal life and make friends with her peers. Homeschooling will shrink her circle to her mother and grandmother. How is that any good for her development?"

"I see your point." Bhumi took off her glasses and cleaned the lenses with the edge of her *dupatta.* "But you guys have been through a helluva lot in the past few years. What harm is there in protecting Esha for a while longer?"

"Life doesn't care about these artificial layers of protection we cocoon ourselves in. So, why bother? I want, no, I *need* Esha to be strong, to realise that once Granny and Mama are gone, she will only have herself to rely on."

"She's a smart girl."

"Smarter than she looks."

"How long has it been since you moved back to Delhi?"

"Nearly four years, would you believe?"

Mira thought back to the moment she had made her decision. Even back then, it had felt absolutely right. India was home, always had been, always would be.

"Hmmm, they've gone by fast." Bhumi slid her glasses back on. "So listen, I'll mark all the bits I think need revision and send it back by the end of the month. Overall, structurally, it is sound, and we can work on the line edits later."

"Sounds good to me."

Their food arrived just then, and as the server laid out the items in front of them, Mira looked at the young couple once again. Would their love last, or would life snatch their happiness from them like it did to so many others?

"...you were telling me about your father..." Bhumi took a slice of the pizza and placed it on her plate.

When had they crossed the professional boundaries of writer and editor and become friends? Was it when she had moved back to Delhi, or was it when she had first confided in the editor she had only ever spoken to online, that her life contained far more drama than her books ever had? It had been a relief to find a female friendship free from the baggage of her past. One in which she could reveal just how much she wanted to and conceal all that she was ashamed of. Over the years, she had unfurled her life in front of Bhumi one petal at a time. The thorny bits she had withheld. And then, there were parts of her life she could not stop talking about. Yes, the boundaries had blurred, but it had never impinged upon their work. Business first, Bhumi had always said, and been true to her word in all the years she had known her.

"Yes, Keshav." Mira sighed. "He was one manipulative son of a..."

"Shhh," Bhumi set the slice down. "Don't speak that way about your father."

Mira grimaced. "It's only the truth. He was in no imminent danger, but he used every dirty emotional trick he could to keep me with him. Then it took him six long years to kick the bucket."

"And he left you a very rich woman."

"Ha! What does money matter when your entire life has collapsed like a house of cards?"

"Money matters, Mira, or you wouldn't be able to sit at home and write your books. You would have had to find a teaching job again, and Esha wouldn't be able to attend these ultra-expensive private schools you've sent her to."

"Fat lot of good they've done, too." Mira scowled as she tore a bite off her pizza slice.

"Did you blame him for everything? Is that why the father character is so vile?" Bhumi tapped on the manuscript again.

"I don't think I ever stopped blaming him. Every interaction I have ever had with any man has always been affected by my feelings for my father. Hugo said as much."

"Hugo?"

"His partner. The guy he left the other half of his fortune to."

"Right." Bhumi nodded slowly.

"Partner as in life partner, not business partner. He shared my father's bed."

"Oh!"

"My father, the proud gay man who went on Pride marches and fought for gay rights, had been a closeted homosexual when he married Mum. But he never apologised, not once, to her or to me. Just wanted what he wanted for himself, and took it, regardless of the cost to others."

"Sorry, I did not know that."

"I don't make it public knowledge, but now do you get why I'm so angry? I could have been with Shyam that day. Maybe if I had been, he wouldn't have felt the need to buy all those expensive gifts to appease me. Maybe they wouldn't have ventured into San Francisco then… All of it could have been prevented!" Her voice went up an octave, startling the people around them. Then, embarrassed, she ducked her head and pulled out her sunglasses.

"There are a lot of maybes in what you just said," Bhumi stated, her voice dry and devoid of sympathy. "No one can change what happened. You are not responsible for their deaths. I have told you this before and I will keep reiterating it until you get it."

"Ah, but," Mira scoffed, "My mother-in-law said that I was. She said that I had brought nothing but misery and misfortune into their lives."

"The words of a grieving mother."

"Yes."

They sat in silence for a while. The afternoon sunshine had given way to a pleasant breeze, the sun retreating behind the clouds.

"You know, Bhumi, it's been ten years, and I just can't…" Mira choked on her words. "I can't forgive myself. Book after book, I try to revive him. I try to absolve myself, but it just doesn't work."

"Maybe that's why your books sell like hotcakes. Something within them strikes a chord with your readers. Your pain and pathos are so relatable."

"I've commodified my life." Mira sighed.

She caught the young girl's eye as she looked towards them again and saw a spark of recognition. She watched her lean forward and whisper something to her companion, who looked over his shoulder at her. Then she watched as the girl rooted around in her bag, grabbed something and came towards her. Mira was glad she had put her sunglasses on.

"Mira Dixit? Ma'am, I'm such a fan of your work. Please, would you autograph your book for me?"

On her drive back home, she pondered Bhumi's parting words.

"Let go of that which you have no control over, Mira."

There was so much in her life that she *had* had control over. In her twenties, it had seemed as if life itself was well within her grasp and she was steering it in the direction she pleased. With time, that illusion of control had revealed itself to be a sham. Yet, she could not honestly say that she was not responsible for the decisions she had made all those years ago. From marrying Monish to falling in love with Shyam, from allowing herself to be persuaded to move to the UK to insisting upon having Esha, there had always been some element of control she had wielded. How could she deny that?

Today, she could look back on her life and regret the many impetuous and ill-regarded choices she had committed herself to. The only one she refused to regret was Esha.

She turned into the driveway of her house, honking the horn for Abdul to open the gate. He came out immediately, unlatching the lock and opening the gates to allow her in.

"Baby *ko* pick up *kiya?*"

"Abhi nahin. Woh boli subah ki school ke baad art class hai."

Mira handed him the keys as she nodded. She had forgotten all about Esha's art class, but dear Abdul always kept track of everything. Mum had been so lucky to find him.

"Nisha*ji andar hain, ki woh bhi class mein gaya hain?*"

"Nahin, woh toh andar hi hain. Shayad so rahin hain."

So, Mum was asleep. Just as well, as Mira was in no mood to repeat her conversation with Bhumi to her. Mum would no doubt chide her too, telling her to stop revisiting the past.

"Ek chai laana, Abdul."

"Ji memsahib."

As he walked towards the kitchen, Mira wondered how old Abdul really was. He could have been anything from sixty to seventy. His diminutive stature, his hennaed beard and the skullcap he wore on his nearly bald head signalled he was old, but he had the strength of a man half his age. Mum had taken him in seven years ago and he had been a loyal and discreet employee. When Mira and Esha had moved back to Delhi, and she had insisted on relocating Mum to her newly purchased home in South Extension, Mum had refused to go anywhere without Abdul. At the time, it had bothered Mira that a strange man would live in the *barsaati* extension to the main house, especially as she had a young daughter, but now, she realised how fortunate they were to have him there.

Abdul was not just Mum's Man Friday, he was a father-like figure to Mira, a rock to their household, a guiding spirit, and a stoic and secure guard to a home that needed some male energy in it. He spoke little of his own son who had cast him out of the one-room tenement they had shared as soon as he'd gotten married. Abdul's past was firmly buried in the past.

Mira flicked through the news on her iPad as she drank her tea. Abdul, through force of habit, had also brought out a small plate of biscuits which she ignored completely. Mum would have polished them off by now, biscuits having replaced cigarettes as her new addiction. Nisha walked in just then, yawning as she yanked at her wrinkled *kurti* which had bunched up around her waist.

"When did you get back?"

"About ten minutes ago. How was your nap?"

"The neighbourhood dog woke me up with his barking."

"Oh. Want some *chai*?"

Mum shook her head and came to sit next to her.

"Where is Esha?"

"Art class. Abdul is leaving in half an hour to pick her up."

"Mmm. Hope she's had a good day today."

Mira's ears perked up immediately.

"What do you mean? Has she been having bad days?"

Nisha regarded her from the armchair, her legs propped up on the coffee table. It was a loaded look filled with censure. Before she could say anything, Mira jumped in.

"Mum, let me talk to her when she gets home. It can't be that bad."

"Okay," Nisha sighed. "Although, if anyone had called *you* the R-word when you were her age, I would have clobbered them!"

"What R-word?!" Mira's heart sank; she already knew, even if she pretended not to. This was worse than she had imagined, although perhaps not as bad as when the boys had locked Esha in a closet for close to three hours. Sticks and stones could break bones, but words cut even deeper. "Who said this? When did it happen? Why didn't she tell me?"

"Because you make light of everything. She pretends she is fine because you want her to be fine."

"That's not true!"

"Oh, but it is. These children have been making her life a misery for quite some time now. They can't stand the fact that she is bright and capable, and talented, albeit a tiny bit slower than them. So they've started calling her names when the teacher's back is turned. *Retarded* was the last one."

A tear trickled down Mira's face. Had she made a mistake in moving back to India? Would they have been better off in England?

But what of Mum, who had point blank refused to move abroad? How could she have looked after her, too?

Nisha's face softened.

"Mira, listen to me. I understand why you've insisted on her being schooled in this way, but in a lot of places in our country, the thinking hasn't evolved. There is still a certain stigma and lack of understanding attached to disability. There shouldn't be, but sadly, there is. Not that Esha is *dis*abled. She is just differently abled. My point is: why put her through this daily trauma when we can just as easily have her schooled at home?"

Mira shook her head to clear it. Shyam had always said that she was stubborn to a fault. Was her stubbornness responsible for her daughter's unhappiness?

"Let her come home, Mum, and we'll talk about it."

❖

"Mama! Look."

When Esha walked in an hour later, holding up a charcoal sketch, Mira was deep into researching her next novel. It took her a minute before her eyes de-glazed and she took in the A4 paper Esha was waving in front of her.

"That's amazing, darling! What is it?"

"Look at it." Esha frowned and placed it on the desk in front of Mira. She peered at it and slowly the picture emerged. There were three female figures, each one standing at a distance from the other, a sliver of lightning seeming to separate them. From the uneven strokes, their features emerged. It was the three of them: Nisha, Mira and Esha.

"It's beautiful, Eshu! It's our family, isn't it?" She looked up at Esha, her eyes filling with tears. "But what is this white zigzag space between us?"

"It's our growing space," Esha responded, her voice soft.

"Growing space?"

"Where we learn to be better." Esha cocked her head and looked at her.

Better? Had Esha picked up on the fact that every day, Mira tried atoning for the mistakes of the past that had paved the way to her present? She did not believe it to be obvious, but maybe it had been. Her decision to give up smoking and drinking, and not swear in front of Esha had been tiny steps she had taken towards becoming a better mother. Practising patience and kindness in her daily life were the harder measures she had taken towards becoming a more decent human being.

Why only her? Wasn't all of humanity constantly in pursuit of change and betterment? Better jobs, larger homes, fitter bodies, bigger bank balances. It never stopped. Every space was a liminal one—a threshold to change, a precipice to something new.

Mira took in the quiet anticipation on her daughter's face and her throat closed up. What need did her beautiful child have to be better? Did she feel she wasn't good enough?

"Oh, baby, you are such a clever girl!" Mira stood up and hugged Esha. "Although, why do you need to be better, tell me? You are perfect as you are!" Mira mock-tickled Esha's tummy as she giggled and tried dodging her mother's fingers. "Now, why don't you tell me what school was like?"

Esha shrugged, and a pang went through Mira. She was so like Shyam when she did this.

"It was okay."

Over the years, Esha's speech had cleared considerably with the many therapies she had undertaken, but there was still the occasional slurring. Not enough to make her incomprehensible, but sometimes one had to listen carefully to understand what she was saying. In this instance, Mira also listened out for what she was not saying.

"Granny was telling me that some children have been saying mean things to you."

"Yeah." Esha fiddled with her skirt as she looked away.

"How bad is it, baby? Please be honest."

"It's not good, Mama." Esha looked her in the eye. "They don't like me at this school. Even the teachers."

"How can that be?" Mira cried out. "I was assured that you would be welcome, that they would make sure you fit in and were included!"

"Yeah, they lied." Esha's slur became more pronounced, the only indication of her distress.

"I'm so sorry, darling! Why haven't you said anything to me?"

"You were busy with your book, Mama." Her almond-shaped eyes were devoid of reproach as she looked up at Mira.

"Never too busy for you, angel." Mira kissed her daughter on her forehead. "You don't have to spare my feelings, Eshu. Always tell me the truth, okay?"

"Okay." Esha grinned. "I don't like *bhindi*."

"Huh?"

"Abdul said we have *daal* and *bhindi* for dinner. I don't like *bhindi*. It's slimy and horrible."

"Esha! It's good for you. Okra is a nutrient rich vegetable."

"You told me to be honest..."

That night, Mira lay in bed researching homeschooling options. This was Esha's third school in four years, and none of them had worked out. Each school had gotten progressively more expensive and given her wild promises they had not fulfilled. All Mira had wanted for Esha was somewhere she could learn, grow, and make friends in a safe environment. Why was it proving so difficult?

Years ago, when she had first come to India with Esha as a toddler, the children had been friendly and accepting of her. The families in Mum's old neighbourhood had petted and pampered her with no sign of pity or discrimination. That feeling of warmth had always lingered in her mind, which was another reason she had wanted to return, to bring Esha up in India. What had changed in the interim?

Mira took off her reading glasses and pinched the bridge of her nose. Shortly after Shyam's murder, Keshav had asked her and Esha to move in with him. She had declined, wanting to hold on to some independence. His persistence had finally worn her down. Once they had moved in, Keshav had tried bringing up the option of a special needs residential school for Esha. In Mira's heightened emotional state, it had been a low blow. It had taken Hugo three days to calm her down.

"He means well, Mira. He just wants Esha to get the best education possible."

"By separating her from her mother? She has already lost her father in the worst possible circumstances! Now this?"

"He means well..."

Mira still didn't know whether he had meant well, or had just not wanted Esha underfoot all the time. For Keshav, appearances were important. Mira, his grieving widow of a daughter, was the right look for a wealthy altruistic father, her daughter with Down syndrome, not so much.

Now she picked up her iPad again and scrolled through all they needed to do to set up home schooling. It still didn't feel right. Isolating Esha would certainly protect her, but how would it set her up to navigate the world later in life? This worry had nagged her right from the start. She remembered Shyam asking her during the pregnancy if this was what she truly wanted. Did she know she was signing up for a lifetime of worry? Was she doing this for herself or for the baby?

The implication had been clear enough. She was being selfish. A child who was disadvantaged from birth would remain disadvantaged throughout life. But was that really true? She had read of children with Down syndrome achieving remarkable feats in the face of tremendous adversity. She had watched YouTube videos of gymnasts and models, of young men working in hospitals full time, of girls who aspired to be singers, and of able and ambitious achievers. Mira believed with all her heart that Esha was equally capable, more so given the right environment and opportunities.

Time and again, she had read accounts of parents saying how

blessed they were to have a child with Down syndrome. The love, the joy, the beauty, the patience they had thanks to being a guardian to such a child was something she could vouch for first-hand.

Esha was more than a blessing. She was an answer to an unspoken prayer, a response to a plea that had blossomed in Mira's heart unbidden. It had taken years for her to fall pregnant and often she had despaired that she would never know the joy of motherhood. So when it had finally happened, she didn't care that her baby carried an extra chromosome which would differentiate her from other children. To Mira, Esha was special, she was wanted; she was a benediction.

A week later, Mira was in the market shopping for shoes when she thought she glimpsed a ghost from the past. Her hand froze, and she broke out in a cold sweat.

Esha looked up at her and said, "Mama, what's the matter? You have gone pale."

Mira could not speak, willing for the woman to turn around but dreading the moment she would. When it finally happened, she allowed her breath to escape in a long exhale. The shoe dropped out of her hand and her mind kept echoing *it's not her, it's not her, it's not her.*

Later, in the coffee shop, as Esha slurped on her hot chocolate, Mira thought back to that moment and felt herself shiver. In a city of nearly four million people, the chances of running into Radha were slim to none. Yet, the fear never ceased to release its hold on her. What if it did happen? What would she say to her? Would she even be able to look her in the eye?

"Mama?" Esha licked at her chocolate moustache. "Granny was saying I will be studying at home now."

"Umm, I'm still thinking about it, baby. Is that what you want?"

Esha cocked her head as she considered this.

"I enjoy going to school. I just don't like the people there."

"What do you like about school?"

"Art class. I like drawing and Mr Bose says that I am good."

It was true that despite Esha's initial struggles with motor development, her talent in drawing had been evident right from the start.

"Well, that's lovely, isn't it?"

"Mr Bose is the only nice teacher. The others think I'm stupid."

"Oh honey, but you're not!"

"I know that." Esha nodded her head before slurping some more of her hot chocolate. "Just because I speak like this doesn't mean I don't understand what's happening around me."

"Esha, you do know that other people's opinion of you does not matter a jot? You are who you are, and we love you just as you are."

"Did Dada love me too?"

Surprised, Mira set her cup of coffee down. Esha so rarely asked about Shyam that when she did, Mira was nearly always taken aback.

"Of course he did, darling! He adored you."

Liar! Her mind screamed. Shyam had loved Esha in his own way, but adored? Most definitely not. He had adored Mira. He had wanted to please her and appease her, and be with her no matter what. Shyam had seen Esha as an encumbrance, as someone who had driven a wedge between them. How could she say all of this to a child whose only image of her father depended on the tidbits her mother fed her?

"Would he have wanted me to go to school?" Esha asked, her almond-shaped eyes filled with curiosity.

What would Shyam have wanted? Mira had stopped asking herself that question the day Esha was born. Shyam had wanted many things in life. Above all else, he had wanted to be successful and prosperous, just like Keshav. In all likelihood, he would have sided with Keshav in wanting to send Esha to a special education school with residential facilities. She decided to fudge the truth.

"Yes, I think Dada would have liked you to attend school, but not if it made you unhappy."

"Hmm." Esha played with the straw in her tall glass. "Mama, you know what makes me happy?"

"What, baby?"

"When you and Granny watch your silly movie and laugh."

"Our silly movie?"

"The one where the men dress up as women."

"Oh!" Mira smiled as she realised Esha was talking about their favourite film, which they watched every New Year's Eve, and which cheered them up no matter what was going on in their lives: 'Some Like it Hot', an old black-and-white comedy that had become such a tradition that it was almost second nature to watch it as the year wound down. When had Esha picked up on the happiness it elicited?

Her cell phone rang just then. She looked at the name on the screen.

"I need to take this, baby."

Esha shrugged and returned to her hot chocolate.

"Hi, Bhumi. All okay? Did I miss something in the last email?"

"No, nothing to do with the book. Although, I have made some notes and I'll be sending those across in a day or two. This is something else. Got time?"

"Yes, of course, but not too long. I'm out with Esha."

"Well, actually, it's about her. I was talking to a friend who has just joined a new school as a teacher, and she said that this school might just be the right fit for Esha."

"In what way?"

"They are quite the pioneers in inclusivity and diversity. Wonderful ethos too. Apparently, while not as flashy as the other public schools, they have been quietly making inroads into becoming a sustainable and environmentally conscious academic institution." Bhumi paused for a moment, as if gathering her thoughts, before continuing. "They have their own farms where they produce vegetables which are sold or used in the cafeteria. They are also hugely into yoga and spirituality, and hold annual camps for the older children aged sixteen and above in their ashram in Nainital. And they have all kinds of children studying there. In fact, they encourage a diverse array of students. Everything I heard sounded really good."

"On paper, all the other schools sounded good, too. Why would this be any different?"

"Because Tripta works there and says that they are truly walking the talk. Obviously, nothing is completely perfect. There will always be problems, but from everything I've heard, I think it might be worth giving it a try."

"Okay," Mira sighed. She was exhausted from trying out various schools, and nothing working out. She looked at Esha, who was sucking the last of her hot chocolate out of the straw. One last try wouldn't hurt. "What's the name of the school?"

"It's called Kinara Public School, or KPS for short. Tripta can organise an interview with the principal if you like. Take Esha with you, and see what you think?"

"Thanks, Bhumi. I suppose it's worth a shot."

"What have you got to lose, anyway?"

Mr Gautam Upadhyay sat across the desk from them. He was a handsome man with a serious disposition. His fingers were steepled together as he regarded Esha. Behind him was a large picture of two hairy dogs. On either side were two smaller framed photographs. One of an older grey-haired lady dressed in a blue saree, and the other of him and a tall, attractive woman, who was no doubt his wife. The rest of the office was tastefully furnished in monochromatic colours with just a few splashes of fuchsia to break the monotony.

"So," he said, looking directly at Esha, "would you like to come and study here, Esha?"

They had already been through the preliminary interview, a tour of the school, and an aptitude test. Esha had responded positively to everything, her eyes twinkling when she had spotted the large art studio. Now, as Mr Upadhyay spoke to her, Mira watched closely to see how Esha would react. In all the previous schools, the head-teachers had always addressed Mira, only speaking to Esha as an afterthought. She could already sense things were different here. Would Esha pick up on it, too?

"I would like to study here if I can have art as a subject."

"I see." Mr Upadhyay leaned back in his chair and smiled. "We should be able to arrange that. You do know, though, that there will be other subjects you will have to study as well."

"That's okay," Esha shrugged and smiled. "I am smart."

Mr Upadhyay's smile got wider. "I can see that you are. W..."

Just then, someone knocked on the door.

"Yes?"

A head peeked into the room. It was the woman from the photo.

"Sorry, Gautam, didn't realise you were busy."

"Come in, Pari. Let me introduce you to our newest entrant, Miss Esha Dixit."

The tall lady walked into the room and smiled at them both.

"Hello. I'm Pari Upadhyay, Gautam's wife. I teach Economics here. Welcome to the school, Esha."

"And this," Mr Upadhyay said without ceremony, "is Ms Mira Dixit, whose books you devour nightly."

"Oh!" she gasped, looking at Mira properly. "I'm sorry I didn't recognise you."

"Not to worry," Mira smiled. "Most people don't. I like it that way."

"I love your books! It will be an honour to have your daughter study here."

"What's the matter with your face?" Esha piped up, pointing to the long, thin scar that ran down her cheek.

"Esha!" Mira scolded. Sometimes her forthrightness could be downright rude.

"No, please, it's okay."

Mrs Upadhyay sat on a chair next to Esha and said, "I was in an accident some years ago, and that's where I got this scar."

Esha put her hand out and touched the scar.

"I think you look real pretty with it." She looked at Mira, then turned her attention back to the lady. "My Dada died in an accident many years ago. If he had lived, he would have had a scar like this from here to here."

Mira saw a look pass between the couple and held her breath. This was the first time Esha had spoken about Shyam's death in front of strangers.

"I'm sorry you lost your Dada, Esha. It must hurt a lot?"

"It hurts Mama more. I'm okay." She shrugged, then looked Pari square in the face. "I would like to join your school. Will you be my teacher?"

Esha had never asked this question before, and in that moment Mira sensed instinctively that this was going to be the right school for her daughter.

CHAPTER 15

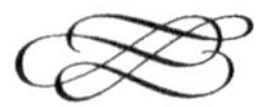

Nisha had lost her bearings again. Who would have believed she had lived most of her life in Mumbai?

"Mum, are you sure it's this way?" Mira asked, disguising the annoyance she was feeling. The holiday had been her idea, but this, coming back to Bandra, had been Nisha's. She had been happy to stay in a hotel in Colaba and show Esha all the usual tourist sights, but Mum had insisted they return to suburban Mumbai and visit the flat she had grown up in.

"Everything looks so different, Mira, I can't tell anymore. Wait! I see it. There's Otters Club, and yes, yes, right next to it is Jogger's Park. Now, if we just follow the road..."

Mira had to admire the taxi driver's patience. They had been going around in circles for a while. He had said earlier, "*Apun* town *mein* drive *karta hai. Idhar ka rasta nahin pata.*"

No problem, Mira had assured him. Her mother knew the area well. She had grown up there. And now, an hour and a half later, that had proven to be a complete falsehood. Luckily, Esha had fallen asleep with her head on Mira's shoulder. Nisha grew more excited as they drove down Carter Road, which was adjacent to the sea. Mira breathed in the salty air, and it took her back to her childhood again.

Why had she been so resistant to visiting? This was where she had grown up, too.

Some days, it felt like she was completely divorced from her life before Esha. That life, those events, the minor and momentous occasions, all seemed to have happened to another Mira. A Mira who had lived in a self-obsessed bubble of her own making. How different she was now from that woman! Today it seemed as if she was going to visit a friend from another lifetime. Would she like her still?

"Idhar, idhar. Right *lena."*

As they parked outside Sea Breeze, the apartment complex at the foot of Pali Hill, she recalled all the days she had spent trudging up the hill to go to Avabai Petit School. There were some happy memories from her time there, even if all her friends had scattered worldwide and she had no contact with them anymore. Did they ever read her books and recall the mouthy, opinionated teenager she had once been?

After she had woken Esha and paid the driver, she looked at Nisha and said, "Now what?"

"Let's go inside and see if the Daruwalas are still around."

"Uncle and Aunty from next door? But they were so old, even back in the 90s!"

"Shush, Mira. Everyone seems old to you, even with all your grey hair." Nisha strode ahead to talk the guard into allowing her entry.

Esha yanked on Mira's hand and asked, "Why are we here, Mama?"

"Because Granny wants you to see where we grew up."

Esha nodded solemnly, holding Mira's hand tight as they walked into the building.

Mum tapped her foot impatiently, waiting for someone to answer the door at Number 1. A stooped lady wearing thick glasses opened the door and peered at them.

"Nilufer aunty! It's me, Nisha!"

A flurry of introductions ensued and then they found themselves sitting on an orange settee, sipping on *chai* and eating fruitcake.

"My, but you are all grown up, *dikdi.* Such a *phataka* you were,"

Nilufer aunty commented, looking straight at Mira, her eyes huge behind the thick lenses of her spectacles.

Mira squirmed. She was glad that Esha wasn't fluent in Hindi or Gujarati, or else the scales would most definitely have fallen in her eyes. Mothers were meant to be safe and solid spaces, not wild, unpredictable teenagers as Nilufer aunty was recalling.

"So, this is your dodder?" She looked at Esha next.

Mira nodded, wary, unsure of what would come out of her mouth next. Nilufer aunty had never minced her words.

"Just like Rustom, she is. My sister's son. He is living in Australia now with his wife."

Mira looked between Nilufer and Nisha, trying to figure out if there was a reason that Mum had brought them down here to meet the Daruwalas. But Nisha remained blissfully oblivious to the loaded looks Mira was throwing her way. As the two ladies reminisced, Mira pulled out Esha's colouring book and pencils. This would take a while.

"You remember when…"

"Dilroz died last year..."

"I'm so sorry…"

"Your parents were good people…"

"Yes, after I lost them, this place did not feel like home anymore."

"But why have you become so fat, *dikdi*?"

"Not so active in Delhi now. Also, I gave up smoking and developed a sweet tooth…"

"You still go *idar udar* on your scooter?"

"Not in Delhi, no. It's not that kind of city, Nilufer aunty."

Mira tuned out. What was the reason she had fled Mumbai? Ah yes, Sam Mascarenhas. The first boy who had played with and then broken her heart. Delhi had seemed a safe option back then. From Mumbai to Delhi to London and back again. It felt as if she had spent most of her life running. She just wanted to set down roots somewhere. Set them down and refuse to be uprooted.

"*Tame su karoch*?" Nilufer aunty asked, turning her gaze upon Mira.

What did she do? What if she said she ran, and kept running, from her past mistakes, her trespasses, her betrayals? Hysterical laughter bubbled up inside her, but before she could say anything, Nisha spoke up.

"She's a writer. Five books." Mum nodded proudly and looked at the shelf of books behind Nilufer's head.

"Very good!" Nilufer stood up slowly. "Now, you must go. I have to take my afternoon nap."

Walking out, Mira looked at her mother, bemused.

"And the point of that visit was?"

"Oh, wait. Look Esha, this is Flat number 2, where Granny and Mama grew up. These are the lawns we both played on as young girls. Come, let me show you."

A man stood by the balustrade, smoking and watching them. He came towards them and the closer he got, Mira started to get nervous.

"Mum, let's get out of here. We're trespassing now."

Nisha ignored her, pointing out all the different flats to Esha, giving her a quick rundown of the families who used to live there.

The man was balding and pot bellied, wearing a lemon shirt with khaki trousers. He came and stood right in front of Mira.

"Mira?" He said, his voice low and raspy.

"Yes?" Her response came out curt and surprised.

"It's me. Sam? Sam Mascarenhas?"

They laughed all the way back to Colaba.

"I can't believe you fancied that boy," Nisha spluttered. "Such a boring old fart!"

"Mum, language!" Mira glanced at Esha, who was fortunately too busy gazing at the rapidly changing vistas from the taxi window to pay any attention to her grandmother or mother.

"Also, why didn't you tell me back then? To think you left for Delhi because of him."

"I was young and stupid. Besides, which daughter wants to divulge all the details of her crush to her mother, eh? That would be weird!"

"Hmmm. Boys have always ruled your life, Mira," Nisha said, changing track abruptly.

"What do you mean, Mum?"

"Think about it. First this Sam boy, then Monish, and then Shyam."

"Nobody ruled my life! I did what I did with the information I had at that time. And I thought you liked Monish!"

"I did like him, but had you told me about the condition he'd put before you, I would have liked him a lot less."

"A condition I agreed to willingly."

"A condition that broke up your marriage."

Mira turned away to look out of the window mutinously. Her mother was the only one who could get to the heart of the matter swiftly and ruthlessly. She blinked back her tears.

"Mira," Nisha said from the other side of her, "it's just that I thought I had brought you up to be independent of men. But to watch you base your life decisions, important decisions, on what they liked or didn't like, what they wanted or didn't want, was quite disheartening. I thought..."

Mira spun around to face her.

"You thought I would be like you! A...mis...misandrist!"

"Now, don't you use fancy words to browbeat me. You know very well that I don't hate men, but after my experience with your father, I never, ever wanted to hand over the reins of my life to a man. So, when I saw you do it, I was disappointed."

"Sorry to be such a disappointment to you, Mum." Mira turned back to look out of the window.

"Why are you and Granny fighting?" Esha asked, her eyebrows knitting together as she regarded them from her corner of the taxi.

Nisha had already turned her back on them and started a low conversation with the driver sitting by her side.

"We aren't fighting, darling, just having a discussion."

"I want you to laugh about that man again."

"Which man?"

"That man who stared at you like you were a *gulab jamun*, all yummy and sweet. The one in the building with the old lady."

"Oh, Esha," Mira smiled at her, pushing away her irritation at Nisha until they got back to the hotel.

There was a lot to unpack in what Nisha had said. Did she truly believe that Mira had given up all independence and agency because of the men who had entered her life? Mira did not see it that way at all. Yes, it was true that she had been fearful of being single like her mother. She liked men; she liked their company, and she liked to be indulged and cosseted by them too. But not at the cost of her sovereignty.

❖

The next few days passed in a blur of activity. They visited the iconic Gateway of India, a historic monument built to commemorate the visit of King George V and Queen Mary to Mumbai. Then they strolled across to the famous Taj Mahal Palace hotel to enjoy cold drinks and club sandwiches in the coffee shop, later stopping in front of the memorial built to honour the victims of the 2008 Mumbai terror attacks. In the evening they enjoyed a leisurely walk along Marine Drive, which was when, as Nisha was explaining to Esha that it was also fondly known as the 'Queen's Necklace' because of its nighttime lights resembling a string of pearls, Mira had a sudden, vivid recollection of her last argument with Monish. It was over a necklace.

"I can't undo the clasp, Monish. Can you help?" She had asked that evening after they had returned from a party.

"Why do you wear this necklace when it's so difficult to put on and take off?" He had said, sighing in exasperation.

"I like it. It's one of my favourite necklaces."

"But you never stop complaining about it."

"Honestly, Monish, if it's such a problem, I'll do it myself."

She remembered him fiddling with the clasp, and then the sudden snapping of the necklace string which caused beads to scatter everywhere.

"Now, look at what you've done!" She had screamed at him. He had taken a step back, his face filling with alarm at first, then a slow dawning realisation.

"This isn't about the necklace, is it, Mira?" He had asked softly, his eyes boring into her. She had been spoiling for a fight that entire evening. The necklace was just an excuse.

That's when it had spilled out of her. This growing desire for a baby, ever since she had heard of Radha's pregnancy. Her wanting to experience motherhood for herself, her biological clock asserting itself entirely unexpectedly. He had listened and then simply said, "No."

It had never been up for discussion. He had always made his feelings clear on the subject. In fact, the only reason he had agreed to marriage was because he had thought she was on the same page as him. No children.

No amount of railing at him, crying, pleading, asking him why, over and over, would change his mind. He had decided very early on that he had no intention of adding to the population of his country or burdening the earth with his progeny. Mira could call it what she wanted, but he was intractable. She had no right to accuse him of cruelty, for she had always known his wishes.

"Are you okay, Mira?" Nisha had stopped by a *bhel puri* vendor. "You don't look too well."

"I'm okay, Mum. You go ahead and order. I'll just sit here for a while."

She sat on the low wall, watching the sun set over the Arabian Sea. The sky turned a fiery orange and the art déco buildings of yore that made up the 'Queen's Necklace' seemed to shimmer with untold secrets. Returning to this city had churned up all kinds of emotions in her. There was a sense of loss and an understanding that there would not be a do-over. Life could not be rewound to start again. Decisions, once made, were decisions one had to live with, whatever the consequences.

Nisha came and sat next to her, with Esha on her other side.

"I'm sorry about what I said yesterday, Mira. I didn't intend to hurt you."

"That's okay, Mum. You were only speaking the truth, but that was your truth. My truth is far more nuanced and complicated than that."

Nisha set down her plate of *bhel* on her lap and sighed.

"I may be your mother, but I have no right to pass judgements on your life. For a moment there, I forgot that."

"No, Mum, you have every right. Just don't expect me to agree with you."

Mira put her arm around her mother and lay her head on her shoulder. No matter how often they disagreed, she knew Nisha would always be by her side, loving and supporting her. She was her captain, her anchor, her stay. Life would have been impossible to navigate if it hadn't been for Nisha's steady hand that had steered her through every storm.

Mira hoped that someday Esha would think the same of her.

On the last day of their holiday, they visited the Elephanta Caves by taking a ferry from the Gateway of India. A World Heritage Site, the ancient rock-cut caves housed intricate sculptures and carvings, including the famous Trimurti sculpture of Lord Shiva.

"Look Esha," Mira pointed to it, "this represents the three aspects of Shiva: the Creator, the Preserver, and the Destroyer."

Esha gazed in awe at the enormous sculpture.

"He looks real nice, even if he has three heads."

Nisha laughed. "Come on, let's go inside."

Mira watched her mother take her daughter's hand as they walked in together. A seventy plus lady in her twilight years, and a thirteen-year-old girl on the cusp of life. Which put her, Mira, slap bang in the middle. She looked up at the sculpture of Lord Shiva and prayed for the same serenity he displayed, sandwiched between the two other aspects that defined him.

❖

Back in Delhi, Mira got busy organising Esha's new school uniform. She gave Nisha the task of buying all the school books, while she explained to Abdul that there would be no more dropping Esha to school. She would be taking the school bus henceforth.

"Baby theek rahegi?" Abdul asked, his brow furrowed in anxiety. He had been ferrying Esha to and from her various schools for the past four years, and not once had he ever been late. He took his duty to the family seriously, and his protection of Esha superseded everything else.

"Haan, baby ko abhi seekhne ko mangta hai." She tried explaining how important it was for Esha to start off on the right foot. She had to become more independent, learn to make friends, and not rely as much on Abdul. He shook his head, unconvinced, and walked away to prepare the evening meal.

Mira chewed on her lip and stared into space. Was this just going to be another expensive mistake? Her gut had urged her to give this one last school a try, and Esha had displayed more enthusiasm than ever before. But…

A loud crash from the garage made her jump. What on earth?

The large blue ceramic pot Mum had made a few years ago lay on the floor smashed to smithereens. Nisha stood staring at it blankly.

"Mum? What happened?"

"I…I'm not sure. I turned around and suddenly it had fallen to the floor…"

Nisha looked shaken.

"Come and sit down, Mum. There." Mira fetched the broom from the corner of the garage and swept the pieces to a side, making a mental note to clear it up later. That had been one of Mum's favourite pieces. Mira looked around at all the different pottery items that Nisha had made over the years. Some of them had even sold on Etsy last year.

When they had moved into this home, Mira had insisted on converting the garage into a studio for Nisha. Pottery was to her what writing was to Mira—an escape. She could not imagine depriving her mother of this outlet. Now she looked at the pottery wheel languishing on the side, the apron bunched up and thrown on the worktable, and the electric kiln with an inch of dust on it, and wondered when Nisha had last been in here.

"Have you not been doing any pottery lately?"

"Huh?"

"Pottery, Mum? Your passion? The reason you moved from Mumbai to Delhi?" She couldn't help the sarcasm that had crept into her voice. Nisha looked at her blankly.

"Mum!"

"What?" Nisha snapped back to attention.

"When was the last time you were in here? This place looks neglected."

"Mira," Nisha's voice got stern, "don't take that tone with me. I'm your mother. I've been waiting for the feldspar to arrive."

"What's that?"

"A flux." Nisha raised her eyebrows. "I need it for the glaze. Any more questions?"

"Alright, okay. I'm sorry. It's just that you seemed to have lost a bit of steam lately when it comes to your pottery. And I just wondered..."

"What did you wonder?"

"If it's got anything to do with Yasuda Shōji's death."

She could have sliced through the silence that followed.

Shōji had been Mum's mentor, her teacher and guide, her self-professed North Star, and for a while Mira had suspected that Nisha had nursed much deeper feelings for him. Whether that had ever been reciprocated, she did not know, nor did she want to ask. This disinterest in pottery bothered her though. It was so unlike Mum.

"Don't you go through fallow times, Mira?" Her mother asked, her voice soft. "Just because I'm not creating with my hands doesn't mean my mind isn't busy." She stood up and moved towards the wooden cupboard at the very end of the garage. She opened the doors of the cupboard. "Look! This is all that I've been making over the years."

Inside were plates, vases, cups, saucers, even oddly compelling, deliberately misshapen figurines of rural women carrying *matkis* on their heads. Everything was glazed in vivid colours of tangerine and amethyst, jade and cerulean, scarlet and amber. And within each of them were delicate lines of gold, highlighting the flaws, showing the beauty that lay in imperfection.

Mira gasped.

"Why have you never shown me these before? They are stunning! You could make a killing with them."

"I don't want to sell these pieces."

"Why not?"

"I made them for Shōji *sensei.* I promised him that someday I'd exhibit them somewhere."

"Mum! Why someday? We should try to do it sooner rather than later."

"What's the hurry? Let another year pass. I want to do it on his death anniversary."

"Ah." It was as she had suspected. "Can I ask you something, Mum?"

"Yes?"

"Why did you never remarry?"

Nisha smiled a tight smile. "You cannot marry someone who is already married. I did not want to be responsible for breaking his home." Her head snapped up, face filling with horror. "I didn't mean..."

"It's okay Mum. You don't need to spare my feelings. I know what I did, and it was a rotten thing to do. If I could go back in time, I would never let my heart rule my head. I would not break up Radha's marriage. But all that is moot now."

"Do you think of her, Mira? That sweet young girl from next door?"

"Who, Radha?" Mira sucked in a deep breath. "Constantly." She looked away. "There are days when I think of little else. Funny, isn't it? The people we wrong are the ones who set up residence inside us forever."

"I wish..." Nisha sat down on her work bench again, her face a picture of misery. "Some days I wish I *had* let my heart rule my head."

. . .

❖

School started with little fanfare. Esha had refused all offers of Mira coming in to talk to her teachers. She said she wanted to start with a blank slate, and despite her worry for Esha, Mira was proud of her. Her little girl displayed so much courage and resilience in the face of all the obstacles she encountered. Not once had she ever wallowed in self-pity or blamed anyone for her lot in life. It was this strength that Mira hoped would carry her through life.

Two weeks in, she received a call from Bhumi.

"Final edits are nearly done. I need you to check it all before I send the manuscript to the proofreader."

"Sure. Say, has your friend said anything about Esha?"

"No, she works with the younger students. Why, has Esha complained? Aren't things working out?"

"No, nothing of the sort. She rarely complains, and that's what worries me. I can't tell if the school is a good fit or not."

"Then ask her."

"She doesn't like to worry me, so she's bound to say it's fine."

"Mira, don't stress unnecessarily. If you can't get the info out of her, get your mother to do it. She talks to her, *na*?"

After Bhumi had hung up, Mira wondered when Esha had made her grandmother her confidante over her own mother. What had Mira done to make her daughter wary of trusting her with her doubts and fears?

She opened the fridge to get a cold bottle of water when she noticed the house keys sitting on a shelf. What on earth?

"Abdul!"

The old man came shuffling in.

"Chaabi fridge mein kyun hai?"

Abdul peered inside the fridge, took in the keys, sitting innocuously amongst the tomatoes and the cucumber, and scratched his head. He looked equally mystified.

"Yeh toh Nisha memsahib ki chaabi hai. Unhi se poochna padega."

The keys belonged to Mum. Why had she put them in the fridge?

"Memsahib kidhar hain?"

He jerked his head to indicate the garage.

Mira had already known the answer. After their little chat, it was as if something had loosened inside her mother, and she had gone back to pottery with a vengeance. Every morning she was in the studio before Mira awoke, and she worked late into the evening, coming in exhausted from her labours. Maybe in her fatigued state, she had absentmindedly put the keys in the fridge.

Abdul stood there as if he wanted to say something more.

"Kya baat hai, Abdul?"

"Miraji, memsahib ki tabiyat kuch theek nahin hai aaj kal."

"Kya matlab?"

Abdul seemed to be implying that Mum was not keeping well. She seemed to be in perfect health.

"Bahut cheezein bhoolne lagi hain."

Mum had never been the forgetful sort. Perhaps it was age-related. She was nearly seventy-seven, after all, and even at fifty-three Mira found herself losing her phone or misplacing her wallet. Still, she had never put her keys in the fridge. She resolved to keep a close eye on her mother, just until she had figured out whether it was fatigue, repressed grief or ill health that was making her behave in this uncharacteristic manner.

The letter that had come from America sat on the sideboard for a week before Mira noticed it. No one had mentioned it to her, and it had gotten buried under the post that had arrived since. When Mira finally got around to opening it, it was already the weekend.

Dear Mira,

I'm sorry to be contacting you under these sad circumstances, but I just wanted you to know that Shyam's mother passed away in hospital last month. It's taken me a while to track you down, and it's only because I remembered someone telling me a while ago that you were an author that I managed to find your details. It didn't help that you had reverted to your maiden name. All this to say that I apologise it took me so long to inform you of her demise.

I'm aware you weren't on speaking terms with Shyam's family, but I know Sangita had always wanted them to make peace with you. In fact, I know for a fact that she had urged Shyam to bring you over with him the next time he visited us. I wish I could have prevented the scene that happened at the funeral, but I had my hands full and could not think beyond my own grief. I had lost my spouse and my children, their mother, but so had you. I should have offered you more support. At the very least, I should have stopped Mataji from saying all those cruel things to you.

Towards the end, she often spoke of Shyam. Somewhere within her I think she wanted to reach out to you, maybe get to know her granddaughter too. However, it was not to be. Mataji carried on staying with me after Sangita and Shyam's deaths. I needed someone for the children, and she stepped in and took over. Perhaps it was the only way we could have coped.

Anyhow, I wanted to let you know that she left a little something in her will for your daughter. Some money, a few trinkets, and a gold chain. If you send me the details of your lawyer, I could arrange for the transfer of these items.

Also, if you ever wish to have a chat, I'm enclosing my number. It would be nice for our children to get to know one another. They are family, after all.

Warm regards,

Hari.

Mira set the letter down with shaky hands. After all these years, she had thought the wounds of that period had healed, but they had only scabbed over. The letter had taken her back to that dark chapter of her life. A chapter in which her marriage had been floundering, and she had been thinking of separation, all before finding out that she had lost Shyam to a random attack in an alley of San Francisco. Layers upon layers of grief and guilt had trapped her in a hell of her own making. Then, as she had stood in a *mandir* somewhere in San Jose, she had raised her tear-streaked face to find Shyam's mother glaring at her, rage and anguish radiating from her.

Her clipped accusations still reverberated in Mira's mind. *Badkismat, badchallan aurat hamaara beta kha gayi!*

She was a jinx on the family. She had taken everything from them. She had no intention of taking any more.

Mira tore the letter into tiny pieces and threw it in the bin.

CHAPTER 16

April had given way to a sweltering May. The mercury had shot up unexpectedly and 40 degrees Celsius was not uncommon in the afternoons. Mira was grateful she had installed air-conditioning in all the rooms, or life would have been unbearable.

She thought back to her time in the hostel at Miranda House, back when she had insisted on joining Delhi University, much to her mother's chagrin. In those days, in the absence of air-conditioning, they wore as little as possible and sprinkled water on themselves, taking turns to sit in front of the pedestal fan. How odd that those tough times, and the extent to which her roommates and she had cursed while they lived through them, were some of her fondest memories of her youth.

The more sanitised life had gotten, the blander it had become. Not that she was willing to sacrifice her creature comforts to some nostalgic nonsense from years ago. Yet, she thought back to that time and recalled the sheer naïveté and insouciance of her younger days with a smile on her face.

Then, as was her wont, her mind wandered to Radha. She had not lied when she had told Nisha that she thought of her nearly every day.

Some days she thought of her with regret, her mind tinged with sadness and guilt. She had always considered herself an innately decent person, but that one episode in her life had altered everything, especially her feelings towards herself. She had sacrificed decency at the altar of selfishness, and now there were times she could hardly bear to look herself in the eye.

Other days, she justified her actions by remembering that Radha's marriage hadn't been the happiest to begin with. A downtrodden wife who, many a time, had resented her husband. Hadn't she come running to Mira with sob stories of how ill-treated she was? Hadn't she complained on multiple occasions? Mira had only taken what had not been held tightly or valued enough. A floundering marriage was ripe for betrayal.

Still.

She was not foolish enough to believe her own lies. She was culpable and no matter how much she disguised it with excuses, finger-pointing and protestations, she knew, deep down, the truth of her murky history. Treachery, after all, was treachery, and over time it had taken a toll on her soul.

What she had omitted to tell Nisha was that now, strangely and habitually, she would have internal conversations with Radha. Conversations that always began with, "I'm sorry..."

Mira had never considered herself maudlin, and although she knew of people who spoke to their deceased spouses or parents daily, that had never occurred to her. As far as she knew, Shyam was gone. She didn't believe in heaven or hell, or even reincarnation. Death was final. If anything existed beyond that, it certainly didn't make itself known to the living.

Her private conversations with Radha were precisely because Radha was alive. As far as she knew, she was alive. Wherever she was, she was probably still wading through life, just like Mira was. And so, she spoke to her as she would to a constant companion who had been wounded in the course of the relationship, and said, "I'm sorry for what I did to you back then. I was selfish and in pain, and I took from you because I thought it would ease my suffering. Forgive me, please."

She did not know whether this daily incantation had any effect on the burden of her guilt, but she carried on regardless.

"Did you know," she said as she brushed her greying curls into a topknot, "Esha is really enjoying this new school. She has settled in and made some friends. She's bringing one home this afternoon." Mira looked into the mirror as she applied a kohl pencil to her eyes. "I'm so excited to meet her."

She stepped away and observed herself. How much she had aged in the last ten years. Menopause had not been kind to her as her slim waist had thickened to twice its girth, and her normally supple skin had turned dry and parchment-like, with wrinkles appearing on her forehead and at the corners of her eyes. She had long abandoned vanity, for it served no purpose in her current life, but she wondered how Radha was ageing. Was it with the same delicacy and grace she had possessed while young?

"You were always such a pretty little thing," she said as she blotted her usual brown lipstick on. "Shame that you never saw it."

As she stepped out of her room, she nearly tripped over her mother's sneakers.

"Mum! Why are your sneakers here?" She called out to Nisha, but there was no response. Abdul had gone to the market and Esha was in school. Was Mum in the studio?

She stepped out of the house and peered at the garage. The door was shut, so most likely she was working. With a sigh, Mira picked up the shoes and placed them on the shoe rack outside the main door. Who was it who had said that as parents aged, they turned into teenagers? That was certainly true of Nisha, who had taken to behaving like one, her clothes and shoes strewn everywhere, an unprovoked tantrum not far behind. Sometimes, even Esha seemed more mature than her mother.

Her mind went back to Esha's friend, a girl named Vandana. Esha hadn't said much about her except that they sat together in the classroom and shared their lunches. It was, Mira hoped, an auspicious start. Esha had never really had any friends. Most children either avoided her or bullied her. This had never shaken Esha's composure or self-possession, and she had to marvel at that. A lesser person would have been wary of initiating a connection, but not Esha. Her disposition was such that she remained open to all, kind or unkind. Mira prayed, with all her heart, that Vandana would be kind.

❖

Abdul had made *poori chhole* at Esha's request, and the aroma of the spicy *chhole* filled the entire house. When Esha entered the room with Vandana, Mira saw her eyes light up. Abdul had laid the table and put a few of Nisha's pottery vases with roses cut from the garden in them.

"Mama, this is Vandana," Esha introduced the slim, shy girl standing next to her, who immediately folded her hands into a *namaste.*

"Hello, *beta,* welcome. Come in, come in. You can put your school bags here. Esha, show Vandana where she can wash her hands."

Nisha came in just then, her hands covered in clay. She looked at Vandana, scowled, and left again.

"What's wrong with Granny?" Esha asked, puzzled by her odd reaction.

"I think she's in the throes of a project, and you know how lost she can get." Mira laughed, trying to make light of the situation. Mum's behaviour was decidedly peculiar. She had never been unsociable, not even during a project.

After the girls had washed their hands and sat down, Abdul started serving them hot and freshly fried *pooris.* Mira sat with them, declining her share, saying she would eat later with Nisha. She was curious about Vandana and couldn't stop herself from asking what she hoped were a few innocuous questions.

"How long have you been at Kinara Public School, Vandana?"

"Just a year, Aunty."

"Do you like it?"

"Yes, very much." Vandana nodded enthusiastically while taking another bite of her *poori.*

"You have other friends too?"

"Yes. There's Suchi, Resham and Vinod."

"That's nice." Mira pondered how to ask the next question. "So, umm, how did Esha and you become friends?"

"She's in my art class, and she's so good, Aunty! I saw her sketch of the school fountain and started talking to her." Vandana accepted another helping of the *chhole*, then carried on talking to Esha as if that was explanation enough.

Mira let go of the breath she had been holding. This was how simple friendships were when you were young. There was no agenda, no ulterior motive; there was just an attraction, a kinship based on the most random event or observation. That was all it took. Only adults over-thought the simplicity of friendship.

The girls played in Esha's room all afternoon. Mira went back to working on the outline for her next novel. She was done with sadness. She wanted something happy and uplifting. When she had floated the idea to her agent, he hadn't been impressed.

"Women don't read Mira Dixit's books for laughs. They want to feel, they want to cry. Why do you want to change a formula that works?"

"Firstly, Ishaan, you're implying that my books are formulaic, which I sincerely hope they're not. And if I'm changing tracks, it doesn't mean I'm going to be writing a romcom. That's not what I'm saying here. All I said was that I want to write something that ends on a hopeful note, something that won't put them in the doldrums."

"Okay, now I hope you're joking! Listen, don't veer too far from the beaten path. Write your draft and let's see how it pans out. If it's going to be a hard sell, I'll tell you outright. You know how it works in this industry, Mira. Even the publishers have come to expect one thing from you and won't be pleased if you serve them another."

They had ended the conversation on a tentative deal. She would write her first draft and he would look it over. If it didn't work, she would go back to it until it fit the parameters of what was expected from a Mira Dixit book.

It dismayed her.

Why did life slot you into a category and expect you to stay there? Why couldn't she write different books? Why couldn't she take up a hobby in her fifties, something she had never done before? Why couldn't she let go of the past and focus on the future?

Nisha came in once again, looking tidier than before.

"Mum, you missed lunch. Shall I heat the *chhole* for you? Abdul is taking his nap."

"No, I had an apple earlier." Nisha shook her head as if to clear it. "Where's Esha?"

"She's in her room with her friend. You know, the one you saw earlier, and didn't acknowledge?" Mira raised an eyebrow at her mother.

"Oh yes. You really must teach that poor child to dance. Life is boring without music and dance."

"Eh?"

"Radha." Nisha looked at her and pronounced her statement with utmost gravity. "Teach her to dance, Mira."

❖

Dr Qureshi was most sympathetic over the phone.

"It's likely that she got confused. That can happen in old age. But if you're worried, you can bring her in and I'll run some tests."

"It isn't just that one instance, though. There have been other occasions where she's misplaced stuff, forgotten something I told her only minutes ago, and even her mood swings have been very unlike her."

"Hmmm. Well, it's hard to say anything without checking her, so I'll transfer you back to my secretary and she can book her in."

After she had hung up, Mira wondered how she was going to convince her mother to visit the doctor. Nisha had nearly always been in rude health, and the thought of doctors and hospitals sent her scurrying in the opposite direction. For Mira, hospitals, doctors, and therapeutic centres were par for the course after Esha's birth. In this aspect, they differed greatly from one another.

Despite her concern for her mother, she couldn't help but be thrilled about Esha's blossoming friendship with Vandana. Shy and sweet-natured, it had emerged that her brother was severely dyslexic and had been bullied his entire childhood. It was only at Kinara Public School (KPS) that he had flourished after being diagnosed and given the right support and encouragement. Her brother's plight had made her sensitive to anyone who had been segregated or treated unkindly. Besides, as Vandana had stated most disarmingly, she liked Esha.

One person, one friend, someone who stood by your side and looked out for you, was all one needed in life. Mira herself had had multiple friends of both sexes as a young woman. She had been fêted and admired by many, but as she had gotten older and her life circumstances had changed, she had lost most of those friends along the way. Her circle had shrunk until it only accommodated her immediate family members. Still, as much as she loved her mother, she was loath to call her a friend.

Friends were people to whom you revealed those parts of yourself that could not be presented to the people who had brought you up and had certain expectations of you. She, like Nisha, did not believe that a parent should be a friend. Parents were there to set boundaries, to help nurture and educate a child. It was not their job to become the child's playmate and partner-in-crime as well.

Her thoughts were interrupted by Abdul entering the room with a pile of ironing in his hands.

"Presswalla aaj phir paise maang raha tha."

"Par maine Nishaji ko pichhle hafta paisa diya tha."

What had Mum done with the money she had given for the chap who did the ironing for them? Abdul seemed flummoxed, too.

"Achcha, yeh lo. Tum hi do usko."

She dispatched Abdul with enough money to cover the bill again. After he left, she wandered over to the garage and knocked on the door.

"Mum, can I come in?"

When there was no response, she opened the door and stepped inside. It had been a while since she had been in there, and from the time Nisha had been spending in the studio, she expected to find lots of pottery dotted around as it used to be. Instead, all she saw were unfinished pieces, some cracked, one still on the pottery wheel, and the other waiting to be placed in the kiln, but clearly forgotten about. Nisha was playing with some clay in her hands, a faraway look on her face.

"Mum," Mira tapped her on the arm and waited for a response. Nisha turned towards her, a puzzled look on her face.

"Yes?"

"I've booked an appointment with Dr Qureshi for next Monday at 11am. Just letting you know before you barricade yourself in here, okay?"

"Why?"

"Just for a little checkup."

"For you?"

"No, Mum, for you."

"Why?"

"Just, uh, you know, a checkup."

"Okay."

Her mother went back to playing with the clay.

"Oh, what about the money I gave you for the *presswalla*. He said he hadn't been paid?"

Nisha carried on ignoring her, behaving as if she hadn't heard.

Mira stood there for another five minutes and when there was no further conversation, she walked out, shaking her head. Something was not right. In all these years, she had never seen her mother placidly agree to visiting a doctor. She had never once agreed to anything placidly. Besides, she had always relied on her to pay the sundry bills on time. This was bizarre and utterly out of character. What was wrong with her?

❖

"Dementia? Are you sure?" Mira set her glass of wine down on the table.

"I'm not sure. I'm not a medical doctor after all, but the behaviour seems to suggest as much. My great uncle behaved the same way." Bhumi waved to the server. "Ready to order?"

They had been postponing their dinner for over a month and now, with the book release set for November, Bhumi had insisted they meet before she got swallowed up in her other projects.

"In those days," Bhumi said, after they had placed their orders, "people used to say *sathiya gaye hain*. No one knew what dementia was, at least, not in the little town my family came from."

"What sorts of things did he do?"

"Oh," Bhumi laughed, "one time he took off all his clothes and ran up to the terrace. He later claimed that *Yamraj* had said that was the only way he could ride in his chariot!"

"Who? What?"

"You know. *Yamraj* is the God of Death, and he comes to take the soul with him. Anyway, my great uncle believed he was dying and wouldn't be allowed on the chariot with his clothes on. So, he divested himself of all such unnecessary fripperies." Bhumi doubled up in laughter. "You can imagine how that went down in our ultra-conservative town."

"Gosh!" Mira frowned. Should she have told Bhumi her concerns? This wasn't funny to her. This was her mother!

Catching her look, Bhumi stopped laughing abruptly.

"I'm not making fun of the situation, Mira. I hope you know that."

"It's just that if that's what it is, how on earth am I going to manage? Mum on one hand and Esha on the other."

"That's why we are called the sandwich generation, sandwiched as we are between our parents and our children."

"Your kids are so much older, though, and they've flown the nest."

"You never stop worrying about them, Mira, no matter how far they fly. Anyway, I'm probably jumping to conclusions. There could be any number of reasons she is behaving the way she is. Best to get medical advice."

"You know what struck me the other day?" Mira swirled the wine in her glass. "Mum never, ever liked Shyam. I don't think there was any love lost between them."

"Why are you thinking of that now?"

"It's because I've never been able to talk to her about him properly, and now I probably never will."

"You don't know that. Plenty of time to have that conversation and loads more, too. Don't start imagining the worst."

The tears came unbidden. It was as if a dam had burst inside her, and as Mira wept, she didn't care who saw her or what they thought. Bhumi handed her tissue after tissue wordlessly, sending the server away. She let her cry for as long as she wanted, waiting, watching, not moving aside from pulling out another pack of tissues from her bag. When the tears finally stopped, she called the server over and ordered another bottle of wine.

"When Ajay and I divorced, it felt a lot like a bereavement." Bhumi leaned her elbows on the table. "It was something both of us had wanted, and it wasn't acrimonious in the least. Still, having lived with someone for over half your life binds them to you in invisible ways. I used to miss seeing his slippers by the bedside, the ashtray full of his cigarette butts, even the dirty underwear that always landed short of the laundry basket. It isn't easy to let go of someone you loved, but sometimes, it is absolutely essential."

She leaned back and sighed.

"You can talk to me about Shyam, if you like. I know it's not the same as confiding in your mother, but I'm here all the same."

Mira pushed the sodden tissues to a side and gave Bhumi a lopsided smile. She knew Bhumi meant well, but she only knew half the story. Revealing the rest of it meant revealing a part of her life that hadn't seen light in over a decade. The only person who knew her dark and shameful secret was Nisha, and if she was slipping away from her too, then that secret would have to remain buried within Mira until her dying day.

"When is her appointment at the doctor's?" Bhumi asked, looking at the menu.

"On Monday. I just hope she doesn't dig her heels in on the day. She's got nearly a week to change her mind, and she was unusually compliant about going, which worries me."

"Cross that bridge when you get to it."

"How do you find coping with elderly parents?"

"Not easy. Mine don't live with me, but I can tell you, as far as they are concerned, I am no older than ten. My father still insists on correcting everything I say, and my mother still packs me food to take home when I visit."

"They sound nice."

"Oh, they are. They're also annoying, want the last word in everything and refuse to accept that I did a pretty good job with my sons. But I love them and wouldn't change them for the world."

"And your sons?"

Bhumi seemed to understand her question without her expanding on it.

"One lives in Sweden and the other one in Dubai. We are close and we talk every day, but who knows how long that will last?"

"Why?"

"You know that old saying: a son is a son till he gets a wife…"

"A daughter is a daughter her entire life," Mira finished for her. "Do you believe that's true?"

"Who knows? Only time will tell. For now, I'm glad I'm employed, self-sufficient, and healthy. I don't rely on my parents or my children, and worst-case scenario, I don't hesitate to call upon Ajay."

"You're still friends with him?"

"Of course! We are divorced, but we don't hate each other. In many ways, we are still family. Just a family that chooses not to live with one another."

"You're lucky," Mira said, thinking how aside from Nisha, she had no family left.

"No, I've just made the best out of a situation that could be perceived as bad. You need to do the same, Mira."

❖

"Mum, wake up! You need to get ready."

Mira tapped her mother's arm, but Nisha stirred a bit, muttered something and carried on sleeping.

"Come on, Mum, Esha has been looking forward to today."

Nisha finally opened her eyes and looked at Mira.

"What?"

"The movie, Mater! Remember?" Then Mira bit her lip. Did her mother remember?

"Oh, that! No, I don't think I'll come today. It's not my kind of movie."

They had planned to see Frozen II for a while. Why hadn't she mentioned this before?

"Mum, Esha will be disappointed if you don't come. We were planning to get some lunch before the film and make a day of it."

"You go. I want to finish something today. I'll explain to Esha." Her mother closed her eyes once again and went back to sleep.

Mira shook her head and walked out of the room. Another thing she needed to bring up with the doctor was this recent ennui her mother had been displaying. Nisha had always been vibrantly involved in life before, excited to be trying new things, actively pursuing new interests, happy to mingle with people of all ages. Now, she seemed to be retreating from life, preferring her own company, at times being wholly reclusive and antisocial. Could all of this be attributed to dementia, as Bhumi had surmised, or was there something else at play here?

Esha was disappointed but still excited to have a day out. In a way, Mira thought it would be nice to chat to Esha on her own without having to worry about Mum.

Abdul dropped them off at Select City Walk Mall, where Mira offered Esha the choice of pizza or Tex Mex, knowing full well that she would choose the latter. As they sat down with their tacos and fries, Esha pointed excitedly towards the right.

"Look Mama, there's Pari ma'am!"

Mira looked in the direction and saw Mrs Upadhyay chatting with another lady. She looked away before they saw her staring.

"That's nice, honey, but it's rude to point. She is enjoying her Saturday, just like we are. We should leave her to it."

Esha pouted. "But I wanted to say hello."

"Maybe later, hmm? I'm sure she wants to spend some time with her friend without being disturbed."

Esha shrugged and went back to her taco. They chatted about school, and she seemed happy and excited, and Mira let go of all her misgivings. This had been the right decision, after all. It was about finding a school which was a good fit for Esha and KPS clearly was.

"Mama, what's wrong with Granny?"

"What do you mean, darling?" Mira paused, setting her French fry back on the plate.

"She's so grumpy these days, and she didn't want to come out with us today."

"She was just tired, baby. I'm sure she's okay, but I'm taking her to the doctor on Monday." Mira crossed her fingers under the table, hoping it wasn't anything serious. She did not want to lie to Esha, but equally, she did not want to worry her. Not until Nisha had been examined. Then, if there was cause for alarm, she would have to find a way to break it gently to her.

Just then, she felt someone stop at their table.

"Hello Esha!" Mrs Upadhyay stood by the table, beaming down at Esha.

"Pari Ma'am!" Esha jumped up and ran to hug her.

Mira stood up as well. She smiled at the slender woman standing next to Pari Upadhyay, who smiled back and said, "Pari has fans everywhere."

Mrs Upadhyay gently disengaged Esha's arms and said, "I'm sorry. I didn't mean to interrupt your lunch. I just spotted Esha and thought I'd say hello before leaving."

"That's alright. Esha spotted you first, but I stopped her from coming over to you. It's your day off, and I didn't want you to be bothered."

Pari laughed. "Never when it comes to my favourite students." She winked at Esha before introducing her companion. "This is Dr Madhu

Yadav, my childhood friend. She is so hard to pin down that whenever I can, I hijack her for the day. We're just heading into PVR to see our movie now."

"What are you watching, Pari ma'am? We are going to see Frozen II!" Esha piped up.

"Not that!" Pari laughed again, and they both waved as they left.

Mira watched the two women walk out and felt her heart clench. Repeatedly, she was reminded of how lonely her life was without a good friend. But those were her circumstances, and she had no right to complain. She had been given a beautiful daughter, a mother who loved her, enough wealth to cushion all her excesses, not that there were many, and a career she enjoyed immensely. People would give anything to have a half of what she did. Besides, Bhumi counted as a friend, didn't she?

Esha yanked at her arm. "Stop daydreaming, Mama! Finish your lunch. Our movie is going to start soon."

Mira rolled her eyes, sighed dramatically and stuffed the last of the taco into her mouth. Frozen II, it was.

Abdul was waiting in the car park for them and as soon as he saw them exit the mall, he ushered them towards the car.

"Memsahib theek hain?" Mira asked as a matter of course.

Abdul plucked at his eyebrow and looked away from her.

"Kuch ajeeb hi rahin hain aaj poora din. Khaana bhi theek tarah nahin khaaya."

So, Mum had been behaving oddly all day long. Her appetite had been iffy the last few months, and while Nilufer Aunty's barb about her weight gain had wounded her, it wasn't like she had set out to diet her way to slimness. After Yasuda Shōji's death, Mum had started eating more than she ever had before, as if she was burying all her emotions in food. Mira understood that all it was, was comfort eating. She had done the same after Shyam's murder. Over time, though, she had realised that pouring her emotions into the books she wrote was far more cathartic than going through a bag of sweets. Mum, she thought, would eventually figure this out too. But this sudden loss of appetite was alarming. What was going on with her? What had changed so dramatically in the last few months?

More things to tell the doctor. Tonight, Mira intended to make a list of all her symptoms and lay it out in front of Dr Qureshi. She wanted to get to the bottom of whatever was wrong with Nisha. Once they had a proper diagnosis, they could figure out how to proceed.

In her heart of hearts, she worried it was dementia. She had been reading up on it, and so much of how Mum had been behaving had fit in with the symptoms. She couldn't bear to lose Nisha in this way. An erosion of her memories and her faculties, becoming indistinguishable to herself, forgetting her loved ones. Oh, she couldn't bear it!

"Mama, you look worried." Esha noted from the seat next to her. "Is it about Granny?"

"No, darling," Mira lied smoothly, "I was just wondering what we should do for dinner. I told Abdul I'd pick something up."

"Let's get biryani, Mama. Granny likes it too, and can we have gulab jamun for dessert?"

"Alright," Mira laughed as she directed Abdul to Biryani Blues in Hauz Khas Village. A slight detour wouldn't matter too much, and Abdul could do with a break from the kitchen.

On their way there, they chatted about the movie.

"I liked it, but it was quite sad in some places." Esha said, biting on her inner cheek. She looked so young at that moment, and Mira felt her heart clench again.

"Life's like that though, isn't it, darling? Happy and sad. We just have to get through the bad bits to get to the good ones."

Esha nodded gravely.

"Are you happy at this school, babushka? You were very pleased to see your teacher today."

"Yes, I'm happy Mama. I got through the bad bits." She grinned cheekily, and Mira laughed in response.

Three quarters of an hour later, Mira was regretting her decision of fetching biryani from Hauz Khas Village. She should have gone nearer to home. They were caught in a typical Saturday evening traffic jam. How could she have forgotten how busy it got on the roads in the evening? Her lack of a social life had allowed a complacency to creep into her movements, and she had completely obliterated the horrors of Delhi's traffic from her mind. Now she was paying for her forgetfulness.

She tried calling Nisha's cellphone, but there was no answer once again. Honestly! Why had she bothered to buy her mother a phone if she never ever answered it?

She tried the landline, which kept ringing without response as well. Where was Mum?

Then a horrid thought entered her mind. Could she have wandered out of the house, gotten confused and lost her bearings? She had read of cases like that. Not that Nisha had ever done anything like that, but there was always a first time. She scrolled through her contacts and found the neighbour's number. The phone rang for thirty seconds before Mr Singh answered.

"Hello? Mr Singh, it's Mira here. Mira Dixit? From next door."

"Yes, yes. How are you, *beta*?"

"I'm okay, Uncle. Please could you do me a favour? Could you just pop over next door and check that Mum is okay? She's not answering the phone and I'm getting worried. We are stuck in a traffic jam here."

"Of course, *beta*. I'll call you back in a few minutes."

Mira rung off and stared out of the car window. She felt Esha's hand on hers.

"She will be okay, Mama. Sometimes she falls asleep with the TV on. Maybe that's why she didn't answer the phone."

Mira gave Esha's hand a squeeze, and her little girl gave her a reassuring smile. It felt strange to be receiving reassurance from her thirteen-year-old. Shouldn't Mira have been the one providing it?

Her phone rang, and Mira answered immediately.

"Hello. Yes?"

"*Haan beta,* I rang the doorbell a few times, but no one answered.

The lights are on and I can hear the television, so your mother must be inside."

"Ah," Mira breathed a sigh of relief. "She is a little hard of hearing and occasionally falls asleep in front of the television. Thank you so much for doing this, Uncle. Sorry to bother you."

"No bother at all. Come over to us sometime. Bring your little girl with you. All our grandchildren are settled far from Delhi now, and Mrs Singh misses them a lot."

Mira thanked him and assured him she would come over soon before hanging up. The traffic started moving at the same time, even if it was at snail's pace.

"You're right, baby. Granny's probably asleep with the TV blaring."

They got home nearly an hour and a half late. The biryani had gone cold, so Mira instructed Abdul to heat it and serve it with some homemade yogurt.

While he parked the car, she unlocked the front door, wondering if Mum had awoken yet or not.

"Mum! Sorry we're late, but I bought us some lamb biryani for dinner."

She walked into the living room and saw that 'Sholay' was playing on the screen, with Amjad Khan threatening his henchman with a pistol. His famous dialogue of "*Kitne aadmi the?*" had just come on. Nisha was so absorbed in the film she didn't even turn around to acknowledge them. Esha went skipping over to her.

"Granny, look what Mama got me!" She had already pulled out the sparkly hairband Mira had purchased in the mall when suddenly she stopped short and stared.

Mira discarded her bag and shopping on the side table before going over to where her mother was seated on the sofa.

Nisha's eyes were open in a fixed stare, her head leaning against the headrest. She sat in her usual spot, her back to the door, her face to the television. On the screen, a gunshot rang out, but she did not react, did not jump out of her skin as she usually did, before collapsing into giggles. Her eyes were devoid of all animation and emotion.

Mira sank down next to her mother, touching her cold, lifeless hand, before moving her palm to her cheek and tracing the contours of her face. With one finger, she moved a strand of Nisha's hair away from her face and tucked it behind her ear. With the other hand, she reached for the remote and shut off the television. Then, gently and with great deliberateness, she allowed her head to rest upon the chest that had nurtured her, listened to her woes and protected her all her life. She strained to hear Nisha's familiar heartbeat, but all she heard instead was a never-ending silence.

CHAPTER 17

Grief had once again sledgehammered its way into their lives. Along with grief came her old friend—guilt. How she had been dreading a diagnosis of Mum's condition; how worried she had been that Nisha would slowly slip away from her. Then the fates had laughed at her fears and snatched her mother away in one fell swoop. There! Take that!

Pain had rendered her insides raw. She could not cry; she felt choked up with a strange indefinable mixture of emotions. Sleep had deserted her, and she spent nights sitting amongst Nisha's pottery pieces, studying them, running her hands over them, trying to understand her mother's state of mind in her final days.

A part of her laughed inside. This is what you get, it said, when you are selfish and fearful. You are not half the woman your mother was, it mocked. She took care of you against all odds, and the thought of taking care of her had already put you in a state of anxiety! Your mother did you a favour, didn't she? She left early because she could not bear the indignity of being in your care.

Why didn't the tears come?

All that remained was a cupboard full of Nisha's pottery, and a heart filled with self-recrimination.

"A subarachnoid haemorrhage isn't as uncommon as you'd imagine," Dr Qureshi had explained, "particularly in older women."

Her mother had become a case study explained away in medical jargon. It hurt to think of her being alone in her last moments, in pain and unable to call out for help. Biryani! What had possessed her? What need had there been to get biryani? Why hadn't she hurried home? Why had she even left?

Mr Singh and his wife had been incredibly kind. They had taken over so many of the preparations, from organising the cremation to the prayer meet. Then Mr Singh had asked her, "What would you like to do with the ashes?"

"I want to keep them," she had said, the words coming from some deep, inexorable need to hold on to her mother's remains.

"Ashes aren't holy," a *pundit* had pronounced, horrified at the thought. "Take them to Benares, or to Kashi. What did your mother believe in? Was she Hindu?"

Nisha believed in everything and nothing. She was agnostic. How could she explain this to the small crowd that had congregated at the prayer meet? Some of them were the men and women Nisha had learned pottery alongside, under the tutelage of Yasuda Shōji. Most of them had spoken of her in reverential terms. She was very talented but so unsure of herself. This was another Nisha, a woman Mira did not recognise. They talked of their times together, how they missed Nisha when she stopped coming to their monthly gatherings.

"Why?" The question had tripped off her tongue before she could stop herself.

"After Shōji san's death..." They had murmured amongst themselves, avoiding looking her in the eye.

She knew, she wanted to scream! It wasn't a crime to love someone; it was only a crime if it brought unhappiness in its wake. Nisha had never allowed that to happen. She was a better woman than Mira could ever be.

Round and round, the thoughts circled in her mind like vultures feasting on the carrion of her memories. She sleepwalked in the day and submitted to sleeplessness in the night. Days melted into each other, every hour just a reminder of everything she had lost. When was the last time she had told her mother how much she loved her? When was the last time she had shown her any appreciation or gratitude?

Why was life cruel enough to snatch someone mid-conversation? *I wasn't done talking to her*! She wanted to scream and scream until she had no voice left. Instead, all she could do was wander helplessly through the house, touching the things that Nisha had touched, feeling her way through the darkness that surrounded her, that threatened to set up residence inside her.

A month after Nisha's death, Abdul came to her while she sat next to the kiln, staring into its blackness with unseeing eyes.

"Mira*ji*?"

Her head felt heavy as she turned to face him.

"Esha baby *khaana nahin khaa rahi*."

She turned away from him. For the first time in her life, she did not want to face the responsibility of her daughter. Buried as she was under the weight of her own misery and guilt, she had barely spared Esha a thought. If it hadn't been for Abdul who fed her, Mrs Singh who dropped in to spend time with her, and Vandana, who called upon her, Esha would have been completely adrift.

A few letters had arrived from the school, but she had left them unread upon the dresser. She did not care, not anymore. Her heart could only house wretchedness, and yes, anger.

She was angry with Shyam once again. Angry at his abandonment of her, angry that she had no one to lean on, angry because she no longer had the strength to carry on. She was angry with Keshav, too. Livid at his treatment of Nisha, of his desire to keep Mira with him in his latter years, his selfishness, his egocentric behaviour that allowed for no one else but himself. Yet, the generosity with which he had treated her was completely at odds with the image she had built up in her mind.

She was confused, too. The same confusion she had felt after Shyam's death, when card after card had announced its sender's sorrow, one card in particular, from some woman whose grief-stricken note had conveyed more, far more, than she had perhaps set out to.

Who were these people—her mother, her father, her husband? Were they even people she knew? What masks did those closest to you hide behind? Could one ever really understand anyone, truly?

"Mira*ji*?" Abdul stood at the door, staring at her.

"Kya?"

"Aap kuchh toh boliye bitiya ko. Uska gham koi kam nahin hai..."

She raised her weary eyes to his red-rimmed ones and nodded, hoping he would leave her in peace, but he just stood there, waiting for her to get up and go console her daughter. Didn't he see it? She was incapable, unworthy, not fit for purpose, not as a mother or as a daughter.

Slowly, she stood up, holding on to the table for support. She followed him inside, allowed him to lead her to Esha's room, and when he had left, closing the door behind him, she looked at her daughter as one would a stranger.

"What has it been? Six weeks?" Bhumi had dropped in unannounced, only to find Mira wandering around in her nightie at five in the evening.

"Yes," Mira sighed, thinking it was actually six weeks and four days, but she did not have the energy to correct her.

"And you haven't left the house in all that time?"

"Everything I need is here." Mira looked at the cup of *chai* and the thin film of cream forming over the brown liquid. When had Abdul placed the tea and biscuits in front of them? She had no recollection of telling him.

Bhumi set down her cup and saucer and cleared her throat.

"Where is Esha?"

Mira gave her a blank look before remembering that Esha was next door.

"With the neighbours. Mrs Singh has taken a shine to her."

"How is she coping?"

"Huh?"

"Has she spoken about her grandmother? After all, it must have been quite a shock for her, too."

"No, she hasn't said anything." Mira omitted the fact that she had not asked either. For the first time in thirteen years, she did not know what to say to Esha.

"Right, I'm taking you to my ashram to meet Swami*ji*. I think you need someone to talk to you, someone who can get you out of this slump you're in."

Mira waved her suggestion away.

"I'm fine. I don't need to see any Swami."

"You're clearly not fine, Mira. You've got dark circles under your eyes, your cheeks are hollowed out, and when was the last time you bathed?"

"Bhumi, please..."

"No! You can't carry on like this. I won't allow it. Now, listen, Chandan, my son who was in Sweden, is moving to Australia. He wants us all to visit and help him set up home. I'm applying for visas and will be taking my parents with me. But before I leave, I want to see you back on your feet."

Bhumi's words barely registered. Everything was white noise now. With Mum gone, she felt as though her feet were no longer on solid ground. Life had developed a hazy quality, as if she was looking at it through a translucent veil. She was drifting through her days now, no longer aware of the time or date, or the reason she was alive.

"I'm picking you up at 9am sharp. Be ready!" Bhumi's parting words sent a strange fear coursing through her. Who was this Swami and why was it so important she met him?

❖

A simple man in a plain white *khaadi kurta*, someone it would have been easy to ignore on the road if he walked past you. Yet here, hundreds of people had thronged to meet him. Unlike the pompous self-aggrandising charlatans she had often seen on television, he appeared almost shy. He didn't want his feet touched; he didn't even want the garland they insisted on placing on him.

"This is why I like him," Bhumi whispered to her. "He's not in it for the money or the fame. All he wants is to impart an age-old message to these millennials and all the various alphabetically named generations."

In any other circumstances, Mira might have laughed at her joke, but today all she felt was resentment. She had been forced to get out of bed early, even though she had barely slept; forced to shower and change; and forced to come out here to the outskirts of Delhi to visit a man in his ashram. What good was going to come from it?

She had known that it would take far more energy to argue with Bhumi rather than just succumb to this one morning. So she had complied, however unwillingly, to this fool's errand.

Today the talk was about tolerance and forgiveness. Using the Bhagavad Gita as his template, the Swami spoke into the microphone, his voice soft and melodic.

"Tolerance will teach us to face all the hardships life presents with equanimity. If one can remain calm in the face of difficulties, then that time will soon give way to better prospects. In tolerance, we also learn that we must desist from using force, even when provoked. A higher soul must practise forgiveness. *Kshama virasya bhushanam.* Forgiveness is the ornament of the brave..."

Mira looked around at the rapt faces of the men and women seated around her. The coir mat was digging into her thigh and she shifted her weight to the other side, half-listening to the Swami, allowing his voice to wash over her. She had read her fair share of religious texts when in school, but as a lapsed Hindu, while aware of the mythology, she had never allowed it to impinge upon her daily life. But here was a man translating the impenetrable Sanskrit into accessible homilies intended to be understood and adapted to modern living. The writer in her could not help but be impressed.

The talk lasted an hour in which several questions were asked of the Swami. He answered them in parables, which often left the audience puzzled initially until he arrived at the answer. Then all became clear. Who was this man? Where had he come from?

At 11am when the temperature headed into the thirties and it became much too warm to continue, he stood up, bowed his head and gave them all a *namaste,* before heading indoors.

"Home now?" Mira asked, turning towards Bhumi, who had covered her head with a white scarf.

"Soon, but first, let me take you inside."

"Inside?"

"Don't you want an audience?"

"A... what?"

Bhumi had already started walking towards the building, and Mira followed her, swimming against the tide of the people heading towards the exit.

"Bhumi! Wait." She caught up with her and held her arm. "How can we go inside? They won't let us. I saw all the guards surrounding him."

"Of course they will. I've known the Swami for a very long time, and he will not refuse me."

"But...but... what am I meant to do?"

"You leave all that to me." Bhumi spoke briefly to a man at the entrance, who nodded his head and stepped aside to admit them.

Inside the large room, a ceiling fan rotated slowly above them, the slight breeze ruffling the mustard curtains drawn shut to keep the mid-morning heat at bay. The Swami sat on a green *divan* surrounded by a small group of people who had been allowed entry. Bhumi sat down next to an elderly woman, gesturing for her to sit as well.

One by one, the people went up to the Swami to speak to him. To some, he only listened and then gave them a single marigold flower in blessing. With others, he spoke in a low voice, placing his palm on their foreheads before they moved away.

The devotees sat in silent anticipation, their eyes fixed on the Swami; their reverence of him reflected on their faces. The only sound was the rhythmic rotation of the ceiling fan and the soft murmur of the Swami's voice.

Time seemed to pause in the room. The outside world, with all its noise and chaos, felt far removed from the proceedings within the sanctum. Here, in the presence of the Swami, amongst all the other devotees, Mira felt an unnerving calm descend upon her as she waited patiently alongside Bhumi.

Twenty minutes later, it was their turn.

"Swami*ji*," Bhumi bowed low, her palms together.

"*Kaisi hain aap*?" His voice was as soft as before, and his eyes remained on Bhumi.

"I've brought my friend to see you, Swami*ji*. She has faced tremendous losses in her life. She was widowed young and just recently she lost her mother. I am worried about her Swami*ji* as I think she isn't processing this loss well. She has a young daughter to care for and needs to be present for her."

Throughout her speech, the Swami's eyes remained on Bhumi. When she had finished, his gaze moved to Mira. The first words he uttered to her were, "You are angry."

Discomfited, she lowered her own gaze. She *was* angry! How dare Bhumi drag her out here to humiliate her in this manner? What gave her the right to lay bare all of Mira's sorrows in front of this stranger?

"Sit, my child."

The kindness in his voice stopped her train of thoughts. She focussed on him once more.

"Do you know the story of Garuda and the little bird?"

She shook her head. If this was yet another parable, she wanted to check out right now.

"A long time ago, Lord Vishnu decided to visit Lord Shiva in his abode on Mount Kailash. While he was inside conferring with Shiva, his mount Garuda, the eagle, who was waiting at the entrance, spotted a beautiful little bird sitting on a rock."

The Swami cleared his throat and immediately someone appeared at his left elbow, holding a glass of water. He smiled and offered it to Mira instead. She took it and swallowed the contents in a gulp.

The Swami carried on.

"Just then Yamdev appeared and stared at the bird in wonderment. Garuda understood the bird did not have long to live, as Yamdev is none other than the God of death. While Yamdev went inside to talk to the Gods, Garuda, in a fit of mercy, picked up the little bird in his claws and dropped it off in a forest thousands of miles away."

The Swami paused and gazed at her. Mira couldn't take her eyes off him. There was a radiance emanating from him that made every word he uttered sound as if the very Divine was communicating through this ordinary man.

"When Yamdev came outside, Garuda asked him why he had stared at the bird in that wonder-struck manner. Do you know what he said?"

Both Mira and Bhumi shook their heads.

"He said that he had seen a vision of the bird being eaten by a snake in a forest thousands of miles away, and had wondered how the little bird could possibly fly there so quickly."

Mira clutched Bhumi's hand.

"You see, my child, death is unavoidable. So, no matter how much it pains us to accept it, we must. *nāsato vidyate bhāvo nābhāvo vidyate sataḥ |ubhayor api dṛṣṭo'ntas tv anayos tattva-darśibhiḥ.*"

The Swami took a deep breath before saying, "The body is corporeal, finite and perishable. The soul is infinite, indestructible, and eternal. Why do you grieve for something that can never die?"

Was her mother still alive? In some other realm, in some other form, was she looking down on Mira, despairing at her daughter's unrelenting grief? The Swami's words continued to reverberate in her mind. She had no intention of becoming his devotee, but a part of her understood the wisdom and kindness of his message. Hindus had always believed in reincarnation; in the body being just a garb to be discarded once a lifetime was completed. Did she believe it, too? She wasn't sure. Yet, it gave her a certain comfort to imagine her mother's soul unfettered from its earthly bonds, free to soar above them all, light as air, no longer subject to any of the sorrows that had punctuated her existence on earth.

Bit by bit, she allowed herself to mourn her mother. It started with her waking up to find her face awash with tears. Then sleep came. Hours and hours of deep, intoxicating slumber where not even dreams could interrupt her rest. Then, a decision to clear out the garage, and make it a storeroom for her mother's pottery, which Mira would hold an exhibition of, just as Mum had planned. If this was Mum's legacy to the world, it would not be forgotten. This was her silent vow to her mother's soul, a promise she would not break.

As she traced her fingers over the exquisite pieces of pottery Nisha had once worked upon, she allowed her grief to declare itself in the tears that flowed down her cheeks, matching the rhythm of the rain drumming against the earth outside. Who could say how much time remained for anyone? There was no visible clock ticking above your head indicating the end was nigh. And yet, so much of that precious time was squandered in anger and dispute, or lost in the fog of indifference and disregard. In the end, all that lingered was a haunting *if only...*

The Swami's words had gone a long way towards stemming the tide of *if onlys* she had been submerged in. Yes, she had lost Nisha. Then again, she had not, not really. Nisha lived on—through her art, through her daughter, and through her granddaughter.

Esha!

It was already the middle of July and the grim realisation of her utter neglect of her daughter slapped her in the face. How could she have abandoned Esha in all of this? She ran out of the garage looking for her. Where was she? Then she realised she was probably in school. It was 10am already.

Mira sighed and went back to her own room. She looked at herself in the mirror. Who was this unkempt, grey-haired, gaunt woman staring back at her? Enough was enough. It was time to pull herself together and be the mother Esha needed, and give her the love and comfort she so desperately required from her.

That afternoon, as she waited for Esha to come home from school, Mira went back to the manuscript she had been working on. Was it too simple, too childish, too romanticised? She had wanted joy to be the main theme of this novel, but could she write about happiness in her current mood? She put the manuscript away. First, she needed to make things right with her daughter. Only then would she return to her writing.

When Abdul brought Esha home from school, she flung the door open to greet her. Esha looked at her in surprise, then walked past her without saying a word.

"Esha?" Mira followed her, only to have the door to her daughter's bedroom shut firmly in her face.

Abdul came inside, carrying Esha's lunchbox and flask. He said nothing either as he set them down in the kitchen and poured himself a glass of water.

Mira felt marooned.

"Baby *kaisi hai*?" She lingered in the doorway, not incognizant of the irony of asking Abdul about her daughter's welfare.

"Chhup hai."

Silent. Uncommunicative. Was this Esha processing grief in the only way she knew how?

Mira went back to Esha's room and knocked on the door.

"Darling, can Mama come in?"

When there was no response, she turned the handle, relieved to find that the door was unlocked. She let herself in. Esha was sitting at her desk, sketching. Mira went over to her and put her hand on her head.

"How are you, baby?"

Esha carried on sketching, behaving as though she hadn't heard her.

"I..." Mira started, then stopped. How could she explain herself to a thirteen-year-old girl? What could she possibly say that would absolve her?

"Mama hasn't been there for you, baby, and I'm so, so sorry. I... it just happened so quickly...and I...I didn't know how to handle it."

Esha carried on sketching.

"Please, Esha, talk to me!"

Her words fell on deaf ears.

"Esha! Look at me!" Mira cried out.

Esha put her pencil down slowly and turned her face towards her. Her eyes were blank, her face expressionless. Mira put her arms around her and wept, all the while trying to infuse her embrace with the depth of her remorse. Esha remained stiff and unyielding.

"She doesn't speak to me anymore, she's shut down completely!" Mira watched Bhumi rummage through the pile of export-rejected clothes in Janpath as she stood next to her, sipping on her cold coffee from Depaul's. In her youth, she remembered having to finish the coffee standing outside the store because the glass bottles needed returning. Now, they could wander away as the coffee was also being served in plastic bottles. Not great for the environment, but the coffee was so good that every time Mira visited Janpath, she had to stop here for one.

"Are you surprised?" Bhumi remarked while picking out a cotton shirt and bargaining expertly with the vendor. "You pretty much abandoned her over her entire summer holidays. Did you even know where your daughter was half the time? If it hadn't been for your kindly neighbours, she might as well have been an orphan!"

"Yes, of course I know I was a terrible mother! But I'm trying to make it up to her." Mira protested, watching Bhumi pay the vendor as he handed over the packet containing the shirt to her.

"Mira, sometimes you are such a child that I wonder how you write the books you do." Bhumi repositioned her handbag on her shoulder and indicated they walk further to another kiosk. "Firstly, you haven't addressed her grief, and secondly, you broke her trust. Now, she dare not confide in you because she doesn't know if you'll pull a disappearing act again. Rebuilding that trust will take time. Start with just being consistently present for her in every way. When she sees you are back to being the mother she knew, she will go back to being the daughter she was."

Could it really be that simple? Mira had been trying to do all of that for the last month, but had only been met with stony silence all along.

"When are you leaving for Australia?" She asked, changing the topic for a bit.

"Early next year, if all goes to plan. I'm trying to get my parents sorted alongside, and I can tell you, that's a job and a half."

"Are they excited to be going abroad?"

"My mother is, but Papa just keeps complaining. He's worried they won't have his medication there. I've told him over and over that I'm taking more than enough for six months, but does he listen?"

"Six months is a long time," Mira said dolefully. It had only just sunk in that Bhumi wouldn't be around to vent to or confide in. She had no other real friends and she could hardly expect Abdul to take Bhumi's place, stoic and dependable though he was.

"I'll be back before you know it. Say, Tripta said something to me the other day, and I clean forgot to mention it to you."

"What?"

They had stopped in front of another stall selling all kinds of junk jewellery and as she watched Bhumi sift through the various chunky metal necklaces; she tried recalling who Tripta was. It came to her in a sudden flash. Tripta was the teacher who had recommended KPS for Esha.

"What?" she repeated, trying to catch Bhumi's attention.

"Oh yes, she said that the school had been trying to contact you for a while and you hadn't responded to any of their communication."

Mira thought back to the past few months and a vague recollection of some letters and phone calls came back to her.

"Right," she nodded. "I've not really opened any of my correspondence for the last couple of months."

"Understandable, but irresponsible. What about your bills?"

"Abdul takes care of all the main stuff."

"Mira, much as I envy you your Man Friday, all this is your responsibility. Besides, the school correspondence could be urgent. If you want to get through to Esha, maybe you need to figure out what's going on with her at school?"

Mira swallowed the lump in her throat. Was this a repeat of Esha's previous school experiences? Was she being bullied again? Had Mira only been seeing half the picture?

Bhumi tapped her on the arm and said, "Lunch?"

❖

Keeping Bhumi's words in mind, Mira kept trying to inject a false bonhomie into all her interactions with Esha, but it fell on deaf ears.

"Say, baby, what do you want to do for your birthday? I was thinking we could go for lunch and a movie? Would you like that?"

Esha shrugged and went back to her book.

Mira observed her daughter. In a few days, Esha would turn fourteen. She was no longer a little girl who came running to her mother for every minor scrape she got into. Esha had already started developing a healthy sense of independence before Nisha's death, but now, the distance between them was less about independence and more about hurt and disillusionment. What could she do to make it up to her child?

"Why don't you call Vandana over? Maybe we can go to Dilli Haat for some shopping instead of a movie? What say, babushka?"

"Don't call me that." Esha looked up, her face severe.

"Oh." Mira swallowed. "Okay, I won't. But what do you think, Esha?"

"I'll ask her."

That was all she got out of Esha, and much as she wanted to press for more, Mira knew it wasn't the right time. She had let her daughter down when she needed her the most. Forgiveness would be a long time coming.

Indeed, even Abdul had withdrawn from her, keeping his conversations to a minimum. She wanted to laugh at her luck. She was being given a dose of her own medicine, as unforgiving as she had been to most people in her life. From Keshav to Shyam, she had meted out coldness when annoyed, been difficult to placate or appease, and here she was, at the receiving end of the same from the two people who comprised her world right now. Irony did not even cover it.

❖

On Esha's birthday, as planned, they went to Dilli Haat. Vandana had said, "Aunty, why don't we eat there as well? There are so many food stalls, and it will be nice to sit outside, won't it?"

Mira had gone along with the suggestion. It was late September, and the weather had finally turned more pleasant. Abdul had driven them to Vandana's house, and once they had picked her up, he had driven straight to Dilli Haat. On the way there, Vandana had chatted away to Mira, who was sitting next to Abdul up front, occasionally directing a comment towards Esha, who remained silent mostly.

"Oh, look Esha," Vandana rummaged in her bag, pulling out a large, wrapped present. "I nearly forgot! Happy Birthday."

Mira watched Esha's expression in the wing mirror of the car as she unwrapped the present carefully. The delight on her face was unmistakable as she pulled out a large sketchbook and colouring pencils.

"I hope you like it?"

"Yes," Esha beamed at Vandana, "I really, really do."

As they wandered past the various stalls selling trinkets and jewellery, skirts and sarees, displaying the wares of artisans from all over India, Mira wondered if Esha's reticence was only directed towards her. In Vandana's company, she seemed happy, albeit slightly withdrawn.

As Esha carried her masala dosas back to the table while Mira paid for the food, Vandana looked up at Mira and said, "Aunty, can I say something to you, please?"

Before she could say any more, Esha was by her side, helping to carry the rest of the food back to the table.

They ate in companionable silence, and when Mira asked if they wanted any dessert, both girls nodded enthusiastically. At that moment, Esha became her old self, happy and carefree. It wouldn't last, but just a glimpse of it was enough to assure Mira that she was on the mend.

Later at night, much after they had dropped Vandana home, and she had tucked Esha into bed, Mira wondered what Vandana had wanted to say to her. Was it important? She had looked worried as she had asked Mira her question. Was it something to do with Esha? She intended to find out as soon as possible.

In early October, Mira finally picked up the large pile of letters accumulating on the sideboard and sorted through them till she came to the three letters emblazoned with 'Kinara Public School' on the envelope. She took her letter opener and sliced through the envelopes, retrieving the letters within. The first two letters were just standard format ones inviting her to meet with the principal of the school to discuss her child's progress. The third one seemed more urgent. This one had come from Mrs Upadhyay, the same teacher Esha and she had bumped into on the day Nisha had died.

Dear Mrs Dixit,

I am deeply sorry for the sudden loss of your mother. This must be a very hard time for your family, and all of us at KPS send you our heartfelt condolences.

You might have received a few letters from the school inviting you for an informal chat. Mr Upadhyay did not want to alarm you, particularly at this sensitive time, hence he kept the letters deliberately short. However, as we haven't had a response from you, may I once again urge you to come in at your earliest convenience?

Please could you ring the office and arrange for an appointment with Mr Upadhyay? If you like, I could be present at the meeting too. As you have probably surmised, this is to do with Esha. Once again, please don't worry, but do set up that appointment. We would like to discuss certain issues with you.

Yours Sincerely,

Mrs Upadhyay.

Mira checked her watch. It was much too late to call now, as school had already finished for the day. First thing tomorrow morning, she planned to set up a meeting.

She heard Abdul parking the car outside and moments later, Esha entered, carrying her large knapsack on her back.

"Hello beautiful!" Mira sprung up from her chair and took the knapsack from Esha before planting a kiss on her forehead. Esha moved away, not acknowledging her or the kiss. She heard her go into the kitchen and open the fridge. Mira sighed. How long would this silence carry on?

That evening, the doorbell rang. It was Mrs Singh carrying a container of *saag* with some *makki rotis* wrapped in foil.

"Esha loves *saag*," she said by way of explanation. "I thought I'd bring some over as I haven't seen her at all this week."

"Do come in," Mira said, hoping she could glean some information from the older lady. Maybe Esha had confided in her?

Over *chai,* they chatted about Mr and Mrs Singh's grandchildren. The ones settled in Singapore and also the ones who lived in Hyderabad.

"It must be hard being so far away from your children, and their children?" Mira asked, still immensely grateful for the kindness this neighbourhood couple had displayed towards her and Esha.

"It is the way of the world. Long gone are the days when families lived together. Our children wanted nuclear families, and then they pursued their careers and their dreams wherever those took them. We can't blame them. We educated them to have ambition, to aspire for a better way of life. So, that's how it is."

There was something reassuring about the lady's calm acceptance of her lot. Then Mira asked what had been uppermost in her mind all along.

"Has… has Esha talked to you about my mother and her death?"

Mrs Singh looked startled by her question.

"No," she shook her head, "she hasn't said a word. She enjoys coming over to play with my little dogs, Pepsi and Coco. I enjoy watching her play and try to make some of her favourite foods. It reminds me of my grandchildren. But no, we haven't talked about her grandmother."

"Oh," Mira responded, crestfallen.

"Don't worry," Mrs Singh patted her hand. "The young are robust. They bounce back a lot quicker than we can imagine."

The next morning, Mira rang the school and was surprised to get an appointment for the same afternoon. All morning her mind had been conjuring up various awful scenarios that could have happened to Esha. Clearly, the Principal and his wife were eager to talk to her. What could be that urgent? It had to be something bad. Something that she, wrapped up in her own misery, had failed to see.

Abdul drove her, and she noticed how taciturn he was of late. He did not engage in the easy conversations that had been their habit before. Something had shifted after Nisha's death. Was he annoyed with her about Esha, or was it because he did not feel the same loyalty towards her that he had towards her mother? Mira resolved to keep quiet. She did not want to provoke a walkout by him. He was the glue holding their family together, and she could not afford to lose him, especially not at this juncture.

At school, she was ushered into the quiet waiting area outside of the Principal's office and offered tea while she waited. She declined politely, tapping her foot, unable to hide her impatience. Now that she was here, she couldn't wait to hear what they had to say to her. Whatever it was, she prayed to Nisha, wherever in the Universe she was, that she would give Mira the strength to bear it.

Ten minutes later, she was called into the office. Mr and Mrs Upadhyay were seated at the small settee together and they rose in unison to welcome her in. Sitting down in the armchair across from them, she marvelled at the couple so in tune with one another that unconsciously they mirrored each other's actions, too.

Mr Upadhyay spoke first.

"Thank you for coming in to see us. I was planning to phone you this week if you hadn't arranged a meeting."

He looked at his wife, waiting for her to fill in the rest.

Mrs Upadhyay tucked a stray hair behind her ear before looking Mira in the face and saying, "We have reason to believe that your daughter has been harming herself."

"Pardon?" Mira's entire body jerked involuntarily.

"I'm so sorry, I realise that this must come as a huge shock to you, but, uhhh," Mrs Upadhyay paused, her eyes filled with worry, "Esha has been cutting herself."

"What?! How...how?"

"One of her friends spotted it and came to us about it."

"Spotted? Cutting? I... I don't understand!" Mira looked at them both, fear and confusion spilling into her words.

"Sometimes young people cope with pain by inflicting more pain upon themselves."

"But I would have noticed! Cutting? Where? How?" Mira couldn't believe what she was hearing. Her little Esha harming herself? How was that possible? Was someone just telling tales? Was this even true?

"Her friend said she cuts herself on her thighs, which is obviously hidden by her school skirt. But at some point, this girl noticed and asked her about it. Esha confessed to her, but swore her to secrecy. Fortunately, the child was smart enough to go to her mother with the information, and the mother contacted the school."

"Is this child Vandana?" Mira clutched at the only clue she could make sense of.

"We really can't divulge the identity of the child, but suffice to say that we are worried, and have been wanting to talk to you directly about it."

So, it was much worse than the bullying she had suspected. How had she not noticed? What kind of mother did not pick up on signs of self-harm?

Mr Upadhyay carried on.

"As we hadn't heard from you, we put our school counsellor on the case. It took a while, but Esha has finally started responding to the counselling sessions."

"That's good." Mira sighed, worrying at the tassel on her bag. "Has she said anything to this counsellor? Has she spoken about her grandmother? Is there… is there anything I…I…could help with?" She stuttered to a halt.

"Well, that's another reason we're glad you set up the meeting today. You see, we believe that if any progress is to be made, it has to be done with the two of you working in conjunction. Clearly, Esha hasn't been coping with her grandmother's death, and perhaps you could help fill in the blanks as to her behaviour at home. Miss Arora, the counsellor, believes that Esha has internalised the emotional distress so much that it is overwhelming her. She is keen to meet you and talk about how to proceed."

As if on cue, there was a knock on the door and Mr Upadhyay said, "Come in."

A slender, bespectacled woman in a lavender *salwar kameez* entered the room, file in hand.

"Tina, we were just talking about you. This is Esha's mother, Mrs Dixit. I'm sure you'd like to fill her in on your observations."

Mira's gaze locked with the woman's soft brown eyes, and her heart lurched. She was older, as evinced by the fine wrinkles at the corners of her eyes, but her girlish charm had barely altered in the last two decades. She wore her hair in a long plait that reached her waist. Her fingers were devoid of any rings, and aside from a thin gold chain and small gold hoops, she had no other adornment. This wasn't the picture Mira had held in her mind for over two decades, but it was her. There was no doubt it was her.

Her assessment took less than a minute, in which she saw her own shock mirrored on the face across from her. How quickly they had recognised one another, after all these years!

The encounter Mira had dreaded for over twenty years had come to fruition in the most unexpected circumstances. Once again, she stood face to face with Radha, the woman she had betrayed all those years ago.

Somewhere in her bones, she had always expected this moment. Only, she had never quite known what she would do when it arrived.

CHAPTER 18

In all the scenarios that had run through her mind in the years past, none had featured her sitting across from Radha, pretending she did not know her. With the tiniest, almost imperceptible shake of her head, Radha had instigated the pretence. Mr and Mrs Upadhyay had understandably put Mira's shocked expression down to the news she had received about Esha, as she remained speechless while Radha sat on the other armchair, setting the file down on the table. No matter what she was thinking, Radha's composure was admirable. Not even a tremor betrayed her turmoil, while Mira's own body was beset by an uncontrollable trembling that could not mask the maelstrom of emotions within her.

"I think I'll get some tea," Mrs Upadhyay looked at her husband meaningfully, while rising to fetch the tea.

"Would you like some time alone with Miss Arora?" Mr Upadhyay asked, rising to his feet too.

"No!" Mira's voice came out louder than she had intended, and, startled, he sat back down.

"I...it's just..." Mira stammered.

"It's best if you stay Upadhyay Sir," Radha cut in smoothly. "Mrs Dixit needs the assurance that we are taking this seriously, and also the fact that we will respect her privacy. As head of the institution, you should be here."

"Very well." Mr Upadhyay nodded, his face grave. "I won't interrupt, but if you need any information from me, please don't hesitate to ask."

Radha turned towards her and picked up the file.

"I have met Esha a handful of times after we heard of her self-harming. At first, she refused to talk to me. I let her draw as I'd heard how well she sketches, and these are the sketches she produced in the first few sessions."

Radha opened the file and took out a few A4 size sheets and passed them to Mira. The first sketch was a heart that had been furiously scratched over and over again until only the mere outline of the heart remained. In the second, a man seemed to be walking away, his face slightly turned to the back as if he was saying something. The third was a replica of the sketch Esha had made of the three of them, with the white spaces in between, except that this time the space between the third figure and the other two was far greater than before.

"I asked her to explain what these sketches meant. The only thing she said was that when people left, they did not return."

"Oh," Mira gasped involuntarily. This was more than she had had out of Esha in the past few weeks.

"I understand that Esha lost her grandmother a short while ago."

"Yes," Mira whispered, unable to look Radha in the eye.

"I'm sorry for your loss."

Mira looked up at Radha and saw genuine sorrow in her eyes. Did she remember Nisha? They had met so many years back, it seemed almost a lifetime ago.

"And her father?" There was the slightest quiver in Radha's voice, slight enough to be undetectable.

"He... he died too."

"I see." Radha's voice was calm now. "Esha has suffered a lot of traumas, and it's no wonder she is acting out. You see, self-harm isn't just about inflicting pain, it is also about control. This is the one thing she can control when everything else in her life has spiralled out of control. *She* decides how much pain she can endure and this cutting is a release of everything, all the hurt, distress, and trauma that is pent-up inside of her."

"How can I make it stop?" Mira looked Radha in the face, just for a moment forgetting their past, and appealing to her as a mother would.

"There is no making it stop. If you confront her, she will find another way. You need to support her in this healing journey, and that will involve sessions of counselling with me where we can unpick all the things that have led her here."

"Does she need to see a psychiatrist?"

"No, I don't think we're at that juncture yet, but if it ever comes to it, I'll be the first person to tell you. Meanwhile, I'd like to have a few more sessions to gauge her state of mind."

"What..." Mira's voice shook. "What can I do to help?"

"First, keep this meeting to yourself. I'd like her to open up to me voluntarily without feeling any pressure from you. Second, just as we will, you need to keep an eye on her. If the self-harm escalates, then an intervention might be required. In the meantime, let us take this one step at a time."

Mira nodded, trying to absorb the import of her words.

"May I ask Mrs Dixit, has Esha been communicative at home?"

"Uhhh...I..." Mira shook her head and swallowed. "I'm afraid I... I was emotionally unavailable after my mother's death, and...and... I failed her when she needed me. She hasn't spoken much to me since Mum's death."

"I see." Radha set the file down on the table. "A mother is a child's mainstay, and you have lost yours. Don't blame yourself, but please, give *your* child all the love and solace she requires. It is not easy being isolated in your grief, and Esha is a particularly sensitive child. I imagine that her condition has set her apart most of her life, and the only thing she has counted upon is your unconditional love. If that is withdrawn, however justified the circumstances may be, it can shake the very foundation of her existence."

Later, as Mira ruminated over the meeting, aside from Radha's soft voice and the import of her analysis, all she remembered were her delicate fingers fluttering over the file like filigree butterflies.

❖

"Will you come with me?"

"Oh, Mira, I can't," Bhumi groaned. "There's too much to do, and we leave for Australia in a few months' time. Go on your own, why don't you? It'll be good for you."

"Will he see me if I'm not with you?"

"As far as I know, he hasn't been granting audiences lately. So, you could just go for the talk."

"But I really wanted to meet him!"

"Okay, I'll call ahead, but no promises. If he doesn't grant an audience on the day, he won't make an exception for anyone."

"Thank you."

"No problem. Now, listen, did you read the email the publishers sent you? I was cc'd in."

"No? When was this?"

"About two or three days ago."

"What's it about?"

"Your book launch has been pushed back to early next year."

"Why?"

"Some celebrity book has taken precedence again."

"I can't believe it!"

"I know, Mira, but those are the rules of the game."

"They don't even write their own books! It's all ghost writers."

"And you think the general public cares? Anyway, consider yourself lucky as you are still one of the star writers in the stable, so they haven't pushed it back too much. The poor first-timers keep getting pushed farther and farther back."

"Yes," Mira sighed, "those are the rules of the game. I just wish the game could be disrupted, you know?"

"I think that's coming, but that's a chat for another time. I really need to go now. Loads to do."

"Bhumi, I'll miss you!"

"Stay in touch. Not like you can't FaceTime me. It's only Sydney, not another planet!"

"I know, but..."

"Mira, you're a lot tougher than you give yourself credit for. Take care of yourself and take care of that sweet daughter of yours. This time is precious. Before you know it, she'll be all grown up and you'll wonder where the years went."

Mira blinked back her tears.

"When you come back, I'd like to talk to you about some stuff from my background."

"Important?"

"Yes, but not over the phone."

"Very well. I can't wait to hear it. Now, I really must go!"

After she had hung up, Mira wondered why she needed to unburden herself to Bhumi? Was it because she was finally willing to come clean about her past? Had seeing Radha triggered something she had been suppressing for all these years?

She still hadn't examined her feelings about Radha. It had been such a shock to come across her, and that too, under such difficult circumstances, that she had been thrusting it away from her thoughts for days now. How long could she avoid it, though? Radha was Esha's counsellor. She was also someone Mira had wronged so grievously all those years ago. Like it or not, she would have to address her past offences. But not before she took some guidance from the Swami.

Mira got to the ashram early, but still found herself in the fifth row, seated behind a group of elderly women who chatted incessantly. Her head was pounding. She hadn't slept all night, and it took every ounce of her willpower not to scream *"Shut Up!"* to the women. As before, *khaadi* clad boys walked around, passing out small bottles of water. A tin container with a 'Donations Only' sign was placed on one side of a small table. She had seen people dropping all sorts of denominations and currencies in there.

While she waited, she fanned herself with a flyer she had picked up at the entrance. The days had started turning cooler in early November, but today was unseasonably warm. She took off the shawl she was wearing and placed it on her lap, looking around her. Most people had come in groups, but there were also couples and families dotted around. She didn't spot any single women around her. Once again, she wished Bhumi had come with her, but handling the travel for two elderly parents and the temporary packing of two different households was understandably keeping her occupied.

Mira examined the flyer she had picked up at the entrance and that she had been fanning herself with. The Swami was going on an all India tour, and it showed all the places and dates he intended to be. Not bad for the modest little man she had met. He didn't seem the sort to seek fame, but maybe fame had sought him out. He was certainly very well known now, judging from the flyer and the swell of people around her. How thirsty people were for wisdom and guidance in their lives!

At exactly 9am, the Swami came out with his entourage following at a respectful distance. He placed his palms together in a *namaste* and bowed low before sitting cross-legged on the elevated platform. One of his guards lowered the microphone and tapped into it, nodding at the Swami to proceed.

"Today," the Swami said, his voice as evenly modulated as Mira remembered, "I will talk about *Karma*."

All the humming and buzzing, the idle chatter in the audience stopped, and the only thing she could hear now was the rustle of the leaves as a gentle breeze blew through them.

"Most people think that *Karma* is the collective result of past action. What they fail to realise is that every action we perform is *Karma*. Your being here, your listening to me, perhaps imbibing some lessons are all *Karma*. So, today, we will broadly speak about the concept of *Karma phal*, free will and destiny."

Mira leaned forward to focus on the Swami's speech.

"When we talk of destiny, we often feel that it is a result of our *Karma* from a previous life, which completely negates any free-will we may have had in creating this destiny. In fact, while destiny may well be the *Karma phal* or the fruits of our previous actions, we still have the capacity to choose our present actions. Those actions which I shall call *Purushartha* are a combination of choice, self-effort, and freedom. While we may not change that which has occurred before, we can mitigate that which is to come by following a life of *dharma*—a life filled with ethics and morality, which leads to inner refinement. Our goal, after all, is *moksha*, that transcendent state of being released from the cycle of birth and rebirth."

The Swami's words washed over her like a healing balm, soothing the turmoil inside. Mira bowed her head and allowed her eyes to close, listening, absorbing, understanding some of what he said, and storing some away to ponder upon later. She had never considered herself religious, but now, here, in the presence of what she believed was a channel of divinity, she allowed herself to be submerged in the spiritual messages that flowed from the simple man on the stage before her.

When the talk ended, he stood up, bowed, and once again joined his palms in a *namaste* before being ushered back to his quarters. Mira leapt to her feet, determined to gain an audience with the Swami. Several people thronged towards the building, and she felt herself being carried along in the crowd. The door remained shut in their faces until a burly guard came out and informed them brusquely that the Swami would see no one that day.

"Please," Mira called out, "Bhumi Chattopadhyay had called on my behalf..."

The guard looked at her and shook his head before reentering the room and shutting the door behind him.

Twenty-odd people waited patiently, but when there was no movement, they slowly started drifting away, until there was just Mira and a tall, slim American woman who leaned against a tree, her eyes unmoving from the door the Swami had disappeared behind. A half hour went by, and it became clear that the Swami would not change his mind. Sighing, Mira slung her bag on her other shoulder before starting her walk back to the entrance of the Ashram.

"Wait!" The American woman called out to her. "May I walk with you?"

Mira nodded, waiting for her to slip her sandals back on. She was wearing a brown T-shirt and printed harem pants with a *dupatta* hanging off her rucksack. Her feet were dusty and her toenails were painted a neon pink. She was attractive in a world-weary way. Her dirty blonde hair was pulled back in a loose ponytail, and her skin had the over-stretched look of someone who had had a facelift some time ago. Judging from her appearance, this woman was no stranger to cosmetic enhancements. Yet, in her careless manner of dressing, her lack of makeup, her simple rucksack, she looked as though she was deliberately eschewing the accepted image of beauty which she may have subscribed to previously. She couldn't have been much older than Mira, but in some ways, seemed decades older.

"I'm sorry," she said. "I just wondered if I could share a taxi with you. It's impossible to get transport from here to the city." The woman gave her a half smile, which Mira responded to.

"I have my driver waiting outside, so I won't be needing a taxi, but I could give you a lift to somewhere you could get a taxi from."

"That's great! Thanks." The woman beamed at her and they walked out together. "So, have you been coming here long?"

"This is only my second time," Mira said, glancing at the woman. "And you?"

"My first time, and I was desperate to meet him in person. I'd heard, of course, that he doesn't do that anymore. The price of fame, I guess."

"Oh, I have met him in person not that long ago, but that was because I was with a friend who has known him from before all this." Mira waved her hands at the expanse of the land. "Honestly, I don't think it's him. It's the people around him who are controlling his movements, and I suppose they want to monetise it all."

"Not surprising! Religion is big business."

Mira fiddled with her bag strap. "What the Swami said wasn't exactly religious… it was more spiritual… more about how we ought to be living our lives."

"No, I'm sorry that came out as a criticism. I didn't mean the Swami. I think he's wonderful. In fact, I was in Kerala at a yoga camp and that's where I heard about him, so I changed my plans and headed here before going home."

"Where are you from, originally?"

"Originally?" The woman laughed. "Minnesota. But I live in San Francisco now. Have you been?"

"Once," Mira swallowed the lump in her throat, "a long, long time ago."

It was a strange journey. From dropping her off at the nearest taxi stand, Mira changed her mind and asked Abdul to drop the American woman off at her hotel.

They spoke of life, of love and loss, of men and relationships, and what being a woman in the 21st century meant. Hefty topics that Mira had never really spoken about to anyone except perhaps Nisha. Even there, she had always felt the weight of Nisha's judgement. Here, she was free from all constraints, speaking to a stranger she was never likely to encounter again.

Now, they spoke about their relationship statuses.

"I've given up on men," the woman called Mandy said, twisting a silver ring on her index finger. "They brought me nothing but unhappiness."

"Oh, I completely get that," Mira laughed. "I swore off men a decade ago."

"Are you divorced?"

"Widowed."

"I'm sorry!" Mandy stared. "Was it an unhappy marriage?"

"No, not exactly. But it wasn't what I had expected it to be. I was married before, and in that marriage, I could be myself intellectually. In my second marriage, I lost myself for a while. I became another woman, someone I wasn't terribly proud of." Mira took a deep breath and looked outside the window, before turning back towards her. "What about you?"

"Married and divorced three times, two long relationships and one abortive one. I guess I'm like you in some ways. I kept trying to find myself in all these different ways with all these different men. It's taken me this long to realise that I really needed to look within for whatever was lacking."

"Did the Swami's words help?"

"In some ways. I wish I could have spoken to him personally, though. Maybe another time..."

When Abdul parked outside the entrance to the hotel, Mandy leaned forward and gave Mira a hug.

"If you're ever in San Francisco, look me up." She scribbled her number on a scrap of paper and pressed it into Mira's hand before exiting the car. Then she turned and waved once before slinging her rucksack over one shoulder and entering the hotel through the large glass doors.

After they had dropped Mandy off at The Maurya Sheraton, Mira wondered at the enigma of life. Had Shyam been alive, Mira and Esha would likely have been living in San Francisco, too. If they could have worked through the problems in their marriage. Would she have been on a spiritual quest then? Would she have encountered this woman Mandy with her insatiable curiosity about India, yoga and the Swami? Could they have struck up a friendship? Would Mum still have died in the way she did? And Esha? Would Esha have been happier, more well-adjusted than she was now?

If the Swami was to be believed, and she truly wanted to believe, then none of it mattered. Everything was *Maya.* Life, as they experienced it, with all their material possessions, their joys and sorrows, their triumphs and losses, their attachments and bereavements, was nothing but an illusion. The only reality was one's attachment to the divine.

With that thought floating in her mind, she lay down on her bed and pulled the quilt over her. Abdul had pulled out the *razais,* their Jaipur quilts, from storage, and as she breathed in the familiar musty smell of it, she allowed it to lull her into a deep afternoon slumber, filled with strange half-dreams of *khaadi* clad men and laughing American women.

When she awoke, it was still light outside, and Esha's body was curled around her. Mira did not dare move. It had been months since Esha had lain next to her; months since she had even allowed her to touch or caress her. What had brought about this change?

She listened to her daughter's deep breathing and felt her heart swell with love. Perhaps she was still a novice in this journey of self-realisation, but her love for Esha was far greater than her love for anyone who had come before, or could possibly come after. It was pure and deep, unconditional and abiding, and despite her temporary lapse, it was as close to the divine as she would ever experience in her lifetime.

In the early years of their marriage, Mira often woke before Shyam. She would lie next to him, observing him sleep, marvelling at the serendipity that had brought him into her life, pushing aside the guilt that inevitably followed. She would look at his face and try to memorise every feature, from his slightly down-turned mouth to the eyebrows that met gently in the middle. Shyam was a very handsome man, and it was his striking good looks that had first attracted her to him. But what had made her succumb was his utter and complete adoration of her. Which woman could resist a man so hopelessly in love?

Yet, even back then, she had tried to restrain herself, tried to reason with him, tried not to capitulate. Until she had. How could she explain this to Radha when all there was, was *fait accompli*? She hadn't just broken Radha's trust, she had broken her heart. And today, in the grandest of ironies, Radha was mending hers. Little by little, Esha had started responding to Mira. A word here, a fond glance there, and Mira understood that the counselling was having its effect.

She dared not address the cutting with Esha yet. Things were still too tenuous and fragile between them, but she was acutely aware that the healing was being provided by the very person she had all but destroyed.

If Shyam was to be believed, Radha had accepted her fate with a grace and fortitude that was almost heroic. He had said that she had understood his love for Mira and his desire to be with her. In some ways, he believed she had even forgiven him.

But what of her? Had Radha found it in her heart to forgive Mira as well? Theirs had been a short-lived but intense friendship, one in which Mira had tried to empower the diffident young woman, tried to make her realise her own worth. Yet, in the deception that had followed, she had also stripped Radha of her confidence, her value, and her happiness. If it were Mira, this had happened to, she would have never been forgiving.

"Mira*ji*?" Abdul stood in the doorway to her study.

"*Haan,* Abdul?"

"*Aapse kuch bolna tha.*" He looked sheepish as he announced his intention to tell her something, and her heart dropped.

"*Kya?*"

"*Hum kuch maheene apne gaon jaana chahte hain.*"

Oh, that was all! At once, Mira realised that in the aftermath of Mum's death, she had completely forgotten to give Abdul his annual leave. Now he was requesting that which was his due, and her momentary panic was far from justified.

"Sorry, Abdul. *Mein bhool gayi thi. Aap kab tak laut ke aogey?*"

Abdul looked down at his feet and shuffled them.

"*Soch rahe the do maheene baad.*"

Two months! That was a lot longer than his usual one month leave. Maybe he saw the shock on her face as he hastened to add, "*Waapas zaroor aayenge, bas kuch zameen baichnee thee.*"

Abdul had land he wanted to sell? This was news to her. As far as she was aware, he had been homeless and penniless when his son had turned him out. Once again, people never failed to surprise. Then, almost as if he had read her mind, he said, "Nisha *memsahib ne paise diye the zameen ke liye.*"

All at once, Mira's eyes filled with tears. Mum had helped Abdul buy the land. She had probably wanted to ensure his financial future, so that he would have a nest egg for his retirement. Another side to her mother that she had failed to recognise during her lifetime.

What qualities had she inherited from Nisha? When she examined her own life, all she saw was selfishness, anger and a disturbing tendency to assume the worst of people. Was this Keshav speaking through her genes? Could she ever rid herself of the father she loved to hate?

"*Haan, aap* ready *ho jao. Mein* manage *kar loongi.*"

After Abdul had left, happy to have been granted his leave, Mira sighed and sat back in her chair. As a fifty-three-year-old woman, was it too late to change herself? She wanted to be kinder, more forgiving, less prone to annoyance and irritation. She wanted to be an example to Esha. As the Swami had said in his talk, "Self-awareness is the first step towards improvement."

She was ready to take that first step.

❖

Mira swallowed convulsively before knocking on the door. The thudding of her heart was so loud she was scared it could be heard outside of her.

"Come in," the soft voice called out, and Mira turned the handle to enter Radha's office.

"Mrs Dixit, please take a seat." Radha waved to the sofa in front of her.

The room had an inviting energy. It was done up in pastel colours, muted lavender and blue, with soft curtains that billowed in the breeze the open windows let in. Radha herself was dressed in a pale green *churidaar kameez*, and once again, her hair was in a long plait that hung down her back. She was seated in a blue armchair, a file on her lap. The wire-rimmed glasses she wore gave her person a serious aspect, and when she looked up at Mira, her face was devoid of any expression.

Mira sat across from her, placing her purse on her lap, tucking her hands under it to hide their trembling.

"It's been over a month since we met last, and I wanted us to compare notes on Esha's progress. Can I begin by asking if you've noticed any changes in her behaviour at home?"

"I..." Mira started hoarsely, then cleared her throat before proceeding, "Yes, I have. Esha is a lot less angry with me. She is speaking more and telling me quite a lot about school again. Vandana has started coming over once more, and I hear them giggling together in her room, which had all but stopped after Mum's death. So, yes, there has been progress, and I wanted to thank you for it."

"Please," Radha took her glasses off and pinched the bridge of her nose, "it's my job."

"Radha," Mira began, but was interrupted by the file being slammed down on the table between them.

"It's Tina," Radha said, steel in her voice.

"Yes, I'm sorry, so it is." Mira looked at her and looked down at her lap again.

"Mrs Dixit, while I understand that there is a shared history between us, I don't think this is the time or the place to discuss it. I am here in the capacity of Esha's counsellor and my job is to make sure that I can help her navigate and make sense of this difficult time in her life. As I said before, we must work in tandem to ensure that we equip her with the skills needed to overcome trauma in a healthy fashion, however long it takes."

She sighed and placed her spectacles back on, then picked up the file and flicked through it. Mira mentally berated herself for her slip-up. All these years she had only thought of the young woman she had known and betrayed, as Radha. This woman, sitting across from her, was not the shy, self-effacing young neighbour she had once made friends with. She was different. Life and circumstances had given her an undeniable solidity. While she still appeared delicate on the outside, she was robust and spirited. This was no shrinking violet, no Radha giving up her Shyam with a resigned stoicism. This was Tina, a professional and accomplished woman, well aware of her position in the world. A part of Mira felt proud of her, of how far she had come. Another part quaked at the thought of what this Tina thought of her. How the tables had turned in the last two decades.

"...and little by little, she is talking about her childhood and her grandmother."

Mira focussed on Tina's words now.

"What has she been saying?"

"I am not at liberty to discuss our conversations, but rest assured that for the most part, she has had a happy childhood. There is someone called Hugo that she talks about. Some sort of father figure?"

"Yes, uhh, that was my father's partner. He was a very kind soul, someone who took a lot of interest in Esha when she was little."

"Is he still a part of her life?"

With a guilty lurch, Mira realised that the last letter she had sent Hugo was nearly two years ago.

"After my father's death, Hugo moved back to Munich, and while we have had an intermittent correspondence, that has petered out in the last few years."

"In this day and age, surely it is easier than ever to keep in touch. Do you not phone one another, or WhatsApp?"

"Hugo is a bit of a technophobe and after Keshav, my father's death, he has also become a recluse. I've tried inviting him to India several times over, but he was reluctant to come, I think, because of Mum." Mira realised how frail her excuses sounded. It was true that Hugo had been everything that Keshav wasn't to Esha. While Keshav had taken on the financial burden of them, it was Hugo who had given them both the sort of love and nurturing they had required after Shyam's murder. How could she have forgotten that?

"Esha misses him far more than she lets on. It might be an idea to reestablish contact with him for her sake. If he isn't willing to come to India, maybe you can visit him in Munich?"

"Yes, I will write to him straight away. I never intended to let all these relationships wither. It just happened." Mira brushed her hair away from her face and looked at Tina.

Tina looked back at her impassively.

"Otherwise, we have talked about death, and how important it is to recognise that while it is a reality for us all, it does not mean that our relationship with the departed has died, too. If we carry on nurturing the love in our heart, the person will remain alive to us for the rest of our days. I have asked her to keep a diary and jot down little notes, do her drawings, write about whatever she feels like. Journaling could potentially be a part of the multi-faceted therapy she requires. We are also looking at mindfulness and distraction techniques alongside Talking therapy and CBT. It is a long road, but Esha has shown that she is willing to apply herself, and I have no doubt that the healing will occur given enough time and patience."

Mira nodded along, listening to Tina's soft voice explain her daughter's situation to her.

At the end of the half hour, when Tina stood up to indicate that the meeting was over, Mira looked up at her and said, "Please meet me for a coffee. We need to talk."

CHAPTER 19

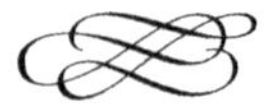

"Mama?" Esha's voice penetrated the fog of her sleep.

Mira opened her eyes, trying to focus on her daughter, who stood at the foot of the bed.

"Are you okay, Mama?"

Mira sat up, felt dizzy, and fell back on her pillow.

"I'm okay, darling, just tired. I was working late last night."

"On the new book?"

"Yes, just doing some outlining for the next part. Are you ready for school?"

Mira observed Esha openly. She looked so much happier now, her cheeks had a healthy glow, and she had taken to talking about Nisha once again. 2019 seemed to have been a turning point for her, and Mira knew that much as her own love and remorse had gone a long way towards making amends, it was actually Tina who had wrought the real change.

"Abdul is just making my sandwich. Mama, can I go to Vandana's house after school? Will you pick me up in the evening?"

"Yes, of course, baby. Just text me the address, will you? Oh, wait, has she asked her parents if it's alright with them?"

"Yes, Mama," Esha rolled her eyes, "she wouldn't have invited me otherwise!"

After Esha had left, Mira closed her eyes again. She was so exhausted from last week. The book launch had gone well, and the early reviews had been positive. Bhumi, frazzled as she was from organising her trip which was only a few days away, beamed at her, saying, "You did it!"

Yet, there was a niggling feeling within her that there was so much more to be said, so much more to be atoned for, and the only way she knew how was through her books. Her stories were her catharsis. Her words were her penance and her reparation.

This constant state of exhaustion and ennui bothered her. She had always been robustly energetic, and suddenly, finding herself so enervated was a strange and disturbing phenomenon. Mum's death had sapped her of so much, but she knew she needed to regain her former self. Somehow, she needed to find the energy within her to be there, to be present for her child. She had let her down once, she would never let her down again.

In all of this, though, the marvel was seeing Esha going back to being a normal teenager, who slammed her door, rolled her eyes and thought all the adults around her were imbeciles. If Mira hadn't encountered the quiet and withdrawn Esha of the past few months, she may not have had any patience for her present avatar. Time and again she counted her blessings, knowing that this change had been wrought at the hands of Tina.

She had tried making a conscious decision to separate the Radha of the past from the Tina of the present. It helped to think of them as two distinct entities, one who had yearned for her to be a part of her life, and the other who had not responded to any of Mira's overtures.

When Mira opened her eyes again, it was nearly 1pm. She sat up, alarmed. Reaching for her phone, she punched in a number.

"Hello?" The gravelly voice on the other end sounded irritated.

"I'm sorry! I know I said 8am."

"It's okay, you are only half an hour late."

"How are you?"

There was silence on the other end.

"Hello? Hugo?"

"Lonely, Mira. I am very lonely."

"Come to India. I'll send you a ticket. Just come. Esha will be so happy to see you. She hasn't stopped talking about you since your last conversation."

She could hear the pleasure in his voice when he said, "She is a young lady now, Mira. I am so happy you called all those months ago, you are the only family I have left."

Mira swallowed the lump in her throat.

"All the more reason to visit us. Hugo, I could arrange for a wheelchair and that will make it easy for you. Please consider it."

"I will."

Even as he said it, Mira sensed instinctively that he wouldn't. If they were to see Hugo, it would have to be in Munich.

"And Esha? Has she stopped hurting herself?"

Mira remembered his surprise when she had told him about Esha's cutting. It had seemed incomprehensible to him that a young girl would harm herself in this manner.

"I think so. I've checked discreetly while she's been asleep, and haven't seen any fresh cuts, just the scars of the old ones. Of course, I got rid of all the razor blades covertly as well. I really hope we've put all that behind us, but I don't want to be complacent about any of it yet."

"You know, Mira, in our time, we drowned our suffering in alcohol and drugs. None of this cutting business."

"Think about it, Hugo. That's also a kind of self-harm, isn't it?"

"Yes, I suppose it is." He coughed a bit, cleared his throat, then asked, "How are you? How did the book launch go?"

"I'm fine, just a bit under the weather. The book launch was good, and the last I heard, the book is selling well. Time for a bit of a breather. But now, my help is planning to take a couple of months off, so I've been looking for a temporary maid to replace him."

"Ah, yes, you are lucky to have all that help in India."

"Could you not get someone in to help you? Maybe a cleaner?"

Mira figured Hugo was probably in his late seventies now. How difficult it was for him to manage on his own!

"Yes, yes." He dismissed her idea and changed the subject once again. "You know, when Keshav was alive, he enjoyed having staff around the house. I could not bear it. All I wanted was a little family. People I could cook for and look after. When you and Esha came to stay with us, it felt like I finally had that. Now, that seems like an eternity ago."

"I guess I never said a proper thank you for those years. I was still so angry…"

"You were grieving."

"Hugo?"

"Yes?"

"How well do you think you knew Keshav?"

"How well? We lived together for over thirty years. I think I knew him well enough."

"Did he confide in you? Tell you all his secrets, his plans, his wishes for the future?"

"Why do you ask me such odd questions?"

"Oh, I don't know. I've been pondering this a lot lately. Whether we ever really know the people we love, or whether something separates the reality of us from the reality of them?"

"I don't understand any of what you are saying, but like Keshav always said, you think too deeply. That is why you are a writer. All I can say is that whatever I knew of Keshav, with all his, how do you say it, 'warts and all'? I loved him, and I know he loved me, too. I wish you would allow yourself to recognise that no matter what happened before you were born, or after your parents' divorce, your father loved you in his own way."

Mira shook her head, then realised that Hugo couldn't see her.

"I am trying, Hugo. Forgiveness has never come easily to me, but I am trying. I suppose, in my own strange, idiosyncratic way, I loved him too."

❖

Mira insisted on driving Abdul to the railway station despite his protestations. She could not bear the thought of the old man fighting his way on and off DTC buses, and knew that even if she had given him the money for a taxi, he would not have used it for travelling in comfort. What she saw as a necessity, he viewed as a luxury.

She sat behind the wheel while he sat beside her in silence as she drove. This role reversal felt strange. Mira was so used to being driven everywhere by Abdul. She would come home from her appointments, and Abdul would rush into the kitchen to make her a steaming cup of *chai*. His guileless happiness at trying out various culinary experiments on them, knowing full well how much Mira loathed cooking, was just another one of his wonderful attributes. Abdul took pride in ensuring they were well-fed and cared for, and she slept easier at night knowing there was a male presence in the house. In a city like Delhi, that last bit was almost a prerequisite to safety. She wondered how much of her sadness was to do with concern for herself and Esha rather than the impending absence of Abdul from their lives. Resolving to set aside her selfishness, she asked him, *"Zameen bechke paise ka kya karega?"*

It was not as if he was likely to make millions out of the sale of his land, but she was curious about how he meant to invest the money.

"Soch rahe the Dilli mein ek chota sa ghar le lenge."

"Dilli mein?"

Why on earth did he want to buy a place in Delhi, even if he could afford it, which seemed unlikely with the sky high property prices, while he had a place with them?

"Ji. Agar aap aur baby phir foren chaley gaye, toh hamara kya hoga?"

In that moment, Mira realised that her thought processes were just as alien to Abdul as his were to her. The fear that lingered in his mind was that she could up and leave India, return to the UK and then where would that leave him? Ensuring his own future was of paramount importance, and she understood that completely. Still, a bit of reassurance from her side would not go amiss.

"Abdul, *hamara aisa koi plan nahin hai, magar hum samajh saktey hain aapka pareshaani.*"

He nodded and looked out of the window, perhaps listening but not really hearing what she meant. April had brought the first wave of heat to Delhi, and while the bougainvillaea bloomed against the wall they were driving past, the school children were already in the summer uniforms, having discarded the winter woollens in March.

Mira thought back to her statement. She had tried to say it in as fluent Hindi as she could manage, and from the sounds of it, had semi-succeeded. When had she lost most of her *Bambaiyya* accent? At first, she had taken great pride in speaking Hindi in the way it was spoken in Mumbai, the genders all a mix, the vowels not so rounded, the language sounding rustic and amalgamated with Marathi. Over the years, however, her Hindi had adapted to the environs, no longer distinguishing her as someone from a different state, a different city; an outsider who was not proficient in her national language. Delhi had become home. Maybe, in some ways, it had always been home. How could she explain to Abdul that this sense of belonging was something she had never felt while living in the UK? He need not worry, she had no plans to relocate to England.

As they neared the railway station, Mira turned towards the multi-storey car park she had researched the night before, but Abdul stopped her.

"Mira*ji, hum yaheen utar jaate hain. Aap aur paise mat kharchiye.*"

Mira stopped the car on the side of the road. She knew he would be deeply offended if she insisted on parking in the car park and escorting him to the station. Abdul, in many ways, had assumed the position of the caregiver and the paternal figure of the family, while also knowing that this was a position they had willingly bestowed upon him. Now, he did not wish to appear helpless or needy, and still wanted to keep his autonomy. How could she take that away from him?

"Baby ka khyaal rakhna, aur apna bhi. Kuch zyaada khaana khayiga, aap bahut patli hoti jaa rahin hain."

Mira laughed off his admonishments and placed a Rs 2000 note in his hand, which he tried to return.

"Please, Abdul, *rakh leejeye. Kaam aayenge.*"

As she drove off, she saw him look down at the money in his hand, then pick up his suitcase and make his way to the station.

At the traffic lights, she pulled down the vanity mirror and looked at her face. Was she too thin as Abdul had suggested? She had been pleased to lose a bit of weight, albeit it had not been in the best circumstances, but had it gone too far? Her appetite had all but disappeared, and prone as she was to abdominal pain and discomfort, some days it was almost easier not to eat rather than forcing food down. Maybe it was time to pay Dr Qureshi a visit. He had been exhorting her for a while to schedule an annual checkup, but she had dodged all his summons. If not for herself, she owed it to Esha to stay in good health. Who else did her child have?

❖

The card arrived in the post a few days later. Not only was she surprised by the contents but also by the venue.

It's time we talked. Come to Bengali Sweet House on the 16th at 11am. I'll be waiting for you.

Tina.

Mira drew in a sharp breath. It had taken five months and several notes and abortive phone calls to get Tina to agree to this meeting. Why was she so nervous now? This was what she had wanted, wasn't it?

. . .

On the 16th of May, Mira dressed carefully. These days, she mostly lived in jeans and sweatshirts. For this meeting, however, she took out an old cotton salwar kameez. It was turquoise-blue edged with burnt-orange embroidery and tiny gold dots scattered amongst the intricate weave. She had always felt beautiful and strong when she wore this outfit. For years she hadn't been able to get into it because of her weight gain, but she had been loath to part with it. It reminded her of the days when she had been so sure of herself and what her path in life would be. Shyam had loved these colours on her as well and always complimented her when she wore the outfit. Now that she had lost weight, she could wear it again, and she needed to. It was silly to be superstitious in this manner, to derive strength from clothes, but it was all she had, and she wanted to look her best when conveying everything that was in her heart.

Bengali Sweet House was just a fifteen-minute walk from P block where Mira lived. Is that why Radha had picked this location? Mira put on a sturdy pair of sandals to navigate the uneven streets that led to the restaurant. On the way there, her heart thudded unevenly and at one point, she felt dizzy enough to lean against a pole. A passing cyclist slowed down, his face filling with concern. She smiled and waved him on.

She peeled herself off the pole and resumed her slow walk towards the market. Her mind was filled with images from two decades ago. A shy Radha bringing them flowers, the first party she had come to in a saree, their walks and long chats, her miscarriage, the pain on her face when Mira had visited. What had she done to that sweet young girl?

Outside the restaurant, Mira paused to collect her thoughts. It wouldn't do to crumble now. Whatever Radha had to say to her, she had to receive it in all humility and repentance, and still keep a shred of dignity if she could. There wasn't much she could say to defend her actions from all those years ago. Even today, she cringed at how appallingly selfish and self-centred she had been. The best she could hope for, at this stage, was the tiniest sliver of understanding. Would Radha, no, not Radha anymore, would Tina grant her that?

Inside, Tina was already seated at a table towards the back. She was reading a book and was so absorbed in it; she didn't hear Mira approaching. The book cover said 'Homo Deus' by Yuval Noah Harari, something Mira couldn't imagine the Radha of yore selecting to read.

"Any good?" Mira asked, standing in front of Tina.

Tina started, then shut the book and laid it on the table.

"Yes," she said without elaborating. Then she gestured to Mira to take a seat.

Once Mira had sat, she started to say, "I'm glad..." but Tina spoke at the same time. "I've been thinking..."

They both stopped and stared at one another, then with a wry smile, Tina proceeded.

"I've been thinking that it is time to lay the ghosts of our past to rest. It's taken me a while to arrive at this conclusion, so I apologise that I didn't respond to your previous missives."

"No, it is I," Mira paused and cleared her throat, "I, who should be apologising... for so much... I don't even know where to begin."

Tina's stare was unflinching. "Why not at the very beginning? Was it always the plan to steal Shyam away?"

"Plan? No! There was no plan. Never! What happened... happened unwittingly. I didn't... I wouldn't have hurt you that way, deliberately."

"And yet, you did."

The server came to take their order, and Tina asked for two cups of tea and a plate of samosas without consulting her.

"I hope that's okay with you. I haven't eaten this morning and I'm famished."

"Of course. Listen, Radha...uhh... Tina, please, can I explain my side? All of your anger and accusations are completely justified, but please, please, just allow me to say something?"

"Alright, go ahead."

"You may not remember this, but Monish and I were going through a very rocky patch in our marriage."

"I remember."

"Oh," Mira looked at her, startled. "Well, it was all to do with the fact that suddenly my biological clock had started asserting itself. I was in my thirties, and while I had always claimed I didn't want children, suddenly, out of the blue, I wanted them, and I wanted to fall pregnant desperately. Your being pregnant...uhh...might have been the trigger."

Mira played with the napkins on the table before carrying on.

"Monish was adamant. He kept reminding me we had both agreed to remain childless and that now I was reneging on my promise. It was at this time that... that Shyam entered my life. I had never viewed him as anything other than your somewhat ass-holish husband."

Tina let out a surprised guffaw. "Ass-holish?"

"You know. From all that you had told me, and even when I first met him, I only thought of him as a misogynistic prick."

"So, what changed your mind?"

"That evening when we went to fetch Monish, when the car had a puncture. Do you remember?"

Tina nodded, not saying a word.

"I was upset with Monish and he...he... consoled me. Things got out of hand, and I started to develop feelings for him. After that, I tried staying away, tried denying that there was something between us. I was concerned for you, worried that I had crossed a line. But... but...Shyam was not willing to let go. He pursued me, he said he could see how unhappy I was... and then...and then...he confessed he had feelings for me too, that he had thought of little else since we'd met. He implored me to...to..."

"Leave Monish?"

"Yes." Shamefaced, Mira looked down again.

"And you did."

"No, it wasn't that simple. I was torn and confused. I still loved Monish and this, you, I couldn't even think of betraying you. But he was persistent, and in the state I was in, eventually, I succumbed."

"So, it was all Shyam's fault?"

Mira looked up, sensing the causticity in Tina's words.

"No. We were both culpable. In some ways, I more than him. I should have followed my instincts and walked away. I should never,

ever have given into my selfish desires. The destruction I caused, the pain I perpetrated! I feel sick thinking about it." Mira wrung her hands together and looked at Tina. "I don't expect you to forgive me, Tina, but all I want to say is that it was never my intention to hurt you. Never."

The server placed the two cups of tea and the plate of samosas on the table.

Tina stirred some sugar into her cup. Mira watched the spoon rotate in the cup with a detached fascination.

"Did you… are you married now, Tina?"

Tina shook her head.

"No, I did not remarry. Out of choice."

"I see."

"Do you?" Tina raised an eyebrow. "Please! Spare me the pity. I've had my fair share of relationships, I just chose not to solidify any."

Mira nodded and looked down at the table once again.

The silence stretched uncomfortably between them. Tina asked for another plate, placed a samosa and some chutney on it, and pushed it towards Mira.

"Here, eat. You look like you need it."

Mira stared at the samosa and the tea, unable to stomach either.

"My life," Tina said, her voice soft, "did not turn out the way I had expected it to. There was a path designated for me by my parents, by society, and by my background. What happened to me, what you did to me, changed that trajectory forever."

Mira opened her mouth to apologise again, but Tina raised her palm and stopped her.

"The divorce freed me from all those expectations. While I grieved at the demise of my marriage, was traumatised by the miscarriage, was incandescent with rage at your betrayal, a part of me realised I was no longer subject to the strictures imposed upon me. Now, I could choose to do what I wanted and be who I wanted."

Tina looked at Mira, her eyes gleaming.

"It took me a long time to realise that you had done me a favour. Today, I called you here to thank you. Everything I am, all that I have become, is because of what happened two decades ago. And none of it would have been possible without you."

❖

Friends? It was clear they would never be friends again. Tina had implied as much. They were ships that had docked together at a port briefly a long time ago, and now, they merely passed each other in the night.

Mira did not know what to make of the self-assured woman who had emerged from the ruins of that long ago time. She felt a strange ambivalence towards her: part-gratitude and part-fear, overlaying the deep affection that still existed within her. With a sudden clarity, she now realised that she could never address her as Radha again. The Radha of the past no longer existed. Tina had reclaimed her identity and her narrative, transforming herself into a woman with means, education, independence, and, yes, power.

Whilst they had parted on civil terms, Mira had sensed that the walls that Radha had once allowed her to breach were implacably in place once again. Tina might have forgiven, but it was unlikely that she would ever forget.

Still, there was a sense of relief in having somewhat cleared the air. Particularly as Esha had developed a great fondness for Tina. Lately, she had talked increasingly about her new 'teacher'. When Mira had probed what subject this new teacher, Miss Tina, taught, Esha had kept things vague or changed the topic.

Today she wanted her hair to be plaited the way Miss Tina did hers. Esha had been growing her hair out and in place of her customary ponytail she had tried herself to plait her hair clumsily. It was at this point that Mira had intervened.

"Why," Mira asked, while combing through Esha's hair, "do you want to copy Miss Tina's hairstyle?"

"I like her," Esha responded simply.

Was this one of Esha's sudden infatuations, like the one she had nursed on Mrs Upadhyay, or was she genuinely fond of the woman who, little by little, was returning her daughter to her previous happy-go-lucky self?

"When will I get to meet this Miss Tina?" Mira asked, plaiting her hair, pretending she did not know of Esha's self-harm or the subsequent counselling that had ensued.

"Soon, Mama." Esha smiled at her in the mirror. "I think you will like her too."

Mira's heart clenched in response. Oh Esha, she thought, if only you knew how much I did, and still do.

❖

"Well, I think a few tests might help figure out the problem," Dr Qureshi said, while making notes on his computer. "So, aside from fatigue, weight loss and lack of appetite, anything else?"

"No, not really. I mean, nothing I can put my finger on. The occasional migraine, but that's normally stress-related. Some back pain that comes and goes. Do you think all this could be the after-effects of Mum's death?" Mira asked, keeping her voice as even as she could.

"Sure. Grief takes a toll on the body and can manifest itself in various symptoms. Just to rule out any real medical cause, let's just get those tests done. What are you, fifty-three, fifty-four now?"

"Fifty-four."

"Right. When was the last time you had a breast screening or Pap smear?"

"Can't remember." Mira knew she sounded flippant, but it was only a cover for her nervousness. She had neglected her health wilfully, knowing all along that she was being foolish.

"Okay, let's put those in as well. So, bloods, urine, stool, bone density and breast and cervical screening. That will take a day. Get yourself booked in with the receptionist and we can take it from there."

"Are all these tests necessary?"

"Necessary if we want to understand what's going on. Worst-case scenario, something shows up. Best case, we rule out any medical issues. Whatever the case may be, Mira, it's time to take care of yourself."

Later, having booked herself in at the clinic for the following Monday, Mira took herself for a stroll in Lodi gardens. In her twenties, she had imagined that she would be the sort of woman who was in full control of her life, a bit like the way she imagined Mum was. Of course, the reality was that no one was ever in full control—not Mum, not Dad, not Hugo, and not even Shyam. Life had a way of wresting the control out of one's hands. All one could do was swim along with the tide and keep one's head above water. Everything that had occurred in her life, whether it was her fault, or whether it was circumstances beyond her sway, had moulded her into the person she was today.

Mira sat down under a tree and closed her eyes. Mum had asked her once if she had made a will and she had responded in the negative.

"Why not, Mira? That's just short-sighted. I made a will as soon as I moved back to India with you as a toddler. You need to sort this out promptly!"

Mira had nodded along and pushed it to the back of her mind. Now she wondered if it was time to do it. Everything she had belonged to Esha, but where Mum would have been the person to administer her wishes, who could take her place now? Bhumi? She was in Australia, and it would be months before she returned. Distant relatives who she had barely spoken to or had any relationship with? Hugo, who barely left his home, let alone the country?

Suddenly she felt achingly alone. When had she gone from being a sociable extrovert with plenty of friends to having not a single person she could rely on or confide in?

Pull yourself together! Mum's voice snapped at her, and Mira opened her eyes. Why this sudden weakness? She had managed all along, and she would manage once again. Chances were that Dr Qureshi would tell her she needed iron supplements and rest, and she would be right as rain.

. . .

❖

"The Pap smear showed some abnormality, and I'd like to investigate this further. Can you come in tomorrow morning?"

"That soon?"

"The sooner the better, Mira. In this sort of thing, the quicker we catch it, the quicker we can treat it."

"This sort of thing meaning…?"

"Let's not get ahead of ourselves. Come in tomorrow and we'll talk." Dr Qureshi hung up shortly after.

Mira stared at the blank screen of her phone, her mind going blank as well. This sort of thing? Hadn't life dealt her enough blows without 'this sort of thing' being added to the mix? Every catastrophic possibility came alive, bringing with it the sort of fear that nothing could allay.

With trembling fingers, she dialled the only number that came to mind.

When the phone rang without response, she nearly hung up but thought better of it.

"Hello?" The voice on the other end sounded perplexed.

"Hugo…"

"Mira? I thought we were talking on Saturday. Is everything alright? Has Esha done something else now?"

"No, no…I…" Mira stopped. What could she say to him? It wasn't as if she had any concrete information she could impart. "I just felt like a chat, that is all."

"Well, I was making a sandwich for lunch. Can you wait a moment? I will bring it here and sit with you."

Mira waited as she heard him shuffle off. Was there any point in worrying Hugo? It wasn't as if he would take the next flight over to see her. Still, he was the closest person she had to family and right now she needed the reassurance that if anything were to happen to her, Hugo would step up.

"I am here." She heard the creak of the chair as he lowered himself into it. "My arthritis has been terrible recently, and I take a long time to get out of bed and do things. But you don't want to hear about my health problems. Tell me, why did you think of me today?"

"Hugo," Mira tried keeping the tremor out of her voice. "I've been thinking. If anything were to happen to me, could I name you as Esha's guardian? As you know, we have barely any family left, and...and..."

"My dear child, I would be honoured to be her guardian. Practically speaking, though, how would it work? We live in two different countries, and I am a seventy-eight-year-old man. Don't you think it would make more sense for it to be someone closer to home?"

"Who, Hugo?" Mira's question came out as a wail. "After Mum, there is no one!"

"Mira? You sound distressed. What has happened?"

"I...nothing. I've had some tests and something abnormal showed up in one of them. I won't know what until later when the doctor does further tests, but I'm scared, Hugo. What if..."

"No what-ifs, Mira! That is no way to live. Keshav thought he'd been given a death sentence when they first diagnosed him as HIV positive, but he lived, didn't he? He lived for a good many years after, and he lived his life with zest."

"I am not Keshav."

"You are more Keshav than you realise. You don't even know what the doctor is going to say to you or what these further tests will reveal. It could be something that is easily sorted, so why are you jumping the gun?"

"It's not that. Mum had always said I needed to sort my affairs out, and I think, well, I thought at that time that she was being unnecessarily cautious. After Shyam's murder, I thought nothing worse could happen to us. But now I realise how stupid and short-sighted I was. Keshav's gone, Mum's gone and I have no one but you. If anything were to happen to me..."

"It won't!"

"But what if it does?"

"Then we will find a solution. Mira, first find out what the doctor has to say, okay? Call me straight after."

After she had hung up, Mira closed her eyes and leaned her head against the sofa. A long ago conversation with Mum floated into her mind.

"A child is an enormous responsibility, Mira. You already know that your baby has Down syndrome. This may be a good time to consider if you want to keep her. Unlike most children, this child will need you well into her adulthood. Have you considered all the possible ways that may not work out?"

She remembered arguing with Nisha, accusing her of depriving her daughter of the joy of motherhood. Railing against her that she did not understand. Maybe Nisha had understood and foreseen far more than Mira could imagine.

Picking up her car keys off the sideboard, she left the house to fetch Esha from school. In Abdul's absence, Mira had taken to picking Esha up from the bus stop. Before starting the car, she looked into the vanity mirror and rearranged her face. Esha was a perceptive child, and she did not want her picking up on her mother's torment.

On their way home, Esha chatted happily about school, her art classes, the bread *pakora* Vandana had shared with her, and her class with Miss Tina. Mira listened, nodding and smiling in all the right places, but unable to bring herself to ask any questions.

At home, after Esha had changed out of her school uniform, she came and cuddled up to Mira on the sofa.

"Mama, why are you so quiet?"

"Oh, am I?" Mira laughed, trying to inject some levity into her tone. "Just thinking about some things, baby, that is all."

"Mama?"

"Yes, darling."

"After Granny died, you went quiet too. I thought it was because you were upset with me."

"Upset with you?" Mira sat up straight and turned to look her daughter in the eye. "Why would you think that, Esha?"

"Because I wanted *biryani.* If we had come home earlier..."

"Oh no, darling! No, no. You mustn't blame yourself." Mira's eyes filled with tears. "I never ever thought that, baby. Listen to me, when it is time for someone to leave, life just allows it to happen. Even if we had been home that evening, Granny may still have suffered that stroke and we may not have been able to prevent her from dying. Do you see, Esha? We have no control over these things."

Esha looked down, then slowly raised the hem of her skirt to show Mira the scars on her thighs.

"I did this, Mama. I hurt myself because I thought you were angry with me, and then I was angry with myself."

Mira took her daughter into her arms and allowed herself to cry alongside her. These tears felt cleansing and true, as if the dam that had locked their emotions of grief and anger behind it had finally burst, allowing them to free themselves of the past.

"Whatever happens, my darling baby, remember that Mama loves you more than anything else in the world." Mira rocked Esha, while praying, *Please Mum, help me! Help me!*

"I'd like to do a colposcopic biopsy today. Nothing to worry about, Mira, and I'll have a nurse present while I perform the procedure." Dr Qureshi took his glasses off and rubbed his eyes. "If the colposcopy does not show any abnormal areas, then we may need to use another method to check for cancer."

"So, you suspect cancer?" Mira watched Dr Qureshi carefully.

"I believe in facts, Mira, not suspicions. Let's get this done and we can talk afterwards."

As Mira lay on the examination table, feet together, knees spread apart, she allowed her mind to float away from the present moment. After yesterday evening, a sense of calm had descended upon her, a feeling that no matter what happened, Esha would be alright. Her child had so much of her mother in her, in her sense of self, her pragmatism, and her instinctive distinction between right and wrong.

Despite the anger, the self-harm, the grief that had briefly derailed Esha, she had the same innate fortitude that Nisha had also possessed.

"The results should be here in a week. In the meantime, I don't want you to worry. Eat well, rest, and keep up with your daily activities." Dr Qureshi said, his dispassionate words doing far more to set her mind at rest than an overload of solicitousness.

At home, Mira went back to her study to work on the book that she had been neglecting far too long. Reading through the previous scenes, she tried imagining what her state of mind had been while writing them. So often when she revisited her work, she saw aspects of her life at the time reflected in it. When she had first started writing this book, she had been happy and comfortable; settled into a life that felt secure. In the turbulent months that had ensued, that fragile happiness had shattered, leaving her feeling unmoored and disorientated. Could she pick up the thread of her narrative and infuse it with the same sense of joy and adventure that she had begun with? In her present condition, was that even possible?

Then she forced herself to write. Abandoning the outline, she allowed her imagination to work unfettered. What poured out wasn't the love story she had been planning, but a story about heartache and disappointment, but also about rejuvenation and rediscovery. Romance didn't have to be a linear representation of love between a man and a woman. It could be about finding love within oneself; replacing self-loathing with self-reflection; understanding one's place in the Universe while also accepting that life was fleeting and unpredictable.

Perhaps she was circling the same themes that she had always addressed in her works, but this time, she felt her words had a deeper meaning, a gravitas that came from love and recent loss, and the knowledge that every human experience was dichotomously unique while also being universal.

When the phone rang, it startled her out of her meditative state. She glanced at the clock and noted that she had been writing for three hours straight.

"Hello?"

"Well, stranger, you've forgotten all about me!"

"Not at all, Bhumi. I was planning to call you soon."

"Liar! How are you?"

"Okay-ish, but we'll talk about that in a sec. How are you? How's Sydney?"

"Good! We've settled Chandan into his new home, and now he's insisting we travel the length and breadth of Australia with him. We're off to Melbourne and Brisbane, and who knows where else? My parents have been miraculously cured of all their aches and pains. This trip has worked like a tonic for them!"

"That's great news."

"You sound a bit distracted. Everything alright on your side?"

"I was just working on the new book, but listen, Bhumi, while you're here, can I ask you a favour?"

"Of course, Mira, ask away. Can't promise I'll be able to fulfil it, but I can try."

This was why Mira had always liked Bhumi. She called a spade a spade and was never shy to say no.

"I was thinking of appointing you the executor to my will. Would you be okay with that?"

"Will? You're younger than me. Why so morbid?"

Mira chewed on her lip, wondering if it was worth revealing more at this point.

"Just. I'm trying to get my affairs in order, and you know, I worry about Esha."

"Rightly so! I'm more than happy to be an executor, but have you looked at setting up a trust for her? That might make things easy in the long run, and I think it would protect her interests. Try talking to a lawyer about it."

"That's a good idea."

"Also, the reason I called was that if you want an audience with the Swami, this Sunday might be the last chance you'll get before he goes on his all-India tour."

"The last time, he didn't..."

"Yes, I know, but I've spoken to him since and ensured that he sees you this time. So, you know, whatever stuff you need to unburden, you can with him. He may not provide solutions, but he will provide succour, that's for sure."

"Thanks, Bhumi."

"You take care, Mira, and I'll call you whenever I next get a chance."

"Enjoy your Australia tour."

"Ha! Chandan will make sure we do."

❖

Mr Singh was watering the plants in his garden when Mira went outside to collect the post.

"Hello, Uncle!" She called out to him. He looked up, startled out of his reverie, and beamed at her.

"All well, *beta*? How is Jyoti working out?"

Jyoti was their maid who had volunteered to work for Mira in Abdul's absence. While she was efficient enough, Mira missed Abdul. She realised, however, how lucky she was that the Singhs had loaned her their maid for the interim. It was near impossible to find help that was reliable and punctual, and fortunately for Mira, Jyoti was both.

"She is good, Uncle. Her cooking is excellent."

"Ah yes, trained by my wife, no less." He grinned at her, his white beard sparkling as it caught the rays of the afternoon sun.

"How is Aunty? I haven't seen her around."

"Her asthma has been quite bad lately, what with this pollution. She stays indoors most of the time. You are welcome to come over, *beta*. I'm sure she could use the company. Now that Esha has gone back to school, we don't see much of her either."

Mira realised with a sudden pang that Esha had not gone to see them for quite a while. It was true that the young moved on quickly.

"I'll bring her over on the weekend," she promised, taking the letters out of the postbox and heading indoors. Inside, she sat down and mopped her brow. That bit of exertion had completely winded her, and in that moment she grasped that whatever was plaguing her, it would take all her might to fight it.

Meanwhile, she intended to make all the arrangements she could for Esha, if the worst were to happen. She had already been in touch with her lawyer, and he had sent her a load of paperwork to read through, which outlined the legal requirements and the process of setting up a trust. Bhumi had agreed to be a trustee, but she wanted to appoint another one. Was Hugo an ideal candidate living as far away as he did? Or Mr Singh, who was old but capable, and in their immediate vicinity? Her mind pondered the possibilities.

Then, suddenly, as clear as day, a memory emerged—a conversation that she had consigned to the recesses of her mind.

"Nisha, what if something were to happen to us, or to you? Who will take care of little Mira then?" Her grandmother's voice, filled with worry. Mira's head bent over her book, ostensibly lost in the story, but present enough to understand that somehow this concerned her.

Then Nisha's voice, answering her mother, saying cryptically, "*Jako rakhe Saiyan, maar sakey na koy; Baal na banko kar sakey, jo jag bairi hoy.*"

Years later, she had finally understood the meaning of Kabir's couplet:

"He whom God protects, no one can kill.

Even if the whole world turns into his enemy, not even a hair on his head can they harm."

Mira took comfort from the fact that these words of wisdom had served her mother, and now, they would serve her, too.

The ashram was even busier than the last time. In the late August haze of Delhi, the out buildings shimmered under the oppressive heat of the Indian sun. Sweltering humidity hung heavy in the air, wrapping its tendrils around devotees, leaving them drenched in sweat. The sky, a canvas of shifting greys, teased with the promise of rain as ominous clouds gathered on the horizon. With each passing moment, the city braced itself for the onslaught of the retreating monsoon, its streets echoing with the distant rumble of thunder. Far from the clamour of honking horns of the city, the ashram stood calm despite the swell of the people, poised between the relentless heat of summer and the impending deluge of the monsoon's farewell.

Now that the Swami's fame had spread far and wide, Mira could sense that these personal audiences were bound to dwindle. Thanks to Bhumi, she was now standing at the door awaiting admittance to see the Swami before he started his *yatra.*

As soon as she entered the quiet room, she noticed that the old sofa had been replaced by a new plush one in cream with matching curtains at the window. The Swami was sitting in an armchair that almost resembled a throne. His slight frame was dwarfed within the large seat, and he looked as if he might be swallowed whole by the overstuffed cushions he was surrounded by. Mira suppressed a grin as she sat on the coir mat on the floor in front of him. There were four people ahead of her and maybe another six or seven behind her. So, she had not been wrong in her assumption that the Swami's private audience had shrunk considerably.

One by one, the devotees approached the Swami and spoke to him. As before, he either handed them a marigold flower as a blessing or said something to ease their burdens.

When it was her turn, the Swami gazed upon her with the same kindness as before. There was no spark of recognition in his eyes. She could have been anyone, a random attendee or just another supplicant requesting the manna of his words.

"What troubles you, my child?"

"Swami*ji*, I am worried about my health. My daughter is still very young, she is differently abled, and we have no family left. If anything happens to me, will she be alright? Who will look after her? How will she get on in life?"

As the questions came tumbling out of her, Mira wondered what she was expecting from him. His talk had been about gratitude and thankfulness, about how everything that happened to us was a lesson we were meant to learn; how life was just like school, and death was when we returned home from school. Suddenly, she felt ashamed for wasting his time. This was a man who dealt with the esoteric and the profound, and here she was, burdening him with superficialities.

The Swami gazed deep into her eyes, then turned around to take a marigold flower from the silver *thaali* beside him. He closed his eyes, chanted a small prayer, then placed the marigold in her upturned palm.

This was all the answer she would get from him today. It had to be enough.

In the waning days of September, Delhi's weather began to shed the stifling cloak of summer, embracing a more temperate disposition. The relentless heat that once held the city in its grip now yielded to the gentle caress of cooler breezes, carrying whispers of the impending autumn. The sun, now less fierce in its gaze, cast a softer light upon the cityscape, painting the sky with hues of gold and amber. A sense of tranquillity settled over the streets, as if the city itself sighed with relief at the departure of the scorching summer months. Yet, traces of the monsoon lingered still, sporadic showers punctuating the days with fleeting bursts of rain, refreshing the earth and nourishing the land.

Mira parked the car outside the clinic and remained seated behind the wheel. Whatever happened today, she knew there was no going back. She had felt so disconnected from herself in the past year. Her body that she had once known so intimately had seemed a mere shell in which her soul resided but lamented for a time before; a time in which she had been happy and carefree; in which neither the guilt of the past nor the burden of the future weighed her down.

She remembered when she had first fallen pregnant with Esha. When, after years of trying, they had finally been successful. Much before she had taken the pregnancy test, much before it was even possible to tell, her body had known. It had conveyed to her that she was now housing another life within her; a life that she, from the very first instance, knew that she would love and protect as fiercely as possible.

When had she stopped listening to her body? What would it have told her if she had listened?

She took a deep breath and turned the ignition off. It was the moment of truth and she had come prepared. It wouldn't do to stave it off any longer.

"Good morning, Mira," Dr Qureshi looked her over as she sat down. "How are you feeling?"

"Not any better," Mira said, her voice calm. "Not any worse, either. So, Doctor, what's the verdict?"

Dr Qureshi tapped his fingers on the desk before clearing his throat.

"Well, I've received the results from your tests, and I'm afraid it's not the news we were hoping for."

She waited for him to continue.

"Mira, I regret to inform you that your condition has advanced to Stage IV cervical cancer with metastasis to the lymph nodes and other distant sites. Regrettably, the disease remained undiagnosed for an extended period of time. Given the advanced stage of the cancer, therapeutic interventions are unlikely to offer significant benefit at this juncture. However, if you wish, we can consider chemotherapy as a palliative measure to help alleviate symptoms and potentially slow the progression of the disease."

Mira remained silent.

"Mira? Do you need a moment? I know it's a lot to take in..."

"What..." Mira started then stopped, then started again, "what are the potential benefits and risks of chemotherapy, Doctor?"

Dr Qureshi took off his spectacles and placed them on the desk.

"Chemotherapy involves the use of powerful medications to target and destroy cancer cells. While it may help manage symptoms such as pain and discomfort, it also carries certain risks and side effects.

These can include nausea, fatigue, hair loss, and suppression of the immune system, among others. It's essential to weigh these potential benefits and risks before making a decision."

Dr Qureshi's clinic overlooked a large park, and from the window Mira observed two young boys laughing and kicking a football between them. She felt a sudden urge to be with them, running through the field, letting the wind blow through her curls, laughing and laughing until she collapsed into a heap.

Instead, she asked, "How long do I have?"

"Based on the progression of the cancer and the available treatment options, I would estimate that you have approximately six months, maybe more. However, it's important to remember that every patient's journey is unique, and we'll focus on optimising your quality of life during this time."

The boys were still kicking the ball between them, and she swallowed the lump in her throat.

"Thank you for explaining, Doctor. I...I think I have to decline chemotherapy."

"May I ask why, Mira?"

"If all I have is limited time, I want to focus on spending it with Esha and making the most of it. I don't want her last memories of me to be of an ailing mother who is lost to her even before it is my time to go."

Now, Dr Qureshi remained silent. When he spoke, she thought she detected a strange note in his voice, but it wasn't one she could identify.

"I understand your decision, Mira. It's important for patients to make choices that align with their wishes and values. We can explore other supportive care options to help manage your symptoms and improve your quality of life during this time."

"That would be much appreciated, Doctor. Thank you for understanding."

"Of course, Mira. I'll arrange for our palliative care team to meet with you to discuss pain management, counselling, and other supportive services. And remember, I'm here for you every step of the way."

Her body had always known. This rogue cell had been living inside her forever, maybe even when she had been in her mother's womb. A cell that had waited for the right time, the opportune moment, to multiply much beyond its brief, creating tumours that would eat her alive from the inside. A tiny ticking time bomb waiting to implode.

Her body had always known.

Yet, she did not blame her body, this mass of cells that had carried her through life. It had done all it needed to for her during her lifetime. She had neglected it, ignored it, put all kinds of toxins in it, deprived it of love and attention, and it had kept going until it no longer could. Soon, she would shed it forever. But while she still inhabited it, she would no longer take it for granted.

❖

"I wish I was there with you."

"What could you possibly do, if you were?"

"I don't know… sit with you, read to you, hold your hand…"

Mira choked back her sob.

"Ah, Bhumi, you can do all that when you return."

"That's not for another three months, and…" Bhumi stopped abruptly and Mira knew it was because she wanted to say what she was thinking. Would Mira still be around?

Abdul had returned earlier than planned as soon as she had sent word. Mr and Mrs Singh had once again proven to be strong pillars of support, and the nurse Dr Qureshi had assigned to her was a lovely young Keralite woman, Tessy, who had been compassionate and sensitive to Mira's needs. All that remained was to tell Esha, who only understood that Mira was sick, not that she was dying.

"Have you spoken to Esha yet?"

"No, I'm scared to. I don't want her self-harm to start again. She's so young and vulnerable, Bhumi, and her life is going to change drastically. I want her to remain innocent and unaware for as long as possible."

"Hmmm. Does the school know?"

"Yes, I sent the principal an email saying that I would be withdrawing her from school after this term."

"And then?"

"The boarding school in England."

"The one you never wanted to send her to?"

"I recognise the irony."

"Oh, Mira!" She heard Bhumi's voice break.

"Please don't, Bhumi. It's all I can do to keep it together. I need you to be strong for me, and when the time comes, I need to trust you to follow my wishes."

"You know I will, Mira. I would have taken care of Esha if it weren't for—"

"No, I can't ask that of you, not with your elderly parents and your boys. Esha will be fine. Hugo has promised to visit her as often as he can."

She remembered the old man breaking down when she had given him the news. All he had kept saying was, *"Du arme Frau... Du arme Frau..."*

When he had finally rallied, she had extracted a promise that he would visit Esha in England. He had agreed, saying it was the least he could do as her godfather.

"I'll call you over the weekend again, okay?"

After Mira hung up, she closed her eyes and drifted off. It only seemed like moments before the doorbell rang. It couldn't be Tessy again. She had only left a few hours ago.

Abdul knocked on the bedroom door.

"Aapse koi lady milney aayi hai."

A lady? Who could it be?

Slowly, Mira hauled herself out of bed. She checked her reflection in the mirror and winced. Then, holding on to the stick, she made her way out into the living room.

Tina was in a pale pink salwar kameez today. She stood up as soon as she heard Mira enter the room. When she turned, her face emptied of all colour.

Mira laughed and said, "I know. I look like death warmed up." She sank into the sofa and called out in a weak voice, "Abdul, *chai laana.*"

"No, I don't want any tea," Tina protested.

"But I do. Come now, have a cup with me."

Tina sat across from her, her eyes scrutinising Mira.

"I just heard today, and came straight over."

"It's good of you to come."

"Esha doesn't know, does she?"

"No, not yet."

"She's a smart kid. I'm sure she suspects."

"Possibly," Mira sighed. "I will need to tell her soon."

"Mr Upadhyay said you are sending her to a boarding school in England?"

Abdul brought in a tray laden with biscuits and *chewra,* and two steaming cups of tea.

"Why," Tina asked, "why can't she stay here?"

Abdul added two teaspoons of sugar to Mira's tea and set it down on the little table beside her.

"Whom with, Tina?" Mira asked, her voice soft. "We have no family left."

"Not even a distant cousin, aunt or uncle?"

"No, not even that."

Abdul gave Tina her cup, offering her the biscuits, which she declined.

"How…how long do they say before…for…?"

"Who knows?" Mira shrugged and looked away.

"Can I make a suggestion?"

"Yes, go ahead."

"Write some letters to Esha. Fill them with everything you would want to say to her as she grows. The advice you would give her at eighteen, at twenty-one, or when she has her first boyfriend, and if she chooses to marry..."

"That's a lovely thought, Tina, but I no longer have the energy for it. As you can see..." Mira pointed to the cup of tea, which she hadn't been able to pick up. "Besides, those milestones you talk about, I don't know if my Esha will ever have them."

For weeks, Mira had held her emotions in check, burying them deep within her heart. But now, as the realisation of Esha growing up alone and far away corralled her, it felt as though someone had punched her in the gut and winded her. She doubled over in pain, allowing a sob to escape her. Her hands trembled and her throat tightened as tears threatened to spill over. She tried to hold them back, clinging desperately to the last vestiges of composure, but wave after wave of sorrow crashed over her relentlessly. With a soft cry, she surrendered to the intensity of her emotions, her body convulsing, each sob tearing at her soul until she felt utterly depleted, drained of the rest of her strength.

Abdul came rushing into the room, but Tina had beaten him to it. She was by her side, holding her, whispering words of comfort, promising to help her break the news to Esha, pledging her support in writing those letters. Tina, her former friend, her erstwhile adversary, was the one whose arms encircled her, who allowed her the briefest glimmer of hope that maybe, just maybe, Esha would have someone by her side once Mira was gone.

Hope was an elusive beacon in the darkness of despair. It possessed a duality as profound as life itself. For Mira, it had been a cruel temptress that had once woven illusions of a brighter tomorrow, only to dash them against the rocks of reality. Its siren song of happiness had lured Mira into an abyss of betrayal, lies and loss.

And yet, despite its treachery, hope had endured within her. It had remained a steadfast companion in the face of adversity. Astonishingly enough, it had brought Tina back into their lives when she was needed most. In Mira's darkest hours, hope had provided the sustenance her spirit needed, breathing life into the embers of an uncertain future.

Its flickering flame refused to be extinguished, and it guided Mira through a labyrinth of despair, leading her once again to the shores of redemption.

Tina, her mind whispered, Tina was where absolution lay. Tina, whom she had allowed to be seen by at her most vulnerable, at her most defeated; who had picked up her scattered pieces and tried putting them back together again. Tina, who she could not help but trust, despite having broken her trust all those years ago.

Tina embodied hope, and within that strange paradox lay everything Mira desired yet feared she would not attain.

What right had she to hope? Yet hope she did. For her child, for Esha's future, and for forgiveness of her past sins. It was all she had now, and she clung to it, tenacious and believing.

Praying to all the Gods she had once known, and all the others she didn't. Praying to Nisha for the help she so desperately needed at this stage, this final liminal space, this threshold that existed between life and death.

Praying, yes. But above all, hoping for a miracle she did not deserve, but asked for nonetheless.

Somewhere in the distance, there was a door. Someone was waiting for her, but she couldn't tell who it was. Her eyes remained closed, but she could hear Tessy's voice talking to Abdul.

"Call baby. It is time."

Time for what? Mira wanted to ask Tessy so many questions, but her tongue refused to move, swollen and heavy in her mouth. Pain had been her constant companion the last few months but had retreated briefly right now, and all she wanted was to see Esha again.

Her eyes remained stubbornly shut, the whooshing noise in her ears urging her to let go. Someone waited by the door. Who was it?

"Mama," she heard Esha whisper to her, her hand stroking her arm softly.

"Darling baby," she said in response, but her lips did not move, and the words remained trapped in her mind.

"Tell Mama you love her," Tina's soft voice urged.

"I love you, Mama. Say hello to Dada and Granny in Heaven."

Heaven?

Was she going to Heaven?

Mira felt scared. She didn't want to leave this life or her daughter. What lay beyond that door? What judgement was she likely to receive? Her fingers moved of their own accord, and she felt Esha's hand hold hers. Her poor, brave child. A tear trickled out of the corner of her eye.

"Don't cry, Mama. I love you. Please don't cry."

Suddenly, the door was right in front of her. All her fear fled, leaving her only with curiosity. Who was it, waiting so patiently behind the door? She needed to find out.

Out of nowhere, Mira found herself enveloped in a sense of serenity, a quiet acceptance of the journey that lay ahead. For beyond that threshold, beyond the confines of mortal existence, awaited the promise of rest, a sanctuary from the trials of the world she was leaving behind. Someone was waiting to escort her into the great unknown, and she no longer wanted to delay the inevitable.

With a gentle sigh, she relinquished her hold on life, her last living memory being the soft clasp of her daughter's hand.

TINA

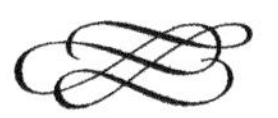

2020

CHAPTER 20

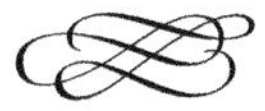

She opened the door to Esha's room, trying to stay as quiet as possible. The bedside lamp was still on, but Esha had fallen asleep, a book open upon her chest. Tina picked up the book, placed the bookmark within it, and set it to one side.

Then she sat on the bed and watched Esha sleep.

There was so much of Shyam in her, and every time she shrugged or smiled, Tina caught a glimpse of the man she had once loved. But how could she deny that Esha was also Mira? Passionate, wilful and stubborn, she carried her mother within her. The Mira that Tina had once admired, then loathed, then pitied, and finally, at the very end, understood.

There was no cure for a lifetime of hurt, but to watch someone as vibrant, as wonderfully alive and gifted as Mira, wither into nothing, becoming a mere shadow of her former self, was far more painful than she had imagined it would be. How she had wanted to hate her! How she had wanted to think that *this*, yes, *this* was Mira's punishment. But she couldn't. This was still Mira, the same woman she had once idolised. The same woman who had given her the courage to rediscover herself against all odds.

In those last few months of Mira's life, she realised that as much as

Mira needed her; she needed Mira and Esha, too. They were the family she had denied herself, the sister and the daughter that she desperately needed to fill the empty corners of her life.

A life that had remained barren of love and friendship after Shyam and Sangita had departed from it. Her strained relationship with her brothers had all but evaporated after her parents' death. Her brief romantic liaisons had brought her little joy and she had soon given up on them, despite her assertions to Mira. Loneliness and freedom remained her only bedfellows. She had buried herself in her studies and work, refusing to acknowledge the lack of companionship; refusing to face the demons of her past.

Yet life had brought her full circle, to the woman who had changed everything for her. To Mira. It had brought her to a juncture where she could choose to stay or to walk away. She had stayed.

Her offer to help Mira with the letters had blossomed into a silent understanding.

"Does Esha need to be sent abroad?" She had asked post one of their many letter writing sessions.

"Yes. She has no one here." Mira had been exhausted and resigned, struggling to finish the letters before the disease vanquished her willpower. For weeks, they had been circling the same topic repeatedly.

"Surely..." Tina had tried arguing against it once more. The idea of sweet little Esha living amongst strangers had nearly broken her heart.

"If it pains you so much, why don't you take care of her?" Mira had asked out of the blue, propping herself on her elbows, her eyes challenging Tina.

And she had found herself agreeing. Agreeing to take on a role she was unprepared for, a role that she had never imagined in her destiny, but realising with a sudden and absolute clarity that she wanted to inhabit with every fibre of her being. There had not even been a moment's hesitation in her response. Not once had it crossed her mind, then, that this was a commitment of a lifetime. All she knew was that despite all her professional accomplishments, she had been missing something crucial in her life. Someone crucial.

A child to love, protect, and nurture. A child she had lost long ago and had never imagined gaining in so unlikely a manner.

She didn't need Mira's money, but Mira had insisted on providing for her in the will. Esha's trust and trustees kept the bulk of the estate safe for her, and Tina understood why these safeguards were in place. Still, Mira had been more than generous in her settlement to Tina. If she wanted, she could give up work and stay home now as Esha's guardian. But she did not want that.

Just as her work had helped bring Esha into her life, there were other children who needed her. Children who processed their traumas in different ways, children who would need her services even more once this lockdown finished.

She was glad Mira had gone before Covid-19 had gripped India in a chokehold. What would she have made of all these rules and restrictions? What would she have thought of this unseen enemy that had invaded their lives, turning the entire world upside down?

Tina thought of poor Mrs Singh, losing her life in the early days of Covid, and Mr Singh being shipped off to live in Hyderabad with his son. She wondered how Gautam and Pari were getting on, trying to manage online classes, trying to keep education going, young minds interested and invested in their futures. She wanted to be there for them after this lockdown ended.

Tina thanked her stars that she had agreed to give up her modest little flat straight after Mira's demise to come live in this house with Esha, admitting that the least amount of upheaval was best for the young girl. When the lockdown happened, she was locked in with Esha and Abdul, both of whom looked to her for direction and comfort.

While their initial few months together had been hard, particularly for Esha, Tina had persisted in talking to her about everything. She wanted Esha to feel every emotion, however punishing and arduous. The only way forward was through the long, dark corridor of anguish and heartbreak.

In the past few weeks, she had sensed something unfurling in Esha. She had found her crying in the bathroom, or lying on Mira's bed, her nose buried in the pillow, trying to recapture her mother's scent. But she had also belly laughed at a silly cartoon on the television and cuddled up next to Tina while reading her book. The day Abdul had unexpectedly brought home an orphaned pup, she had squealed in delight, begging to keep him. She had named him 'Batman' after Mira's first dog.

❖

Esha's eyelids flickered, and then, as if sensing Tina's gaze upon her, she opened her eyes and smiled at her sleepily.

"I was dreaming of Mama."

Tina pushed the hair off her forehead and smoothened the stray strands with gentle strokes.

"And what was Mama doing?"

"She was running and laughing."

"She was happy?"

"Yes," Esha nodded. "She looked happy."

"And you, Esha? How are you feeling?"

"I think," Esha paused and furrowed her brow, "I think I am happy I'm with you. Mama said to call you *choti mama.* You are my 'little Mama', and I love you, too."

Tina felt her heart swell with an unspeakable joy. She had hoped that someday Esha would see her as a substitute mother, not there to supplant Mira, but as someone who created her own small space in Esha's life. Little had she known that Mira had already planted those seeds in her young mind.

She kissed Esha on the forehead and breathed in her warm scent, holding back the tears that threatened to spill; biting the inside of her cheek to keep her composure. She tucked the covers around Esha and said in a soft undertone, "Go back to sleep, darling. Maybe Mama will show you what else she's up to."

Esha smiled, squeezed her hand in response, then closed her eyes and fell back into a deep slumber almost immediately. Tina watched her for a few more moments before standing up and switching the lamp off.

She made her way outside, leaving the door open a crack, so that if Esha called out to her, she could be by her side in an instant.

Fate had brought this beautiful child into her life. Yes, she wasn't like other children. Her journey was marked by challenges and obstacles that others could never comprehend. But to Tina, those differences were not barriers to be overcome, rather threads that enriched the fabric of their relationship. In Esha's laughter, Tina found solace; in her unguarded moments of wonder, she discovered profound beauty.

To Tina, Esha was perfect.

She embraced the gift that fate had bestowed upon her, knowing that she would spend the rest of her life giving this child all the love that had been bottled up inside her for years.

Together, they would embark upon a new chapter in life.

THE END

AFTERWORD

Did you know there are three other books in 'The Friendship Collection'? You can check them out here:

The Intimacy of Loss

A Quiet Dissonance

Intersections - A Novel

Please do remember to rate and/or review this book on your preferred site. It helps other readers discover this novel. Thank you!

If you enjoyed this book, you can sign up to hear more about my new releases and any special offers.

Do visit www.poornimamanco.com to keep abreast of all my news.

ACKNOWLEDGMENTS

My deepest gratitude to Tanya for reading an initial draft of the book, and helping me craft a believable character in Esha. Having no personal experience of raising a Down syndrome child, her input was invaluable. Any mistakes I may have made in representation are solely mine.

Also, a big thank you to Laura O'Neill (MBACP), dearest friend and practising counsellor, who helped me with the nuances of the various therapies that would be provided to a child in Esha's situation.

Finally, my sincere appreciation to my wonderful editor, Charulatha, my cover designers at MiblArt and all of my ART team for your reviews and feedback.

ABOUT THE AUTHOR

Poornima is an award-winning novelist whose short stories have been published in The Guardian and The Telegraph newspapers in the UK. Born and raised in India, she still retains a deep connection to her motherland, which reflects in all her stories and books. Poornima lives in the UK with her family.

ALSO BY POORNIMA MANCO

Parvathy's Well & other stories

Damage & other stories

Holi Moly! & other stories

The Intimacy of Loss

Twelve - stories from around the world

Parvathy's Well & Other Stories: The India Collection

Eight - Fantastical Tales From Here, There & Everywhere

Six - Strange Stories of Love

A Quiet Dissonance

Intersections - A Novel

Printed in Great Britain
by Amazon